Liane J [illegible] ales, in 1958, a [illegible] uthor of three r [illegible] l, THE DREAM [illegible] 2 Betty Trask Award:

'One of the most enthralling books of its kind I've ever read' Celia Brayfield

'Quite lovely' *Bookseller*

'Everything a bestseller should be: thrilling, compelling, sexy and sensational' *Sunday Express*

'Impressive fictional debut . . . sweeping and affecting' *Mail on Sunday*

'A rich escapist read' *Yorkshire on Sunday*

Painting the Dark

Liane Jones

Riverside Books
Fairview Farm
Littley Green
Essex CM3 1BU

ISBN 1 904154 59 X

Printed and bound in the United Kingdom

ACKNOWLEDGEMENTS

To Sara Fisher, my agent, and Jane Morpeth and Andi Blackwell, my editors: much thanks. To Jamie, as ever. To Siobhan Patterson, for all that good-humoured wrestling with Harry and for your company. To Eve Jones my mother, for stepping in many times. And first, middle and last, to Alan Jones my father, for your generosity with your scholarship, your time and your endeavour.

Prologue

Judith was lost. In the great city of Jerusalem, where they had warned her of the dangers and told her to stay close by her father and his cousin Benjamin, she was lost.

Ahead, the flax sellers stood by their trestles; beyond them were the men sitting by piles of figs. In the curve of the street was the crowd she'd seen before, gathered round the merchant with his loaded camel. That meant she was near the Strangers' Gate again, although she could have sworn she had been walking away from it a minute ago. There was no sign of her father, nor of Endeyeh, her servant.

The noise was coming at her from all directions, like the sound of the big rains, except that these noises were all dry. Dust dry; harsh, city dry. Judith's throat was parched; she wished she hadn't finished her small cask of spring water.

She crossed the street into the shade. The streets of Jerusalem were wider than those in her own city; there, two men couldn't walk abreast. This street was broad enough for the flax sellers to set up their benches and display their wares and still leave enough room for a woman to lead her donkey past. The loaded camel wouldn't fit, however, which was why it was stopped in the crook of the wall, attracting a stream of people down to inspect the goods. They jostled her as they passed.

Judith flattened her back against the wall. The sun had only just slipped below the ramparts and the baked mud was still hot; it made her feel sick. She tried not to panic. If she stayed in one place, her father or Benjamin or someone else from Benjamin's house would eventually pass by.

'What are you doing?'

Judith looked round sharply. It was a boy, squatting on the ground, playing dice. At least, from her initial glance at the top of his head she'd taken him for a boy; now the soft growth of beard on his face and the breadth of his shoulders told her that he was a young man, about her own age.

'Waiting for my father,' she said haughtily. 'Why?'

'I wouldn't stand there. That's where the guards pour their slops down the wall.'

Judith moved hastily away. The young man grinned.

'You're not from Jerusalem, are you?'

'No, I'm from Bethulia.'

'And where's that?'

'On the northern edge of the mountains, looking out over the plain. You needn't sound so superior,' she added, annoyed. 'Bethulia guards Jerusalem. If it wasn't for us, enemies could get into the mountain pass and come straight down here.'

'You've personally stopped some of them, have you?'

'No, but my father has. Ten years ago when Judas Maccabee was leading us all in the holy fight against the Syrians, Bethulia was attacked by Syrian reinforcements. My father and the other men fought them off. He met Judas Maccabee himself and Judas Maccabee said that if it hadn't been for Bethulia, the reinforcements would have got to Jerusalem and the unholy Syrians would have held onto it much longer. You Jerusalemites might never have been able to overpower them and lock them into the Acra. Imagine.'

The young man put his dice away and stood up. His eyes were hostile.

'Imagine.'

'Well, yes. What's the matter?'

'You think it's a good thing that the reformers are shut into the Acra?'

'Of course it is.'

'All right then, come and look at them.'

'What? Why?'

'I want to show you something.'

Judith stared. The young man had gone pale and he stood bent towards her, his fists clenched.

'I've got to wait for my father,' she said cautiously.

'It's not far, you'll be back in ten minutes. What's the matter, scared?'

His scornful smile infuriated her. Judith lifted her robe, picked her way over the litter strewn around her feet, and began to walk uphill.

'Come on then,' she said into the young man's face as she overtook him.

'There. That's the Acra. These are the guards. And up there on the steps are the unholy reformers' children.'

Judith stared up at the fortress-like walls. On her way through the city yesterday, when they'd been going to Benjamin's house, she had looked away from the Acra, as her father had told her. 'It's the one unholy place left in Jerusalem,' he had said in his gentle voice. 'The people who were once our oppressors and their wretched followers live in there now.

They're not allowed out, and one day they'll be forced to leave. Don't look at it. Good Jews turn their eyes away and pretend it's not there.'

She had obeyed him, willingly. But now, nervously and yet a little excited by the challenge, she looked.

The walls were high and in disrepair. Small trees grew in clefts in the masonry and every few yards the ground was littered with small stones which had come loose.

Through openings in the walls Judith could see people moving around inside; all looked thin and moved slowly. Here and there emaciated, matted goats were tethered. The steps the young man was pointing to were on the far side of the Acra, emerging from inside the enclosure to end in a broken platform. They were covered by children who sat, squatted and lay curled up, some crying, some squabbling but most quiet.

'What are they doing?' she asked fearfully. 'Why aren't they playing or helping their families?'

'With what?' said the young man. 'There's not enough food for everyone to cook. There's not enough room for the children to play. They've got no sheep to mind and no vines to tend. No grain to grow. What would you do except sit on the steps and look out at the luckier ones?' He sounded angry, but in a way Judith had never heard before, as if he were sick deep down but well used to it.

'They could leave,' she pointed out. 'No one would stop them.'

'Yes, they could leave and they will. They'll go in the end, and try to scratch a living from some hillside where they'll be attacked by the villagers and the wild animals, and where there's already too little to go round. So then they'll split up and die in the wilderness.'

'So? They're bad people, they break God's laws. What's it to you?'

The young man looked at her as if he would hit her. Then he looked back at the fortress.

'My mother's sister and her two brothers are in there,' he said quietly. 'And my six cousins – at least there used to be six of them. I don't know how many are still alive. Still,' his voice was suddenly coarse, and he grimaced at her, 'that's their problem, eh? There's always losers. Coming? *I've* seen enough.'

He wheeled round and walked off fast, not waiting for her. Judith grabbed her robe in both hands and hurried after him. She caught up with him as he clambered over a broken-down cart and as she hopped through the splintered planks, she looked at him sideways. She could see it now, a Syrian flatness around the brows, and although his hair was dark there were giveaway tawny lights in his half-grown beard.

'Your mother's a Syrian?' she panted.

'Was. She's dead.'

'And what about your father?'

'He was a Judean.'

'And you live here in Jerusalem?'

The young man stopped. 'What's it to you?' he mimicked.

Judith glared at him. She didn't know what it was about this boy that interested her, but she was reluctant to let him go.

'It's nothing to me at all,' she said, 'but you've got me lost now, so the least you can do is show me the way back to where we were.'

In the shade of the doorway, their legs drawn up out of the way of passers-by, they took it in turns to drink from his flask.

'They kicked us out,' he said. 'For eight years we lived here without any trouble and then your people, the Maccabees, got the upper hand and we were out. My father could have stayed if he'd divorced my mother and disowned me, but he wouldn't.'

'Why didn't you go into the Acra with your mother's family?' Judith asked.

'My father knew how it would end up. And he was angry, he didn't want to stay here. So we left for Syria but my father got sick and died on the way.'

'What did you do then?'

Her companion stared at the legs, sandals, baskets that bobbed and jostled in front of them.

'We went back to my mother's village. And when I was twelve I joined the army.' He straightened his back. 'I've been on three campaigns,' he said casually. He passed Judith the flask; she felt a tremor of daring as she put her mouth where his had been.

'Have you killed anyone?' she asked, copying his tone.

He laughed. 'Four people for certain,' he said, 'and I hurt another three pretty badly.'

'How did you do it?'

'With a spear, three of the four. I used a sword on the other one. And my wounded I got sometimes with a spear, sometimes with a sling.'

Judith didn't know whether or not to believe him. In Bethulia people told stories of battles but they seemed a long time ago and nothing to do with daily life. This was different. The young man talked of killing with a matter-of-fact pride, like someone boasting about their vine harvest.

'Have you killed Jews?'

The boy's face darkened. 'No,' he said shortly.

Judith passed him back the flask and wondered if he was

angry because he wanted to kill Jews and hadn't, or because he was insulted by the question. After all, he was half a Jew himself.

It was strange to think of it that way round. In Bethulia, they had always been taught that anyone who married a foreigner or went to their temples forfeited their Jewishness. That was what had happened to the hill villagers, a long time ago, and because of that they were condemned to live on the barren slopes, looking towards the Godless places that had entered their blood. But this young man lived in the heart of the Godless place, with Jewish blood in him. He looked back angrily towards Judea.

'What are you doing here now?' Judith asked curiously.

His scowl cleared. 'I heard there's a general coming through, one of our allies in Macedonia. He's recruiting men for an expedition there and I want to be one of them. There's all sorts of action happening in the west now. Macedonia's up for grabs; the Romans have taken over in Carthage; Demetrius, who would have been king of Syria if his uncle hadn't pushed him out, is hiding out in Crete. The west is the place for a young man who wants to make his name, and that's where I'm going.' He smiled, and for the first time he looked boyish; there was a flush of excitement on his hair-patched cheeks.

'I'll be hearing all about you then,' said Judith sarcastically. His confidence, and his eagerness to turn his back on everything she knew, peeved her. 'You'd better tell me your name, so I can listen out for it.'

Her companion narrowed his eyes teasingly. 'You're jealous.'

'No, I'm not!'

'You are. You wish you were going to do things like me,

instead of being stuck in your hill city following rules and regulations.'

'You don't know how wrong you are. I'm not going to be stuck anywhere, I'm going to be someone.'

'Oh yes, who?'

Judith hugged her knees and let the smile spread all over her face. It was good to be able to tell a stranger; it made it seem real to her all over again.

'I'm marrying an elder's son. His name is Manasses and he's handsome and clever. We're going to be rich – he's already doubled the yield from his portion of land, and he's buying more for our marriage. His father, Chabris, is giving my family a great big bride price for me, *and* my own servant. She's called Endeyeh and she's with me here in Jerusalem.' She smiled at the young man, feeling her triumph blaze out around her. 'We're here buying cloth for my wedding dress and special drinking cups and platters for the house.'

The young man gazed at her and grinned. 'How old are you?'

'Fifteen.'

'And how old's this Manasses?'

'Seventeen,' Judith said proudly.

'And he's known you all your life? He hasn't been in much of a hurry to marry you, has he? Why didn't he snap you up years ago? I would have done.'

'He wanted to do things properly,' retorted Judith. 'He thought I was worth waiting for.' She grimaced at him but at the same time couldn't help a smile. Heat stole into her face. He was making fun of her, which was infuriating, but she liked the way he was looking at her. It disturbed and excited her. *I would have done.*

'Your Manasses is right. I'll wait for you, if you'll wait for me. When I've made my name I'll come and get you.'

'Don't be stupid.'

The young man was still looking at her, his smile playing round his face. 'Oh well, it's your funeral. It's a pity though, you'll be wasted in Bethulia. And you won't be happy with Manasses for long.'

'How do you know?'

'I can see it in your face. You like your freedom, and there's not much of that in Judean towns these days. It's going to get worse too. But like I said, if you'll wait for me I'll come back and get you.'

Judith shook her head, smiling foolishly. She found herself holding the young man's gaze and suddenly, bewilderingly, there were tears in her eyes. She looked hastily away.

Emerging from a knot of people at the lower end of the street was Endeyeh. She started when she saw Judith and waved anxiously. Judith sat very still for a second, then waved back.

'Who's that?' asked the young man.

'Endeyeh.'

'Oh yes, your very own servant.'

Judith blushed. 'Well, she's my friend too, really.'

He nodded, then got to his feet in one quick movement. 'You'd better be going.' He reached down his hand and helped her up. His grip was tight and Judith could feel calluses on his palm. 'Good luck, Manasses' bride,' he said. 'Have a parting drink before you go.' He released her hand and placed the flask in it.

'It's nearly empty.'

'That's all right. Finish it.'

Judith swallowed the last mouthful of water and handed the flask back. Out of the corner of her eye she could see Endeyeh approaching.

'My name's Judith,' she said quickly. 'What's yours?'

He smiled. 'Whatever seems like a good name at the time, mostly. I tell you what, for you I'll be . . . Holofernes.'

'That's an odd name. What does it mean?'

'Who knows? Perhaps you can tell me when we meet again.'

The young man shoved the empty flask into his belt and disappeared into the crowd.

Chapter One

Rain: streams of it running down the windows, pressing and spreading against the glass; it rattled on the roof and little swirls and pools appeared on the skylights overhead. So many people hated rain, but Cathy had always rather liked it. Now it made her think about its opposite: heat and sunbaked buildings of reddish stone, with a blue sky arching above. That was where Matthew was going.

He had been excited on the telephone. Cathy knew Matthew's voice well and she had been able to hear, through the casual tone he adopted, that half-husky low note vibrating. As always, his excitement had infected her, and now she sat in her office, her stomach knotting as she wondered what exactly he was going to tell her when they met.

'Rome,' he'd said. 'For about a month at first, perhaps longer. I might stay on through the summer. Come to lunch, please, Cat. I want to talk to you about it and I can't do it over the phone.'

Cathy picked up her shading pen and began to work away at the right-hand figure on her design rough. Rome: it was a long way away. And all summer was a long time for Matthew to be gone. Her stomach felt oddly hollow and she abandoned the rough and began painstakingly filling in squares on the graph paper.

'Isn't it time you went?' Nick straightened up from his drawing board and looked at his watch. 'It'll take you quarter of an hour to get there, probably more in this weather.'

'Yes,' Cathy said, not moving. 'I'm just about to go.'

Five minutes later, Nick looked up again. His freckled face looked quizzical.

'Well, go on. What's wrong with you? Don't you want a free lunch and something to distract you from that bloody awful book cover?'

'Yes, yes, I'm going, I'm going.' He was right, she was late. Cathy got up and put her coat on, looking in the little wall mirror. Her eyes were darker than usual and her face slightly flushed; it was the haste, and the conflicting emotions. And the anticipation of seeing Matthew.

'Have a good time. I'd look for a bus if I were you. You didn't bring your umbrella in this morning, did you?' Nick always covered all the bases.

'Oh, I'll just walk,' Cathy said and waited for the protest.

'You'll get soaked.'

'I'll run.'

'You'll still—'

'I'll buy an umbrella downstairs.' She slipped out onto the landing, laughing as his protesting 'But you've already got one at home' was cut off by the closing door. Suddenly she was exhilarated. She was going to see Matthew; he had asked her to share his celebration. Wherever he was going, and whatever new twist it would put into their relationship, she could be his friend today.

Cathy ran down the four flights of concrete stairs and out

onto the street. She turned into the big corner branch of Boots but she didn't buy an umbrella; she bought a stick of kohl and drew faintly smudgy lines round her eyes, as a kind of talisman.

There was always this edge of excitement when Matthew and Cathy met. They were partners in so many ways: step-siblings, intimate friends, artist and art exhibitor. They were partners in personality too, after a fashion. Cathy was quieter than Matthew and more stubborn; he was the impulsive, quicksilver one. At least, that was how their families described them.

Cathy and Matthew had several families. Cathy's mother had died when she was five; Matthew's parents had divorced when he was six. Two years after his wife's death Richard, Cathy's father, had married Louise, Matthew's mother. From then on they had shared a home, at first just the four of them, later on with Sammy and Conor, their little half-brothers. The household in the dark green belt of Buckinghamshire was their chief family, but of course there were others on the fringes of their lives. There was Matthew's father, living in Hampshire with his new wife and her two daughters. There were Cathy's grandparents on her mother's side, who loved her desperately for her kinship to their daughter; and there was a network of aunts and uncles and cousins deriving from all five parents, who throughout the years had invited Cathy and Matthew to stay with them, sometimes separately, sometimes together.

Cathy and Matthew were less than a year apart in age, and at the beginning they had seemed to resent one another fiercely. Seven and three-quarters and eight and a half when they became stepbrother and sister, they had fought furiously and bitterly. And inventively.

After six months, the head of their local primary school had invited Louise and Richard in for a discussion. There was a problem, he explained, with the two children. They continually ganged up on the other pupils and sometimes on the teachers; they took advantage of their cleverness to disrupt classes and when they were made to sit at opposite sides of the room they reduced everyone to fits of laughter by miming behind the teacher's back. Richard and Louise had been astonished. It had never occurred to them to look for an alliance beneath the fighting.

The alliance had survived separation when, at eleven, they had been sent away to different schools 'to widen their experience'. Cathy and Matthew had both enjoyed their schools in a way; they had made plenty of friends, grown, changed, and met up again at home every school holidays. With adolescence, the reunions had become unpredictable, sometimes moving, sometimes disappointing, but always prefaced by this physical excitement which was pulsing through Cathy now.

In their last years at school, they spent less time together as holidays became broken up by stays with friends, trips abroad, exam revision. Then at eighteen they had left school and home. Matthew had gone to Cambridge to read history and Cathy to Goldsmith's in London, to study art.

Cathy and Matthew were now twenty-six. For the last few years they had both lived in London and, in very different ways, pursued careers in art. Matthew, having firmly rejected all their parents' proposals for his future – Foreign Office, banking, the City, computers – had done an MA in art history and got himself a series of short-term jobs with galleries and museums. For a while he had been notorious as the organiser of illegal exhibitions in disused warehouses. That had earned him friends among the artists he showed and enemies among existing gallery owners in about equal measure; Louise and Richard, needless to say, had been horrified. After a year of this 'cultural terrorism', a phrase Matthew had coined to get publicity, he had decided that it was time to mend some bridges. He had started applying for regular jobs and eventually got one at the Clerkgate, a prestigious gallery on the edge of the City. He had been there for eighteen months and was doing well.

Cathy was a painter. She painted abstracts and had been one of Matthew's regular artists in the warehouse days. She had received some useful attention then and had sold pictures to a few private buyers and to the Arts Council. Since then, she had continued to paint, to show occasionally – usually in mixed shows – and to sell in small quantities. She didn't earn nearly enough to live on. For regular money she relied on doing illustrations for book covers and other commercial work, and she shared the small bare office with Nick, a fellow artist, for that purpose.

Through the last few years, Cathy and Matthew had shared one another's ups and downs. When Louise and Richard had been predictably discouraging about Cathy's painting, Matthew had said, 'Don't be bloody ridiculous, of course you're an artist,' and had found her a cheap studio to rent. He had forced her to finish work in time for his warehouse shows too, and introduced her to the critics he managed to lure to them.

In turn, Cathy had designed fly-posters and leaflets for the shows, gave Matthew her sofa whenever he was between flats and defended him against the attacks of their family and more respectable friends. Twice she had hidden him from angry warehouse landlords.

Those precarious days were now over. Sometimes Cathy

missed them. There had been aspects of them which she held very dear, days and nights when she and Matthew had almost been able to shut out the rest of the world.

But then there had been the other things: the anger, the jealousy, the struggle that would go on between them – over what, they weren't sure, but it would rage relentlessly for days on end, stringing them both tighter and tighter. Louise had told her years ago that she and Matthew were not good for one another and it seemed she'd been right. No, not seemed; Cathy had known at the time, when Louise had said it during that healthy woman-and-stepdaughter walk in the woods, that it was true. 'You and Matthew are very alike. You have a lot to give each other but you need to be careful. You especially, Cathy. Don't let him take you over.'

Cathy had been seventeen then, and racked with jealousy because Matthew had decided to go on holiday with a new girlfriend. She could still recall the sensation now.

She could recall so many feelings connected with Matthew. They would always be close, she was convinced of that. But the blank spot in their relationship troubled her. The gap where love and antagonism, rivalry and a fierce tenderness bled into one another. Sometimes Cathy wondered exactly what it was they wanted from one another.

Passion often hovered very close, and last year they had come to the verge of being lovers. Cathy had been the one to pull back. She hadn't done so for the reasons with which Matthew angrily taunted her: emotional cowardice, failure of nerve, a complete inability to face up to their parents' outrage. Those things had certainly played their part, but her main fear had been a deeper one.

She and Matthew were stepbrother and sister, childhood

allies, rivals and friends. What would they turn into once they became lovers too? Matthew seemed to want so much of her and to call out a similarly devouring need in herself. Surely love wasn't meant to obliterate you. Yet when Cathy tried to imagine what it might be like to become Matthew's lover, even to have a brief affair with him, she saw only darkness.

Still, they could be friends, no matter what happened. And now that Matthew had accepted her decision, they were. That was why he had called her before anyone else, to celebrate his promotion. And that was why she was hurrying through the crowded lunch-hour streets to meet him.

Cathy put her head down and ran through the slanting rain, listening to the thudding of her feet on the pavement.

Matthew was waiting at the table in Benni's. He was sitting in front of the mural, so that a red and purple sunset blazed behind his head. It made him look like a brooding angel: pale face, shadows in the hollows of his cheeks, his black hair damp and curling.

He was drinking wine and looked happy. As she drew nearer, Cathy realised he had chosen the seat as a joke: above his left shoulder hovered the seven hills of Rome, crazily diminished in an attempt at perspective.

'Very funny,' she said, leaning over to kiss him. He grinned and squinted sideways at the hills.

'The Capitol, the Palatine, the Aventine, the Quirinal,' he chanted. 'The – er – well, I can't remember the others.'

'The Esquiline, the Viminal, the Caelian.'

'God, how do you know that?'

'From school. You know how ferocious my memory is.'

She sat down and held out her glass for the bottle of wine he was brandishing. It gave her a good excuse to drop her eyes.

She had indeed learnt the names of the Roman hills at school; but she'd done it to bring her thoughts closer to Matthew who had been away in Rome at the time on an art trip organised by his own school. Cathy could still remember sitting in the history lesson, repeating the names to herself, savouring them. Their outlandish syllables had seemed to conduct her secretly to where Matthew was, had made her feel she was there with him.

Oh hell, why was she thinking about things like that now?

She raised her glass and smiled at him. 'Congratulations. I'm really pleased for you, you deserve this.'

'Yes, I do, don't I? All the same, Exhibitions Officer for the Clerkgate . . .' Matthew pulled a wry face. 'It's not exactly storming the barricades of art, is it? For a second back there, when Greg offered me the promotion, I almost wanted to say no.' He smiled wickedly. 'Almost. Just to see what the family would say.'

'"Aaaagh!" I imagine. You don't really have any doubts, do you? After all, you'll have much more influence now. It's quite something, you know, to be the person who's opening up the Clerkgate for new artists.'

'Yes, I know. And there's the other side of it too, persuading people that they might get to enjoy some of this funny new art. It gives me a real kick whenever I hear someone coming out of an exhibition saying, "Actually I rather liked that installation thingy." Not that they do very often.' Matthew shrugged. 'Oh well, let's hope I can make a go of my first big exhibition. Let's order, and I'll tell you about it.'

He reached for the menu and put it flat on the table so that they could both see it. Their heads bent close together over it and Cathy was very aware of him. She couldn't make herself read about lasagne and spaghetti alla vongole; instead, shielded by her brown hair, still damp from the rain, she watched his darker curls falling on his face. She could see his lashes moving as he blinked, casting shadows on his crooked nose.

Suddenly his hand came up and lifted her hair from her face. Cathy looked at him, startled; his touch was gentle, his fingers rested with perfect steadiness a millimetre from her cheek, but his gaze was serious. In the shadow cast by his hand, his pupils had widened, greedy for light; they made his eyes look black.

'Thank you for coming, Cat.' His voice was even but she recognised the intent note in it. For a second she felt a rebellious happiness, then came the ripple of unease.

'That's all right.' She made herself sound surprised and amused, and at the same time she moved gently, pulling her hair free of him. 'You couldn't celebrate alone. You are paying, though, I hope.'

There was a little pause, and then Matthew withdrew his hand and smiled.

'Oh yes, I'm paying. I can even afford it now that I'm such a big shot.'

'Ah, you get a pay rise, then. Is it a decent one?'

'Yes. Quite a decent one, thank you, nearly two thousand. Enough to buy me a plate of calamari. What are you going to have? Whatever it is, leave room for a pudding, because they've got that brilliant zabaglione today. And let's have some more wine, too.' He sat back and gestured at the bottle. 'I seem to have sunk half a bottle waiting for you. Why are you always so late?'

The moment had passed safely.

Over the calamari, Matthew explained the details of his

promotion. He was being made into a fully-fledged exhibitions officer and would have responsibility for organising one major exhibition and at least two smaller ones every year. He would also continue to do authentications in his specialist area, the early seventeenth century, and he might also continue to do a small amount of restoration work.

'I know it sounds like an odd mixture,' he said, 'but that's because of the way it's happened. You see, I've been promoted in a hurry because a rather big job has – er – come my way.'

'Come your way?'

'Yes, an important exhibition.' He put down the calamari ring he had been forgetting to eat. His face showed an odd mixture of pleasure and wariness. 'Look, this is confidential at the moment.' He filled up both their glasses to the brim. 'You'll see why in a minute. Basically, it's quite a coup for the Clerkgate to get this, let alone for me. It's going to be an exhibition based on the private collection of one family, which has been built up for generations. Have you heard of the Bonaventuras?'

'The Bonaventuras? As in the Bonaventura auction house?'

'That's right, the Christie's of Rome, except that it's still controlled by the one family. It's their collection.'

'Wow, that *is* impressive.' Cathy was astonished. Matthew was grinning over his wine and she wasn't surprised; the Bonaventuras were shy of publicity but most people connected with the art world had heard of them. They were an old Roman family who had started an auction house two hundred years ago and who still refused to sell out their majority shareholding, despite the wealth it would bring them. According to regular and respectful mentions in the art press, Enzo Bonaventura, the current head of the firm, lived in a beautiful old palazzo in

Rome, along with the family art collection which was full of esoteric pieces by minor artists. He was secretive about it; you had to be a scholar or an art expert to be invited to see the collection, and even then you were usually shown only the works in your specialist area.

Cathy had known that the Clerkgate had some dealings with the auction house. Matthew had told her that the Clerkgate's specialists sometimes did authentications and restoration work for them, but she'd never known he was personally involved.

'That's amazing,' she said. 'God, Matthew, that really is a coup. I had no idea you were remotely connected with the Bonaventuras. How on earth did it happen?'

'Luck, initially. Or serendipity, being in the right place at the right time. You see, it turns out my choice of MA subject wasn't so useless after all. Enzo Bonaventura has a special liking for early seventeenth-century Italian art, and I'm the Clerkgate's specialist in the area. I did a few authentications for Bonaventura's over the winter and Enzo took to me. I took to him too, actually; we've had some very good discussions.'

'So you've met him face to face!'

Matthew laughed. 'Yes, several times. He's not a recluse, you know; he just doesn't like nightclubs and the newspapers. He was in London for the big seventeenth-century sale last winter – that was when we first met. I'd already done several jobs for the firm by then so I was wheeled out to meet him. And we got on well. He was very friendly, nothing like the mystery figure the press make him out to be. Well, all right, if he takes against you I'm sure he could be chilling. But if you share an interest with him, and he likes you, he's good company.'

Cathy looked at Matthew closely. He evidently knew Enzo

quite well. 'You never told me,' she said, trying to ignore the pang inside her.

Matthew touched her hand fleetingly. 'I know, I'm sorry. I wanted to, but I was hoping something might come of it and, well, I suppose it was superstition. That and the fact that he's a stickler for discretion and I didn't feel I should tell anyone that I was talking to him.'

'Were you talking to him about the exhibition, even then?'

'Oh no. We were talking about individual artists and their paintings, mainly seventeenth-century ones. But after a while he was obviously sounding me out for what I knew about other areas. There had been rumours about a possible Bonaventura exhibition some years back, which came to nothing; I had that in the back of my mind, so I did wonder. And then last week Enzo rang the director and said he'd decided to mount a definitive Bonaventura Collection show and send it round Europe. He wanted us to handle it for him. And he wanted *me* to be the organiser.'

Matthew lowered his voice as the waiter came to take their plates. Neither of them had eaten much. He waited till the waiter had gone and leaned forward, his elbows on the table, his hands playing with the stem of Cathy's glass.

'So now I can tell you, though I'd rather you didn't tell anyone else for a while. It's official, but it's a pretty huge step up for me, and I want it to come out as slowly as possible.'

'Of course. I won't tell anyone.' Cathy smiled, refusing to listen to the treacherous whimper inside her: *when are you going away? How long before I see you again?* 'Matthew, this is brilliant. God, you have kept this quiet.'

Matthew hunched his shoulders, something he always did when he felt awkward. 'I wanted to tell you,' he said. 'You were the one person I really did want to tell. But until I was sure, I had to play it safe.'

'Of course, of course. I don't mind.' Cathy spoke quickly; she suspected she had fooled neither of them. 'So tell me about Enzo. Wasn't there some sort of tragedy with his wife?'

'Yes. It was ages ago, back in the sixties. Alessandra, the wife, had a crack-up when she and Enzo had been married just a few years, while their son was still a very young child. She went missing from the palazzo and there was a big hunt for her. The police finally caught up with her in the south of Italy; there was a car chase and a crash and a man who was in the car with her died. Enzo took her back to Rome and she killed herself.'

'Why?'

Matthew shrugged. 'She was having a breakdown. She was mentally ill. I only know what other people say, and what's reported in the old newspaper cuttings in our library. She seems to have been having delusions at the time. At the scene of the accident she said she needed to get on board the ferry and "go home", to her own country, before she did something terrible. She said someone who knew she was wicked had told her to kill a man. If the press reports are anything to go by, it was a terrible scandal at the time.'

'Was any of it true? That she was told to kill someone?'

'God, no. Everyone who knew her said she was a gentle woman, the last person you'd ask to do anything violent. It was all delusions, Cathy, she was mentally ill.' Matthew paused. 'It must have been awful for Enzo.'

'And their son. How old was he?'

'Six or seven, I think.'

'How sad. And Enzo's never remarried?'

'No. I've never talked to him about it of course, but I think he must have been devastated by it. He virtually retired from active work in the business for several years and locked himself away in the palazzo with the child, Danilo. The business started to slide but Enzo wouldn't go back to it. When he did emerge from mourning he went off on a series of foreign trips with his son, for about a year. When they came back, things had reached crisis point and there was talk of Enzo having to sell up.'

'But he didn't.'

'No. He opened up the palazzo again, put Danilo in school and said he was ready to get back to work. It took five years before Bonaventura's was back in profit, but since then it's been up and up.'

'Quite a story,' Cathy said. 'He must be an extraordinary man.'

'He is.'

'What about his son? He's just a few years older than us, isn't he? Doesn't he run the American end of the business now?'

'Yes, he does. Of course, Bonaventura's are too small to compete in a big way in the States; they operate mainly through association with one of the international houses there. But Danilo's been out there supervising it for the last four years. I've never met him, but I think I'm about to quite soon.' Matthew sounded unenthusiastic.

'Is he likely to be a problem?'

'He's got a reputation as an ice man. He's very, very protective of the Bonaventura name and especially of the collection. He's been doing some aggressive buying for it – buying other pieces by artists already in the collection. His methods have been quite ruthless and it seems to be just for the sake of it – some of the pieces aren't up to much. I have a feeling that he doesn't want Enzo to do this exhibition; there was a definite hint of warning in the way Enzo said, "My son will be coming home soon. You'll be working with him, of course."'

Matthew was a good impersonator and in his voice she could clearly hear another man's tones; charming, cultivated, with a hint of steel in them. 'Like that, is he?'

'Yes. Danilo's going to be a challenge, all right,' said Matthew, misunderstanding her. 'Look. This was in *Artworld* last week.' He pulled the magazine out of his briefcase and folded it back at an inside page. 'There.'

The article was headed 'Danilo In The Lions' Den' and was about an American auction house deal. But Cathy's attention was immediately caught by the photograph. It showed a man in his late twenties, wearing a well-cut suit, about to cross a busy road. It was a classic posed man-in-a-hurry shot, except that the man at the centre of it had an unexpected stillness. Danilo Bonaventura looked out at her, a tall, slightly heavy man, with dark eyes and straight features, and Cathy felt a small, violent tap of recognition.

'I've seen him before,' she said.

'Very likely. The press have been getting quite keen on him since he's been in America. You've probably seen other photographs.'

'No, I've seen him in the flesh.' Cathy frowned. Had she? She couldn't be sure. In that instant of recognition she'd had a memory of him standing a few yards away, half-turned towards her, but now she tried to place it, it shifted and became indistinct.

'Maybe not,' she said slowly. 'No. Do you know what I

think it might be? He looks like one of those portraits of Renaissance noblemen. You know, young men with experience on their faces. Young men who stand by curtains and look out with thoughtful eyes.'

Matthew laughed. 'You always were a romantic. When Danilo's thoughtful, his mind's on making money and promoting the Bonaventura family interests.'

'Just like Renaissance noblemen, in fact,' she said. But she looked again at the photograph and felt sure Matthew was wrong. That face did not belong to a cold man. The eyes looked up at her with a complicated expression, very direct. It made her rather uncomfortable and she handed the magazine back to Matthew.

'It'll be interesting to hear how you get on with him.'

Matthew nodded. 'You'll hear, don't worry. I'll probably be on the phone grousing about him every day.' He rolled the magazine into a cylinder; Cathy sat watching his hands. The talk had died away between them, leaving a silence. She tried to break it, but her throat hurt.

'I'll miss you,' Matthew said suddenly. He looked up into her eyes. 'Why don't you come out and see me?' he said steadily. 'I'm going to be there quite a while. It's a lovely time of year in Rome. I could get you a room in my hotel and you'd have lots of time to work.'

For a moment Cathy didn't speak; she couldn't, she was overwhelmed by the desire to say yes. And Matthew knew that, damn him.

She shook her head. 'Don't tempt me. I've got much too much commercial work to do and, besides, I can't afford it.'

'I see. OK.' Matthew's face was suddenly angry. He ducked his head and dropped the magazine back into his case. When he looked up again, his expression was neutral. 'What's all this work you've got on?' he asked.

Cathy began to tell him about the book-cover commissions and the posters, but it was hard to concentrate. After the Bonaventuras it all sounded very dull, and Matthew's invitation seemed to hang in the air, mocking them both. She talked on brightly about Nick and the office, putting a wall of words between them.

After lunch, the two of them walked down through Covent Garden together, across the Strand to the Embankment. The rain had stopped and the clouds had broken up. A freshening wind drove high across the sky, and the moisture clinging to the new leaves glistened in the sun.

'The start of an English spring,' said Matthew. 'I'll be in Rome by the time these leaves are fully out.' He reached up and picked a stray blossom from her hair. 'It's all right,' he said irritably, 'there's no need to flinch. Just count the days till I'm safely gone.'

Cathy turned abruptly away. 'Leave it, Matt.'

She stared at the river. The grey body of water stretched before her, but another image was vivid in her mind. Narrow streets and orange stone and tall, thin windows shuttered in green, behind one of which Matthew would be waiting. Like Matthew himself, it lured her and warned her away at the same time.

[illegible]

Cathy sat at the [illegible] and [illegible]

[illegible] would handle [illegible]

[illegible]

paintings [illegible] against the wall [illegible] to inspire [illegible] All [illegible] during the day and evenings [illegible] canvases.

So there she was, waiting to board the [illegible] would she [illegible]

Chapter Two

Cathy sat at the plastic-topped bar and sipped her kir, keeping an eye on the flight information screen. She ran her mind over the various arrangements and items of business she had left with Nick. No, there was nothing to worry about there; Nick would handle them all impeccably. Not that she had ever had serious doubts. From the moment she had recognised Matthew's writing on the envelope ten days ago, Cathy had known she was going. She had not even needed to open it and read his words.

'My pensione is quiet and has a spare room next to mine. There are so many things I'd like to be seeing with you. Please think about it, Cathy.'

As if she needed to think. She was sick of London. Winter had given way to a dull grey spring. At the office the book covers were finished and her next task was to get on the phone and drum up more work. At home in her studio her latest paintings were propped half-finished against the wall, failing to inspire her. All she had to cheer her up were Nick's banter during the day and evenings spent with friends in pubs and cinemas.

So here she was, waiting to board the plane to Rome. It would be a fortnight's stay; a holiday. Nick had been encouraging. 'You've been looking down recently,' he'd said. 'It'll do you good. Don't worry about this place. I'll ask Howard if he'd like to take over your desk for a couple of weeks, then if anything urgent comes in he can deal with it.' Howard was a friend of Nick's who sometimes took on overflow work for them; Nick had promptly phoned him, he had agreed, and that had been that.

It was, after all, very simple to go away on holiday; people did it all the time. And a holiday was all it was.

Cathy took another mouthful of kir and opened her street-plan of Rome. The pensione where she would be joining Matthew was in a side street near the Spanish Steps; on the map it appeared to be quite a way from the Ghetto where the Bonaventuras had their house, but she knew that Rome was small. Matthew had said it was less than ten minutes' walk, and he had chosen the pensione because from his window in the morning he could smell the baskets of cut flowers which were laid out for sale up and down the steps.

Cathy had been to Italy only once before, with a friend when they were students. They had gone to Florence and to Venice using student rail cards, and their money had run out before they could get down to Rome. She had seen photographs and films of the city, of course, but they tended to show this or that landmark, at best a jumble of ruins, restaurants and churches. She had no sense of how the city worked as a place in which to live.

She thought of Matthew walking through the streets, under the shadows of the domed churches, through the ancient Ghetto to the Palazzo Bonaventura. 'You would like Enzo,' Matthew had written. 'He's fascinating company and very interested in young artists.' He hadn't mentioned Danilo.

Over on the edge of her vision, the flight indicator whirred. Her flight was boarding at gate 11. She finished her drink and started off down the series of ramps and corridors.

It was a three-hour flight, and after two hours Cathy gave up trying to read. She bought a second gin and tonic from the trolley and stared out of the window. The Alps passed below in folds of brown, streaked with white; sometimes she could see the coastline and a section of wrinkled blue sea. It was hard to get any real idea of the land through such a small opening.

It was hot and she felt her eyes closing. She welcomed the idea of sleep but as she drifted deeper, so the heat increased and made it hard to breathe. The air in the plane was dry and smelled dusty. Soon it caught in her throat and she wanted to gasp; she forced her eyelids apart and tried to sit up, thinking that if she surfaced from sleep for a few seconds, she could turn the cool air flow onto her face.

At first she thought there was something wrong with her eyes. She struggled to focus on the seat in front of her but instead of its blue upholstery and plastic tray there was an indeterminate criss-cross pattern that went down and up as far as she could see. She turned her head to the window. The criss-cross was there too, and on the other side where the aisle should be. She blinked and waited for the play of light to disperse; instead, it solidified and became more distinct. She was looking at a lattice of branches.

The lattice stretched around her on three sides. The boughs which made it up were small and pliant and here and there parched leaves were twined among them. The wood was unevenly spaced and light came through the gaps – bright light, cutting into the gloom. Noises came in too: shouts and cries, scraping and banging, animal noises. Some of them came from a long way off and as she turned her head to hear better, grit stung her eyes and dust blew through the latticing into her throat.

In the dream, then, she was out of doors. But she was enclosed in some kind of hut. She felt very curious. Once or twice in the past she'd become caught between waking and sleeping, but those half-dreams had been confusing and rather panicky, not clear like this. In this dream so far there was no emotion. It was like watching a film come into focus around her. And it was all around her. She looked up and saw that over her head more branches, darker and twisted and sprouting fresh leaves, were loosely heaped to make a roof.

She turned to look over her shoulder and behind her it was different: a dark cloth hung there, its end seemingly anchored to the ground – it was taut and didn't stir when the breeze rustled the leaves in the roof.

She was shaded by the lattice and the roof, but it was very hot. It was a heavy, thick heat, and as she thought about it, it intensified and filled with the smell of the branches, and of her own sweat, and of something sickening and oily. She gasped and breathed through her mouth.

Then other sensations began to come. Her knees hurt and the muscles in her legs ached, and along her back, and in her neck. She put her hand to her thigh, then onto the earth. She was kneeling; she had been kneeling a long time.

Voices sounded, nearer than the other sounds had been. They belonged to two women, and they rose over one another and dipped again in a string of guttural syllables. They were having a conversation, emphatic, full of expression, but the words were completely alien.

Suddenly Cathy was frightened. And then, as if the fear had

let them in, other emotions came searing through her. There was misery and grief and anger, but most of all, so strong that all the others went down before it, there was guilt. It coursed through her body, pressed on her eyes, weighed down her tongue . . .

'Are you all right? I'm sorry, but you seemed to be in discomfort. Is it hay fever? Would you like an antihistamine?'

The lattice was gone and in its place, very clear in the crystalline light of the cabin, was the plump woman in the flowery dress in seat B. To Cathy's eyes, the flowers on her bosom were much too bright and too large; her coral lips were overpowering. She stared, trying to get her bearings; her eyes fell on the gold cross and chain round the woman's neck and for a strange second she wondered what it meant.

'Do you need a doctor?' the woman said.

'No.' Cathy found her voice. It was uncertain. 'Thank you, I'm all right. It was just so hot.'

The woman looked puzzled. Cathy felt a draught against her face and realised that the air conditioning was working perfectly; in fact, the cabin was rather cool. She rubbed her forehead to get rid of the sweat, and to shield herself.

'That's better. Thank you. I'll just ring for some water.' Her throat was so dry, she was finding it hard to talk. She smiled self-consciously. 'Was I asleep a long time?'

The woman looked baffled. 'You were hardly asleep at all, dear. You'd only closed your eyes a second.'

'Oh.' Cathy leaned back and pressed the button to call the stewardess. She wanted to be left alone so that she could recall the dream, but even as she turned to the window, she realised it was too late. She could remember the individual elements of it – the hut of branches, the chattering voices, the anguish – but they had become fragmented. It was like seeing pieces of a jigsaw puzzle instead of the real thing.

The stewardess arrived and Cathy asked for a glass of water. She drank it with relief; it was soothing on her throat and she imagined it washing away not only the thirst, but the sense of oppression that still lingered.

Matthew was waiting for her just the other side of Customs. It was a small airport – her cheap flight came into Ciampino, in the south-east of Rome – and not very smart. Matthew was leaning on the metal barrier, between a group of young girls in nun's habits and a man with a piece of cardboard reading 'J. Sykes APL'. Matthew looked more rested than when she'd last seen him; his pale skin had a patina of health and his face was relaxed. One of the young nuns was watching him with interest.

When he saw Cathy he gave a quick smile and dodged under the barrier.

'Cat. You really came.'

His hands were light on her shoulders and his mouth barely touched her temple in a kiss. Then, amid an easy flow of chatter and exchanged questions, he picked up her suitcase and they strolled through the arrivals hall and out of the doors. A green and brown landscape greeted Cathy, and a surprising heat. She had a moment's disorientation, remembering her dream.

'The bus goes from over there,' said Matthew. 'Come on, you'll have to dodge the taxis.' He took her hand and pulled her across the busy forecourt. Cathy's mind spun: they were running across the playground together again; she felt a childlike freedom mingled with love and desire and for a second she was completely happy. They gained the bus stop laughing and she looked away, leaving her hand in Matthew's longer than necessary.

The bus arrived half full of people, and once the small bunch of new passengers was settled, it drove busily and noisily out of the forecourt. It was evidently a local bus service, for it rattled along a series of country lanes, stopping at unlikely spots to let people on and off.

'Where's the city?' Cathy asked, surprised.

'Not far away. Rome's small – a fraction of the size of London. It does have suburbs, but they tend to be ten minutes from St Peter's on the bus.'

'What's going on there?'

A furious argument had broken out at the front of the bus, between an old man and a very old woman who had just got on. The volume rose above the sound of the revving engine and increased steadily; the torrent of words was too fast for Cathy to follow.

Matthew hid a smile. 'They're arguing about that window seat up there. It's reserved for certain categories of people – war amputees, victims of industrial accidents, old people. There's a strict hierarchy. She's telling him that she's older than he is and a woman and so she should have it; he's saying that he was injured in a – hold on, I can't quite make it out – in an accident when he was driving a Red Cross ambulance in the war. She's saying that doesn't count as a war injury. Those cards they're brandishing are their identity cards which carry all the details.'

'But there are plenty of free seats back here.'

'That's not the point. They both think they're entitled to that free seat up there.' Matthew shrugged, amused at Cathy's astonishment. 'You'll see quite a lot of it. Taking precedence is very important for old people here. It's the pay-off for a lifetime of having to let their elders take precedence over *them*.'

Cathy looked down the aisle at the two old combatants. The woman seemed to be gaining the upper hand. As she watched, the man launched into a sudden spate then, still hectoring, pulled himself away by the hanging straps and struggled down the bus into one of the unreserved seats. The woman seated herself, glaring straight ahead. After ten seconds she looked across at her adversary and gave him a stilted nod. He returned it. The formal exchange had a kind of grace about it.

This was so different from the way British people would behave. Cathy wondered what it must be like to live in a country where the people were vehement. She glanced at Matthew and saw that he was looking across the aisle, reading the back of someone else's newspaper. He looked very much at home.

Once or twice in the past Cathy had seen a resemblance between Matthew and young men in Italian paintings. Now she realised that he wasn't unlike some of the other passengers on the bus. The young man two rows in front of them, for instance, had the same combination of long nose and pale skin, with the eyes set rather far above the cheekbones. And the old woman who had won the seat had a similar cast of features; when she was younger, she must have looked remarkably like Matthew. And in his own way, Cathy reflected, filtered through an English upbringing, Matthew was vehement and prepared to fight for what he wanted – for work, for ideas, for people. He had fought for her during the last few years, and it had taken all her strength to keep him away.

But he did not look as if he were fighting now. He looked

happy. There was a new confidence in his eyes. Cathy dropped her eyes to his hand, lying several safe inches from hers, and told herself that she was glad. Perhaps, she added to herself, averting her gaze to one of the other passengers, Matthew would find his spiritual home here. He already seemed changed and more at ease with himself; perhaps he would stay with these people and never come back.

'Cathy, you're glaring at that poor man.' Matthew's fingers pinched the back of her hand gently, the warning sign they had devised as adolescents for use at table, to ward off family rows.

She pinched him back, smiling into his face, and felt better. Then she moved her hand out of reach. She settled to looking out of the window. They were on the outskirts of the city now. Modern apartment blocks alternated with older, thinner buildings. The place had a Mediterranean air, but so far there was nothing she could recognise as Roman. A sign ahead of them read 'Roma Centro', and Cathy craned her head to see if she could catch a glimpse of the city proper. Beyond a line of mid-rise buildings she saw trees, and something flashed up from their midst.

'Oh my God!' Cathy wasn't able to control her start.

'What's the matter?'

Her heart was beating uncomfortably fast. 'What's that?'

Matthew followed her pointing finger, but the bus was lurching to the left to overtake a lorry. As they came onto the straight again, the huge object reappeared in the distance, a jagged tooth of stone, dark against the bright sky.

'Ah, that. It's the baths of Caracalla,' said Matthew. 'They're enormous when you get close up to them. It's quite a shock, isn't it, seeing the old city break through like that?'

A ruin, that was all; old stones, nothing to worry about. So why did they seem to remind her of something awful?

Cathy rested her fingertip against the window to steady it and breathed out. 'I hadn't expected the ruins to look so big,' she said.

'Oh, they're huge,' said Matthew. 'Much bigger than most of the medieval and Renaissance buildings. They built things on a different scale.'

Cathy nodded and smiled and went back to looking out of the window. The bus was trundling along a wide straight road now, leaving the ruins behind. She stared over the shoulder, watching as the change of angle revealed more uprights and arches behind the first.

The dream on the plane: that was where she had felt a similar emotion. God, she was in a state. It must all be displacement about Matthew. She must try and relax; she would be seeing plenty more ruins before they reached the centre of Rome.

All the same, she found it hard to tear her eyes away from the baths. Their broken silhouette spoke of age-old violence and she kept twisting to look at them, almost superstitiously, until the modern buildings obscured the view.

The city was beautiful. Long before the bus reached its terminus, Cathy's eyes were dazzled. Domed churches stood on every other corner; muscular statues perched on parapets and rose triumphantly out of fountains; the sloping streets were lined with narrow buildings of red, brown and ochre. On the ground floor of the old buildings, plate-glass windows flashed, the shop goods laid out confidently behind them. On the upper floors, signs jutted out of stone balustrades and announced 'Scuola', 'Hotel' and 'Farmacia'.

Cathy hadn't imagined anything like this. She had vaguely

supposed that the historic monuments would be grouped in one area, and that the rest of the city would be pretty but businesslike. Instead it was all jostling together: smart and shabby, secular and Christian, modern and ancient.

And the streets were alive with people.

'Most of them are on their way home,' Matthew said, 'doing the shopping on the way. Many of the little shops shut for siesta then open again in the late afternoon and stay open till evening. No one wants to shop in the heat of the day.'

'What time is it, then?' Cathy was confused by the day's travelling.

'Just gone six. You'll need to change your watch, we're an hour ahead here.'

They changed buses in front of the station. The great forecourt was filled with people, teeming round the green buses as they arrived and left. They squeezed onto one, with Matthew struggling to find room for the suitcase, and travelled along a wide road which dipped downhill, then turned right. The bus was too crowded for Cathy to see out of the windows and she was surprised when Matthew said, 'Here we are. Come on, we have to get off at the front door.'

They stepped down into a warm evening in the middle of a large irregular piazza. Opposite them steps flew away up a steep hill, tier after tier of curving yellow stone, finally giving onto a small church with angular towers, far above.

'The Spanish Steps,' said Matthew. 'With the Church Trinitá dei Monti on the top. The tumbledown building on the right-hand side of the steps is where Keats died. He had a little room in there, with one window giving onto the steps. And there,' he pointed to the far side of the steps, where a back street emerged, 'is the Pensione Flora.'

* * *

Seeing Cathy in the pensione bedroom filled Matthew with a strange mix of feelings. He had wanted her to come so much. He had imagined just how she would look, walking across the polished tiles, sitting on the bed, brushing her hair in front of the mirrored wardrobe door. When he had inspected this room for her, he'd visualised it all.

And now she was here, paler than in his imaginings and slightly tense, but he would soon put that right.

'Do you like it?'

'It's lovely.' She went to the tall window which he'd just opened for her, and leaned out. The slanting light touched her dark hair with reds and browns, and cast her shadow across the floor behind her. Matthew was looking at two Cathys: the flesh and blood one with her back to him and the insubstantial one who seemed to stand alone in the centre of the room, watching both of them.

Two Cathys; or Cathy and Cat, as he had sometimes thought of them: his stepsister and his potential lover. Up until now, the lover had been forced into the shadows by the Cathy who cared about what their family would think, who worried about the world's censure. The Cat he loved was able to live only in fits and starts, when Cathy allowed her to. Would she allow her to now?

Cathy had come to Rome. Matthew knew it must mean something. But she had moved towards him before, only to back away again. Eighteen months ago, when they had come nearer than ever before, so near, they had ended up making that stupid vow to each other. He had kept it, reluctantly. He'd had no real alternative, as Cat had hurled herself into Jonathan Fielding's arms.

She still wore Jonathan's ring, he noticed, but she hadn't mentioned him for a long time now. And she was here.

Longing, hope and frustration were weaving their usual mesh inside Matthew. The hope was strong and growing stronger, but he didn't dare encourage it. There were other things too: compassion for Cat's uncertainty and an oddly down-to-earth, brotherly devilment that made him want to tease her. *Come on, Cat, what's the matter? Scared?*

'I hope you don't mind looking onto the back street. I wanted to move in here myself and give you my room, but the patrona wouldn't have it. This is very much her home, you see, and what she says goes. She pretended to get miffed when I said this room wasn't so nice, so I had to give in, but you can always use my room during the day. There's a connecting door.'

Matthew turned the key to unlock the door. He'd had quite an argument with the patrona over that. She'd wanted to keep the door locked during Cathy's stay, and he'd had to make great play of the fact that Cathy was his stepsister before she would supply the key. She still wasn't happy about it; he hoped Cathy hadn't noticed her searching looks as she'd shown them in.

He opened the door and held out his hand to Cathy. She came across the room and stopped next to him. After a second's hesitation she took his hand.

'My kingdom,' he said jokingly. 'It's all yours.'

Cathy laughed. 'I can't see a thing.'

'Just wait till I open the shutters.'

Cat looked happier now, standing on his balcony in the late afternoon sun. The flower-sellers at the foot of the steps were packing up their baskets and the scent of their blooms wafted up through the dust and exhaust fumes, and the smell of coffee from the bar below.

Matthew went to his corner cupboard and got out a bottle of red wine and the two large goblets he'd bought yesterday.

'Here you are. A drink to the city.'

'Thanks.' Cathy lifted her glass and raised her eyebrows at his. 'Why is yours so much smaller? Are you on a temperance drive?'

'Hardly. It's work. I've got to go over to the palazzo for a little while. I'm really sorry to go as soon as you arrive, but I won't be long – an hour probably.'

'That's all right, I know you've got a lot on. How's it going?'

'Well. Very well.' He smiled at her. It was good to be able to confide his pleasure. 'The collection is incredibly eclectic, such an odd mixture of things. At the moment I'm feeling my way round. I still haven't seen everything they've got.' He sipped the wine; it tasted warm and loose on his tongue. 'That's one reason I need to go over there now. A French scholar is coming to look at some of the early seventeenth-century paintings; Enzo will be showing them to her and I'd like to be there just in case he decides to show her a certain painting I'm interested in. I've never seen it yet, but I know it must be in the palazzo.'

Cathy laughed. 'That sounds very roundabout. Can't you just ask to see it?'

Matthew thought of Enzo's reticence, and of the quiet palazzo waiting for him now, and of the yellowed newspaper cuttings tucked away in the bottom pocket of the records file. 'No, I couldn't; it's got too much history attached to it. You remember the story about Enzo's wife?'

'About her breakdown, you mean, and her suicide?'

'Yes. Well, I was looking through the files in the palazzo archives, doing some research on when various pieces were bought and where, when I came across some newspaper cuttings from the time of her death. Several of the Italian papers printed pictures of Alessandra and the palazzo, and of Enzo. And one also showed a reproduction of a painting which had apparently been Alessandra's wedding present to Enzo. It was only a fuzzy repro, of course, but the painting looked – rather fascinating.' Matthew paused. Was 'fascinating' the word to describe the sensation he'd had on seeing that blurred black-and-white image? 'The thing is, I've never seen the painting. It's from the turn of the sixteenth century, so it's my special period, but it's not kept with its contemporaries, and Enzo's never mentioned it to me. What's more, when I looked it up in the official catalogue, it wasn't there.'

'Perhaps he's sold it,' Cathy suggested.

'No, the sale would be in the records.'

'Perhaps he keeps it in his bedroom. It must mean a lot to him, after all. Couldn't it be that he just doesn't regard it as being for show?'

Matthew nodded slowly. 'It could be. I'd thought of that. In which case, how do I get to see it?' He was speaking half to himself and was slow to register Cathy's quizzical expression.

'Do you *have* to see it?' she said. 'If Enzo wants to keep it to himself, isn't that his business?'

'Oh yes, of course,' he said at once. 'Yes, it is.' But Cathy had heard the reluctance in his voice.

'Oh dear, you're on the trail, aren't you?' she said. She leaned back against the balcony railings and lifted her face to the setting sun. 'What's your idea? To put the painting in the exhibition?'

'If it's good enough, yes. For now, though, I'd just like to see it.' Matthew's voice trailed off. Cat was basking, her eyes closed; for the first time she looked truly relaxed. He wished he didn't have to go out now, painting or no painting.

From opposite sides of the piazza, church bells began ringing the half-hour, out of synchronisation.

'I have to go,' he said. 'What'll you do when I'm gone?'

Cathy opened her eyes. 'I'll have a shower, then I think I'll go out for a walk.'

'Why don't you come to the Ghetto and meet me? It's not far, only about fifteen minutes, and then we can go to dinner in Trastevere, just across the river. Hold on a minute, I've got a map somewhere.' Matthew went back into the room, now hazy with evening light, and rummaged through the papers on the small writing table. 'Here.' He held out the street map on which, when he'd first arrived, he'd inked the route to the Ghetto. The black line wriggled through the middle of the city and he drew his finger down it, feeling obscurely proud, as if he were showing Cathy something of his own. 'When you get to this square here, Piazza del Tempio, the Palazzo Bonaventura is through an arched doorway that leads into a courtyard. There's a cafe on one corner of the piazza – Cafe da Bruno. Take one of the tables if I'm not already there. Is that all right?'

'Fine, don't worry about me. Good luck with the picture hunt.'

He resisted the urge to kiss her. 'See you later.'

Matthew glanced at his watch: five to eight, and Enzo, having given Marie-Laure Laffont forty-five minutes of his time, was drawing the interview to a close. They had visited two rooms in the west wing and Ms Laffont had made an appointment to return next week to spend an afternoon taking notes in one of them. That was all. Enzo had given no sign that there was anything else to interest her in the collection, and Ms Laffont was obviously more than pleased with what she'd got.

Well, that was fair enough. Alessandra's painting had no great claim to artistic importance; it was only Matthew's fancy that led him to pursue it. But it was frustrating to have spent an hour there on Cathy's first evening and to be no further forward.

Matthew smiled as Ms Laffont turned to say goodbye to him, and shook her outstretched hand. Perhaps once she'd gone he could get Enzo to broach the subject of the Giuditta.

The Giuditta. That was the name the newspaper cutting had used for it. The Judith. Logical enough; it was, after all, a fairly straightforward treatment of the Judith and Holofernes story. Caravaggio had painted the subject, so had Gentilleschi and Antonisz. The Bible story of the young woman who seduced an enemy general and cut off his head had appealed to generations of artists throughout Europe. Matthew had never been particularly keen on it till now, but there had been something about the Bonaventura Giuditta, poorly reproduced as it was, which tantalised him. He couldn't analyse it. Since he'd first made the discovery he'd gone back to the file several times, but it was always impossible to say, when he looked at the murky reproduction, why he was so sure the original was beautiful.

But he was sure. Matthew held the central image now in his mind's eye: the kneeling woman with a sword laid across her lap, her hands clasped round the severed head of the general, her pale face swimming out of the darkness to confront the onlooker. That face: the details were indistinct, but he carried an impression of strong features, with arching lines and a broad, vulnerable brow.

Ms Laffont didn't know what she was missing.

'Matthew, will you walk Ms Laffont to the door? And then can you give me five minutes before you go?'

Matthew admired Enzo's ruthless courtesy. Alone with Matthew, Enzo was often informal, even robust. But whenever he wanted he could erect his perfect manners round him like a barrier.

'Of course.'

As he escorted Ms Laffont down the stone staircase into the hall, Matthew quickened his pace to discourage her from loitering. He was eager to get back to Enzo's study and hear what he had to say. If an opportunity arose to mention the Giuditta, Matthew decided, he would take it.

But when he strode back up the stairs, two at a time, he heard voices coming from across the landing. He checked his pace and listened. That was Danilo's voice – Matthew hadn't realised he was in the palazzo – and Enzo must have gone into the drawing room to talk to him. Damn it, he wouldn't get Enzo on his own now.

Reaching the landing, Matthew had a clear view of Danilo through the open drawing room door. He was standing by the fireplace, one hand resting on the marble mantelpiece. He turned towards Matthew and paused in what he was saying.

'Is that Matthew?' came Enzo's voice. 'Come in here.'

'Good evening,' Matthew said to Danilo, bypassing him and trying to look relaxed. Danilo always made him jumpy; he could feel the man's level gaze boring into him, as if he were appraising him like a painting and finding him of doubtful quality.

'Good evening.' Danilo sounded as suspicious as he always did. 'I hear the French researcher had a fruitful time.'

'Yes,' said Matthew simply. He tried to keep his conversation with Danilo to a minimum; apart from anything else, Danilo had a habit of addressing him and Enzo together, which made it awkward to know how to reply.

'She saw room number four *and* room number five?'

'Yes.' Matthew nodded pleasantly.

'That was very quick.' Danilo looked at his father accusingly. 'I was hoping to talk to her before she left, find out some details of her research.'

'You should have told me.' Enzo shrugged, making his jacket wrinkle across the shoulders. He was a stocky man, several inches shorter than both his son and Matthew, and although all his clothes were expensive he wore them without elegance. 'I didn't know you'd be interested.'

'You know I always like to meet the people we grant access to.'

'You have met her – last year, at the Academy. And you can meet her again next week, on Tuesday, Wednesday and Thursday, when she comes back to make her detailed notes.'

'I'd have preferred to talk to her today, at the same time as you. And Matthew.'

'I'm sorry,' Enzo spoke with good humour. 'I didn't think you'd consider her so important. Her research isn't especially original. Would you like a drink, Nilo?'

Danilo looked at his father for a split second. 'Yes please. Vodka.'

While Enzo busied himself with the tray of drinks, Matthew

looked out at the terrace and walled garden. Why did Danilo do this? He was surprised that he didn't have more sense. So Danilo didn't like the idea of the exhibition; so he was suspicious of Matthew and jealous of his relationship with Enzo. Matthew could understand all that, even though he thought it was completely unnecessary. But what he didn't understand was why Danilo, with his business experience and his ice-man reputation, behaved so obviously. The man seemed driven to interfere in everything he and Enzo did. He was continually calling round at the palazzo to check on them. He was always having these sub-confrontations with Enzo, hinting that they were trying to shut him out of something. And Enzo always reacted in the same way, half snubbing, half humouring him.

God knew what was going on. Some complicated father-son struggle probably, and nothing to do with him at all; it was just his bad luck to be caught in the crossfire. He had no idea how long Danilo intended to stay in Rome. He'd assumed he was coming over briefly, but Danilo had been here three weeks now and showed no sign of going back to the States. Matthew supposed he should be grateful that at least Danilo had his own apartment in the Ghetto and so wasn't living here at the palazzo.

'Aren't you having a drink, Matthew?'

He turned and smiled. So Danilo was turning on the Bonaventura manners now. 'No thank you. I have to leave in a minute to meet someone.'

'Oh yes, of course. Your stepsister. She arrived today, didn't she?'

'Yes, this afternoon.'

'And it's Cathy's – Cathy's her name, isn't it – Cathy's first time in Rome?'

'Yes,' said Matthew shortly. What was this sudden personal interest? He didn't feel inclined to let Danilo know anything about Cat.

Danilo nodded, smiling. 'You could have asked her to come here, couldn't he, Father? You must show her the Ghetto. Too many people never step inside it.'

'For which you've often said you're very grateful,' said Enzo drily. He handed Danilo his drink. 'I didn't think you wanted to encourage tourists.'

'Cathy's hardly a tourist, Father. She's Matthew's sister.'

'Stepsister,' said Matthew quickly. Then, as he saw Danilo's eyebrows shift very slightly upwards, he regretted it. The last thing he wanted was to draw Danilo's attention to his relationship with Cathy. He couldn't have said why, but the idea made his skin feel hot. He smiled deprecatingly and turned to Enzo. 'Was there something particular you wanted to discuss?'

Enzo, however, seemed to have lost concentration. He shook his grey head and flashed Matthew his sudden illuminating smile. 'Ah no, it can wait until tomorrow,' he said. 'It was good of you to come in and I don't want to make you late for your stepsister. Did she have a good journey, by the way?'

'Yes, thank you.'

'Excellent. Do you know, Matthew, I should like to meet her. Please invite her to come here and have a drink with us. Six o'clock tomorrow would be a good time. If it doesn't interfere with her plans, of course.'

'I'm sure she'd like to.' Matthew was taken aback. Enzo wasn't known for inviting strangers to the palazzo. From the way Danilo was looking at his father, he was surprised too, and not best pleased. Matthew couldn't suppress a rush of competitive pleasure. 'Thank you, Enzo,' he said.

'Good. You'll be here, of course, and Danilo can join us from the auction house, can't you, Nilo?'

'Yes, naturally,' said Danilo, a touch stiffly. 'I'll look forward to it.'

Cathy followed the route on Matthew's map and found herself negotiating a maze of streets and piazzas. Most of the shops were closing and the restaurants were beginning to serve food. People strolled at a leisurely pace and teenagers gathered in knots on corners. The traffic had abated only slightly, though; cars shot down narrow streets and swerved round one another at intersections, and every so often a tourist coach would lurch by, perilously close to the pavement.

Even on this relatively short walk, the streets kept changing character. Turning a corner, Cathy was confronted by a huge round building with a shallow dome: the ancient Pantheon, built in the second century AD. Soon afterwards, she skirted an elegant oval piazza, starred with cafes. After another little web of alleys she crossed a busy road and came out on the river bank. The river was green, just a few hundred yards in span, and curving. On the far bank the enormous white dome of St Peter's hovered above some trees.

She turned her back on St Peter's and followed the river for a few minutes till she drew level with a small island, shaped like a boat and linked to both banks by bridges. On the far bank was Trastevere: a jumble of buildings and campaniles. On this bank, immediately to her left, the buildings rose up a small hill and a side road opened to show a silver-grey dome glinting behind trees. She had arrived in the Ghetto.

Before coming to Rome, Cathy had read up about the

Ghetto. The city's Jews had been confined here during the sixteenth century, hence the name, and it had remained a strongly Jewish neighbourhood ever since. There was a large synagogue, built at the turn of the century and adorned with a curious aluminium dome; apart from that, the streets had remained largely unchanged for hundreds of years.

As Cathy entered the small network of streets, she was struck by the quiet. She walked over flattened cobbles, past the synagogue on her right and a row of food shops running uphill to the left, and then followed the road down into a slight dip. Three streets ran off at different angles here. She took the middle one, followed it round a kink to the right and was in Piazza del Tempio.

It was nondescript, more a space than a piazza. There was a bakery and a shop selling fresh pasta, an ironmonger's and the cafe Matthew had told her about. The other buildings were obviously residential. They were built in stone, with once-ornate carvings on the door lintels. Many of the windows were now unshuttered and stood open to the cooling air. It was a tranquil place but not strikingly beautiful; she could see nothing that resembled a palazzo entrance.

An arched doorway, Matthew had said. There were several, and Cathy walked round the rim of the piazza, taking the longest path to the cafe so that she could peer in to them. The first two archways turned out to be simple front entrances, the heavy wooden doors propped open to let air into the hallways. The third had no door. As she drew level with it, she saw that the arch led under the façade of the building – the passage was no more than ten feet long, so the rooms above it must be small – and then gave onto an inner courtyard. She caught a glimpse of greenery and unevenly spaced windows.

She had an impression of great stillness.

Cathy went into Cafe da Bruno and sat at one of the two tiny tables. She felt self-conscious; she was so obviously a tourist in a local people's cafe. She ordered an espresso and sat sipping it, watching the local people come in and out of the buildings to shop and talk and part again. They did everything with an air of great purpose, even when it amounted to hanging around chatting. Every so often she looked at the windows above the archway. If all of the courtyard inside belonged to the palazzo, so must these.

There were three rows of windows above the ground floor. Many were shuttered, but here and there a few were open to the early evening. At the right-hand end of the first floor, someone was at work in an office. It wasn't Matthew; a young woman answered a telephone and Cathy saw her turn and call to someone else who stood out of sight. Matthew had told her there were several other people employed at the palazzo, to maintain the collection and keep the Bonaventuras in touch with their various businesses.

The remainder of the first-floor windows were closed. On the second floor two were open but the interiors were too dark for her to see in. Up on the third floor, everything was shuttered. Cathy watched idly, so idly that when a hand appeared between the slats in the top left corner and the shutters were pushed open, she forgot to be discreet. She gazed at the young woman who stood in the window, noticing her long features and the arched eyebrows. It was a strong face, and beautiful in its way. It was also angry. She seemed to be looking for something. She was leaning slightly forward, and as she braced her arms on the sill, the dark fabric Cathy had taken for a jacket slipped backwards and showed bare arms underneath. The woman stared down into the street, looking from one person to another, and her face turned towards Cathy.

Cathy looked away abruptly. She was embarrassed to be caught staring and she was also disturbed. The woman was younger than Cathy had thought at first glance, not much more than a girl, and there was something intimate about her dishevelment.

Cathy stared fixedly at the archway, refusing the temptation to glance back upwards. Out of the corner of her eye she could see that the girl was still there. Was there a daughter of the house? Or was she perhaps Danilo's young lover, or even Enzo's? She must ask Matthew.

Where was Matthew? It was past eight o'clock now and she had finished her espresso. There was a flash of colour in her peripheral vision and she looked up to see the girl slipping back behind the shutters. At the same time, movement disturbed the shadows in the passage opposite and Matthew came hurrying into the piazza.

Danilo had been walking for twenty minutes when he saw them. They were in the square that marks the beginning of Trastevere, sitting at one of the many outdoor tables. Candles flickered in glass shades all around the piazza, adding their dancing light to the glow of the restaurant interiors and of the street lamps, and the dark, brilliant reflections that came off the river.

Danilo slipped into a crowd of people waiting for a bus. Over their shoulders he could watch Cathy and Matthew unobserved. He let his eyes feast on Cathy's face. She looked radiant, her slightly sharp bones softened, her eyes at that distance appearing as dark as her hair. She had grown into her face now; its planes had lengthened and slimmed and she had lost that awkward forward tilt to her head. She had become a woman.

Danilo felt no shock or surprise; none of the violent reactions he had anticipated. On the contrary, he felt a deep, quiet joy. She was here.

Across the table from her, Matthew Forse refilled her wine glass. He smiled as he did it, and Cathy laughed at whatever it was he'd said.

Matthew Forse. Did he have any idea what his stepsister meant to him, Danilo? Or what Matthew himself meant, for that matter? Until now, Danilo could have sworn not. But looking at the two of them as they drank and talked, he was no longer sure. There was a bond between them, a special tension. It made them look alike, though that was really an illusion, the leaping candle flame emphasising their fair skin and dark hair.

Danilo wanted to detach himself from the crowd and walk over to them. He wanted to feel Cathy's eyes on him and to watch her react to him. Would she be frightened? Would she be pleased? Would she remember at all? At the thought of it, his lungs tightened. He had to be careful. Matthew already disliked him, and even if the dislike was born of instinct rather than conscious recognition, Danilo did not want to provoke him. Then there was his father who had noticed something amiss this evening. His father was so quick to pick up on Danilo's state of mind, and so ruthless when it came to controlling it. That was the purpose of the drinks invitation: Enzo wished to make sure that any meeting between Cathy and his son took place under his eye.

And so it would. Danilo had waited years to find this woman; he could wait a little longer. He felt exultant as he looked at her. Then he glanced at Forse. He was smiling at Cathy again, and leaning across the table to point something out to her. Danilo couldn't be sure but he thought their hands touched.

He stood dead still. He tried to fight it off but it was no good: he recognised that intimacy and the way they held one another's gaze. So it had begun already. But how far had they gone and how much did they understand? A needle was driving into his breast, bringing a new kind of fear. Danilo was coming late to the game. He would have to play with all his wits and all his ruthlessness if he was going to win.

[illegible]

[illegible]

Sightseeing [illegible] was strange. By [illegible] o'clock she had seen the Spanish Steps and [illegible] much of the [illegible] seen the Trevi Fountain, [illegible] paintings in the Palazzo Doria Pamphili.

She had [illegible] lunch at a restaurant [illegible] the Corso, the long straight road that ran through the centre of the city and down which [illegible] she could [illegible]. She [illegible] and was now [illegible] Rome, with the [illegible]

[illegible] have a look at [illegible] Giulio, according to the map she should be able to get from one to the other quite easily.

First, though, she had to negotiate Piazza Venezia, a huge open space in front of Rome's [illegible] building, the Vittorio Emanuele monument. Daisy [illegible] from her side street onto the piazza and was engulfed by the roar of traffic.

CHAPTER THREE

Sightseeing alone was tiring. By four o'clock, Cathy had climbed the Spanish Steps and visited the church at the top, seen the Trevi fountain, and inspected the paintings in the Palazzo Dora Pamphili.

She had had lunch in a restaurant off the Corso, the long straight road that ran through the middle of the city and down which, so her guidebook told her, chariots used to race. She had returned to the pensione for an hour, washed and changed, and was now taking a leisurely stroll through Rome, with the Palazzo Bonaventura as her ultimate destination.

She hadn't realised it would still be so hot outside. The fumes of a whole day's traffic hung in the air, intensifying the heat, and tiny particles of grit blew against her arms and legs. Cathy wound her way through the side streets, trying to keep in the shade. She meant to wander down to the Roman Forum and have a look at it from the outside. It was not too far from the Ghetto; according to the map she should be able to get from one to the other quite easily.

First, though, she had to negotiate Piazza Venezia, a huge open space in front of Rome's ugliest and silliest building, the Vittorio Emanuele monument. Cathy emerged from her side street onto the piazza and was engulfed by the roar of traffic.

She began walking arduously round the perimeter of the square, squeezed by the crowds and feeling hotter and hotter. The sunlight seemed to bounce off the huge white monument and, checking her map, she realised that she needed to go all the way round and behind it to reach the Forum.

Two-thirds of the way round, having inhaled the exhausts of several buses, she gave up. To her right a smaller square opened, giving access to two flights of steps. One climbed steeply to a flat-faced church; the other was wide and graceful and led to a raised courtyard with long buildings around it. Another look at the map told her that this was Michaelangelo's staircase, leading to the Campidoglio, a sixteenth-century courtyard whose palaces were now museums. From the road Cathy could see trees and bushes growing around the edges of the raised court and it had an air of peace. She set off thankfully up the steps.

It was beautiful at the top and the two palaces facing each other across the courtyard had colonnades, offering shade. Cathy walked slowly through them, examining statues, busts and fragments of much larger sculptures which had been arranged on the stone slabs. She was one of only a few loiterers. Through the windows she could see people touring the palace interiors in groups, but out here it was quiet. She came to the end of the colonnade and passed into a gap between two buildings. She walked a few yards down a path towards some trees.

She stopped and her hands flew upwards. Instinctively, she pressed herself against the wall, seeking protection. It was as if she were looking out at the scenc of an earthquake or a nuclear war. In front of her the ground fell away and from far below reared up fragments of buildings: huge broken arches, shattered columns, stone platforms that stood alone, their steps torn away. It was as if half the city had been silently destroyed.

It was the Forum. After the first split second, Cathy recognised it. Oh, for God's sake, she said to herself, you idiot. She stepped away from the wall, glancing round to see if anyone had noticed. There was no one at this end of the courtyard, no one to see that her fingers still fidgeted nervously against her throat.

Shock was an odd thing. It must be something to do with the sheer scale of the Forum. Cathy recalled her aesthetics theory. Didn't they say that if you suddenly came across an object on a vastly bigger scale than its surroundings, it induced a kind of sensory panic? That must be what she was feeling now. That was why, despite the competent reasoning of her brain, her heart was still squeezing in her chest and she wanted to shut her eyes.

Interesting. Yes, very interesting. If only the reaction would hurry up and go away.

To encourage her heart to return to normal, Cathy got out her map and began to calculate her position. She must be standing at the top of the Capitoline Hill, looking across a drop of about one hundred feet towards the broken buildings of the Forum. Her view from here was restricted by the corner of the third palace, but if she went to the end of this path, she should be able to see the whole site.

She walked the ten or so yards that remained of the path and stopped by the railings. Beyond them the ground fell away abruptly, like a cliff, and from its foot stretched the ruins of the old Forum.

Stretched was the word. The remains of the old city, whitened in the sun, reached into the distance. The perspective was strange. At first, looking down from her high perch, Cathy had an impression of breadth and openness. It was only when she focused on the bright little figures moving among the ruins that she realised how high were the walls, how tall the columns. The tourists were dwarfed by them; they craned their necks upwards, helped one another to scramble over the broken pavements.

The sight made her feel dizzy. In fact, she felt uncomfortable all through her body and mind. Though the initial shock had passed, she still had to force herself to look down at the ruins. There was something naked and frightening about them, and her eyes kept wanting to veer away.

She sat down on a stone bench, in the shade of a tree, and began flipping through her guidebook. She would read the historical facts about this place, and that would put it all in context. Then she could look at it with a more informed eye, and perhaps even form some aesthetic judgements. It would be useful to have some intelligent ideas at hand for conversation this evening.

But that was easier said than done. Once she started to read the guide, Cathy realised that she was looking at the remnants of hundreds of years of Roman public life. The Forum had had several incarnations: buildings which had been put up in one period had been altered, enlarged, burned down and rebuilt in others. She had a plan, but it was hard to make it tally with what she saw on the ground. And besides, looking down at this buried city and reading about its destruction, its rebuilding, its destruction again, oppressed her. Cathy felt as if she were rifling through the belongings of a dead person.

She checked her watch: there was well over an hour to kill. She would stop trying to be well-informed and instead take advantage of this quiet corner to relax for a while; perhaps she would even do some sketches. She had her small sketchpad and pen in her bag, as usual, and the ruins made some interesting shapes.

Cathy often drew objects, as preparation for painting. Although her work was completely abstract, she would use the shapes and spatial relationships, and the play of light and shade that she had observed. Now she took out her pad and pen and eyed the pathway along which she had just walked. Together with the walls on either side and the glimpse of the Campidoglio courtyard beyond, it made an intriguing combination of shapes. She started in the middle of the page as usual, and began drawing outwards.

She had all the main structures in place and was starting to work on the textures when she began drawing something that wasn't there. It started as a roundness some way up the wall, lengthened to become a body beneath it. Angles took shape under the pen and became shoulders; downstrokes thickened and bulked and became robes.

Cathy worked on, puzzled, and the figure grew clearer: she was standing in the shadows, in the crook of the wall, and she had one arm drawn across her breast, wrapping her cloak round her. Her head was turned to one side, as if she were listening for the approach of footsteps. Cathy began to draw her features: curving nose, the mouth just opening, the eyes – tiny movements of the pen, contrasting white with black – looking at her.

She laid her pen down softly on the bench. From the pad on her lap, the girl looked up at her: guarded, stealthy, hunted.

She had drawn the girl in the upstairs window. For quite a while, Cathy sat examining her. Yes, there were the long eyes, the same emphatic brows. The nose – she hadn't realised yesterday that it was slightly crooked at the bridge. She had caught her so well, and in such detail.

But she couldn't draw people. And why the fugitive air to her? This wasn't how the girl had looked yesterday. Leaning from the window she had seemed purposeful, determined; though now Cathy came to think of it, there had been a haste about her movements. She remembered the sudden withdrawal, coinciding with Matthew's appearance in the square.

Cathy looked around the empty terrace and the path. She was all alone here, her limbs dappled with warmth and brightness as the sun, milder now, shone through the leaves. Her heart was beating rapidly; it was a pleasant sensation.

She gazed down at the drawing again. There was, she thought, an appeal in those eyes. Slowly, she tore the sheet off the pad and slipped it between the blank pages, to keep it flat. Then she swivelled so that she was facing the Forum and took up her pen again.

'Hello, sis.' Matthew smiled from behind the heavy door. 'You're timing's good, we've only just finished work. Have you just come from the Forum?'

'Yes, how did you know?'

'Don't look so startled, I saw you coming down the hill. We were in the west wing and I spotted you. Enzo was impressed with your sense of direction; you didn't look at the map once.'

'Oh, I could see the palazzo from up there. Besides, I'd looked at the map earlier.' Cathy smiled to cover the fact that she felt flustered. She'd spent too long drawing and had had to rush to get here. Luckily she had found her way easily; in fact, the medieval streets had simply seemed to open up before her and usher her in. Before she knew it, she'd been walking beneath the arched entrance, to arrive in the courtyard. She'd had a sense of being watched as she'd crossed the cobbles, beneath rows and rows of windows, to get to the main door. But now it seemed that she had been observed long before.

Matthew drew her in and shut the door behind her.

'Enzo's upstairs, in the drawing room. Danilo's not here yet.' He lowered his voice. 'What do you think of it?'

Cathy looked round. The hall was square and elegant, with a single wide staircase rising to the left. There was a domed skylight high above, and arched windows on two walls – behind her, looking into the courtyard, and ahead of her, giving onto a terraced garden. The hall was lively with late sunlight and surprisingly unadorned with art. There were a few small sculptures and some unassuming oil paintings on the walls, mostly landscapes.

'It's lovely.' She spoke quietly too. 'Very livable in. I was expecting wall torches and rows of ancestral portraits.'

'Oh, Enzo has the portraits. Fourteen of them, of greater and lesser artistic interest. Mostly lesser, unfortunately. They're upstairs, in one of the collection rooms.'

'So these don't count as part of the collection?'

'For insurance purposes, no. The collection pieces are supposed to be kept on the first and second floors so that there's no direct access to them from the ground or the roof.'

'Locked rooms?'

'Some of them. But there are plenty of things that aren't locked away. You'll be seeing some in a minute. Come on.'

Matthew's hand was on her arm again as he led the way to the staircase. His touch was very light, as it had been ever since she arrived in Rome, and not quite casual. He seemed edgy. Cathy wondered how much of it was to do with her and how much was apprehension about this evening. Last night he had been both pleased and surprised by the invitation.

'It's not usual for Enzo to invite strangers to the palazzo,' he'd said. 'Not socially, at any rate. When he's not working, he likes his privacy. Of course, you're not exactly a stranger, because he knows me. The odd thing is, it was Danilo who pointed that out. Unexpected, hey? Who'd have thought Danilo would extend hospitality to my relations?'

As they reached the top of the flight, Matthew let his hand fall. Cathy felt oddly vulnerable without it. They were now on a wide landing. It ran round three sides of the hall but only at the back were there rooms giving off. The two arms were merely decorative walkways, with pictures hung in them. A second, slimmer flight of steps rose from the furthest, right-hand walkway. The main landing turned a corner at each end; round these, Cathy realised, the palazzo must continue into the west and east wings and ultimately into the façade which enclosed the courtyard.

Matthew pointed to the double doors in the middle of the landing. One stood open and Cathy stepped through it into a rectangular room which seemed to be all pale blue panelling and white carving. Amidst a row of tall windows, a pair of painted doors were wedged open, and the garden she had glimpsed downstairs rose up in terraces and smothered the balustrade with climbing flowers.

Through the windows she saw a man moving about on the terrace. He was grey-haired and slender and wore a suit. He had a tiny watering can in his hand. Another man stood in the room with his back to her, sorting something into dishes on a side table. He, too, wore a suit, but his neck and shoulders were bulky and pulled the fabric tight.

This must be a member of staff. Cathy turned resolutely towards the windows, at which point the man at the side table turned.

'Miss Seymour. How nice of you to come. Please excuse me, I've been handling olives.' He came forward to meet her, wiping his hands on a white napkin. There was a quiet amusement in his broad face, as if he knew what she had been thinking.

'I see you're looking at the garden. It's unexpected, isn't it? When Giovanni has finished, we'll go out there. The scents are best at this time of day, just after watering.' The amusement deepened into a smile, and two long creases appeared on either side of his mouth. 'Welcome to Rome.' He shook her hand. 'It's your first visit, I believe. And yet you studied art.'

'I know,' Cathy said. 'It must sound awful. I did come to Italy, but I ran out of money before I could get to Rome.'

'It doesn't sound awful to me. I sometimes think we're too much in thrall to the past, particularly in the art world. And it must be interesting to discover Rome as an adult.' His English was accented but flawless.

'It is. Though I think I'll take it more slowly than I did today. I wasn't prepared for the heat.'

'What would you like to drink, Cathy? I may call you Cathy? I was just going to open a bottle of wine from my brother-in-law's estate in the north. It's not always very good, but this particular year is one of their better ones.'

'Thank you, that would be lovely.'

Enzo began uncorking the wine. 'What about you, Matthew? A glass of Luca's eighty-nine?'

'Er, yes please.'

Enzo laughed. 'Don't worry, this really is much better than the ninety-two. I wouldn't subject you to that again. We had a truly terrible bottle of Luca's wine last week,' he said over his shoulder to Cathy. 'And now Matthew's lost confidence in my cellar.'

Behind Enzo's back, Matthew gave Cathy a quick smile; he was obviously relieved at the way things were going. She felt quite surprised that he should have been worried; Enzo seemed quite at his ease with her.

She watched him uncorking the bottle. He was much stockier than she had imagined, and shorter, just a couple of inches taller than she was. He looked younger than his sixty-three years too. His tight-knit muscles gave the impression of fitness and his skin had an olive sheen but as he turned back towards her, Cathy saw that around his eyes there was a telltale greyness – the sign of a man who had been working too hard for too long. He was very different from the elegant, cosmopolitan gentleman she had anticipated. He would have looked at home in a factory, or on the land.

He poured three glasses of wine. He left the fourth glass on the tray empty.

'Your very good health,' he said when they each had a glass. 'I'm very pleased you could come tonight, it's a pleasure to meet one of Matthew's family. Ah look, Giovanni's finished outside. Shall we go and see the garden?'

It was cool in the garden and the air was full of the scents of evening flowers. Enzo led them along the paths and pointed out the various plants with a pride that Cathy found rather endearing. It was not a very big garden, no more than a quarter of an acre, but the different levels seduced the eye and steps and trellises tempted one into private corners.

When Enzo had shown them round, they climbed back up to the stone balcony. They were still standing there, drinking wine and chatting, when someone else arrived.

Enzo and Matthew both had their backs to the room, so Cathy saw him first. He came into the drawing room hurriedly, then stopped dead and looked around him. She recognised him at once as Danilo. He was very like his photograph, but, just as Enzo was smaller than she'd expected, his son was bigger. There was a physicality to him that the photo hadn't captured.

Cathy watched him scan the room and catch sight of the empty wine bottle. A look of anger snapped onto his face; he hunched his shoulders and turned back to the hall, but then Enzo laughed and the sound must have reached him, because he went still.

Cathy looked away hastily as he turned round; she felt that she had just seen him in a vulnerable moment.

'Is that Danilo?' said Enzo. 'We're on the balcony, come and join us.'

Danilo came towards them quickly. As he stepped onto the balcony, he seemed relieved.

'I'm sorry I'm late. I couldn't get away from the acquisitions meeting, and when I did there was a broken-down car blocking half of the Via Arenula.'

'Ah well, you're with us now.' Enzo touched Danilo's arm. It must have been a light touch; although his hand was large, it didn't disturb the fabric of Danilo's sleeve. 'Cathy, this is my son, Danilo. Nilo, Cathy Seymour.'

'I'm very happy to meet you.' Danilo's expression was formal but within it there was a slight smile. Cathy felt a disturbance inside her as she looked back at him and when she took his hand, it intensified.

She felt self-conscious and was glad when Enzo began asking Danilo about the meeting he'd just attended. Danilo was a good-looking man; he probably had this effect on many women. And of course he was rich and powerful too, which didn't hurt. She hoped no one else had noticed her reaction. She didn't want Matthew to be jealous, or Enzo to think she was some kind of predictable gold-digger.

'Cathy,' Matthew touched her arm. 'Danilo's asking you if you'd like another glass of wine.'

She was flustered; now she had seemed rude. 'Oh, yes please,' she said.

Danilo reached past her to the stone balustrade where her glass was balanced. 'Excuse me,' he said politely. 'What is it, Father, the eighty-nine?'

'Yes. I've decided to leave the more recent vintages for a very long while yet. And as for the eighty-eight, we'll have to see if we can sell it on to our restorers as cleaner.'

'You were in Trastevere last night, Matthew tells me,' Enzo said to Cathy. 'What did you think of it? It was the most densely populated part of Rome in the Middle Ages, you know, and it has a dialect all its own: Romano.'

'Yes, Matthew was trying to teach me some phrases. So far all I've got is "*Nammio*".'

'Ah yes, Romano for "*Andiamo*". The phrase is overused in both Italian and Romano. You could at least have shown some creativity, Matthew.'

Enzo and Matthew began some aimiable sparring over Romano phrases. It was obvious that they got on very well; in fact Enzo seemed more relaxed with Matthew than he did with his own son. Cathy let her glance wander to the drawing room. Inside, Danilo had just finished opening another bottle of wine, but he didn't fill the glasses at once; instead he poured himself a large vodka, swallowed it in one, and topped up his glass again.

When he rejoined them on the balcony, he handed out the wine glasses and stood quietly for a while, listening to Enzo and Matthew discussing Romano.

Eventually he turned to Cathy. 'I understand this is your first visit here. So what do you think of my home? Not this house, the city.'

'It's beautiful. But it's a bit overwhelming.'

'You're a painter, aren't you?'

'Yes,' Cathy said cautiously. She hoped he wasn't going to ask about her work; she'd never acquired the knack of talking easily about it.

He grinned, and suddenly looked much younger. 'Don't worry. I'm not going to ask you if you've come to paint the Colosseum. I'm just surprised that you haven't been here before. Your stepbrother seems to be personally acquainted with every painting in every gallery in the city.'

'That's his job.'

'Yes, I know. He does it very well, too. I suppose I assumed he must have started young, that you'd come on family visits here.'

'No. Matthew came here on a school trip in his teens, that was the only time either of us came to Italy before we left home. Our parents weren't very interested in art, or in Europe.'

'So Matthew got to know Rome on his own, quite recently?'

'Yes. He came here twice in his college holidays, and then of course there have been business trips since.'

'Yes, I know he's been over several times to advise our

auction house. He's well thought of in his field.'

The formal note was back in his voice. Matthew was clearly right when he said that Danilo was suspicious of him. Watching Matthew laughing with Enzo, Cathy wondered how much of it was jealousy. Danilo's mother was dead, he lived the other side of the world from his father, and now he had returned home to find Matthew in his father's confidence, entrusted with opening up the family collection to the public and apparently winning his father's affection as well. Cathy felt a twist of sympathy for him.

He was looking at her thoughtfully now, making her worry fleetingly whether he could have read her mind.

'So what is it that you find overwhelming about our city?' he asked.

'The volume of it, I suppose. And the way the different ages co-exist. I can't get used to seeing car hire offices in medieval courtyards and computer companies in Renaissance palaces. And today I seemed to be for ever walking up hills in the blazing sunshine.'

Danilo laughed. 'You probably were. This is a city built on hills. We've grown used to climbing.'

There was something proprietorial in the way Danilo identified with the city. Our city; we Romans. But it wasn't the exclusive manner that some people used when talking to visitors; it was more as if he were inviting Cathy to join them.

Despite telling herself that she was imagining things, Cathy felt flattered.

It was Enzo who broke off the discussion with Matthew and asked where he and Cathy were going for dinner. The conversation became general as they talked about the different quarters of Rome, and restaurants Enzo and Danilo knew. As they talked they began drifting back into the drawing room. It was clearly time to go.

'Has my father asked you to dinner on Friday?' said Danilo as he picked up Cathy's bag for her.

She looked uncertainly at Enzo, who was replacing the glasses on the table. 'I don't think so.'

Enzo turned round. 'Not yet, Nilo, I was just about to. You've managed to anticipate me.' It was said with good humour but he fussed for a few seconds with bottles and the ice bucket, frowning slightly. 'Cathy, Matthew, would you have dinner with us on Friday? You never know, Danilo,' he interrupted himself, 'they might be going away for the weekend. To Naples or Perugia, for instance. Or perhaps they simply had other plans. And now they'll have to deny them and accept our invitation because they're well-mannered.'

Cathy wasn't sure how to take this; nor, evidently, was Matthew. They stood awkwardly, glancing at each other. Then Enzo burst out into a sly laugh.

'Very funny, Father,' said Danilo. He turned to Matthew and Cathy. 'We'd be delighted to see you on Friday, if you'd like to come.' He addressed them together.

Cathy waited for Matthew to accept, but he just stood looking puzzled. In another second, the pause would become embarrassing.

'Thank you, we'd like to,' Cathy said. 'Wouldn't we, Matthew?'

Chapter Four

'What do you think Danilo's playing at?' Matthew said.

They were standing side by side at the river wall. Behind them traffic whizzed cheerfully by; ahead, across the water, squatted the great round fortress of Castel St Angelo. Matthew was staring at it, his eyes screwed up in an expression that was half smile, half frown.

'Need he be playing at anything?' Cathy said reasonably.

'Something's going on. He steamrolled Enzo into that invitation.'

Cathy remembered the way Danilo had looked at her; a surreptitious pleasure stirred.

'Yes, he did a bit, didn't he? Enzo didn't look very pleased.' She glanced at Matthew. 'Why don't you sound him out and find an excuse to cancel? I don't want to go if he doesn't want us.' She watched his face. She *did* want to go; she felt drawn to Danilo and intrigued by the tension between him and his father. Matthew's position in the household was delicate and she didn't want to jeopardise it.

Matthew shook his head. 'I couldn't do that, Enzo would be offended. Besides, it's not that I think he doesn't want us. He obviously took to you. And I know he likes me – I've been to dinner there often, usually just with him. But the couple of times Danilo's been there, the atmosphere was not pleasant. So I'm a bit surprised to hear Danilo handing out invitations.'

'Perhaps he's decided to make an effort with you. He might have decided that if his father likes you, you can't be all bad.'

'Hmm. It's more likely he's decided to make an effort with you. I saw him being quietly charming all over you.'

Cathy's stomach turned over. Matthew was smiling, but it was no disguise for the jealousy in his voice. For the first time since her arrival, their easy-going tone was broken and naked emotion showed through. Danilo receded from her thoughts; she stood very still, watching Matthew while he drummed his fingers against the wall and peered at the water.

'He wasn't being charming. He was just talking.'

'Danilo never just talks. He was being charming, and you fell for it.' Matthew wouldn't look at her. Suddenly he swung himself up so that in one ragged movement he was sitting on the wall. His body rocked, swaying out over the river far below.

'Don't do that!'

He raised his eyebrows at her, teasingly. 'What? Say cynical things about little Nilo?'

'Don't sit up there. If you fell – don't. It's such a long way down.'

'I won't fall. People sit on the walls all the time. Look, no hands.' Matthew laughed defiantly and waved his arms in the air; then, still laughing at her, his face froze.

'Matthew!' Cathy's breath stopped. For a terrible second, there was no wall beneath Matthew and he hung in the air, his face grey. He looked directly at her, and there was horrified comprehension in his eyes.

Cathy couldn't move. She stood and watched him and knew

that he was going to die. Then she jumped forward and grabbed his leg, just as he righted himself.

'It's all right. I just lost my balance for a second. My fault for being stupid.' Matthew pushed himself down from the wall, his hands gripping the top tightly. 'Sorry,' he said shakily. 'Sorry.' He saw Cathy's face and, with a quick apologetic movement, put his arm around her. 'Hey, I'm all right, you know. There's no need to look like that.'

'No need? Jesus! You should have seen yourself.' Cathy was trembling with shock and anger and wanted to push him away but she couldn't stop holding on to his waist. The image of him falling seemed stamped on her eyes; the terrible way he had looked at her. 'God, you're an idiot sometimes! I feel like hitting you.'

'Yes, sis. Oh, come on, I've said I'm sorry. Let's go and get some dinner, shall we?' Matthew turned her away from the river and steered her along the pavement, his arm still tight round her shoulder. They walked in silence, their bodies fitting into one another, and neither released their hold.

They had dinner in a restaurant on Piazza Navona, the lovely elongated piazza Cathy had crossed on her first walk to the Ghetto. Had it really been only yesterday? It seemed a very long time ago now.

The piazza was humming with people; Matthew and Cathy sat under the awning of one in a row of restaurants and amidst the social bustle their table was like a little oasis of intimacy.

The atmosphere between them was highly charged. Neither of them had any desire to lighten it; instead, they talked through their activities of the day, knowing that it would lead them sooner or later to more dangerous, more exciting things.

'You didn't get round to asking Enzo about that painting,

then?' Cathy said, as Matthew described his day's work. 'The one you can't find – what's it called?'

'The Giuditta. No. I was looking for an opening to mention it but it never came. And it seems so bald to ask about it out of the blue. Enzo hardly ever speaks Alessandra's name in front of me and when he does, his voice goes hollow. I keep feeling as if I'm trespassing, even knowing about her painting.'

'Perhaps you are. I think maybe you should let it go, Matthew.'

'Mmm. I'll see how it goes. What about you? I saw you had your sketchbook in your bag. Did you do anything?'

Cathy peeled a fleshy leaf off her deep-fried artichoke. 'Yes. As a matter of fact, I did some quite good drawings from above the Forum. Of people – or rather, one person, a girl I saw yesterday.' She bit into the succulent leaf and smiled.

'You look very pleased with yourself. Are you telling me you're finally satisfied with one of your own figures?'

'Yep. At least I think so. Perhaps when I take another look at them, they'll be awful.'

'I always said your figures weren't as bad as you thought. Can I see them?'

'Yes, hold on.' Cathy wiped her fingers and took the pad out of her bag. She had put the two sketches in the middle of the blank sheets for protection; now she felt a ripple of pleasure as she passed the pad to Matthew. Handing them over without looking at them again was something she would have done for no one else; it felt like giving him a present.

She tensed a little as he lifted the top sheets and slid out the drawings. She watched his head bend over them and was pleased to see him stiffen in surprise. He looked at them for a long time. When he straightened up, his face wore an odd expression.

'Cat, are you playing some sort of joke on me?'

'No. What do you mean?'

'This woman you've drawn, where did you see her?'

'At the palazzo. When I was waiting for you in the bar yesterday, she came to one of the windows. Does she work there?'

Matthew laughed. 'No, not exactly.'

'Who is she then?' Why was Matthew staring at her like that?

'You didn't mention her last night,' he said.

'Why should I have done?' Cathy frowned. Matthew was supposed to be talking about her drawing, not the woman. Woman: that was Matthew's word for her, and yet Cathy was sure the person she'd seen was young, still in her teens. An unwelcome suspicion brushed her. 'So who is she, Matthew? Do you know her?'

'In a sense. I don't know how the hell to explain this, Cat, but you've drawn the Giuditta.'

Cathy refilled her glass and toyed with the remains of her artichoke. Matthew had been poring over her drawings for nearly ten minutes and he was making her uneasy.

'You're sure you're not imagining the resemblance?' she said, half jokingly.

'Sure,' said Matthew. He looked from one drawing to another yet again and finally handed them back to Cathy. 'The outline of the cheek, the eyebrows,' his free hand drew an unconscious curve in the air, 'I'm sure I'm not mistaken. But there's only one way to prove it and that's to show these to Enzo.'

Cathy slipped the drawings hastily back into the pad. The

underneath one came loose and for an instant she looked into the eyes of the girl in her second pose: stepping out from the shade of a broken arch, pushing briars aside. Briars? There were no briars in the well-tended Forum.

'I think we should leave Enzo out of it. If the likeness really is there, it might upset him. And if it's not, you'll look stupid.'

'It is there. I swear it. Come on, Cat. This is really weird. He *should* see them.'

'Well, I don't know.' Cathy buckled the strap on her bag and held it on her lap, with her arms round it. She felt possessive towards these drawings; she didn't want them handed over to Enzo, to be discussed and examined. She didn't want anyone else touching them. 'I'll think about it,' she said vaguely.

Overhead the sky was dark, dark blue shading to sapphire above the rim of the buildings. The first wave of diners had gone and the restaurants were filling up with the late crowd. At Cathy and Matthew's table the food was finished, and the wine, and they were drinking their second brandies.

They had long stopped trying to talk. Increasingly, they were listening to the silence and watching one another. The surface of Cathy's skin glowed from the consciousness of Matthew's glance, and yet so far there had been no touch.

Her hands ached. She ran her finger round the top of her glass, trying to make it sing. Matthew sat watching her, his eyes smiling.

'You never could do that.'

His hands were creeping forward across the tablecloth. When Cathy let go of the glass, he picked up her right hand and began to play with her fingers. A needle-sharp heat ran through her.

'I'm glad you came, Cathy. I told Enzo today that I want to spend more time with you in the next two weeks.'

'Good.' She didn't make any protestations about not wanting to distract him from work. They wouldn't have been true.

He fiddled with her emerald and pearl ring. 'Do you still see Jonathan?' His voice was low.

'Now and then. He's got a new girl friend, called Sally.'

'Do you mind?'

She shook her head. 'No. Not one bit.' She looked up at him. His face was shadowed in the hollows, his eyes very dark and undefended. 'But I've sometimes wished, for all our sakes, that I did.'

Matthew was silent. Then his mouth twisted in an apologetic smile. 'I'm sorry I wasn't nicer to him. I tried to be, but I was jealous.'

They were both silent now. They had often argued over Matthew's behaviour towards her boy friends; it had been one of the things that warned Cathy against pursuing their love. If Matthew was jealous now, what would he be like once they'd made love? But this time Cathy made no comment.

Matthew took hold of both her hands. She felt his palms pressing against hers, the warmth and strength of his grasp as their fingers entwined. Throughout her body, responses were igniting.

It was Matthew who finally spoke. 'Jesus, Cathy, what are we going to do?'

In the silence, Cathy's mind was full of clamour. The moment had come. She loved Matthew, and she had to decide if she was going to cross the line and become his lover. If the answer was no, she would have to leave. In fairness to them both, she would have to leave tomorrow, bid him goodbye and commit herself to a life of decent men like Jonathan, who even now waited for her.

Cathy touched her fingertips very slowly to her stepbrother's lips. 'Let's go away this weekend,' she said slowly. 'Leave Rome and go somewhere else.'

'Somewhere that's not the Pensione Flora?'

'Exactly.'

'And afterwards?'

She shook her head. Her mind was dark; she couldn't think about afterwards.

They didn't kiss. They held each other briefly in the doorway to the pensione and she stroked Matthew's cheek. Then they walked upstairs decorously, not touching, and said goodnight in the corridor. They could hear the patrona talking into the telephone.

Cathy's body was burning with desire and pent-up energy. She washed and undressed and put on one of Matthew's old shirts, long since borrowed to use at night. She wandered round her bedroom, looking at the reflections of the lamp in the mirror on the wardrobe door and in the brass drawer handles. She wondered if Matthew were lying in his bed next door, listening to her. Or was he, too, pacing round his room, unable to rest?

Cathy finally switched off her lamp and slid into bed. Lying in darkness, listening to the many tiny sounds of the night – squeaks and rustles, car engines outside, distant doors and voices – she felt that she was travelling through space, spinning towards an unknown future.

The heat of the day was abating. The viciousness had gone out of it, but it still pressed down on the skin like a blanket. Judith climbed the steps carefully and paused halfway up, pressing herself into the tiny strip of shade next to the house wall. She had come out too early, but she couldn't stand to be downstairs any longer, with the servants and the house slaves and the tent-dwelling family they had taken in, and her mother telling her over and over again what the elders were saying.

'Where are you going?' her mother had demanded as she put her stool away.

'Onto the roof. There are some figs to press.'

'Figs. What we need is grapes. I don't know, your father thinks the plan to send men out to the vines could work. And if they brought back enough, we could make wine for a couple of days, maybe three, and by then help might come from Jerusalem . . .' Rachel's eyes had been bright with intelligence and anxiety.

Judith had nodded respectfully and said, 'Shall I call Endeyeh to sit with you?'

'No, she's busy. I'll go and see if I can help her. We must all pull together now. Then I'll take Reuben home. Your father will be back from Ozias's house soon. Oh Judith,' as Judith walked towards the blinding sunlight of the courtyard, 'be careful. Stay in the shade. We should all be careful of the sun.'

Her mother's face stayed uncomfortably with Judith as she climbed the last few steps onto the roof. It had been troubled and full of love. Judith straightened up and felt the searing force of the sunlight as it poured down from the sky and bounced back at her from her own roof, and from the scores of other roofs stretching out around her, scattered with stools and shelters and bowls and mats but empty of people at this hour.

She walked quickly along the eastern arm of the house onto the main southern part; from here, in the corner occupied by her prayer hut, she could see over the city walls. She went into the little lattice-branch shelter and stood on the stool. Through the plaited wood she looked out, past the knot of sentries talking and sharpening their swords on the wall to the plain far below. She knew exactly what she would see, but she still savoured the shock of it.

In the distance the familiar red-brown rock stretched to the horizon, but closer to the hill the earth had disappeared beneath colours and shapes. It was like a vast, living cloth. At first, it was baffling, but after a while she could pick out where people stood in crowds and where tents offered respite from the sun.

The army had been camped there for thirty-three days. It ringed the foot of Bethulia's hill and guarded not only the spring but the paths which led up to the city. The army's sentries stood halfway up the hill, in clusters; they didn't dare stand higher, as spears could reach them from the walls, but their presence there was enough to keep the people penned inside the city limits.

Ozias had told them there were three thousand soldiers here alone, and it was rumoured that more were marching to join them. It was a huge force to threaten such a small city, but then their object was not Bethulia itself but the mountain pass which Bethulia defended.

No one in Bethulia quite knew how it had come about. They had all been aware, of course, that King Demetrius of Syria was stirring again. Stories had been coming in along the trade routes for months. Enraged by threats of invasion from the Parthians, their northern neighbour was arming again. Demetrius had begun recalling his generals from their foreign missions; he was conscripting young men; he was levying a defence tax.

Then they'd learnt that they as Judeans were being asked to contribute. There had been surprise and indignation. It was only two years since Demetrius had exempted Judea from his taxes. That had been seen as an acknowledgement of their independence at long last – in Jerusalem the ruling families had celebrated by dancing into the temple.

All the same, a powerful neighbour was a powerful neighbour, even if his influence was on the wane. No one knew that better than the inhabitants of a hill citadel like Bethulia where attacks had been made before. So the elders had organised the local payments, trying to work out how little they could get away with sending. And then, incredibly, they had received news that in Jerusalem the priests were preparing everyone to resist.

Events had moved swiftly after that. The city elders had barely reached Jerusalem to argue with the priests when the force had been sighted and they had had to rush home to prepare Bethulia's supplies and fortifications against attack. Debate and recriminations had passed furiously up and down the country and within Bethulia itself the arguments were bitter. Many people had suffered in recent years under the elders' increasingly restrictive rule; now, they muttered, look where their word of law has led us.

Judith had been one of those who had suffered. Perhaps that was why she couldn't feel as she was supposed to. During these last thirty-three days she had prayed with the others, worked with them, held her mother and allowed herself to be held, stroked her little brother Reuben's hair and brought him into her house to play with the tent dwellers' children. Once, when she had seen tears in her father's eyes, she had burst into a storm of weeping. But always there was this little silence inside her.

It was as if she stood at a distance from the people around her. Generally she managed to conceal it by throwing herself into the work imposed on them all by the siege. No one was more active than Judith in providing for her household, especially now that she had taken in the largest and least popular family of tent dwellers. But there were times, like this one, when she listened to the rebellious voice and stole away from the others.

Now, standing inside her prayer hut with the sun beating down through the lattice of palm branches, she filled her eyes with the sight of Bethulia's enemies.

Stay in the shade. We should all be careful of the sun. Her mother must have been thinking of Manasses, Judith's husband, when she said that. Was that why she'd looked at her so painfully? Did she believe she was still mourning Manasses?

The death of her young husband had meant the loss of many things to Judith. And the gain of others. But the gains had been slow and her mother would not wish to hear the truth about them.

Judith had never told anyone what the last four years had done to her. Endeyeh, her maid, knew some of it. Her father-in-law Chabris, the third city elder, sometimes seemed to guess at it too. But then he had supervised the long mourning, overseen the fulfilment of her duties; it was under his eye that Judith the young, wilful wife had been gradually transformed into Judith the devout, submissive widow. For which she would never forgive him.

When Judith heard her neighbours mutter angrily against Chabris and the other elders, she said nothing. She did not believe anything would come of the resentment; the people of Bethulia were used to following the elders' lead, no matter how much they grumbled. It had not always been so. Judith could remember a more easygoing Bethulia. But in the last ten years the elders had tightened their grip on the community and one by one the people who resisted were brought to heel or forced out. It was part of a movement that was taking place all over Judea, in cities and villages further south and in Jerusalem too. But here in Bethulia it was particularly stifling.

He had been right, that Syrian boy. She had put on shackles when she married Chabris' son.

The Syrian boy, Holofernes. It was such an unusual name. As it had passed from mouth to mouth in the last thirty-three days, she had listened and changed her mind a hundred times. It must be him; no, it couldn't be, the boy had been flippant when he'd told her his name – 'For you I'll be Holofernes,' he'd said. This Holofernes would be some Syrian general, older than her father. And yet they said the man laying siege to the city had Judean blood.

Judith had told no one her suspicions. She hadn't even confided in Endeyeh. She waited until everyone was busy and then she came up here and hid herself behind her screens and looked for him. She had seen him several times, far below, walking through the camp with lieutenants on either side. She had known it must be the general from the way the others behaved, and from the stir among the sentries on the city walls. But he was only a tiny figure, utterly unrecognisable; and yet she pressed her hands against the woven lattice and thought, What if it is him?

The question whispered in her mind, calling up no answer.

They were talking. Abishag and Rebekah, her neighbours, were standing close together, nodding and gesticulating. They had moved away from the tent dwellers, as a mark that they remembered their rank, but it was clear that whatever they were discussing was being shared among the tent dwellers too. Around the stone mills, where they were crushing the last of the olives, the women clustered and the children hopped, half-eager on the scent of gossip, half-bored. Everyone looked at Judith as she came down the steps into the courtyard, but no one bothered to break off their chatter or address her.

She had a moment's dread: Are they talking about me? It took her back to the weeks after Manasses' death, when the town had been rife with rumours about her. Rumours that were lacerating because they were true.

Judith had killed Manasses. She had been a wicked wife, an unnatural woman, and she had driven him to his death.

She had married him with such hopes when she was fifteen. On her marriage day she had thanked God for guiding Manasses to choose her out of all the girls in Bethulia. Her young husband was handsome, well-born, ambitious – and at the slightest touch of his hand, her body rippled with the strangest, most tantalising sensations, like fire on water. It was bitter to remember how she had welcomed those feelings, for they had fed poison into the marriage.

It had begun at once, on their marriage night, when Judith had found her fears washed away by the excitement of Manasses' body. The pain had been sharp but the heat of his skin and his hardness inside her aroused an appetite she had never imagined. It had not been satisfied that first night. She had looked forward to the next night and then, as that only intensified her desire, the next.

Judith had sought Manasses' touch eagerly in those first weeks of marriage. He was often reluctant, but following some inner prompting, she began to caress him when they lay together and discovered how to bring him to hardness even when he was tired. Judith was happy, but Manasses had seemed troubled. At the time, she hadn't understood; she had simply tried harder to please him. But he had shaken off her loving gestures and had begun spending more time away from her, working the land. He often came back to the house very late, after passing the evening with his brothers. And two months after their marriage, he had unrolled a separate sleeping mat and told Judith she was not to disturb him in the night.

Judith had worried about his health. She'd put healing herbs in his food and waited for him to get better. But he had only grown more withdrawn and impatient of her attention. Finally, puzzled and aggrieved, she had asked him whether she was doing something wrong.

'Immodest. Unwomanly. Unclean.' Those were the words he had used. Judith could hear them now, years later, and see the disgust on his face. Even after so many other sufferings, the shock of that moment could still set her trembling.

It had been the beginning of the struggle between them. At first Judith had tried to behave as Manasses wanted, with circumspection. But he was no warmer to her. He continued to stay away, working long hours, eating meals at his parents' house, going on trips with the merchants to buy and sell produce. Judith had been lonely and wretched and people had begun to gossip.

It was then that Judith had grown angry. Unable to turn to anyone for advice, she had become proud and secretive with the other citizens. At home she'd fought back against Manasses' coldness with silence and small gestures of rage. Their marriage had turned into a hidden war. Yet her passion for him hadn't died, it had simply turned to hatred.

It was Manasses who had died. Just one year after their marriage, he had worked so long at the wheat harvest, refusing to come in from the blazing heat of the fields, that he had been struck down by fever. Two days later, he was dead.

And then the rumours, which had been mounting steadily, had burst into a swarm.

Judith never admitted even to knowing what they said about her. Neither did Chabris, Manasses' father. At the burial he had told her that she was to come and live in his house as a member of his family, and he had led her there that same evening, his four surviving sons closing protectively around her as they moved through the streets. But Chabris had heard the talk; only to look into his face made Judith sure of it. And during the months that followed, she had paid the price.

Not once did her father-in-law accuse her, nor did he punish her in any way that the people of Bethulia might recognise. He did not load her with heavy tasks and beat her, as Sarra did. Instead, he turned on her his learning and his authority as the town's third elder. 'You are now the daughter of this family,' he had told her, 'and you must become a model of virtue, for all the citizens to see.' So Judith's days had been divided between working for Sarra and taking instruction from Chabris. She could already read simple documents, but now she had to study the complex holy stories. She sat behind Chabris's younger sons when they had lessons and struggled to memorise what they were taught. She spent nights learning long passages to recite to Chabris the following day. She prayed for hours. She came to know every description of lustful and wicked women by heart, every curse pronounced against them, every admonishment on how to live a chaste life. They branded themselves into her mind and burned her tongue as she repeated them to Chabris.

Weeks became months and months became seasons. For much of the time, Judith had been kept in seclusion. She didn't mind much; her shame had become so great that she felt unfit to take part in city life, or have people look at her. She meekly accepted every new restriction: being shut in the house for the first twelve hours of any feast, the new headdress that covered her face to its chin, the interdiction on going to the city gates. These were new measures that the elders were enforcing against all young unmarried women, but Judith knew that whereas the other women complied out of obedience, she did so as an acknowledgement of shame.

Shame and pride, meekness and rebellion: during all of that long penance in Chabris's house, they had warred inside her. Sometimes shame and meekness were uppermost, and she felt as if she would never have the will to be angry again. But the anger always came back eventually, and with it the urge to rebel. Judith did not rebel; she knew she could only bring worse on herself.

And then, gradually, news had filtered in to Judith that people were asking about her. Her mother, visiting her, brought a gift of dates from her aunt. Eleazar the second elder had praised Judith's regular prayer-making to a group of young girls. And then Endeyeh, the servant nearest in age to Judith, who had often looked at her with sympathy, told her that she was to be sent back to her old house.

Judith had never been sure why they'd let her return. At the time Chabris had told her that the elders wished her to 'live openly in the town, in the devout way you have followed in my house. We want you to be an example to younger women.'

Endeyeh had whispered that it was more likely at Sarra's insistence, to get Judith away from her sons. Surely Judith had noticed that Simon was taken with her? Judith had shaken her head swiftly, suddenly afraid that this was a trap, and that Endeyeh would report back and get her punished.

But she had indeed been allowed home, to this house that Manasses had built. She had not come alone. Sarra had sent Endeyeh with her as her servant (Sarra had never liked the girl) and Chabris had installed the widow Abishag, his cousin, to act as his eyes and ears.

Judith had been home nearly a year now. She had done nothing to incur Chabris's wrath. There were few tales Abishag could carry back to him. But then Judith lived dutifully and quietly – she had no temptation to do otherwise – and only Endeyeh knew how trapped and restless she felt. The two of them had become friends, secretly and with the minimum of words. Judith lived in dread of Abishag realising this, and having Endeyeh removed.

Was that what she was talking about now, with Rebekah? But no, of course not. It would be to do with the siege, everything was these days. Judith skirted the tent dwellers' children and moved quickly up to Rebekah and Abishag.

'Has any more news come in?'

Rebekah glanced at the older woman, waiting for her to speak. Abishag looked directly at Judith. 'There's going to be a council this afternoon,' she offered. 'The elders and the leading citizens. Ozias' two youngest sons are sick with fever, and Ozias is proposing to go into the camp himself to negotiate.'

'I know,' said Judith. 'I heard this morning.'

Rebekah shuffled expectantly.

'There's something else,' said Abishag. 'Something that

concerns you and your household.' Her eyes moved from side to side, brimming with her secret knowledge. Judith felt the clutch of apprehension again.

'What is it?'

Abishag chewed her lip, maddeningly.

'Tell me! Is it my father?'

'It's Rechab, Endeyeh's husband.'

'Oh!' Judith's eyes flew instinctively round the courtyard, seeking Endeyeh. Rechab was a travelling merchant and there had been no word of him since the start of the siege. There had been plenty of rumours though, and Endeyeh suffered with each one. 'What do they say this time?'

'He's in the Syrian camp and not as a prisoner. He's enlisted with them, against his own people.' Abishag stood very erect. 'He's a traitor,' she added softly.

'I don't believe it. Who said so?'

'Joachem, Eleazar's boy. He's on sentry duty today and he saw him this morning, with his own eyes. Rechab was leading the Syrian General – God curse him! – along the paths at the foot of the hill, showing him the different routes up.'

'You can't possibly recognise anyone from that distance.'

'Rechab was wearing that cloak of his, that he bought from the Phoenecians. That's how Joachem spotted him.' Abishag primmed up her lips. 'You know how he always boasted that there was no other cloak like it.'

Judith gazed at Abishag and longed to slap her triumphant face. Abishag wanted this story to be true because she liked condemning people. She would enjoy bringing unhappiness to Endeyeh, especially as Endeyeh's shame would inevitably taint Judith too.

'We all know how Rechab boasts,' she said calmly. 'And

we all know not to believe half what he says. There are probably a hundred cloaks like that on the backs of all kinds of people. Rechab's a good-hearted young man under the swagger and I don't believe he'd betray his people.' But as she spoke she had a moment's doubt, remembering Rechab's last stay in Bethulia, and how he had teased Endeyeh with tales of his exploits. They said all sorts of men had ended up in the Syrian force unwillingly, and Rechab was just the kind who would be unable to resist an encounter with soldiers if he thought he could take money off them.

'Ach, Judith, this is war. We can no longer afford to think the best of everyone. Now's the time to look beyond the sweet words and expose corruption where we find it.'

Judith looked sharply at Abishag. The older woman smiled at her. By her side Rebekah, who was Judith's own age and had once been a friend, flushed. Judith smiled back and nodded.

'Yes Abishag,' she said. 'We must all pray hard to keep our deeds and thoughts pure.' She turned her back on them both and walked away towards the stores to find Endeyeh.

Endeyeh was sitting with her back to the door, dividing bags of barley into smaller packages. She didn't look round at the sound of Judith's footsteps.

'It's Judith, no one else.' Endeyeh didn't respond. 'You've heard what they're saying, then? Oh Endeyeh, it's probably just a rumour like all the others.'

Endeyeh nodded. Judith moved round to sit opposite her, where she could watch the door. 'It's because of the cloak the soldier was wearing. And that doesn't mean anything.'

'It did to Joachem,' said Endeyeh. Her lips were pale. 'And it does to the elders.'

Judith dropped her voice. 'And do you think the elders are always right?'

Endeyeh smiled stiffly but shook her head at the same time. 'Hush Judith,' she murmured. 'Now's not the time to take risks.'

Judith watched her. Endeyeh's face had smoothed into a frightened blankness. It made her look younger than her twenty years, much younger than Judith herself, yet there was something in her eyes that was old and watchful.

'*Do* you think he's there, Endeyeh?' Judith's voice was barely audible. Endeyeh looked up from the barley.

'I don't know,' she said at last. 'So many rumours. So many different stories. Two days ago they said he was dead, now they're saying he's a traitor. I don't know what I believe.' She flexed her hands, dusty from the grain.

'There'll be another story in a few days' time. One of the scouts will see him on the mountain pass, safe and well.'

Endeyeh shook her head. 'Ah no, they'd never say just that about Rechab. If he was sighted, he'd be doing something dishonourable, you can be sure.' Her voice was bitter.

Judith took Endeyeh's nearest hand and squeezed it fiercely. 'Don't listen to that kind of thing. It's just vicious old crones like Abishag, who can't stand anyone young.'

Endeyeh glanced over her shoulder at the doorway.

'And Chabris,' she said in a stifled voice. 'This is a gift to him. He'll make me divorce Rechab now. You know he never liked me marrying Rechab.'

'Yes, I know.' Judith remembered Chabris' feigned pleasure at the marriage. He had been forced to agree for fear of offending Ozias, Rechab's father having once been a favourite servant of the chief elder. 'It was the best thing that happened while I lived in that house,' she added.

'And now he has a chance to end it.' Endeyeh brushed Judith's hand away and bent her head down again to the barley. Her hands moved blindly, scooping, measuring. Judith couldn't argue with her: only the previous week the elders had made a new bride divorce her merchant husband when the scouts caught sight of him selling to the army.

'If only I could see for myself.' Endeyeh spoke in a low voice. 'Here we are, forbidden to go on the walls, kept inside, hearing all these stories. Meanwhile my Rechab might be in the camp or miles away. He could be injured or in danger or dead. I keep thinking if only I could get down there, too, and look, someone would have news of him.'

'You wouldn't get very far. If our sentries didn't get you, theirs would.'

'You don't understand what it's like. Everyone you care about is here in the town. When you look out from the roof you just see the enemy but for me – Judith, what if your man was thought to be in the camp? Wouldn't you want to go down there?'

Judith's heart was thumping. Endeyeh was staring at her fiercely – did she know? Had she somehow guessed? Judith put her hand over her mouth.

'What's the matter?' Endeyeh frowned, then wariness flashed across her face. 'I'm sorry,' she said abruptly. 'I shouldn't have said that. I didn't mean . . .'

Judith took her hand from her mouth and placed her fingertips on Endeyeh's bare arm. She could feel the dampness of Endeyeh's sweat. She watched Endeyeh fall silent, bewildered. 'There is someone I know there,' she said, very low. 'Do you remember that boy I met in Jerusalem, when we were preparing for my marriage?'

Endeyeh's eyes travelled over her face. 'That half-breed boy?' she asked eventually. 'The little soldier?'

'Yes. Come closer, Endeyeh.' Keeping one eye on the doorway, Judith drew her servant into the deepest niche of the storeroom. 'I want to tell you my secret.'

'Sounds fascinating.' Matthew reached for his tiny cup of espresso and threw the last of it down his throat. At the same time, Cathy saw him glance at the clock on the wall. They were standing in a bar at the far side of the Piazza di Spagna and it was nearly 9 a.m. Cathy had been supposed to lie in bed and relax this morning but she was charged so full of energy that she had been up and dressed by the time Matthew knocked on her door, and had insisted on accompanying him to his usual breakfast spot. She had begun telling him about the dream as soon as they left the pensione.

'You mean, "Shut up about it, I'm late,"' Cathy said.

'Let's just say I'm late. Cat, I really have to go. Not that you look as if you'll mind so very much.' Matthew glanced at her as he dug into his pocket for change. 'You're still there, really, aren't you?'

'Where?'

'Bethel or Bethlehem or whatever it was called.'

'Bethulia.'

'That's the name given in the Bible story, isn't it?'

'Is it? I've got no idea.' Cathy allowed him to put his hand on her back and guide her towards the door. He'd done it so often in the past; sometimes it had been truly innocent, sometimes it had quickened with potential. And there had been times when it had felt like a threat. Now she had promised him that this embrace would soon be real. It seemed to Cathy that everyone in the bar had only to look at them to recognise it.

Out on the pavement, they stood and stared at one another, forgetting to move apart. People swerved round them in the morning rush.

'I must go,' Matthew said again.

'Yes, of course. Matthew, I wanted to ask you, is there an English library here?'

'Yes, the British Council library, about ten minutes away. Why?'

'I need a Bible. I want to read the Judith story again.'

Matthew cocked his eyebrows. 'It *must* have been a powerful dream.'

'I told you, it was.'

'And the Judith in your dream was the same woman you saw in the palazzo window? The one you've been drawing?'

'Yes. But Matthew, you're not going to say anything to Enzo about this, are you?'

Matthew smiled provokingly.

'You're not, are you?' Cathy's hand shot out and grabbed his arm.

'Ow! Shit, sis, you haven't forgotten how to fight, have you?' His brow creased but he didn't flinch, despite the fact that Cathy had found the sinews below his elbow and was trapping them, a trick she had learnt long ago.

'Matthew. Promise me you won't say anything unless I agree to it.'

Matthew's free hand closed on her fingers and gradually prised them apart. When he'd removed her hand from his arm, he held it in mid-air for a few seconds and drew his thumb gently across it. The infinitely light touch sent shudders through her.

'I promise. Though I don't see why it has to be such a secret, especially when it could help me get to the Giuditta. If Enzo could just, say, catch a passing glimpse of those drawings, he'd be bound to raise the subject himself. And then we could compare—'

'I know.' Cathy tugged her hand away. She was smiling against her will. 'You went through it all last night.'

'Well, will you help me? After all,' Matthew grinned wickedly, happily, 'you are my stepsister.'

Cathy shut the heavy book and sat staring at the red cover which had faded in patches from the sun. There was dust collected in the spine; few people bothered to take the Bible off the shelves these days.

Looking at the next table, Cathy saw a nun taking notes. Yes, well, she would have her own copy at home. It was a long time since Cathy had turned the pages of a Bible and she didn't know what to make of the story she had just read.

The Book of Judith. Sixteen pages of close print had disclosed a triumphalist story: Judea comes under threat from its powerful neighbour; the hill town of Bethulia is besieged and virtuous young widow Judith, respected throughout the town for her beauty and her devotion to God, goes down into the enemy camp, makes the enemy general Holofernes mad with desire for her and cuts off his head. She then carries the head back to Bethulia in triumph, the enemy flees, and after many days and nights of thanksgiving, Judith retreats into a life of prayer.

Cathy frowned. There was something odd about the story. The language was sensuous, and in places violent; long poetic passages were devoted to Judith's prayers, and yet when it came to describing what she did in the camp, the prose seemed to lose character. It was almost as if the narrator were trying to avoid something.

The story contained within these covers was easily recognisable from her dream. But it seemed garish in comparison. Garish and clinging, like one of those commercially-bred roses that swarm over everything and choke off the smaller, intricate blooms that grow wild.

The Judith of her dream flickered like a flame in Cathy's mind. She had been young and fierce, and full of pent-up longing. Cathy hoped she would dream of her again, but of course that was unlikely. You couldn't call up dreams to order.

She stood up and replaced the Bible on its shelf. Then she picked up her bag and made her way towards the door. She could feel something inside her bag digging into her hip as she walked: her sketchpad and her pens. She flexed her fingers experimentally. Perhaps she would do some more drawing later.

CHAPTER FIVE

'Cathy, I thought it was you.'

Danilo stood several yards away, on the flagstone path. He was wearing a business suit and carrying a slim case, and he looked incongruous in the leafy courtyard. How long had he been there?

Cathy had been sitting in the courtyard more than an hour, and for most of the time she'd had it to herself. The place was one of Matthew's discoveries, just round the corner from the auction house but hidden away from the bustle of the streets. 'You'll be quiet here,' Matthew had said. 'Hardly anyone goes through it. It's so tucked away, people don't realise it's there.' So she had sat there on a stone bench, in the shade of a tree, and whiled away Matthew's absence with sketching and thinking. She had plenty to think about; plenty she needed to get straight in her mind before this evening.

There were the Judith drawings – five of them now. And that dream, which still burned in her memory, as bright and elemental as if it had only just left her.

Today was Friday and Cathy and Matthew were going to the palazzo for dinner. They had finally agreed that, at some stage in the evening, they would tell Enzo about the drawings; then if he asked to see them, Cathy would show him. She had been reluctant at first, but over the last few days, as Judith had reappeared again and again under her pen, she had begun to feel the need for an impartial and expert eye. Were these drawings really as good as she thought? And was the likeness to the Giuditta as strong as Matthew seemed to believe? She was keeping Matthew to his promise to say nothing about the dream, however. That felt too personal to share.

Cathy had come here to wait for Matthew and to think but her thoughts hadn't progressed very far before she'd found herself drawing again. Just the one sketch this time, but it was enough to give her that odd, hazy-excited feeling. And now Danilo had materialised, only yards away, and God knows how long he'd been watching her.

Cathy stood up hastily and turned her sketchpad face down.

'I'm sorry,' Danilo said. 'I didn't mean to disturb you. You're working, aren't you?'

'No, not really. I'm just resting – and waiting for Matthew.'

'Ah. He's at the auction house?'

'Yes. Is that where you're going?'

'It is. I expect I'll see him.'

It had been a mistake to stand up. Cathy was now hovering in front of the bench, feeling awkward. She and Danilo were several yards away from each other, too far apart to shake hands and yet too close to nod and say goodbye. Besides, Cathy didn't want to let him go. She had the feeling there was something they should be saying to one another, though for the life of her she couldn't work out what it was.

'I like this courtyard,' Danilo said. 'I often come here when I want time to think. Did you just stumble across it?'

'No, Matthew brought me here.'

'Ah. I didn't realise he knew about it.' Danilo said it

pleasantly but there was a hint of something painful in his face. Loss? Resignation! 'I'll leave you to your rest. I hope it restores you. Our city can be an exhausting place for a holiday.'

'I think it's beautiful,' Cathy said, surprising herself by the fervour of her tone. She felt a peculiar urge to confide in Danilo. Her eyes flickered to her sketchpad.

'Yes, it is.' His dark eyes, a softer, richer brown than Matthew's, followed her glance.

'What time is it?' Cathy asked quickly. It suddenly seemed very important that they shouldn't start talking about her drawings.

The bell in the church tower just behind him struck the three-quarter hour. Danilo turned and looked at the large clock face that dominated the courtyard.

'A quarter to six,' he said politely. Through her discomfiture, Cathy thought she saw a smile in his face. 'And I must go. I'll see you later, at the house.'

'Danilo came through earlier.'

'Bad luck. What did he have to say?'

'Just hello and goodbye. He seemed surprised you knew about this place.'

Matthew grimaced. 'That's Danilo, always convinced he's got the inside line on everything. He'll be trying to introduce us to each other next.'

'I thought you were getting on better this week.' Cathy finished doing up the buckles on her bag and stood up. Matthew put his arm through hers.

'We are. He chats to me sometimes; it's unnerving.' He pulled her gently towards the small fountain at the far side of the courtyard. Their limbs moved with disturbing compatibility.

They had strolled arm in arm very often before; and very often they had been aware of more than sibling affection when they did it. But it had never seemed so highly charged as this.

These last three days, as they lived in anticipation of the weekend, everything they said and did trembled on the edge of the forbidden act. It couldn't go on much longer; they were both dizzy from trying to keep their balance.

Every touch of Matthew's bruised her. Every casual kiss left her throat parched for a deeper one. They never discussed it, but Cathy knew Matthew felt the same. His eyes had become fervid and the skin beneath them translucent. And then sometimes he smiled at her as if he didn't have a care in the world, as if it were all simple and there was nothing to worry about. But Matthew had always believed that they could and should be lovers; it was Cathy who had put up resistance.

She put up her hand and ran her knuckles down his cheek. The spray from the fountain cooled her forehead and dampened her hair. 'You and Matthew have been brought up as brother and sister. To your father and me, you are our joint children.' Louise had said that to her, and Cathy had heard the warning in it. Their family would never accept them. She had known that all along.

She felt Matthew's mouth on her temple and closed her eyes. 'Shall we go and get a drink?' she said. She leaned her head against his shoulder. 'I've got another drawing to show you.'

'OK.' She felt rather than heard him pause. 'Cat, I've been thinking. Are you sure about this? You know, if you don't want me to tell Enzo about the drawings, I needn't.'

She shook her head quickly. She didn't want to start interrogating her motives now, there simply wasn't time. She only wanted to move on, to this evening and beyond. 'I'm sure. If it'll help you get to that painting, then that's what I want too.'

They had been at the palazzo half an hour, and the lights were burning brightly in the drawing room. It was clear to Cathy now that no other guests were coming. That at least was a relief. She had been anticipating a social dinner, with some neighbours or art world colleagues invited along, and she had been wondering where she would fit in. She wasn't sure her Italian would stand up to a high-powered evening. But instead it was just the four of them. They were speaking English and the atmosphere was intimate and gently festive, as if it were someone's birthday.

Under the dark gold shades of the wall lights, Enzo talked to Cathy. He was quieter than on Tuesday and showed a more thoughtful side. He asked about her work and her views on her contemporaries. Matthew had evidently told him the kind of work she did and Enzo began asking her about her influences and which other abstract painters she most admired. He was a skilful interlocutor; after a while, Cathy realised that she was telling him a good deal, not only about her work but about herself.

'That's a very modern way of looking at it,' Enzo was saying, after eliciting her opinion on a fashionable Italian sculptor. 'I can see that it would have certain attractions for you. But tell me, have you never wanted to paint figuratively?'

Cathy shook her head. 'When I was a teenager I did, and even when I first went to art college, but I was hopeless at it. My life studies were terrible. My tutor once said they were an insult to the human form. So I gave up.'

'And you have never been tempted to try again? Matthew tells me you're a good draughtswoman. Don't you ever draw a person from life now and then, to see if you can prove the tutor wrong?'

'No, I don't,' she said firmly. She was slightly annoyed at the hint that abstract work was second best. 'I'm really much more interested in abstract. I haven't drawn from life for years.'

Matthew looked up from his talk with Danilo. There was a quizzical look on his face and it was directed at her. It lasted barely a second but it was enough to jolt Cathy. What the hell was she thinking of? She'd been drawing the Judith woman all week and Enzo was due to learn about it later on. Yet somehow it had never crossed her mind to equate that woman with drawing from life.

She looked away from Matthew, bewildered, and caught Danilo watching them both. His eyes were very dark and attentive.

'Of course, for someone with your ideas about distance and closeness, and the relationship between touch and vision, abstract painting can seem the richer discipline.' It was Enzo, leaning forward to claim her attention again.

After a second he smiled at her, and then the murmur of Matthew and Danilo's conversation resumed. Distracted, Cathy tried to hear what they were saying but Enzo was speaking again. 'Forgive me, Cathy, I didn't mean to interrogate you. Let's interrupt Nilo and Matthew and make them continue that piece of gossip at the dinner table.'

So far, Cathy had been talking almost exclusively to Enzo. On the way to the dining room, however, the formation changed so that she and Danilo walked ahead of the others.

The dining room was at the back of the hall, set below the drawing room and to one side. As they crossed the marble flags towards it, Cathy had the impression of dimness and shifting light, and for a second she wondered if someone had lit a fire in there despite the heat.

But when Danilo stood back to let her go in, she saw that it was candlelight. Most of the candles were round the edges of the room, on the mantelpiece and on a pair of delicate side tables, one below each window. Then in the middle of the table was a branched candelabra which gave off a rich glow. The atmosphere in the room was peaceful and mystical. It was also alive. The flames moved unceasingly and were reflected in the glasses and the silver and the big oval mirror above the fireplace. Cathy drew in her breath.

Danilo, who had followed her into the room, looked down at her. 'I hope you don't mind. I always do this when I'm at home. I'm only half-Jewish and I don't practise, but I like to mark Friday nights.'

'Oh, I didn't realise. Do you have prayers?'

'No. When I'm alone, I bless the food, but not when there's anyone here. It was my mother who was Jewish, you see, and she converted when she married my father. I was brought up a Catholic.'

'And are you a practising Catholic?'

'I go to confession now and then.'

'I see.'

Danilo held a chair out for her. 'You find it strange.'

'No, just unexpected.'

'My father thinks it's strange. He thinks it's a morbid way of remembering my mother. But it's not. It's a way of reclaiming the other half of my heritage.'

Cathy glanced at Enzo. He was showing Matthew one of the pictures on the wall and didn't seem to have heard Danilo.

'I'm a mixture, you see,' Danilo went on. 'Traditionally Catholics believe their faith is passed down by the father, and Jews believe Judaism goes through the mother. So I can belong to either. And both.'

'Do you go to the synagogue?'

'Sometimes. It's quite interesting inside. I'll take you there if you like.'

'Danilo, would you serve the wine?' Enzo's voice cut across the table. He had turned to speak over his shoulder.

Danilo moved obligingly to the side table, just behind Cathy. 'It's ironic,' he said, as he opened the bottle. 'This house originally belonged to some Jewish merchants. Pope Paul the Fourth confined the Jews of Rome into this Ghetto in the sixteenth century, and within a hundred years they'd become quite a thriving community. Some of them grew rich and built houses like this one. So eventually the Christian citizens moved in and dispossessed most of the wealthy Jews. It's a continuing cycle that Jews undergo, you know: displacement, growth, displacement. But when my father married my mother, Jews came back to the house.'

Cathy looked at Danilo, his head bent over the corkscrew. He was speaking with a quiet satisfaction; his half-Judaism meant a lot to him. And yet there was an odd note of defiance in his voice, as if he expected someone to start arguing with him.

'The Ghetto is so fascinating,' he said. 'It doesn't give up its secrets lightly, you have to know where to look. You should explore it. It makes an interesting contrast to the more public and grandiose parts of Rome. If you like, I could—'

'Nilo.' Enzo turned back to the table again. 'Oh, I'm sorry for interrupting, Cathy. Forgive me. Nilo, I can't remember the date we settled on for this Spanish school St Jerome. Matthew thought the sixteen forties. Would that be accurate?'

Danilo looked at her expressionlessly for a second, then straightened and answered his father's question. Cathy sat quietly, listening to the discussion about attributions, dates and expert opinions. Enzo had not been sorry to interrupt at all; he had done it on purpose, and he had done it twice. He evidently didn't think it a good idea for Danilo to show her round the synagogue, or the Ghetto, or anywhere.

Cathy wondered if he were thinking of the trouble it might cause with Matthew. Enzo Bonaventura was an observant man and she thought he'd looked at her and Matthew rather searchingly several times tonight. She looked at Matthew herself: he was leaning against the back of a chair disputing some detail of art history with Danilo. In the candlelight his face was all motion – dark eyes, sliding shadows, swift-moving mouth. He looked like one of Caravaggio's boys.

It was pleasant to feel Danilo's interest in her. No, more than that, he stirred her, quite deeply and in a way she wasn't sure she understood. But he had come too late. Matthew, her stepbrother, had long ago touched her to the quick. Cathy watched him hungrily. Danilo was leaning towards her to fill her heavy crystal wine glass. He was speaking to her, asking her a question, and she knew Enzo was watching them both, but it was several seconds before she could tear her gaze from Matthew's face.

Matthew finished eating his pear and carefully wiped his hands. Across the table, Cathy was talking to Danilo but he knew that her attention was half on himself. She was waiting for him to speak.

Throughout the meal, Matthew had been listening to the rhythms of the conversation and watching Enzo's expressions. Enzo seemed relaxed, even expansive. He certainly gave the impression of enjoying Cathy's company. He had joined in her discussion with Danilo now – the three of them were talking about a Pinturrichio fresco Cathy had seen this morning.

There was Danilo's voice, steady and intent. God, why did he always have to talk as if empires depended on his utterance? And Cat followed on, with some flight of fancy about the background figures she'd noticed. And now here was Enzo, teasing her: 'I'm surprised at you. So very unabstract. You'll be giving them names and addresses next.'

Cat made a tiny movement with her head – or was it just her eyes? She was looking at him. Come on, Matthew, speak. The trouble was that the leaping candlelight had lulled him; that and the wine, and the sight of Cat's face with the shadows gently stroking it. And there was something else, a nagging sensation that he had missed something. It was connected with that strange dream she'd had, and which she'd described to him so vividly the day after they'd last been here. He felt that there was something she hadn't told him about that dream, but which he knew all the same. And if he could remember it, he would understand more about the drawings.

But he must concentrate. Enzo had caught Cat's glance; he, too, turned towards Matthew. Matthew looked from him to Cat, just a fraction hesitantly.

'Well,' he said, 'Cathy's not quite so hardline abstract any more, are you?'

There was a second's silence. 'I suppose not,' said Cathy.

Her wary expression threw him. He could have sworn it was genuine. Hold on tight, as she used to say to him in the playground.

'I mean, you've been doing one or two figurative drawings since you've been here, haven't you?'

Cat nodded.

'The thing is,' Matthew turned to Enzo, 'Cathy's been doing some very interesting work. Do you remember when we were upstairs and she said she never drew from life? I suppose strictly speaking that's true, but she's certainly started drawing people. Or rather, one person.'

Enzo raised his eyebrows. He glanced over at Cathy, smiling quizzically. 'Should you be telling me this, Matthew? Cathy doesn't seem very comfortable. Perhaps she doesn't like you discussing her work as if she weren't here.'

'No, it's all right.' Cathy spoke quickly, with a nervous laugh. 'I don't mind Matthew telling you. You see, I'm drawing someone I saw in the palazzo. Or I *thought* I saw her in the palazzo. But Matthew says I can't have done. He says . . .' she looked embarrassed. Matthew couldn't tell if it were real or assumed. 'He insists I've drawn someone who's been dead for nearly four hundred years. Perhaps longer. He thinks the woman in my drawings is the same person who's in one of your paintings. But that doesn't make sense, because I've never seen it.' She smiled, rather hectically Matthew thought, and folded her arms in front of her. As well she might; she couldn't have made it sound more crass if she'd tried.

Danilo was watching her with a faint smile. Matthew glanced at Enzo, wondering if he would be annoyed or simply amused, like his son. He was neither. To Matthew's surprise, Enzo sat pressed against the back of his chair and it was as if all the muscles in his shoulders, neck and face had tightened, shrinking him.

'Forget it,' said Matthew. 'I'm probably wrong. You're right, Enzo, I talk too much.' He made a deprecating gesture with his hands, more to attract Enzo's attention than anything else. But the old man was looking straight ahead of him, at a silver salt cellar. The old man: that was suddenly how he seemed.

'It was only a passing likeness,' Matthew went on, 'and as a matter of fact I've never seen the painting itself, so I'm almost certainly wrong. All I've seen is—'

'Which painting?' Danilo spoke quietly.

'I'm sorry?' Matthew played for time; he did not want to name the Giuditta under these circumstances. Enzo was already upset, though at what, he couldn't tell.

'This likeness you saw; it was to which painting?'

God damn Danilo. His tone was so measured, so politely disbelieving.

'The Giuditta,' said Matthew reluctantly. 'The Annalisa Genzanese painting.' Out of the corner of his eye, he thought he saw Enzo twitch to attention.

'Yes, thank you,' Danilo murmured. 'I know who painted it. But I didn't know you were familiar with it.'

'I'm not. As I said, I've only ever seen a reproduction.'

'How is that possible?' Enzo turned to Matthew. 'There are none that I'm aware of.'

Matthew was relieved to hear Enzo's voice sounding quite normal. Perhaps that had been just a physical tremor a few seconds ago. Matthew knew that Enzo took heart pills. At any rate, the mention of the Giuditta didn't seem to have done permanent damage.

'There's an old newspaper picture in the library, in the cuttings files,' Matthew said. He didn't like to add 'from when Alessandra died', but judging by Enzo's expression, he was remembering for himself.

'Ah yes,' he said.

'You must have been going through the files very thoroughly,' Danilo said. 'Mustn't he, Father?'

'I asked him to,' Enzo said. To Matthew's ears, it sounded defensive. 'I thought it would help him get an overview of the works in the collection and show him which ones have been lent to exhibitions over the years.'

Danilo was looking at his father searchingly. Trust Danilo to suspect everyone's motives for everything. Perhaps Enzo shared some of Matthew's irritation, for he didn't smile at Danilo or say anything further to reassure him. Instead he turned to Cathy.

'If you wouldn't object,' he said gently, 'I'd very much like to see one of your drawings, so that I could judge for myself.'

Cathy looked at him, wide-eyed. During all this discussion, she had been sitting in silence, her hands folded on the table. Now she seemed to be regarding Enzo almost with fear.

'Yes, of course,' she said. 'I'll go and get my bag.'

'Don't disturb yourself. I'll ring for Giovanni. Thank you, my dear.'

The few minutes that elapsed while Giovanni fetched the bag were awkward. There seemed to be nothing to say and the tension was broken only briefly when, at Enzo's request, Danilo poured out liqueurs. When Giovanni brought in the bag, Cathy bent over it for a few moments and shuffled the pages of her notepad. She handed Enzo two drawings. As they passed over the table, Matthew saw that she had given him the first and the most recent of the Judith drawings. Cat sat back in her seat without looking at him; her eyes were on Enzo. Danilo sat very upright next to her; he, too, watched his father.

The first drawing, of the woman looking stealthy in the cloak, was uppermost. Matthew watched Enzo square it in his hands, lay it down on the polished table and then look. Nothing happened. There was no shock, no jolt of the head or shudder. No exclamation. With a steady hand, Enzo lifted the drawing to one side and looked at the next. In this one, which Cat had shown Matthew a few hours ago, the woman was only a small figure, standing on the top of what seemed to be a high wall. Urgency was written in every line of her tiny figure as she looked out at the world.

Enzo studied both pictures at length. The small movements of his head were familiar to Matthew: Enzo was scrutinising Cat's drawings with scholarly interest, just as if he were in the auction house or in his office upstairs.

'Remarkable,' he said at length. 'It really is a striking likeness. And these are good in their own right. I think you've proved your tutor wrong, Cathy. May I show them to Danilo?'

'Yes, of course.'

Matthew noticed that, as Enzo passed him the drawings, Danilo leaned back. He hesitated before he took hold of them, then laid them swiftly down by his plate. He glanced at Cathy and then looked at the drawings; he scarcely bent his head to do so but, like his father, he looked for a long time.

'You can see the likeness, can't you, son?'

'Oh yes,' said Danilo without emphasis.

'And you don't believe you've ever seen a reproduction of our Giuditta?' Enzo asked Cathy.

'No.'

'You based your first drawing, in fact, on a live person? Whom you saw here?'

'I thought I saw her here. I was sitting across the road in the cafe and I saw her at a window.'

'Which window?'

'The end one on the top floor – the left-hand side as I looked.'

'How extraordinary. That's where the Giuditta is kept.'

Matthew's mind tripped. The Giuditta was kept on the top floor? But all works officially in the collection were housed on the first and second floors, with specially designed security.

'Perhaps I saw the Giuditta. Perhaps I glimpsed the painting and then confused it with the face of the woman I'd seen.' Cathy offered the explanation brightly, as if they were making polite conversation.

'Oh no. That wouldn't be possible, would it, Danilo?'

Danilo looked up from the drawings reluctantly. 'No, Father.'

Matthew watched father and son look at one another. Danilo had shuttered all expression from his face. Enzo, meanwhile, was giving off an odd, dark energy. Matthew had the impression that he was communicating with Danilo long before he spoke.

'I believe, in the circumstances, I'm going to show our friends the Giuditta.'

Danilo didn't move a muscle.

'I think that would be a good idea, don't you?' Enzo continued.

'I don't see the need,' said Danilo.

'Don't you? I do. We've kept it hidden away up there too long. It's time it was brought back into the light.' Enzo was speaking very gently. He waited, but Danilo made no reply, only looked at him. In his calm face, his eyes were suddenly burning. 'Cathy, Matthew. If you've finished, perhaps you'd like to come with me.' Enzo rose and, with brisk movements, pushed in his chair, discarded his napkin and led the way to the door.

Matthew walked along the corridor side by side with Cathy. Enzo was still leading them; behind came Danilo. Matthew listened to Danilo's regular tread; for a big man, he was light on his feet. The corridor was familiar to Matthew – they were in the east wing, on the second of the floors that housed the collection. Closed doors were ranged on either side of them, electronic eyes winking as they passed. He had often been in these rooms during the day, initially with Enzo to escort him, more recently entrusted with the keys on his own, and as they passed the doors he mentally named them: seventeenth-century Florentine; Claude and followers; Genovese portraiture. The categories were reassuring.

At the very end of the corridor was a door he had never seen opened. Enzo was taking them into the internal staircase which connected the east and north wings. It was normally kept locked for security. Enzo switched on an electric light and they followed him in. Stone stairs led upwards and downwards in a tightly twisting spiral; they were in the crook of the building here, enclosed by walls painted a faded blue. They climbed to a small landing above them, and Enzo unlocked another door, a heavy wooden one, studded with brass.

Matthew glanced at Cathy. She immediately looked away, staring at Enzo's back. From her tense profile, Matthew could tell she was unhappy. He brushed the back of her hand with his knuckles; for an instant she pulled away, then she returned the pressure. Out of the corner of his eye, Matthew saw Danilo looking at them. Had he seen? In an atavistic surge of rivalry, Matthew hoped he had.

Enzo shepherded them through the doorway and at once Matthew was able to orientate himself. They were on the top floor of the north wing, above the offices. Before them the corridor led out wide and dark-tiled, with doors at evenly spaced intervals on the right-hand side and recessed windows on the left. Down there was the central courtyard. Light from the ground-floor windows and the garden lamps shone into the corridor and made silhouettes of leaves on the wall.

The proportions of the corridor were lovely but it felt abandoned. There was a smell of floor polish and dead air.

'Here we are,' said Enzo. He blinked at them and seemed to hesitate. His gaze lifted over Matthew's shoulder to where Danilo stood. 'When my wife was alive, she used to work up here. We converted this end room into a studio for her.'

He turned and began unlocking the nearest door; he had to try several keys before he found the right one. Then, when the lock gave, he walked quickly into the room, not pausing to turn on a light. Matthew and Cathy had to follow him blind.

It was not entirely dark in there. Light from the courtyard reached in across the threshold and showed scattered objects that might have been furniture. Matthew had to step away from Cathy to avoid tripping over something squat and hard. As he stepped round it, Danilo's figure blocked up the doorway and for a few seconds Matthew was completely disorientated. He heard a stumble and Cathy's intake of breath; then a shuffle and someone murmuring, 'Careful.'

The light came on. Enzo was standing by a wall switch; Cathy was in the middle of the room, between two wooden crates, and Danilo was close behind her. His hands were moving away from her shoulders.

'As you can see,' Enzo said quietly, 'we've never really cleared up in here. At first I couldn't bear to come in here, then it seemed too final a thing to do. It was wrong of me to have left it so long, though. Alessandra herself would be annoyed. She didn't generally work in such disorder. But she wasn't like herself for the last weeks of her life.'

He looked around, taking stock. It was a rectangular room, with bare walls and no furniture beyond one hard and one soft chair. Boxes and trunks were spread around the floor; there were concertina files stacked on shelves and against the far wall stood a line of easels. All except one were empty and that was covered with a sheet. Enzo took one corner of it and looked at Danilo. Danilo didn't move.

'This is the Giuditta,' said Enzo wryly.

The sheet came off awkwardly, flapping in front of the painting. At first Matthew thought Enzo must have mistaken the picture, because surely this was an abstract. Thick swathes of paint, dark and intense, crowded into the canvas, fighting one another. There were whorls and diagonal flashes and fierce horizontals, and other, more subtle lines which seemed to struggle through them.

Then, as his gaze settled, he understood. The delicate lines were not random, they made a pattern beneath the others. The dark paint was only an overlay, crudely and frantically splashed on top of what already existed, obscuring the detail and yet not able to destroy the outline of the woman. Through the attempted destruction, Matthew could see that the woman was kneeling; that something long and bright was falling across her lap, and that in her hands she cradled a round object.

Yes, this was the Giuditta he had seen smudgily

photographed in that cutting. But Holofernes' severed head was a mass of overpainting, and the woman's face, which had haunted his memory for weeks, was disguised under a criss-cross of black paint. Only one part of her was left untouched: from the thick strokes which pressed against her face like a mask Judith's eyes gazed out, full of anguish.

From Cathy, standing a few feet away, Matthew thought he heard a sigh.

'This is the Giuditta,' Enzo repeated. 'This is what my wife did to her before she died.'

[illegible]

[illegible] said Matthew. [illegible] along the [illegible] the water, the [illegible] Matthew's [illegible] since leaving the [illegible]

[illegible] hands to her [illegible] woman [illegible]

"And [illegible] imagined [illegible] someone [illegible] What [illegible]

[illegible]

[illegible] think [illegible]

[illegible] what you [illegible]

[illegible] at home [illegible] What do you [illegible] talking about [illegible]

[illegible] She [illegible]

Chapter Six

'Jesus, how desperate she must have been,' said Matthew. They were walking along the river bank. Across the water, the great dome of St Peter's bruised the night sky. Matthew's words were the first either of them had spoken since leaving the palazzo.

Cathy pushed her hands in her pockets. 'Poor woman.'

'And poor Enzo. Imagine having to watch someone you loved going mad like that. Did you see his face when he told us?'

Cathy could still see it very well. And she could hear his measured voice too, not quite managing to flatten out the pain. *My wife was severely mentally ill towards the end. She believed the Giuditta was speaking to her and telling her to do terrible things. It was schizophrenia, of course. It was too much for her to bear. She tried to silence the voice by destroying the painting.*

'I don't want to think about it,' she said abruptly.

'No.' Matthew sounded subdued. 'I know what you mean. God, what a lot of unhappiness there's been in that house.' He was quiet for a while. 'What do you think they're talking about now?'

'I've got no idea.' Cathy walked a little faster. She didn't want to go on with this conversation. She didn't want to have to remember Danilo's pallor, or the atmosphere in that shuttered room. Most of all she didn't want to think about the painting.

She filled her eyes with the night-time sights all around her: the river, the cars, the street lamps, the people walking. But it didn't work. She could still see that canvas, dark and chaotic. She saw the young woman, half hidden in the turmoil of paint. And she knew her from the dream.

'Oh God.' She stopped and breathed deeply. 'None of this makes sense.'

'What doesn't?' Matthew looked at her cautiously.

'Well . . .' Cathy paused. She tried to organise her thoughts so that she could say something rational. 'Well, why am I doing these drawings, for a start?'

'Er – haven't we just spent the last hour discussing this with the Bonaventuras? I thought we'd settled on the you-must-have-seen-a-reproduction-and-forgotten-it explanation.'

'Yes, yes, I know. It just bothers me not being able to remember it, that's all.' Cathy twitched her shoulders and set off walking again.

She would have liked to believe in that explanation, but there were too many things that didn't fit. There was the dream. There was the girl she had seen in the window. There was that odd panic attack she'd had on the plane, when she had felt almost as if she had entered into someone else's body. And that had been somewhere hot, with a familiar dusty smell which came back to her even now, stealing into her nostrils, dry, acrid and choking . . .

'It's time we got away from these Bonaventuras.' Matthew's arm was suddenly through hers. 'They're an intense pair and we're getting dragged into their unfinished business.'

'That's a bit much. It was you who was so dead keen on getting to see the Giuditta.'

'Hey, calm down. I'm not blaming anyone, I'm just stating a fact.' Matthew stopped walking and forced Cathy to stop too. She looked angrily past him, until he put up a hand to her face. 'Cat? I'm sorry if I made you do something you didn't want to.'

Cathy closed her eyes and concentrated on the touch of his hand. It was like a foreshadow of caresses to come. Tomorrow: this time tomorrow they would be a long way away from here.

'You didn't make me do anything. Oh, take no notice of me, it's just been a bit of a gruelling evening.'

'Do you want to go and have a drink?'

'Definitely. Let's find somewhere bright and noisy.'

'Suits me.' Matthew took her arm again and they crossed the road, zig-zagging to avoid cars. 'By the way,' said his voice in her ear, 'what was Danilo doing pawing you in the studio?'

'He wasn't pawing me, you idiot.' Cathy stepped briskly up onto the pavement. 'He just steadied me when I nearly fell.'

'I didn't like it.'

'Neither did I, especially.'

Matthew laughed. 'Good. Just checking, sis. Here's a bar. Is it noisy enough for you?'

'Perfect.' Cathy went eagerly into the crowded bar, trying not to think of Danilo's touch in the darkness, and the puzzling familiarity of it.

Was it last-minute nerves about the weekend that made her feel so strange? Or was it the events of the evening? Perhaps it was the alcohol. Three whiskies had seemed an excellent idea in the bar. They had melted the hard edges of her consciousness and eased her into a pleasant free fall; walking back to the pensione, Cathy had felt quite radiant.

But now that she was lying in bed, and sleep was approaching, she had to keep reminding herself where she was. Her mind seemed to wander between Rome and London and Judea. Memories of her shared past with Matthew overlapped with thoughts of Enzo and Alessandra's tragedy, and with the scenes she had been drawing. In muddled anticipation, she kept looking ahead to tomorrow and seeing herself and Matthew leaving the city, only it wasn't Rome; it was a hill city, buildings and streets jumbled behind high walls, and in her imaginings the bus carried them along a tarmac road that kept changing into a mountain track, and she leaned forward eagerly in her seat, craning her neck to see further into the desert landscape ahead.

Judith trudged through the street, her mother's soiled clothes rolled up under her arm. The smoke was already rising from the wasteland immediately behind the upper gate: this evening's burning had begun. Every day the citizens collected the fouled belongings of the sick and dead, and took them to this spot to be destroyed. It was all they could do to try and check the spread of the sickness.

Seventy-four people had died and more fell ill each day. There wasn't a household left untouched. Judith's mother had survived this time: her fever had lessened and she was sipping the melon juice Judith had found for her, but she was badly weakened. She would not be able to nurse her husband or her son and Judith had noticed with dread that little Reuben's lips were cracking and his eyes were dull. Endeyeh had taken him back to Judith's house, and he would stay there tonight. Judith muttered a prayer for her brother, but without any hope that it would be answered. God had deserted Bethulia, that was clear. Everyone thought so: last night at the city gates, people had shouted angrily at the elders and blamed them for their inaction.

'We have sent again to Jerusalem for help,' Ozias had said. 'We have received a promise of supplies and some armed men.' His words had been drowned by furious protests. 'We've had promises for weeks and nothing comes!' someone had shouted. 'Nothing's going to come, they've betrayed us!' Recriminations had broken out. The citizens had rounded on one another as well as on the elders. Some wanted to evacuate the city and seek refuge in the towns further along the hill pass; some urged negotiation; others came up with plans for night-time strikes on the camp, for sending out parties of men to recruit support by force from the surrounding villages, for ambushes and the taking of hostages. They were desperate plans, doomed to failure, and everyone knew it.

Finally, Ozias himself had gone down into the camp, as he had done several times in the past weeks, and attempted to negotiate. General Holofernes had ordered him from his tent and sent him back to the city with a curse, and a promise to kill the next man who came out of Bethulia with any offer short of surrender.

Now the elders were in council again. They had been locked away in Ozias's house for hours. And citizens were drifting restlessly through the streets, asking one another in vain if they'd heard any news. 'No word from Jerusalem?' 'No word.' 'A scout came back.' 'Only to say that he's met nothing on the pass.' 'I heard Ozias is thinking of going there himself, to petition.' Judith listened with a dull rage. After all this time, the people were still hanging on the decisions of the elders. If Ozias went to Jerusalem, half the city would die before he returned.

For the first time, Judith felt that death was very close. The danger posed by the Syrian army had terrified and thrilled her. She had felt drawn to it, as if it sent a personal challenge to her. She remembered the culmination of that feeling – the moment six days ago when she had confided her secret to Endeyeh, in the close dimness of the store room. And Endeyeh, tormented by her own longing for Rechab, had put trembling arms around her and whispered 'Oh, what can we do?'

The question vibrated inside Judith now. In the last terrible days, it had seemed to gather urgency. Bethulia was dying. Everywhere she looked she saw sickness and hopelessness. She had grown to hate the sight of the city walls: no longer comforting or protective, they now seemed to be crushing the life out of the people within. Judith hated them as she had once hated the walls of Chabris's house.

She had reached the upper gate. She joined the crowd pushing its way through the opening, into the wasteland beyond. The smell of soiled garments and bedding was terrible and Judith hurried to the fire and threw her bundle on the flames, retreating swiftly. She stood blinking against the smoke, hugging herself. *What can we do?* She had an idea, a vision of what they might do, which had been growing inside her for days.

At first she had seen it as a wild dream, the kind of thing men and women did in the holy stories. But then she had begun to think it through. It was a frightening, desperate idea. And yet she knew it was possible.

The crowd around the fire was thinning. People were making their way back to the gate, jostling each other in response to noises from inside the walls. Judith lifted her head and listened. It was news of some sort; the elders must have ended their council. A murmur of bewilderment was travelling from mouth to mouth. 'Surrender,' she heard. 'We're to have special prayers for three days and if there's no answer, we'll surrender.'

Amid cries of dismay and fear, Judith was swept towards the gate. She heard the noise as it swelled, but only distantly: a sudden silence was on her. She let the crowd carry her back inside the walls then, as the others surged down through the city to confront the elders, she turned into a side alley and walked swiftly home.

'He's asleep,' said Endeyeh, moving away from Reuben's mat. They were on the roof, where the air was cool. 'He's drunk some more of the melon juice and it hasn't made him sick. I think he might escape.'

'Thanks to God.' Judith touched her breast. 'You've heard what the elders have decided?'

Endeyeh gestured at the groups of people on the surrounding roofs, all calling frantically to one another. 'I've heard.' Her eyes were frightened. 'There's no hope for us, then?'

'Not if we follow the elders,' said Judith. She sank onto the baked earth of the roof and beckoned Endeyeh to join her.

'What else can we do?' said Endeyeh quietly. Their faces were only inches apart and she watched Judith with apprehension.

'Do you remember what you said to me in the store room?' Judith spoke quickly. 'About wanting to go into the camp to look for Rechab?'

'Yes.'

'Do you still want to?'

Endeyeh put her hands over her eyes. 'I don't know. I don't

know if I could stand to see him, if he is there.'

'You think he's guilty of treachery then?'

'No! No, of course I don't. Even Chabris had to admit there was no proof of that! It's just – oh, but what's the use of talking like this? We can no more go into the camp than go to Jerusalem.'

Judith gulped for air. 'There is a way, if you really do want to go. Listen Endeyeh, we could offer ourselves as hostages.'

Endeyeh sighed. 'Oh Judith, why would they care about having us as hostages? They'd laugh at us – or more likely rape us and kill us.'

'No,' Judith said steadily. 'I don't believe the general would hurt me.'

Endeyeh looked at Judith again. It was a sharp look, touched with bewilderment. 'I see. You're still thinking that name's significant.' She shook her head. 'I don't know why it's so important to you.'

'I'm sure it's him, Endeyeh.' Judith spoke softly. It was vital that she caught Endeyeh's full attention now; she must make it clear that she was serious. 'I've been listening to everything people say of him, all the information that's been coming out of Jerusalem. It's the same man.'

Endeyeh stared. 'So?' she said at last.

'So I should go into the camp and speak to him. Claim his protection for Bethulia, or at least his mercy.'

'What?' Endeyeh spluttered a disbelieving laugh.

'I'm saying that I should go to the camp and present myself to the general. I'll remind him of who I am and where we met. I'll come to no harm – he looked after me in Jerusalem.'

'Looked after you! The boy you met insulted you, forced

you to go to the Acra and blamed the Judeans for shutting the profaners in the Acra.'

'Reformers,' said Judith, smiling faintly.

'What?'

'He called them reformers.' Suddenly she could see the angry, dust-stained boy very vividly.

'In the name of God, Judith, if it is the same man, isn't that all the more reason to be afraid?' Endeyeh's voice rose. 'He hated Judeans even then for what we did to his people. Now he's leading an army against us and he's sworn to starve us into surrender. Why do you think he's going to show any mercy?'

'You're wrong, he didn't hate *us*. It was the priests and elders he blamed. He told me I'd suffer too if I went ahead and married Manasses, and he was right, wasn't he?' Judith was rigid with tension but she spoke calmly, determined to make Endeyeh understand. She had thought about this again and again in the last few days, recalling the boy's words, seeing his face, at once taunting and sympathetic.

The image of him was there now, keeping them both company on the roof. Then Endeyeh leaned forward and touched her and he vanished. 'Judith.' Endeyeh's voice was gentle. 'You remember the boy you met, but even if he is now the Syrian general, can you be sure that *he'll* remember *you*? Or care about you?'

Judith slipped her hand from Endeyeh's fingers and looked out across the city roofs to the walls, which were alive with people. They moved incessantly, a human barricade shifting in the failing light.

'Of course I can't be sure. But it's a chance. And what other chance do we have? Three nights from now the city will surrender and those of us who are still alive will be the army's prisoners. Aren't you afraid of that?'

There was a very long silence. 'Yes,' said Endeyeh finally. She reached out again and clutched Judith's robe. 'Of course I'm afraid, we all are, but I try not to think of it.'

'That won't help anyone, will it?' Judith spoke angrily, fighting down her own terror. Endeyeh didn't answer at once, but sat for a while, kneading the rough fabric of Judith's robe. When she finally raised her head and spoke, her voice was steady.

'Very well. What do you propose?'

Judith felt the blood roar in her ears as she turned quickly. Endeyeh nodded. 'Go on,' she said. Was she truly going to listen? Judith began talking quickly.

'I want to be sent into the camp as an official envoy. With you as my companion. And with the – the blessing of the elders. We'd need their permission to get out of the city, of course, and we should take gifts from them, to show respect. We would ask to be taken to General Holofernes' tent. And then . . .' she faltered.

'Then?'

'I'll tell the general who I am and plead for Bethulia.'

Judith looked away. She had invented scene after scene in her mind; some were triumphant, some were terrifying, but all were fragmented. She could not properly visualise the face of the boy transformed into the great general; and though she could sometimes hear his voice, deeper and with more authority, she could not order his words.

The doubt that always accompanied these imaginings suddenly pierced her. She hugged herself and looked apprehensively at Endeyeh. In the gathering darkness, Endeyeh's eyes were wide. 'If Rechab is there,' she said eventually, as if speaking to herself, 'I'm sure it's not as a traitor. Once I find him, he'll help us.'

Judith drew a long breath. 'You're willing to come?'

'Yes. You're right, it's a chance.'

They stared at one another. Judith felt her hands creep onto Endeyeh's lap and clasp her friend's strong fingers. They clung together mutely. Judith could hardly breathe for the beating of her heart.

'How are we going to persuade the elders to let us go?' Endeyeh sounded afraid but, now she had pledged herself, utterly practical.

'We'll let the people at large know what we're planning.' Judith fell in at once with her tone. She felt a surge of confidence. 'Now's the best time we could have chosen for it. The elders have lost their authority. Once people hear that there might be another way than surrender, they'll force the elders to agree.'

They both jumped as from the courtyard came the sound of groaning and Abishag's voice, calling for water.

'We'll talk later,' said Judith. 'Abishag's awake and people are coming back from the gates. Lay your mat next to mine on the roof and we'll talk when everyone's asleep.'

They had talked, murmuring low, for hours. Now they had moved their mats apart and lay still, each one tangled in her own thoughts. They had planned all they could plan; they had agreed on what to say and do. In a few hours, it would begin.

What was Endeyeh thinking of? Rechab, the husband she hoped and feared to find? Her family? The great camp itself, quiescent for now in the desert night?

Judith turned her head and watched Reuben as he slept

restlessly. She prayed that he would not worsen. Silently, she begged God to keep him safe while she was away. She asked the same for her mother and father too. But when she tried to ask it for herself, her inner voice failed. She could not imagine what would take place in the camp. The silence fell in her mind again and as she looked up at the stars, she wondered if it would put her beyond God's hearing too.

The idea was too frightening to bear. Judith closed her eyes and summoned up the scenes that would surely await her if she won the city a reprieve. They were there, ready for her; throughout her nervous planning, she had often sustained herself with them. She could see how the people would dance, and hear their songs of joy. Ozias and Eleazer would bless her; even Chabris would have to join in the tributes. And it would not only be Bethulia, but Jerusalem too, for if the siege were lifted the whole nation would have reason to thank her. She would go in a litter to the temple. They would praise her with cymbals and strew her with flowers.

In Judith's visions, the last traces of her old shame were washed away from her by the anointing oil, the feasting wine. The visions became dreams, richly coloured, all-enveloping.

Then a wind stroked her face. She opened her eyes to find the night fading, and Endeyeh already awake, crouched on her mat, watching the new light edge over the eastern ramparts.

Cathy awoke gently. She seemed to glide out of the dream; it retreated from her without hurry, she could almost see the images drifting past into the darkness.

She was wide awake and refreshed. The confusion she'd felt just before falling asleep had gone. She lay quietly for a while, thinking of Judith. She had been so clear, so real. Was this what it had been like for Alessandra when she'd heard Judith speaking to her?

Oddly enough, Cathy didn't feel frightened. She felt . . . she searched her mind for the word. Honoured. That was it. She felt that she had been visited by something extraordinary; that she had been awarded a precious insight.

Into what, though?

She got out of bed and walked to the window. Through the slats in the shutters a bluer light filtered into the room, breaking up the darkness. The night was ending, but it was not yet over. Cathy enjoyed the sensation of warm air on her skin, and the cool touch of Matthew's cotton shirt; she wished she could give the simple pleasure to the girl in the dream, so young, so passionate and thwarted.

She opened the shutters as quietly as she could and stood in the open window. It was still very dark outside, but up above the apartments opposite where the corner gave onto the Piazza di Spagna, the air was indigo rather than black and as she watched the colour intensified and spread and gradually became the bruised purple of heartsease.

It went on changing, faster now. Quite soon the darkness was no longer darkness but a deep blue light, and she could see the mouldings around the windows opposite. Next the mass of shadows at the end of the street resolved into buildings, steps and lampposts.

At first, she thought the shape at the corner was part of the Spanish Steps, a balustrade perhaps or a piece of architectural exuberance. Then it moved and, staring at it, Cathy saw that it was a person. He or she – she couldn't tell which in the half-light – was sitting down, elbows on knees, in the kind of attitude that suggests a long wait. She leaned out of the window to get a better look. Without her contact lenses everything looked indistinct, but the breadth of the shoulders told her that it was a man. She thought his face was turned towards her and she withdrew quickly.

Cathy rummaged in her suitcase for her glasses and put them on. The room snapped into focus. She looked out of the window more cautiously this time, using the shutter as a shield. The stone bench at the end of the street was empty but she could hear footsteps and when she craned her neck she could see a man walking away into the piazza.

Her mood was spoilt. It might not have been Danilo, of course; probably it hadn't been. Half the men in Rome had wide shoulders and dark curly hair. And although he had looked tall, it might have been a trick of distance. But Cathy felt exposed and uneasy and her dream no longer seemed quite so benign.

Who was this Judith and why had she come to her? Cathy half closed the shutters and went to sit on the bed. Then she pulled the sheets over her.

CHAPTER SEVEN

The bus drove away, its exhaust billowing as the engine strained to pull it up the gradient. It climbed the country road and vanished suddenly round the side of the slope. Cathy and Matthew were left standing by the roadside, looking at the wooded gorge and the viaduct ahead. Around them the land wrinkled into hills; to their right, across the small bridge, the village of Caprarola clambered up a slope.

'Oh God,' said Matthew. 'The guidebook did say there was a pensione here.'

Cathy glanced down at her hands. 'I think perhaps I should wear a ring.'

'What? You're wearing several.'

'But not on the right finger. Look over there.' On the other side of the bridge stood a group of old women, dressed in black and watching them as they dithered.

'Ah,' said Matthew, 'a welcoming party. Oh, come on, Cathy, they're just sizing up the foreigners. Don't let it get to you.'

'All the same.' She took the emerald ring off her right hand and slid it onto the fourth finger of her left. 'At least they'll think we're engaged now.'

'To bloody Jonathan,' said Matthew. 'You can't wear that

when you're with me. Take my signet ring instead.'

It was too big for Cathy's finger, and she had to hold her hand cupped to keep it in place. They walked self-consciously across the bridge, and at the far side Matthew spoke politely to the women and asked where the pensione was. They all stared at Cathy, while one of them gave directions.

A little way above the bridge was a piazza, with a horse trough and trestles stacked against a wall, waiting for market day. Some old men stood talking in a bar and outside it three teenagers were gathered round one scooter. Cathy and Matthew walked past a dark little grocer's and turned up a street that ran uphill to the right. The pensione was halfway along. It had a small metal sign hanging vertically by the door but made no other concession to hospitality.

Inside, it was a pleasant but bare village house. As she signed her name under Matthew's, Cathy was acutely conscious of the signet ring slipping on her finger, but the elderly woman taking down their passport details showed no interest in it. Cathy peered at the register and saw that the last entry was for the previous week. Business was not exactly flourishing; probably the landlady needed all the custom she could get. And after all, it was the late twentieth century, even in this village. A second glance at the register showed that all the recent entries were for couples. Perhaps this was a well-known trysting place. Matthew had picked it out of his guidebook at random.

They were shown to a square, sparsely furnished room on the first floor. Its window was at the back of the house and looked over a small garden with vegetables growing in it.

'Love among the runner beans,' said Matthew when the door had closed.

She went to gaze out of the window. The garden was divided into neat earth beds, with vegetables staked and netted. A path led down one side of them to a child's swing at the end of the garden, and a small girl was kneeling down by a hutch, feeding whatever fluffy animal was inside. Watching her, Cathy was struck that with all the glamour and anonymity of Rome at their disposal, they should finally have come here, to a room above a domestic garden, to make love.

In its odd way, it was very erotic.

'Cathy.'

She turned. Matthew was at the foot of the bed, a few yards away from her. And suddenly there was nothing in the little room but blank walls, the wide flat bed, and Matthew.

She had assumed that they would lead up to it gradually, that they would wander through the countryside, eat lunch and drink wine, and grow used to the touch of one another's hand discreetly, in public. But now she saw that there was no point in that.

They walked towards each other uncertainly. When they met, on the small cotton rug by the bedside, they put their hands up and touched palms. The feel of Matthew's hands were gentle but surprisingly strong. His fingers pushed through hers and she looked down at them and thought of all the ordinary, brotherly things she had seen them do – opening doors, turning the pages of books, mending a tennis racquet.

He slid one hand free and lifted it to Cathy's face. She rubbed her cheek against it and then, suddenly desperate, she pulled his head down to hers and pressed her face against his shoulder, his neck, the edge of his jaw. She could feel his lips trembling slightly and his breath was sweet.

She turned her head so that their mouths met. They hesitated, then tasted each other. His mouth was so soft and hot, it shocked her. Her first instinct was to pull away, but she held steady and then she grew used to the gentleness of him and she didn't want to stop. After a while, when she needed to pull away to swallow, she couldn't. She couldn't bear to lose him and she went on tasting him and sucking his tongue.

Their hands were clasped round one another's heads. Cathy felt his ears and the sharp angles of his jaw. His fingers stroked her hair back from her temples again and again. It was as though their hands were talking now that their mouths were silent. They were saying all the things they had denied themselves through eleven years of being stepbrother and sister.

Matthew moved away first. He took his mouth from hers and stood back, very slowly. Cathy had thought they might both cry when it came to it, but he was as dry-eyed as she was. He looked into her face and began to undo the buttons down the front of her dress.

They moved quite quickly after that. They were trying to be deliberate but Cathy was clumsy and had trouble taking off his T-shirt. The sensation of her knuckles brushing against his skin distracted her, and meanwhile he had unfastened her dress and pushed it back from her shoulders; his hands were on her breasts. She tugged at his T-shirt, trying to get one arm free, but it wouldn't come and in the end he had to take it off himself.

The last time Cathy had seen Matthew bare-chested was a year ago, when he'd had a shower in her flat. He was browner now and though he was still thin, it was no longer a boy's skinniness. His sinews moved, shadowing his flesh, as he unbuckled his belt. 'Let's undress,' he said. 'Properly. I want to be naked with you.'

'The window,' Cathy said. Matthew turned and pulled the thick lace curtain across. The light in the room became grainy, but she could still see him quite clearly as he climbed out of his jeans and his underpants. They stood naked, an arm's length apart. Cathy opened her mouth to say 'You're beautiful,' but she couldn't speak. Instead, Matthew stepped up to her and she closed her lips on his skin.

Her mouth and hands were full of him. She couldn't get enough. His hands were inside her and his tongue sucked at her. The bed sagged as they curled their limbs round each other and entwined fingers and mouths, and then finally, tenderly, almost as if they still had a choice in the matter, Matthew lifted her hips and pushed himself into her.

There were three faces: one broad, one long, one with sick yellow cheeks. They all wore beards close-clipped, then long at the chin, and their mouths moved to different rhythms. A moment ago she had understood what they were saying but now the sounds were unintelligible. Cathy struggled to hear clearly and to stop the faces receding, but in a way it was a relief to let them go. She felt herself move away from Judith. As if sensing her departure, Judith turned towards the door. Her eyes dilated, and Cathy knew what she must be seeing. 'It's only Matthew,' she tried to tell her, but Judith couldn't understand and for a second Cathy felt her uncomprehending fear and saw Matthew through Judith's bewildered eyes: a strange and ominous figure.

'Ssh. It's all right. Are you awake now?' Matthew was sitting up in bed, one hand on her stomach, as if she was a young child he was soothing. 'Are you awake?'

'Yes. I am now.'

'That was a tenacious dream you were having. You've been trying to come out of it for ages. What was it?'

Cathy looked away from him; his face was too real and complicated, she wasn't ready to look into it yet. She looked up at the ceiling instead.

'I was talking, having an argument,' she said slowly. 'Well, I wasn't, someone else was, but I was there.'

'What was it about?'

'Whether or not this person could leave the city.'

Matthew lay down beside her and trailed his hand across her ribs. 'Someone else? This person? What on earth are you talking about?'

'Judith,' Cathy said softly.

Matthew's hand stopped. 'What?'

'I was having another dream about Judith. Or it was having me, I don't know which.'

'You've had a second dream? Now? It really has got to you, hasn't it?'

'Actually, it was my third dream. I had the second last night.'

'You didn't say anything.'

Cathy reached for his hand and lifted it to her mouth. 'No. I've had other things on my mind.'

Matthew spread his fingers across her lips and stroked her mouth and her cheeks. 'God, Cat, you're all there's room for in my mind. Do you know what I dreamt just now? About us making love. I wasn't even sure where the real thing stopped and the dream began, I was so aware of having you here in my arms. Yet you've been skipping off to ancient Israel and frolicking about in legends.' His mock-protesting tone didn't quite work.

Cathy put her arms round his neck. He resisted her for a second, then rolled on top of her. His weight was comforting.

'But I was aware of you too,' she said. 'Very aware. That's the odd thing about these dreams, they seem in some way to be all to do with us.' She thought of Judith's mingled excitement and fear, of the longing she felt. 'You're there in the dreams, not so much as a person, but I feel you, all through them.'

'Do you? Really?' Matthew's face was patched with sun and shadow where light filtered through a gap in the curtain. He looked like a harlequin. white-dark and vulnerable.

'Yes, but I can't explain it.'

'I think I'm going to give up trying to explain things. If you try to find a reason for everything, and a justification, you make things vanish.' His hands tightened on her fractionally. Cathy's heart contracted with love and pity. Matthew might seem the strong, reckless one to other people – indeed, he had seemed so to her – but she was beginning to understand how vulnerable he was.

'I'm not going to vanish,' she said.

'You're not going to change your mind? Because if you want to walk away, you should do it now. After this, I won't make it easy for you.'

'I don't want to walk away.' Cathy began to tremble. She had spoken the words quietly and now, like an aftershock, their meaning spread through her. She felt as if her flesh were breaking up.

Matthew looked down at her steadily. His face had no colour at all. 'My Cat,' he said eventually, and kissed her mouth.

They got up and dressed at five o'clock. The village had

suddenly sprung to life and they walked through it, saying '*Buona sera*' to everyone they passed. They stopped for a drink at the bar in the marketplace. Standing at the counter, they swallowed glasses of sticky Martini, then as the warmth stole down into their stomachs they strolled across the bridge and walked along the straight road towards the viaduct.

As they walked, Cathy told Matthew about the dreams. Last night's dream was easy; it had been coherent at the time and lay intact in her memory. This afternoon's was harder to describe. Indeed, she could recall it only in fragments.

She knew what it was though: Judith putting her proposition to the elders, Judith trying to persuade those three authoritarian men, one of them her father-in-law, that she should be allowed to go into the enemy camp to sue for peace.

The atmosphere had been highly charged, pungent with emotion, and images had flashed at her: Judith walking with Endeyeh through a narrow street; a door opening to admit Judith alone; the three bearded faces of the elders. Cathy had known their names and who was who. The thin one was Ozias, the muscular man was Chabris, while the man with the sickly face was Eleazar. She had watched them with Judith's sharp eyes and shared her knowledge of their characters. Judith had been concentrating fiercely; there were so many expressions for her to read, so many objections for her to overcome. She had started to speak, the emotions in the room had intensified and become claustrophobic and the argument had spun away from her to the men and back again, a pattern of logic and learning and reason, outrunning Cathy's understanding but somehow forcing her to stay with it. And all the time she had been aware of the steady tension in Judith, a hope that was almost indistinguishable from fear urging her forward.

'What do you think it's all about?' Matthew asked when she'd finished.

Cathy looked at the viaduct whose tall arches seemed to shift as they walked towards it. 'I think it's a kind of mime. A message from my unconscious to help me get together with you at last.'

'You mean Judith is really you?'

'Oh, she isn't me!' Cathy paused and frowned, surprised by her own vehemence.

'Well, she must be a part of you,' said Matthew reasonably. 'You've dreamt her. She's a product of your unconscious, with a bit of help from the Bible and the Giuditta.'

'Yes, of course, but what I meant was she doesn't *feel* like me. I don't identify with her. She feels like a friend I'd forgotten about, someone who's been hiding away for ages and now she's suddenly emerged to say to me, "This is what you want. This is what you can do." And she's showing me through her own actions.'

'I see,' said Matthew. 'You mean, you and she are parallel. She's trying to get out of Bethulia and find Holofernes again, and at the same time you're trying to get free of your inhibitions and find me.'

Cathy laughed. 'Something like that.'

'I see,' said Matthew again. It took Cathy a second to realise that he wasn't laughing with her.

'What's the matter?' she asked.

He shrugged and gave a wry smile. 'You're still fighting me, aren't you, Cat? You've come here and we've made love but you're still not sure. For a moment there I thought you were doing this because you wanted to, not because your dreams said it was OK.'

Cathy blinked at him; he was serious.

'I am doing it because I want to. Matt, you said yourself that Judith is a part of me. These dreams are just my way of understanding myself.'

The words weren't quite convincing, but she didn't think the false note was strong enough for Matthew to have noticed. She hoped not, for along with it had come a sudden memory of the man who looked like Danilo, slipping away into the daybreak. She wrenched her mind away.

'This dream Judith is very real to you though, isn't she? Very persuasive. What if your next dream has her changing her mind and staying in Bethulia like a good little widow?'

Cathy put her arm through Matthew's. 'It won't,' she said calmly. 'She's gone too far to go back now; like me.'

The radiance had gone from the light by the time they reached Caprarola again. They were ravenous, so they called in at the bar for cakes, which was all the food the place had, and another couple of Martinis. They had long since stopped talking about Judith or the dreams. Cathy had resolutely led the conversation away and after a while the length of the walk and the curious hilly landscape had done the rest. It had taken them an hour and a half to reach the viaduct and the exercise had drained the tension from Matthew. He had kissed her under one of the impossibly high arches and apologised. Since then he had looked carefree and young again.

Cathy had not felt like this for years, not since that day when she was fourteen when she had looked into Matthew's face and realised for the first time that she loved him. Catching sight of their reflection in the espresso machine, Cathy felt that everyone who laid eyes on them must know. But of course there was no reason to hide it here. She leaned forward and kissed him briefly, publicly, as lovers do.

Half an hour later, still hungry, they climbed up to the village's one hostaria.

Six tables were set in a room which had a clean, deserted air. They ate alone, listening to the sound of television floating in from the kitchen. The food was delicious and so was the wine. The television noise gave them the privacy to talk. Not that they said anything of great account; it was intimate talk about their feelings, episodes from the past, incidents which had snagged the emotions of one or both of them and which they could finally discuss.

They left at what seemed a very late hour; when they reached the pensione they were amazed to discover it wasn't even ten o'clock. They opened their bedroom window and sat on the ledge for a while; it was a clear night and stars shone on the vegetable patch. Then they began touching one another, more gently this time. The darkness, and their tiredness, made it an oddly childlike experience, and their shared past seemed to hover at their shoulders. Cathy's desire felt pure and fierce, and every sensation was intense.

Later, they both slept long and peacefully. When they awoke, the room was full of sunlight and Cathy realised she hadn't dreamt.

'Nothing? Nothing at all?' Matthew smiled teasingly, and put out a hand to help her over the rocks. 'I think I'm a bit disappointed.'

'Are you?' She paused for a breather and watched him bask in the sun above her; then she scrambled up to join him. 'I'm not.'

'You didn't miss the excitement?'

'No.'

Matthew kissed her hand, then laughed. 'Your wedding ring seems to be back on my finger. What will the villagers think?'

'I don't care.'

'Good. Cathy, are you going to stay here with me?'

'Yes.'

'For how long? I might be here several months. Even all year.'

'I'll stay. I'll stay until it's time for us to leave. I can't think about time limits at the moment.'

Matthew nodded. At that moment, they weren't touching; they stood opposite each other, bathed in noonday sunlight. 'What will you do about Nick and the office?'

'I finished all my jobs before I came away. Nick can take over anything new that comes in; I don't think he'll mind. I don't think he'll be very surprised either.' Cathy recalled his expression at her parting words: *I'll be in touch if I'm going to stay longer*. She must already have known then, at some unconscious level, what she was going to do. So much for Judith as dream guide. 'And Howard's there now,' she added.

Matthew nodded. 'We'll move out of Pensione Flora,' he said. 'Start again somewhere else. Perhaps we could even get a little apartment. I get a good allowance for being out here and we can live cheaply enough, you won't have to earn any money. You can paint. It's time you got down to some real work again.'

'Cracking the whip already?'

'Always,' said Matthew happily, putting his arms round her. 'You know what I'm like, you'll get no peace with me.'

Cathy looked down at the village directly below them and

the river and road beyond. They were very high here, she could see over the far side of the valley to the tops of further hills. To the west, the viaduct spanned its dark crevasse. It was unfamiliar landscape, full of hidden dangers.

Matthew's body was taut against her and she could feel his heart beating against her back.

'Who needs peace?' she said.

Chapter Eight

Judith paced the little storeroom, watching Endeyeh. She had put the cruse of oil into the bag and taken it out again twice now. Once more, she pushed the stopper further into its neck and folded the cloth round it.

'Shall I do it?' Judith said impatiently.

'There's no need, I'm doing it, it's just difficult to make sure it won't spill. Oh God, listen to them. What are they doing?' Endeyeh's eyes darted up at Judith as the noise in the street rose and became a roar.

'They're waiting for us. And they'll be waiting another hour unless we finish in here soon.'

'I'm nearer finishing than you are. Once I've done this, there's only the bread for offerings. If you're going to start with ceremonial prayers, then you've got to finish dressing. You haven't even braided your hair.'

'I can't do it with these bracelets on. And if I take them off, it'll be impossible to get them on again because my flesh will swell.'

'Come here. Sit by the sack. You wrap the oil and I'll braid your hair.'

Endeyeh's hands grabbed at Judith's hair and began separating it into hanks. Judith slapped at her arms. 'You're hurting me!'

Endeyeh slapped back. 'Stop it. You arranged this, it was your idea. Now we've got to do it properly.'

'Oh, so you don't really want to go at all?' Judith's arm stung where Endeyeh's fingers had struck her, but she was principally aware of the shivering which had suddenly started and which she couldn't contain. 'What was it, then? You just said you wanted to go in order to impress me?'

'Of course I want to go. And I don't need to impress you. It's you who's frightened. I'm not.' But in Endeyeh's truculent voice was a distinct note of panic.

Judith laughed, heard the touch of hysteria, and stopped it by rubbing her mouth. She reached over her shoulder and fumbled for Endeyeh's hand. 'I'm not frightened.' She clutched the hand for a second, grinding her knuckles against her friend's. 'Listen to them outside. And what will it be like when we get down there?'

Endeyeh leaned against Judith's shoulders. 'I don't know. Dark, I expect.' She laughed unsteadily and her fingertips traced the groove that Judith's armlets were already cutting into her flesh. 'Your bracelets are much too tight. They'll be hurting by tonight.'

Tonight. They were both silent as they thought of where they would be. Outside the sound of the people swelled again. There was no going back now.

The streets were crammed. People jostled in every doorway and ran up and down the streets alongside Judith and Endeyeh. The roofs were covered with people too, they teetered on the very edges and clustered on the steps, shutting out the western light. Some cheered, some prayed; many were silent.

As they turned onto the street where Judith's parents lived, her mother came out. Her face was sunken, and she paused an arm's length away from Judith and gazed at her. For a long moment, Judith looked into her mother's eyes. All kinds of feelings, beyond words, travelled between them. As well as love and fear and grief, there was something reluctant in her mother's expression, something that recoiled from the sight her daughter was forcing on her.

Judith couldn't bear to see it. She stumbled forward and buried her head in her mother's neck, clinging to her. They stood that way for a long while – much too long for the crowd – but Judith couldn't let go. This might be the last time she ever touched her mother. She had thought of that before, when she was piecing the plan together, but it hadn't seemed real then. Her mother's arms were fierce round her, as they had been when she was a little girl. Other people separated them in the end, and ushered her mother along by her side.

Further down towards the gate, Endeyeh's family came to embrace her. Endeyeh's youngest sister wouldn't let her go and they had to walk on more slowly, with Jael clutching Endeyeh's skirt.

Then they were round the last corner and in the open space by the gates. It was packed with people. By the gates themselves stood the elders and, with them, Judith's father and little Reuben. Across the gap, Judith looked at them; her father's face was pale; Reuben looked bewildered and excited.

The matter was out of her hands now. Ozias began to speak.

'Citizens, we are in great danger. We have prayed and fasted for thirty-four days, and still the enemy is camped around us. The weak amongst us are dropping in the street from thirst and disease. No help has come from Jerusalem. As you know, we have only two days left from this evening before we must surrender. If no support comes from our brothers in Jerusalem, and God does not intervene to turn away the enemy, then we shall have to surrender for the safety of our women and our children, and to preserve as much of our temple and practices and godliness as we can. We are God's people, and we owe it to God to save ourselves for him.' Ozias raised his voice firmly, to quell any disagreement. But from somewhere to the left a man's voice broke through clearly.

'Raped and enslaved, we owe him that,'

'It has been a hard and bitter decision,' Ozias went on at once. 'Some citizens have argued against it. Among them was Merari, the father of Judith. He and his daughter have spoken and prayed together and he, in his loving wisdom as a father and she, in her devout obedience to him and to God, have offered our city the sacrifice of her safety.'

Judith gasped and stared at her father. He looked impassive but she could tell from the way Reuben flinched that his hand must have tightened on the boy's. She sought her father's eyes but had to wait several seconds before he looked at her. The doubt in his face was awful to see. *It's not true*, she said to him silently. *I'm not doing it because of you, he's lying.*

But Ozias was talking on, reminding Judith's neighbours of her long mourning, her knowledge of God's word as taught to her by her father and father-in-law; her humility and her obedience to civil and religious laws.

Humility and obedience, thought Judith; humiliation and suffering. She glanced at Chabris, standing silently next to Ozias. *I hate you*, she thought. *I hate you and now I am escaping you.* When she looked back at her father, he was watching her sadly. She exchanged a long look with him. He had never spoken to her of her marriage or her years in Chabris' care, and she had often wondered how much he allowed himself to understand.

Ozias had reached the high point of his address. He was a practised orator and he was carrying the crowd with him. Judith listened to his valediction numbly; it no longer seemed to be anything to do with her.

'Judith, daughter of Merari, will go with her servant into the enemy camp as a token of our faithfulness to God. She will observe dawn and evening prayers when she is there. She trusts in her heart that God will keep her safe and that her presence there will weaken the resolve of the enemy. We know that they have heard stories of other wars, when our God has protected us and led us to victory; we know that many of their troops are afraid to attack us for that very reason. Go, Judith, and demonstrate by your steadfastness that we are not afraid. God keep you and your servant safe.'

Then he turned to the stone altar, set up on its slab on the eastern side of the gate, and called for oil and bread. There was a scuffle just inside the crowd and Eleazar's son emerged, dragging one of the few remaining kids, its hooves tied together. There was to be a special sacrifice for Judith's safety.

The ceremony seemed to pass very quickly. Teams of men began opening the gates and Judith and Endeyeh turned to their families, stretching out their arms for one last embrace. Judith endured the touch of the elders with bowed head, clasped her father, pressed her hand to his face and kissed her brother. She was still looking for her mother when she found she was moving forward with Endeyeh at her side. They passed through the first set of gates with the crowd surging round them, then everyone fell back as the outer gates were heaved open just wide enough for them to pass through. There was no time to turn for a last look. Judith stepped through first, then Endeyeh, and they were out on the mountainside.

It was eerie. Little groups of men were scattered at intervals across the rocky slope. They stood back to back, every one of them alert, and they each held a spear or a sword or a sling in readiness. Each one had his head turned towards Judith and Endeyeh, but none moved.

There was much shouting further down the hill and a strange, dulled noise of footsteps and chanting seemed to be trying to escape from the walls behind them, but on this stony platform there was utter quiet.

'What's the matter?' Endeyeh said in a horrified voice.

Judith blinked across the rocks, unable to make any sense of it. Then a scraping noise came from far above them and she suddenly understood. 'The soldiers on the walls have drawn their weapons,' she said. 'And the Assyrians have drawn theirs in response. They won't come any nearer because then they'll be in range.'

'Oh yes. Of course. I see.'

'We'll have to go forward to them.'

'Yes.'

'We'll go very slowly. We'll stop when we're near enough to call to them.'

As they picked their way carefully, Judith held her head as high as she could. She tried to picture herself in the soldiers' eyes, an unexpected figure, exotic and proud. The light was gold and violet and her shadow moved before her, rippled by the rocks.

After ten paces, she could see faces under the soldiers' helmets. After fifteen, she could see that the rumours were true – they were a mixture of nationalities, some Moabite, some

Ammonite, two who did indeed look Judean. But more than half of them wore the short tunics and the copper necklaces of Assyria.

'Who are you?' The man who shouted was young, not much older than herself. He had straight hair which was flattened across his forehead by his helmet. 'Stop where you are. Why have you come out?'

They stopped, and Endeyeh lowered the bag to the ground.

'I am Judith, the daughter-in-law of Bethulia's third elder.' Judith's voice sounded very high in her own ears. 'I have come out with my maidservant on behalf of the people of Bethulia. I must go to General Holofernes, I have something to say to him.'

The soldier stared and gradually a smile crept over his face. 'I bet you do.'

The men on either side of him laughed, and somehow – Judith wasn't sure how because they were too far away to have heard him – the soldiers in the other groups also began to grin. Laughter and obscene gestures spread from one to the other.

'It's a trick,' a man shouted from one of the groups to the right. 'Keep your weapons ready.' The laughter lessened as the men tightened their grips on their arms and their eyes went from the women to the town ramparts.

'Yes, the walls,' someone else shouted. 'Watch the paths where they come round the side. They might be trying for an ambush.'

Judith saw heads snap left and right and didn't know whether to be heartened or afraid that the soldiers were so alert. It meant they still feared the people they were attacking – much, much more than they needed to. But what did that mean for her? She held the gaze of the man who had challenged her and who, after one swift glance around, was now looking closely at her again.

'It's no trick,' she said and succeeded in making her voice resonate as if she were confident. 'If you'll give us an escort, we'll come down to the camp now.'

'What's your business there?'

'I've told you, to see your general.'

The man narrowed his eyes. 'All right. Come forward.'

He stood still and watched while they came towards him, saying only 'Move aside' in a blank tone to the men who flanked him. 'Stop there,' he said quietly as they arrived within a few feet. He stepped sideways, walked past them, peered up at the ramparts for a long time. Then he came back and made a slow circle round them. 'Well, here you are. Out of range of your people now. And you want to see the general?'

'Yes.'

'All right then, I'll take you down. Who did you say you were again?'

'Judith. I'm the daughter-in-law of Chabris, the elder. I'm one of the town's most devout and well-respected women.'

'Sure you are. Well, come along, Judith. Let's get you down to the general. Don't worry, I'll take care of you. By the way, you're not in any hurry, are you?'

His arms went round her waist; he grabbed at her breasts and thrust a hand between her legs. Judith struggled and screamed, but it was an ineffectual noise and he laughed.

'Stay on guard!' he shouted at the soldiers who were beginning to break from their positions. 'Come on! Bring the other one!' he ordered his two immediate companions.

'Right, Captain,' yelled one. He seized Endeyeh and at once got an elbow in his mouth. He swore, grabbed her hair, and doubled his arm round her neck, this time successfully.

Judith was already being forced into a stumbling run down the hill. She could just see Endeyeh being half dragged, half lifted, her fingers clawing at her captor. Alongside them thundered the third soldier, whooping and carrying the sack and his friends' discarded weapons.

Over the captain's forearm which was levering her chin up, Judith could see other men coming up the hill. 'Look what we've got!' the captain yelled happily. 'They're sending their whores out to us now!'

'Just as I was getting bored of Agar and Bel-Malain!' shouted the soldier with the bag.

'Over here,' said the captain, suddenly slackening his pace. He stopped abruptly and clamped Judith against him, then turned her towards some thorn bushes. Her legs were tangled in his and she strained to get free. 'All-ll right,' he said in her ear. 'All right, stop those legs, you'll have plenty of reason to kick them around in the air in a minute or two. There's a good bitch, a nice little – what did you say you were? – well-respected widow.' He pushed her down onto her knees in front of the bushes.

Judith looked at her grazed hands holding her off the ground, and at the muscled legs straddling her. The captain had one hand on her shoulder, pressing her down. She saw the grain of his skin and the black hairs that curled across it, and wondered why she hadn't started fighting back earlier. Next to her Endeyeh was squirming and biting the second soldier. Following her lead, Judith twisted and dug her nails into the captain's calf. Immediately he kicked her and thumped her between the shoulder blades, and her head smacked down onto the ground, stunning her.

She tasted dirt and nausea and the cheek that was pressed to the ground stung agonisingly.

'Captain, look,' said one of the other soldiers, and the man above Judith laughed.

'Look at them come running for it! Hey! It's all right!' He was shouting, his voice painfully loud just above her head. She felt the weight of him on the small of her back and already his hands were tearing at her dress. 'There'll be lots for everyone, no need to— Oh shit.'

His voice had dropped again; then his hands lifted away from her and dust sprayed into her eyes as he stood up reluctantly. Had he hurt himself? She should run now, but her eyes were blinded and it was all she could do to get her nose clear of the ground and breathe.

'Better let her go,' she heard, and there was a scrabbling, followed by gentler hands on her. Endeyeh was kneeling next to her and trying to lift her head.

Judith pulled herself into a sitting position. She tried to see what was happening but her eyes were streaming as the sand in them stung.

'We should run,' she muttered to Endeyeh. 'Help me up, we must run back.'

'No, it's too late. Sssh. Judith, keep still. Someone important's coming. I think it's your general. You've got to convince him who we are.'

'What do you mean? We're from the city. He'll know that.'

'These men think we're prostitutes. You've got to show him we're not.'

Endeyeh's face loomed in front of Judith, much too close. Her mouth looked bruised. The urgency in her eyes made Judith panic.

'Where is he? I can't see!'

'Keep still. He mustn't see you yet. Now concentrate, Judith, we've only got a minute.' Endeyeh's hands plucked at Judith's hair and dabbed at her face, hurting it; they wiped her eyes and brushed the earth from her arms. Judith tried to think, but she felt sick and shocked, and somewhere behind those sensations, flowing in like a gritty river, was anger.

The voices and footsteps which had been sounding distantly for some time were much nearer now. Endeyeh glanced hastily over her shoulder and helped Judith to her feet. She bent down for the cloak which had been torn off, and for an instant Judith saw the captain going to meet the advancing crowd. A small knot of men led them, and one of those must be Holofernes. Then Endeyeh blocked her view again and with shaky hands fastened the cloak round her neck.

'Are you ready?' she whispered. 'Remember what you were like with the elders. In God's name, make him believe us.'

She moved aside. Judith looked at the four men – the captain and three newcomers – walking towards her. Why couldn't she recognise Holofernes? She had seen him from the city walls, at a much greater distance than this. But her eyes were filmed with dust and couldn't make sense of what she saw.

She turned shakily to the soldier still holding the sack and said loudly, 'Give my servant her bag. There are offerings to God in there. How dare you try and steal them!' The words gave her courage, even if her voice was not quite steady.

The soldier hesitated and looked at the men approaching. They were only a few yards away now. Judith's eyes skidded over them. Besides the captain there was a pale man wearing copper armlets, a handsome young man with rings on every finger, and a thickset one with tawny dark hair and a tightly curling beard. Which; which? She gazed at the handsome young man – a boy-man almost, with laughing eyes. If this was Holofernes, he had grown very tall.

'Offerings to God?' It was the tawny man who spoke. She turned quickly towards him: that voice plucked at her memory and he was staring at her curiously. He too was young, she realised, but weatherbeaten, making him appear older. His eyes didn't laugh but moved slowly over her face.

'I've come from the city with messages for the general,' Judith said. 'I've brought offerings to God so that I can make devotions while I'm in your camp.' Immediately, she regretted her tone. Instead of being dignified, she only sounded defiant.

The young man frowned in disbelief. 'You're coming to stay in our camp?'

'I am Judith, the widow of Manasses and daughter-in-law of Chabris the elder. I'm well respected in Bethulia. I'm sent to you as an envoy and as a hostage, to talk on behalf of our people with the general.'

There was a silence. Judith was looking straight into his eyes, trying to find a response. She thought something had moved in them at the mention of her name, but it could have been surprise, even amusement. Was she wrong after all?

'You want an audience with the general?'

'Yes.'

'Which general?'

She raised her head slightly. 'General Holofernes.'

'You're speaking to him.'

There was another pause. Judith had rehearsed this moment. She was going to sink down on her knees, her back straight. She would look at him with glowing eyes and then slowly, gracefully, reach out her arms and prostrate herself on the ground. Holofernes would watch her all the way down. Then he would step forward and help her up, and escort her personally to his tent.

But now she stayed upright. There was a question in Holofernes' eyes that put her on the alert.

'I bring you greetings from the Bethulian people, General Holofernes,' she said, falling back on the words the elders had given her. 'And I beg that you'll allow me a private audience.'

Bend, she told her knees; bend. And finally they began to obey her and she started to sink. But Holofernes wasn't waiting. He shrugged and turned away.

'All right. But lady, when you get back, tell your people that any messenger would have got safe conduct. They didn't need to send a woman.' He turned to the captain, who saluted. 'Bring them down. Treat them as official hostages. Don't harm them, don't touch them, don't insult them. Can you manage that?'

The captain flushed and nodded.

'Good.' Holofernes looked back at Judith and Endeyeh and gave an abrupt bow. 'You'll be safe now. Nicanor, please find them a tent,' he said to his handsome lieutenant. 'And a guard with some manners. I'll see them later.' He made a dismissive gesture with his arm and walked away.

Waking was peculiar, like swimming up through a waterfall into the warmth of day. Cathy opened her eyes and lay for a few seconds, getting her bearings. She felt wound up and full of energy. She swung her legs out of bed and stood up, feeling the prickle of blood as it ran into her muscles. She opened the shutters and light sprang into the room. She wrapped the lace curtain round herself and stood at the open window, breathing in the many scents of a Roman morning.

'She went!' she said aloud. 'She went and she found him.'

The next instant she wondered, rather sheepishly, why it should matter to her so much. It was, after all, only a dream, and dreams were unpredictable things, so it was foolish to have expectations of them. What if, last night, Judith had been stopped from going, or had changed her mind?

But she wasn't stopped, Cathy answered herself. She didn't change her mind. She got away and now she's in the camp, and Holofernes is going to give her an audience later. She looked up at the sky, the blue, Roman, European sky.

Matthew came in. His hair was damp from the shower and he was buttoning his shirt cuff.

'Hallo Cat, how are you?' He shut the door behind him and smiled at her. 'You look very happy, standing there,' he said softly.

'I am.' Cathy shook herself free of the curtain.

'Any special reason?'

'You.' Cathy went across and kissed him. The decision not to tell him was made in a split second. Why complicate the moment? Matthew *was* the reason for how she felt. Any significance the dream had was drawn from him and her feelings for him. 'What are we going to do today?'

Matthew held up his right hand so she could button his other cuff. 'I've got to go into the palazzo for a couple of hours.'

'But that's not until later, is it? We can have breakfast first.'

'No we can't, it's ten o'clock already. We've slept late.' Matthew laughed at her surprise. 'I looked in on you an hour ago but you were sleeping so nicely I didn't have the heart to disturb you. Look, I can't hang around. Why don't you have a shower and a leisurely breakfast and I'll meet you back here at twelve thirty. Enzo's already said I can have the afternoon free, so the rest of the day is all ours.'

Cathy looked up with a start as the clock struck twice for half past twelve. She'd been so preoccupied that she'd lost track of the time; she hoped she hadn't missed Matthew. She was at the cafe immediately below the Pensione Flora so she should see him coming. It was too lovely a day to wait in her room, and besides, she felt like having company.

Once the initial exhilaration had worn off, she'd felt an odd hangover from the dream. There had been some disturbing elements in it: the violence, and Holofernes himself. Had he recognised Judith? It bothered Cathy that she couldn't tell. Surely, as the creator of the dream, she should know, in her heart of hearts, what her protagonists were thinking. You always did, didn't you?

Now, as she drank her orange juice, she found herself once again trying to interpret the expression on his face. And once again she could recall it perfectly but she couldn't read it.

Perhaps she would tell Matthew about the dream after all – later in the day, when they were both relaxed. Here he was, dodging the group of students and heading for the corner.

'Matthew!' Cathy waved one of the newspapers she had bought for the accommodation columns. He stopped and his head turned sharply. He looked flushed, she noticed; he must have been hurrying.

'Cat. Good idea. I was looking up on the balcony for you.' He pulled a chair from a neighbouring table and sat down opposite her. 'What are all these?'

'Newspapers which advertise places to live. I thought I'd have a look through, see if there's anything suitable.'

'Ah. Yes.' He glanced at her. His eyes were bright, and Cathy felt a pang of disquiet.

'What do you mean "Ah. Yes"? Is something wrong?'

'Oh no.' Matthew began playing with a corner of *Il Giornale*. 'Nothing's wrong, quite the opposite.'

'Don't be maddening.'

'I only meant that we might not need to look for an apartment. You see, we've just been offered one.'

'Have we? Where?'

'In the palazzo.'

Something folded over swiftly in Cathy's chest. 'I don't understand what you mean,' she said.

'Enzo has come up with a proposition for us. It seems we're not the only people to have made some big decisions this weekend. Since Enzo showed us the Giuditta on Friday, he's been discussing with Danilo what they're going to do about it. As far as I can gather, they've had arguments about it for years – Enzo's suggested several times that they should get it cleaned up, but Danilo won't let anyone near it. He's very protective of his mother's reputation and he thinks the story of her destroying it would get out once they had someone working on it. But now you and I have seen it. And I have restoring skills. And the long and the short of it is, Cat, that Enzo has asked me if I'd restore the Giuditta for them.'

'My God.' Cathy stared at Matthew. He was trying to appear calm but his eyes were dark with excitement. She thought of him standing in front of the Giuditta, his hands skilfully lifting the disfiguring paint from her, and she felt a fierce stab of jealousy. 'My God.'

'It's incredible, isn't it? I'm going to work on it. Last week I thought I might never even see it and now I'm going to be restoring it.'

'Will you get it for the exhibition?' Cathy was aware as she asked that she wasn't sure what she wanted the answer to be.

'Perhaps, if the restoration works well enough.' Matthew didn't sound very bothered. It seemed that the exhibition was no longer the focus of his attention; the Giuditta had taken its place.

He shook himself. 'The thing is, Enzo suggested that I move into one of the apartments at the palazzo. There are several in the west wing – that's on the right-hand side as you walk into the courtyard. I think Danilo had rooms there before he moved out altogether. Anyway, as Enzo said, I might as well make use of them and it's more comfortable than a pensione. And when I told him that you were going to stay on and we were looking for a place together, he just said, "How splendid. You can have the first-floor apartment, it's the largest."'

'Matthew, we can't move into the palazzo.'

'Why not?'

Cathy gazed across the pile of newspapers at him. In her mind, the palazzo walls danced elegantly, seductively, the water in the fountains whispering to her. 'We're lovers,' she said, her voice low. 'Enzo knows us as stepbrother and sister. We'd have to pretend all the time.'

'No we wouldn't. We'd be as independent there as anywhere. The apartment's self-contained and the west wing has its own entrance which we'd use. Our windows aren't overlooked except by collection rooms, and at the back there's a little private garden.'

'You've seen the apartment?'

'Enzo showed it to me.'

'I don't know, Matt.' Emotions were conflicting inside Cathy and she was playing for time. 'There are so many things to think about. How does Danilo feel about all this?'

Matthew made a face. 'He seemed all right this morning; hardly enthusiastic but he was quite civil to me. He said that he had reservations still, but he felt that his father was probably right and it was time to get the painting restored. Though I did understand, didn't I, that it needed careful handling – you know what Danilo's like.' Matthew folded his arms on the table and looked at her. 'I'm sure he won't mind *you* moving in,' he said with a lilt to his voice that was both teasing and sharp. 'He sent you his regards.'

'Oh, that was nice.'

'Wasn't it just? Anyway, that's the proposition. I haven't said yes or no – oh, I have to the Giuditta work, of course, but not to the apartment. I said I'd talk to you about it. Enzo said if you'd like to have a look round before making up your mind, they'll be at the palazzo at five.'

Danilo heard them coming up the stairs, Enzo and Matthew talking, Cathy quiet except to say 'Oh, excuse me,' once. He waited until they were almost at the top before he walked out of the study onto the landing. He wasn't sure how well he could control his expression.

His father was leading the way. He looked relaxed – at least, he would seem so to Cathy and Matthew, but Danilo noticed that he'd shoved one hand into his cardigan pocket and was kneading the soft cashmere out of shape. Danilo had bought him that cardigan and Enzo was spoiling it, just as he was deliberately spoiling more precious things.

'Ah, here's Danilo,' he said.

Matthew had his hand out for the usual brief shake and Danilo met it. Then he had to force himself to turn to Cathy and kiss her cheeks. He would much rather not have touched her this evening. Embracing her in front of his father made him feel that he was giving something away.

She held herself stiffly but he could have sworn a tremor went through her as he brushed her skin with his mouth. He moved away quickly to look into her face. Her eyes were guarded.

His heart began to beat fast. Danilo never needed to fidget, but now he pushed the sleeves of his sweater up to cover his sudden surge of hope. Had she remembered something? She had been awake at dawn on Saturday; like him, she had been keeping a lonely vigil. Could it be that she was beginning to know him?

His father put a hand on Cathy's elbow and steered her past him, towards the study door.

'I thought we'd talk in here. After all,' he said briskly, 'strictly speaking this is a matter of business.'

Danilo sat at right angles to Enzo, his arms loosely folded on the desk edge in the attitude of one content to listen. His father was doing the talking for the moment, putting his proposal as succinctly as he had done to Matthew this afternoon. God, he was shrewd; Danilo could see that Cathy was reassured by this matter-of-fact approach.

Don't do it, he willed her. *Stay away. Resist him.*

Cathy glanced at him. Her eyes lingered on his face, no longer guarded but anxious; they seemed to be asking him a question. It was hell having to keep his expression bland. But his father was watching him, Danilo knew, and Matthew's gaze kept flickering over him, and the only way to play it was by refusing to give anything away.

He knew that Cathy was bound to come. Whatever intimations of the truth she was receiving, they wouldn't be strong enough to withstand persuasion from both Enzo and Matthew. Pain burrowed into Danilo as he saw the way Matthew was sitting so close to Cathy. Their shoulders were very nearly touching and there was a new possessiveness in the way Matthew looked at her.

It must have happened at the weekend. He'd seen it coming, but it didn't make the pain any less violent. Danilo's hand jerked involuntarily. Enzo looked at him and suddenly Danilo saw the anguish in the old man's eyes, like an echo of his own; then it was as if a veil fell over them. Steady, Danilo said to himself. Steady. You've waited so long, you've overcome so many obstacles. This is just another one and you can handle it.

But it was almost too much to bear. Now not only was Matthew being invited into their home and given access to the Giuditta, but Enzo was sanctioning his affair with Cathy. Enzo was furnishing them with a roof and a bed, and his unspoken blessing. His protection against Danilo.

Why was his father doing this to him?

'It's lovely,' Cathy said. They had walked the length of the apartment now and were standing once more in the airy sitting room. As Matthew had said, it was perfect for them. It had two bedrooms, a kitchen and a bathroom. The sitting room and the smaller bedroom looked into the courtyard; the other rooms overlooked a little walled garden which they could reach by a back staircase.

This wing felt quite different from Enzo's residential wing, and from the collection-dominated east wing through which they had walked on Friday. It was decorated with a touch of skittishness – walls in pale blues and yellows, with painted birds and cherubs and soft fruits appearing here and there round doors and stair panels. 'One of my nieces did it last year,' Enzo had said, laughing. 'She's taking a very expensive course in interior decorating, so we let her have her head.'

The sense of separateness was all the stronger because they had entered the wing through its outside entrance. In fact, Enzo had already handed the keys to Matthew who was swinging them silently in his hand. Cathy met his eyes and looked quickly away, feeling the blood creep into her cheeks. Immediately, she intercepted Danilo's gaze. He was standing quietly by the open window, one hand resting on the sill. She moved impulsively towards him.

'It's a lovely view,' she said.

'Yes. If you like citadels.' He spoke very softly. Standing beside him was like stepping into a force field; Cathy could feel his sadness, it seemed to draw her towards him. She had been feeling it ever since she saw him at the top of the stairs.

Their coming to live here and Matthew's commission on the Giuditta – these were things which hurt Danilo. And yet his pain wasn't oppressive, nor did it make her feel guilty. Instead, it was like a secret which he whispered under the surface of the conversation and which she alone could hear.

'Citadels.' She said it hesitantly; the word brought the exotic flavour of her dreams into the room. 'Aren't they places that keep you safe?'

'Or trapped.'

She looked at him; her mind felt suddenly still, as if a wind had dropped. 'Is that why you felt you had to move out?'

'No, not really.' He spoke very low again. 'There were other reasons for that. But the palazzo's a powerful place. And an intimate one, good for secrets. Cathy—'

'Danilo, what time was our meeting with the German bankers?' Enzo's voice cut in from across the room. Danilo straightened, still looking at Cathy.

'Six fifteen, Father.'

'That's a shame. I should have liked to show Cathy her studio.' Enzo smiled at Cathy's surprise. 'We are clearing out the studio for you to use. As soon as it's ready, I'll give you the keys and I hope you'll treat it as your own.'

'Alessandra's studio?' Cathy turned instinctively to Danilo. 'But I couldn't! I mean, it's very kind of you, but are you sure?'

'Quite sure,' said Enzo. 'Please don't refuse, Cathy. It would please me very much if you worked there.'

Cathy's throat was dry and she had to swallow. 'Thank you,' she said, forcing a smile at him. She glanced up at Danilo. He was watching her with something like compassion. He gave a tiny nod.

'We'd better go, Father,' he said. He leaned forward and pulled the window closed. For a second his body shielded Cathy from the others. 'Cathy, you know where I am if you need me.'

Chapter Nine

The window was open and on the warm air sounds of activity came drifting in from the courtyard – the snipping and scraping of tools as the gardener tended the plants, the buzz of a distant telephone, a murmur of voices from an open office window. Matthew wandered round the sitting room and savoured it. He loved the way the palazzo hummed with life during the daylight hours and then withdrew into quiet as evening came.

It had been three days now. In one sense the time had flashed by, full of activity, yet Matthew already felt he'd been here much longer. The apartment felt like home. Lying in bed with Cathy, watching the moonlight cast shadows of leaves on her skin, was surely something they had been doing for years. Yesterday he'd been crossing the courtyard when he'd seen Cathy come in through the archway, her arms full of fruit from the Campo dei Fiori market. His throat had clutched. She had looked so absorbed and natural, walking along in the morning sun.

Being close to Cat was like a drug. As much as he had of it, he wanted more. Matthew had thought that once they lived together, his longing for her would be fulfilled and he would attain an equilibrium with her. But that wasn't happening. In some odd way, he felt that she continued to elude him –

physically, this morning. He had come over here to grab a coffee and a talk, but she was still in the shower – he could hear the water in the bathroom. Damn. He could only spare another five minutes and he really wanted to see her before he went back to the lab.

It wasn't that he doubted her feelings for him. She was passionate in their love-making and affectionate when they were simply spending time together. And she was keen to involve him in the arrangements for her new studio. Yesterday afternoon, when Enzo had shown them into the now cleared-out, pristine room, she had immediately asked Matthew for his advice on what materials to buy. Today they'd planned to go to Trastevere together, to the art supplies shop. She had even talked about the work she intended to do first – abstracts, she had said firmly. The series she'd left unfinished in London hadn't worked, so she was going to try again, using more blues this time.

It was just that, behind all the activity and the confiding chatter, Cat sometimes seemed to be listening. As if there were sounds in the palazzo which only she could hear. He would catch her at it now and then: a stillness would come over her and different expressions would pass across her face – puzzlement, wariness, once he had seen pleasure. And despite his casual questions she never wanted to talk about it.

Matthew didn't press her. He suspected that the story surrounding the Giuditta and Alessandra's madness had upset Cathy more than she liked to admit. He could tell that she felt sorry for Danilo. It was slightly awkward, the two of them living here while Danilo stayed in his apartment three streets away.

At least Danilo was keeping his distance. They'd hardly

seen him since they moved in. Matthew would be glad if it stayed that way; the mutual antipathy between him and Enzo's son was becoming hard to disguise. These days, their presence in the same room made his skin prickle. He could point to nothing tangible by way of proof, but he had seen the way Danilo looked at him, and at Cat, and he knew the man was a threat.

He'd had the same instinct about Cat's Judith dreams. He didn't know where they'd come from or what they really signified, but he had understood at once what they meant to Cathy. Too much. The way she had talked about them in Caprarola, as if they were showing her the dictates of her heart and telling her what she could and couldn't do – it had made him feel horribly out of control.

She hadn't had any more of them since Caprarola, thank God. Nor had she done any more Judith drawings. Matthew felt less glad about that. He had liked them. They were unusual and had a curious directness. Whenever he looked at them, he felt excited. Perhaps it was just because he could see her with his own eyes, whereas Cathy's dreams were invisible to him. He thought of the way he held her in the night as she twisted restlessly in her sleep. He frowned.

In the bathroom the water finally stopped. Matthew put his head into the corridor and called, 'Cat, it's me. I've only got a few minutes.'

'Oh! Hold on.' There was a rattle as she pulled the towel off the loose rail. 'I didn't hear you come in.'

He went back into the sitting room. Two hours ago he'd left her wearing one of his old shirts, saying she was just about to get dressed. What had she been doing since then? Sketching? Her pad, he saw now, was lying face down in a corner of the sofa. He went over to it, hesitated, and turned it over.

There was no drawing on it but there were lines of writing. They were oddly arranged. He looked down at them, trying to understand.

Seeing Danilo in the dawn	
Judith girl in the window	Can't explain
My Judith drawings	
My Judith dreams	
My feelings for Danilo	Sexual obsession?
Matthew and the Giuditta	? coincidence?
Enzo inviting us	
Danilo's words on Monday	
The studio	

The last three lines had nothing written opposite them, but Cathy had been doodling on the far edge of the page. She had crossed out what she'd written but when he peered Matthew could see the letters looping faintly through the grid of ink: Ghosts Ghosts Ghosts.

Cathy came through the door and saw Matthew gazing at her sketchpad. He was white. Oh Christ, she was too late. What was she going to say? A headache, which had been hovering all morning, sharpened and began to throb at her temples.

But she felt relief, too. It had been difficult not confiding in him these last few days. Several times she'd tried to broach the subject but then lost her nerve. What could she say? 'Matthew, I'm frightened my dreams are taking me over'? 'Matthew, I'm afraid to draw Judith any more because she's getting too real'? Whichever way she framed it, it was going to sound hysterical. Matt would be bound to think it was all displaced anxiety about the two of them – if he didn't simply think she was mad.

She was using up so much energy not dreaming. She refused to dream until she could understand what was going on; this only meant that she went to sleep every night thinking doggedly of other things and then later, when the images began their seductive approach, she had to fight her way up to semi-wakefulness and cling there until exhaustion took her back down again.

This morning, as on every morning, she'd started out tired; even worse, her fingers had itched to draw. The urge seemed to grow stronger with each day and this time it was almost overwhelming. She had very nearly given in; she'd even sat down with her sketchpad and felt the sweetness stealing through her blood.

And then she'd become alarmed at that very sweetness. What was happening to her? Instead of drawing, she'd managed to focus her mind and, slowly, with the sensation of feeling her way into a mist, she had written down that list of impressions and incongruities – which Matthew was now staring at. Uneasily, she remembered writing Danilo's name, more than once.

Matthew looked at her. He didn't speak immediately, and when he did, his voice was uncertain. 'What's going on Cathy?'

She tucked her towel in to give herself time to think. She must lead the conversation away from Danilo – Matthew was jealous enough as it was. And yet she knew she needed Matthew's help.

'I don't know, Matt. That's what I've been asking myself. I

thought if I wrote it down, I might be able to work it out.'

'Work what out?'

Cathy sat down on the arm of the sofa. 'Listen. Don't you think there's something very odd about us being here?'

'With the Bonaventuras, you mean? I suppose it's unusual, yes.'

'It's more than unusual. Take the facts: for twenty-five years, the Bonaventuras have kept the Giuditta locked away in Alessandra's studio, too grief-stricken to be able to deal with it.' Then we come along. You find an old newspaper photo of it and fall in love with it. I see – or think I see – someone who's the image of the woman in the painting and start drawing her. I dream about her too. We show Enzo and Danilo the drawings and the next thing we know, we're living here, you're restoring the painting, I'm installed in Alessandra's old studio.'

'So? There's no mystery. We know Enzo had thought about getting the Guiditta restored before – it was Danilo who blocked it.' Matthew paused and Cathy's heart sank as she saw comprehension grow in his eyes. 'Danilo. As in your list.' He looked down. '"My feelings for Danilo,"' he read. '"Sexual obsession."' He was silent for a while. '"Seeing Danilo in the dawn,"' he said at last, painfully. It seemed ages before he finally looked up. '"Danilo's words on Monday." I'll ask you again, shall I Cat? What's going on?'

'Nothing like what you have in mind.' Cathy felt a surge of impatience, fuelled by guilt. 'You might not have noticed, but some pretty strange things have been happening to me recently. I'm seeing people who don't exist, drawing versions of a painting I've never seen, and having dreams out of some kind of alternative "Tales From The Bible".'

'I thought they'd stopped.'

'They have, but only because I'm not letting them happen. I can feel them there, trying to come through.'

'All right, but what's that got to do with Danilo?'

'The morning we left for Caprarola, I woke early and looked out of the window. There was a man sitting on the edge of the Spanish Steps: I thought it was Danilo but by the time I got my glasses he was gone. And,' Cathy pressed on, feeling that she was skating on perilous ice, that it was important not to falter, 'ever since we came back from Caprarola I've felt that he knows about us. I don't know why, but I feel as if he's watching us, me especially.'

Matthew smiled faintly. 'You think he's sexually obsessed with you?'

'No.' Cathy felt heat spread across her face. 'I think I might be sexually obsessed with you, and it's affecting my judgement.' She glanced at herself in the mirror above the fireplace. She wasn't flushed; in fact, she was rather pale, but she continued to feel uncomfortably hot. When she'd written 'sexual obsession' she had been thinking of herself and Matthew, but now, with a little shock, she recognised that she did indeed think Danilo wanted her; and what was more she desired him in return.

She lifted her wet hair away from her neck and began systematically to squeeze the moisture out. She had to keep her composure while Matthew was here; she couldn't start getting confused now. Once she had reassured Matthew and he'd gone, she would allow herself to think about the implications, and how she was going to deal with them.

Matthew watched her and thought that her face looked shadowed. A pain was coalescing inside him. He had been right to worry. Despite leaving London and throwing in her lot with him, Cat wasn't happy. *Sexual obsession.* Was that how she felt about their love for each other? That it was some kind of unwholesome fever that would pass? And what exactly was the nature of her sympathy for Danilo?

He wanted to take her face in his hands and kiss the tension away, but his instincts told him not to. Cathy needed space. He mustn't crowd her now; he must let her feel that she was free to be herself. She loved him, Matthew was sure of that. He had fought hard to bring her towards recognition of it and he was prepared to go on fighting, doing whatever he had to do, even if it meant more waiting and more denial.

But it was very difficult. His hands shook as he laid down the sketchpad and wandered over to the mantelpiece. He caught sight of himself in the mirror. God, he looked haunted. He smiled and exhaled, trying to force his shoulders down.

'I don't think there's much wrong with your judgement,' he said in a reasonable tone. 'I'm not sure about dawn vigils, but Danilo's an observer by nature and he feels possessive about the palazzo and the Giuditta, so yes, in general terms he probably is watching us. Besides Cat, a blind man could see he's attracted to you.' He grinned teasingly. 'You don't have to be so modest.'

Cathy looked at him warily, then colour stole into her face. 'Well, yes, it had struck me that he was quite attentive.'

'Exactly. Look, I'm sorry if I jumped down your throat about him just now. It's just that we don't get on very well and I feel in an awkward position here. You're right, everything has happened very fast. But honestly, Cat, I don't think there's anything to get worried about.'

'No, I suppose not.'

'But what?' said Matthew gently.

'It bothers me that Enzo's given me Alessandra's studio. Doesn't it seem peculiar to you, when he's had it shut up and untouched all these years?'

Matthew felt relieved. This, at least, had nothing to do with Danilo. Or with him, for that matter.

'No. I think Enzo's making a determined attempt not to be morbid. Doing a new broom thing with all his Alessandra memories.' He paused as something in her face struck him. 'Are you worried about having to work in there?'

Cathy rubbed her hair with a corner of the towel. 'A little bit.'

'Is that why you're being so particular about your paints suddenly? You're putting it off?

Cathy shrugged. 'I suppose so.'

'Oh hell, I don't know what to say. We can't really tell Enzo you want another room when he's been so kind to us.'

'No, of course not. I know that.' Cat towelled her hair hard, shook it away from her face and sat up. 'It's OK, Matt, I know I'm overreacting. This afternoon, when we've chosen some new materials, I'll take them into the studio and start making it my own. Giovanni told me that all the clearing out and cleaning should be finished by then and I'm sure that'll make a difference.'

'So am I. The only thing is, I can't come with you to Trastevere. That's what I came over to say. I'm taking delivery of the new chemicals this afternoon and I've got to be in the lab to check them – you know they sent over the wrong kind last time.'

'Oh. Never mind.'

'I'm really sorry. If I can get free, I'll come over to the studio when you're back.'

Cathy shook her damp head. 'It doesn't matter. Don't worry about it, I'll be fine. I'll probably enjoy myself.'

Matthew pushed himself away from the mantelpiece, wondering if he'd overdone the light touch. Cathy was looking rather puzzled. He walked towards her and bent down, meaning to kiss her, but then he had second thoughts. Would that seem importunate, intense even? He stopped halfway down and ruffled her hair instead. She stared up at him, and there was no doubting her puzzlement now. Oh shit, thought Matthew wretchedly, why was it that when you tried to be sensitive to someone, you started doing everything slightly wrong?

'I've got to go,' he apologised. 'I'm expecting Enzo in a few minutes. We're going to go over the painting again, to agree on my approach. I'll be starting the work tomorrow.'

'Great.' Cathy got up in a sudden energetic flurry. 'You must be really excited. Good luck.' She was standing very close. Matthew wondered if she was going to say something else, but instead she put her arms round him and held him tight. He clung to her for several long seconds before he pulled away.

It was mid-afternoon and Enzo had finally gone. On Matthew's workbench lay three sheets of paper covered with notes from their long session. He wouldn't be in any doubt about which way to proceed now. In fact, as Enzo had acknowledged apologetically, the instructions left nothing to chance. 'But you understand, Matthew, this is very important to me. Bear with me. And I'll try to bear with you when you depart from them.'

Next to the notes were a couple of plates, with the remains of the lunch Enzo had ordered from the kitchen. Antipasto and olive bread, Matthew noticed belatedly; at the time he'd barely tasted it.

He felt talked out. He switched off the electric panels overhead and at once the stark, eye-hurting brightness was gone and he became aware of the golden sunshine flooding in through the windows. Over by the store cupboard was the box of chemicals which had been delivered earlier. He had opened it and checked the contents: all present and correct this time.

He went over and transferred the containers onto the cupboard shelves. It took him quite a long time, not because he was weary but because he enjoyed the simple, repeated actions and had no wish to hurry.

When he'd locked the cupboard door, he looked at his watch. Nearly four o'clock. Cat would almost certainly be in her studio now. He could go and see her. Workmen had been busy this morning installing a new intercom for the courtyard entrance. If it worked, he would be able to buzz his way in from outside and climb up the corner staircase to see her, like a lover in an old tale.

Catherine, Catherine, let down your dark brown hair. Did she want him to climb up and reach her, though? Matthew felt miserably uncertain.

If he went to see her in her tower room, he would be gauging her reactions and wondering how to behave. The thought was painful. All sorts of thoughts were painful. He wasn't sure how far he believed her explanations of this morning. He could still see the list she'd made, short phrases in dark blue ink, seeming to mean far more than they divulged. And Danilo's name had been there in three places.

Cathy's sighting of Danilo in the dawn – was it accurate? Had he really been loitering outside the pensione like a tom cat? Or had she only imagined it? In which case, what did that say about her?

God, stop it. Stop thinking about it all. His mind suddenly felt like a marsh, choked with weeds and rotting vegetation.

No, he wouldn't consider it for a while. Instead he would look at the Giuditta again, now that he was alone. In the old days, when he had done quite a bit of restoring, he'd always spent time simply looking at a painting before he began; not analysing or planning, but simply being with it. So far, he hadn't had a chance of being alone with the Giuditta.

Matthew walked deliberately round the end of the workbench and stood in front of the draped easel. They had covered the Giuditta before Enzo left. Now Matthew breathed out several times, allowing his mind to clear. As the troubling thoughts seeped away, he felt anticipation rise in him. The Giuditta. It was under here, waiting for him.

Carefully, he lifted the cover and hooked it over the top corners of the canvas; then he stood before it for several minutes, quite still. The afternoon seemed to stretch out and recede from him. Earlier, with Enzo, he had been looking at the painting as a scientific problem. Now it hung in front of him as a mystery. There she was, the woman, visible in glimpses, beautiful, challenging, but shadowed and obscured, trapped behind the dark screen.

She seemed to call to him, asking him to release her.

This was something to which he could and would commit himself. While he stayed his hand with Cathy, and kept a close, discreet watch on Danilo, he would draw comfort from this, his work. Freeing the Giuditta would be his own personal quest.

Chapter Ten

It was like a great city. The tents were goatskin and well-constructed, they stood close together, rising up above Judith and Endeyeh's heads. Behind the tents were more tents, and behind those, more. Fires burned on the clear ground between, and pots stood over them. Everywhere people were coming and going.

Few of the men down here looked like professional soldiers. There were men in shepherd's clothes and in field workers' tunics; some wore the aprons of various town trades. Hardly any of them carried weapons; instead they were doing business or standing in groups, talking. Young boys slipped through the groups with an air of being in on important events. Around the fires and milling through the tents were women.

Judith looked with special interest at the women. There were far more than she'd expected and it was clear that some of them were prostitutes. It wasn't so much their clothes or appearance, more the way they were talking to the men. Yet just as many of the women seemed respectable and were busy with the sort of tasks Bethulia's women would now be doing: cooking and seeing to children. They were talking to each other like family as well.

The noise was fierce. At first it made no sense to Judith and she thought everyone must be speaking in strange languages. But then voices nearby detached themselves from the cacophony and became intelligible. She heard the accent of the sea coast, and that of northern Samaria, then several more which she didn't recognise. The words seemed distorted and were spoken in odd rhythms, but if she concentrated she could understand.

'Tomorrow, first thing, before first light – '

'No, the cask is ours, we want it back now. I know you, if you pack it with your tent we'll never – '

'Basot's men lead, then the Cretan century. We're to follow.'

'Hello mate, what are you doing with this one? Very pretty. Your sister, is she?'

The question cut through the noise and instinctively Judith looked round. The man was squatting just a few feet away, sharpening a long blade on a whetstone. He grinned up at one of the escorting soldiers and then winked at Judith. He waved his blade; the flesh of his arms bulged between thick leather thongs.

'I asked,' he shouted more loudly, and then stopped as he saw the good-looking lieutenant at the head of the escort. 'Ah, hmmmph, I see. Oh well, we can always hope, can't we?' He winked at the soldier this time, and went back to his sharpening.

The young lieutenant turned. Judith thought of Holofernes' instruction to treat her as an envoy, and waited for him to slap the man down. But he only gave her a scornful look. 'Please walk faster,' he said shortly. 'The sooner we get you to your tent, the better.'

Judith's face burned. She didn't dare look at Endeyeh. Holofernes had made no sign of recognition and now this Nicanor with the rings and the commanding face was making it clear that he held her in contempt. He turned away and strode on, increasing his pace as if he wanted to be sure of keeping a distance between them. Judith quickened in order to keep up with him.

Her heart quickened too. She had just understood the meaning of the activity all around her: they were preparing to attack Bethulia. She had hardly any time left.

At last they reached their tent.

It was a soldiers' tent, but comfortable. The weapons and armour had been moved out, and the old blankets removed. Several sacks of provisions and two casks lined one side of it and soon more comforts arrived. A voice outside announced itself as belonging to Bagoas, Holofernes' servant, and a slender man with hair oiled flat to his head came in, carrying a mound of sheepskins.

'General Holofernes wants you to be comfortable,' he said, with a faint air of amusement. 'I'm to bring you anything you want. What do you want?'

Judith asked for fresh water and drinking cups, and a basin for washing. Bagoas bowed and disappeared. Judith and Endeyeh had just begun to whisper nervously to each other when his voice called out again and he brought in a small stool on which he set a bowl of water and a pitcher, and two beautifully made copper cups, decorated with animal figures.

'Thank you,' said Judith. She wasn't sure whether to admire the cups; they were finer than anything she was used to in Bethulia, but would commenting on them show her up as unsophisticated? Bagoas seemed to be waiting for her to say something, but before she could speak he bowed and withdrew, then came back in at once with two squares of linen and a polished copper reflecting plate.

'I thought you'd like to look your best,' he said. 'For your audience with the general.' And then he was gone again.

'Come on,' said Endeyeh, picking up one of the linen squares and wetting it. She thrust it out towards Judith. 'We'd better hurry.'

It was difficult to prepare for the interview in the gloom, with the candles casting an inadequate light and the noise of their neighbours so loud that they kept expecting them to burst in through the tent walls. There were flaws in the copper plate which distorted Judith's reflection, and when she turned the plate round, her features kept looking and retreating. She had to keep checking to make sure the smudges on her skin were shadows and not bruises. Her eyes looked frightened. Beside her, Endeyeh was seeing to her own face, colouring her eyelids and fastening Rechab's gemstones into her hair.

'Madam. Are you ready for me to come in?' It was Bagoas's voice. No, Judith was not ready; not nearly. But Endeyeh hurried to the flap, only pausing at the last instant to turn and direct a hunted look at her.

'Yes, we're ready. Are you alone?'

'I am. I've come to take you to the general.'

The outer canopy of Holofernes' tent was crammed with people. They sat on the ground in groups, drinking and talking raucously. There was an air of feasting about them, though the only food seemed to be figs and nuts. Their mouths were stained with wine. Most were men, and the women who were present were not the matronly types Judith had noticed in the wider camp.

'Move aside, move aside for our visitors,' Bagoas called out in a sing-song voice, but Judith had to step over people's legs to reach the tent flap, and her cloak kept catching and threatening to overbalance her.

Bagoas preceded her through the flap, said something which she couldn't hear above the hubbub, and then held the curtain aside for her. She walked in, Endeyeh close behind her. A long table ran down the right-hand side of the tent, loaded with the remains of food. There was half-eaten meats, bread loaves, fruit, nuts, bowls of honey, large cruses of oil. On the left-hand side, cushions and sheepskins showed where the crowd had been sitting, and a servant was squatting down, sweeping the floor clear. Holofernes was alone. He stood in the middle of the tent, no longer wearing his breastplate, and Judith could see that he had a thick band of scar tissue on his left shoulder. It showed white against his dark skin and no hairs grew on it. The sight of it shocked her.

He was standing in the same aggressive way that had struck her in Jerusalem, years ago, but now it seemed less comical. In the last weeks Judith had thought often about violence and death, and about the Syrian boy's rise to generalship; now the two were brought together in front of her, in this damaged flesh.

She looked into his face, feeling confused. This was very much a man standing before her; there was a brutality in the muscle and weight he had put on. But she still saw the boy. The general stared, but gave no sign of recognition. Judith sank carefully onto her knees.

'My lord, Holofernes. Thank you for receiving me.'

'I didn't expect a woman,' Holofernes said abruptly. 'Why did they send you? Are your men afraid to come themselves?'

'You said you'd kill any man who came here from Bethulia.' Judith went on looking at the ground. 'The men were willing to come, but the women stopped them. We decided one of us should come instead.'

'Here, madam, take my hand.' Holofernes strode over to her and helped her up. Feeling him so close to her and smelling the oil on his hair, the sweat and eucalyptus on his skin, Judith was suddenly embarrassed. As she rose nearly level with him she met his eyes. They were bright and intrusive. She ducked her head quickly in a pretence of losing her balance and didn't look at him again until she was steady on her feet and he was already turning away.

He went to the table and picked up a knife. 'Are you hungry?'

Judith hesitated. She was so hungry that saliva pooled in her mouth at the sight of the meat and the bread.

'Yes, I am hungry, my lord,' she said, trying to keep the eagerness out of her voice.

He nodded and started rifling through the provisions. 'You must be. You look ill. The city's beginning to starve now, isn't it, as well as go thirsty.'

'Oh, we're not starving. We've got food and drink to last us quite a while.' It sounded unconvincing, even to her own ears. 'But I fasted and prayed to God all day before I came down here.'

'Did you? Well, that might be good religion but it's bad tactics. Take a tip from a hardened soldier. You should build yourself up before you go into enemy territory.' Holofernes pulled a half-carved lamb's head towards him, cut a thick slice from the cheek and handed it to her. Then he dipped a cup into the wine cask and gave that to her as well, wiping it first on his girdle.

Judith stared at the food. She felt that it would be demeaning to eat it at once and tried to resist, but her appetite took over. She took a small bite, then another, and as Holofernes turned back to the table, she pushed the whole slice into her mouth and chewed fast. She was still chewing when Holofernes finished cutting the second slice and walked calmly past her to where Endeyeh stood, just inside the curtain. Endeyeh bent over his hand as she took the meat.

'Bethulia *is* starving,' Holofernes said, going back to the table. From among the dishes he picked up a heavy silver cup and dipped it into the cask. 'But thirst is the real problem.' He drank deeply, watching her. 'You'll be out of wine by now. What are you using? Melon pulp? Cistern water?'

Judith swallowed the meat with difficulty. The action brought tears to her eyes, and she blinked them down angrily. He had asked the question curiously, as if the fact that there were people dying of sickness and fever behind the city walls meant nothing. The wine shimmered in her cup, inviting her to drink it, but suddenly it seemed like an act of betrayal.

Holofernes was facing her again. He shrugged. 'Drink,' he said quite gently. 'It won't help your people if you pass out.'

Judith drank.

When she had finished, Holofernes took her cup and dipped it in the cask again. He gestured to the cushions. 'Sit, madam,' he said. 'I'll bring you food. Drink and eat first, then we can talk about your town.' He returned to the table and began sorting food onto a platter. 'Here, Bagoas,' he shouted, and Bagoas reappeared swiftly through the curtain. 'See to the servant woman.'

While Judith leaned back on the cushions and ate and Endeyeh had her own meal at the far end of the tent, Holofernes stood by a tall chest and looked at scrolls.

Had he recognised her? If so, he hadn't betrayed it by a flicker of a muscle. Yet she had told him her name and her connection with the elders; surely memory must be stirring. There had been something in his eyes when he asked about Bethulia. Was this how he would behave with an unknown woman who came as official envoy? There was none of the stateliness Judith had expected, just a rough dignity – the same as that shown by the sunburnt boy in Jerusalem, years before, when he had offered the lost girl his drinking flask.

Holofernes moved round the chest, opening a side door and pulling out more scrolls. He walked with his legs splayed outwards, and Judith was reminded of something else she had forgotten: the boy's curved back. It had grown more pronounced with manhood.

He was not handsome; he was not even conventionally attractive, but his physical presence was very strong. Judith found it hard to keep her eyes away from him.

Eventually, he put the scrolls away and turned to her. 'Have you eaten all you want?'

'Yes, my lord general. Thank you.'

'Well then, you'd better deliver your message from Bethulia, from these elders who don't dare risk their own lives but send you instead.'

'They didn't send me, I asked to come. I thought you might remember me, General Holofernes.'

'I remember you all right.'

Judith watched him, waiting, until her eyes stung, but he said nothing more. He was waiting for her to speak. She had already decided that a supplicating tone would be no good; besides, she didn't want to speak to him like that. She chose her words with care, clearly, steadfastly, allowing her intellect to lead her.

'General, we don't want war. We don't challenge the Syrian

borders. Your king Demetrius exempted us from paying taxes to him three years ago. Why has he sent you to attack us?'

If Holofernes was impressed, he didn't show it. He rounded on her at once. 'Rulers with armies attack places. Didn't you know that? Don't the elders teach that? No, I suppose not. It doesn't slip down easily with the books of law and ancestry, does it? Too much like the real world.' Holofernes' voice was scornful; he shook his head, as if he were shaking off tiresome insects.

'You're attacking us just because you have the men to do it? Even though the Syrian king has all but recognised us as independent?'

'All but. You said it.'

'But why? Why should he want Jerusalem now?'

Holofernes sat with his elbows on his knees, looking at her sombrely. He seemed to be calculating whether or not to answer her. Then to Judith's astonishment he smiled. It was an unwilling smile and a weary one, but it spread irrepressibly across his face. The boy on the dusty road was instantly back before Judith's eyes, and the effect was, oddly enough, to make her feel in greater danger.

'Jerusalem, Jerusalem. I agree, why would anyone want Jerusalem? Look, madam.' He appeared to have taken a decision. He stood up and paced a circle. 'Can I explain a few facts? The truth is, people send their armies out for many reasons. Some are political, some are financial, most are both. Do you think we want to occupy or destroy every place we go to? No, hardly ever. But we might go out as enforcement for a pact that might be dishonoured, or as a warning to a vassal state that's getting restless. Or we go to an area that has strategic interest, as an invitation to another interested party to open negotiations. That's how things work.'

Judith watched his scar flash silver as he strode up and down, one hand curled over the shaft of his knife, and wondered how many people he had killed on his expeditions. She pulled her mind away from the idea; he was waiting for her to speak again. She thought quickly, trying to apply what he had said to this situation, now.

'Judea's made no pact with you, and we already have our independence. Who else is interested in us, besides Demetrius?'

Holofernes smiled. 'You're very sharp, Judith. I told you once, didn't I, you'd be wasted in Bethulia.'

'Is it Phoenoecia?'

'Who?'

'Parthia?'

Holofernes made a derisive face. The local threats that seemed so frightening to her were laughable to him.

'Not a neighbour then. A power. There are only two of those: Macedonia and Rome.'

Holofernes folded his arms.

'Which is it?'

'Go on, you're doing well. Work it out.'

'We have an alliance with Rome. Simon Hasmon signed it the year after I was born, and we've had no trouble with them since. It must be Macedonia.' Judith faltered, and Holofernes shook his head.

'No, no. You're looking at it the wrong way. If Macedonia was planning to attack Judea, Syria would probably send forces to defend it. Make common cause, get tributes and taxes from Judea in return. Besides, Macedonia's finished. Rome's the only power now.' He stopped and looked at Judith for a long while. She found that she could hardly breathe. Her head was crowded with impressions, like scenes glimpsed through a lattice, scenes of armies, and men in council, chests piled with money, messengers passing in palace corridors, rooms and shady rooftops where brilliant men and knowing women dealt in events like these.

Holofernes got up and it was as if the images swirled round him like a cloak. He began to walk up and down, talking fast.

'Syria has to treat with Rome, and Syria needs to keep Rome's respect or else it gets the worst of every exchange. So when Demetrius wants something from the Romans, he starts off by showing them that he means business. What he wants from the Romans now is help in fighting off the Parthians, so he has to make it look worth Rome's while to give him that help. That's the thinking behind this manoeuvre – show Rome that as long as Syria's threatened from Parthia in the east, it'll be tempted to consolidate on its western edge. Then Rome will ask, what the hell's going on? And Demetrius will say, help me pin back the Parthians and I'll leave Judea and the rest alone.

'That's why we're here. But we're not going to be here much longer. There's a Roman general, Lucius Tullius Bestia, who's been on an expedition to Galatia. He's on his way home with his troops, and I've had my orders to strike camp and march with five hundred men to meet him. The rest of the forces here will go to the north-east, just in case the Parthians decide to make another move. You'll be rid of us tomorrow. No hard feelings, I hope?'

Judith could only stare. She felt as if she had been sitting in the open mouth of a lion, and now the beast had plucked her out with a velvet paw and set her down on the ground. And was now laughing at her.

'You're leaving? Abandoning the siege?'

'That's it. Didn't you notice people packing up as you came through the camp?'

'Yes, but I thought it was preparations to attack.' Her voice was very weak.

'No, preparations for withdrawal. We're moving on. This time tomorrow we'll be gone and Bethulia can get back to its normal business. Sorry we spoilt your vine harvest.' Holofernes put his head back and exhaled.

Judith watched the sinews tighten in his neck and then loosen as he let his shoulders relax. She should have felt exultant, but she did not.

'You don't look very convinced, madam,' he said. 'This is no trick, I'm telling you the truth.'

'I believe you. I – I thank you.'

'Don't thank me, I'm only following orders.' Holofernes stretched and sighed, as if he'd been tied up for hours. Then he lowered his arms and looked at her and suddenly the look was one of simple interest. 'Look, madam – Judith. We were friends when we met last time. Will you stay with me for a while, before you go back to your tent? You can't leave before tomorrow anyway; then I'll get an escort to take you back at first light. In the meantime, will you stay and drink to the success of my mission?'

Judith hung onto his gaze. Her body suddenly felt very alive against the soft cushions.

'I will. Happily.'

'Your servant.' Holofernes looked at Endeyeh, standing at the far end of the tent. 'Will she be staying too or shall I send for someone to take her back to your tent?'

Judith looked through the shifting light and saw Endeyeh

gazing urgently at her. She turned back to Holofernes. 'Endeyeh has been married two years; she thinks her husband might be in your camp. He's a trader, Rechab. Do you know if he's here?'

'He might be, we've got some Judeans.' Holofernes walked towards Endeyeh. 'I don't know of any Rechab, but then he might be going under a different name now. Names change where armies march.' He stopped in front of her and smiled, not unsympathetically. 'And then of course some people come into service as hostages, or are sold in by their creditors. The man in charge of the Judeans is Jonathan of Beth-horon. Talk to him about it. Bagoas!' He moved rapidly to the tent flap and began giving Bagoas instructions.

Judith walked over to Endeyeh in silence. She had felt oddly excluded from that last exchange. Was it because Holofernes had turned his back on her? No, there was more to it than that. There had been a straightforwardness in the way he spoke to Endeyeh which she would have liked for herself.

She took Endeyeh's hands and looked into her face. 'Will you be all right with Bagoas and this Jonathan?' she asked.

Endeyeh nodded. 'There'll be a woman to escort me too,' she muttered. 'I've just heard the general order it. I'll be all right – as long as I find Rechab.' Endeyeh's face was alight; she looked almost demonised. Judith felt a little tap of fear. Endeyeh was about to go off into this foreign, unholy camp, seeking her husband. And she herself would be left here with the Syrian.

'Remember,' Judith said, reluctant to let Endeyeh go, 'even if he's not here, they might be able to give you news of him.'

'He's here, I'm sure of it. I feel it in my insides.'

They embraced; then with a bow to Holofernes and a

murmured 'Thank you, General', Endeyeh followed Bagoas out of the tent, and Judith and Holofernes were alone.

There was less than an arm's length between them; had he wanted to, he could have reached out and touched her. But Holofernes only said, 'A lot's happened to you, hasn't it?'

'Not as much as has happened to you, General.'

'Oh, nothing has happened *to* me, I've worked for it all.' He tapped his chest. Judith was aware of his strong body, with the curved back and the damaged tissue. She could smell eucalyptus again.

'I work too,' she said sharply. 'I run a house and some land, I study the Pentateuch. I help teach my brother and some of the younger children of my neighbours.'

'So I've heard,' said Holofernes. He hunched his shoulders and gave her a quick sideways look. 'Surprised? I told you we had Judeans in the camp. There are one or two who've been through Bethulia in the last four years. They've kept us informed.'

There was something in the way Holofernes said it, a husky note of sympathy, that brought the blood into Judith's face. So he had heard the gossip. All of it or only some? She couldn't bring herself to look at him.

'You've been very brave, coming into the enemy camp like this. Stupid but very brave. I salute you.' He had moved away from her; he padded over to the cask of wine. He seemed much lighter on his feet now. He scooped up their cups, dipped them into the wine and held them up with a stealthy grace. It was as if he had taken off some invisible armour and could now move freely. 'Judith.' She looked up from the shadows clustering round the wine cask and into his face. It was clear of all mockery. 'I drink to you.'

* * *

Hours had passed, Judith didn't know how many, but the noise from the outer canopy had quietened to a murmuring and the lights had burnt low. Only two wicks were left now, one on the table and the other on the ground by the chest. Some time ago Holofernes had wrapped a fur round her shoulders and she sat warm inside it. Holofernes sat next to her. She watched his hands as they rested on his knees, and his face as he talked – about Rome. He talked brilliantly, compulsively about Rome.

'It's an incredible place. As long as you've got some property or, if you're a foreigner, a position, then you can make something of yourself. God help you if you're a foreigner and poor, but then that's the same anywhere. Don't I know it. The first time I went, when I was enlisting for Macedonia, I couldn't work out what I was seeing. I kept trying to trace the family lines and entitlements. They have them of course, but they're not written into law. Just because your brother and father and grandfather have all held office, it doesn't give you a right to it. Any freeman with the minimum property can come and challenge you and if the citizens prefer him, he'll get it. Do you know, they've got a first generation smallholder as one of their consuls now. His father was a bondsman. It's like your servant Endeyeh's son getting to be one of the temple priests in Jerusalem.'

Judith strained her tired eyes. They had been wide open for so long in the dim light, watching Holofernes. She had been concentrating on him hard, to block out her thoughts.

'But surely they don't let foreigners like you become – what are they? Consuls?'

'Well, no, that's true. But you can be adopted by a consul and that means you can rise to a high rank in their army. I met a

Greek Samarian there last year. He'd been alongside Scipio Marcellus on their Pydna campaign and he'd made a fortune. He had a villa on the Palatine Hill and he went to the Forum every day. He was Marcellus's right-hand man and military adviser.'

Holofernes touched his cup to hers.

'The women have a better time of it too,' he said slyly. 'They have their married matrons who keep house, then they have women who are . . . companions and hostesses to the public men. And they're educated, these women. Clever. They eat with the men and discuss with them; they know who's coming up and who's on the way out and what's happening among the chief citizens. They entertain artists and the great teachers as well. They're respected. So now some of the matrons are doing that too. One of them, Cornelia Gracchus, is a consul's wife. She's got ambitious sons and she's started inviting the powerful men to her villa. And someone was telling me the other day that the men are keen to be in with her now, because if you go to her house, you meet the people who matter.'

Judith put her cup down. It was empty. She had been listening for a long time and drinking while she listened. She had lost count of the number of times Holofernes had filled her cup from the pitcher; now he did it again. She picked it up at once. The act of drinking helped the direction of her thoughts.

'If Rome is so marvellous, why did you leave?'

'It wasn't the right time to stay. I had to bring back a deal for Demetrius. I wouldn't have done myself any good by walking out on his commission. You must know, Judith, that there are times when you have to wait and other times when you must act.'

Holofernes' face was glowing with a subtle light. Judith knew what he was doing. All along he had been teasing her, tempting her with stories of his adventures and his chances. He hadn't tried to hide the dangers from her and much of what he'd told her about his life was sordid. He had lied, often, and cheated. He changed allegiance as it suited him. He took squalor and violence in his stride. But he lived.

And she was trapped. He understood enough about her to see that, Judith was sure. She had tried to act and she had failed. There was to be no triumph for her to claim as her own, no passage to Jerusalem. All her hopes had been centred on Bethulia being in her debt, but now she would be at best the bearer of good news. She would be welcomed for it and expected to resume her old life just as before. If anything, Chabris would watch her more closely; she knew that she had aroused his suspicions. She could not go back to that.

'So you are thinking of going back to Rome?' she asked cautiously.

'Yes.' Holofernes filled his own cup and looked at her. 'Soon.'

'Once you've finished this commission.'

'No, before that.' He narrowed his eyes. 'I didn't tell you the truth earlier. I will be striking camp tomorrow and going back to Syria. But I won't be carrying out Demetrius's orders. Nor will Nicanor. He's the leader of the Achaeans, who are – or have been – Syria's allies. When we get to Apamea, Nicanor and I are going to close an alliance with Lucius Tullius and sail with his ships for Rome.'

'Why?'

'Because the time is right. Demetrius is finished. It's only a matter of time before the Parthians take over in Syria, and I'm not waiting around to be an exile in my own country again. I met Lucius in Rome last year. He's young and ambitious and brilliant, but he's not a military man. Not by instinct. He could do with partners like me and Nicanor.'

Once again, exotic scenes passed before Judith's eyes, brightening the quiet tent, but this time she could see herself in them. There she was, in a courtyard where trees grew; and there again on a wide pavement, while Holofernes walked shoulder to shoulder with another man. And in the middle of an alien crowd she recognised herself, wearing robes draped diagonally from shoulder to sandal, and with bronze clasps keeping up her hair. The visions called to her with a wild, low allure. Yet to follow them would surely lead her into danger. Once out there, she would be beyond the reach of her family and her people, beyond the protection of God.

'Judith.' Holofernes' voice was curious. 'What will happen to you when you go back to Bethulia?'

She looked into his face. He was sitting very close to her, one knee folded up under him and the other leg stretched out. What would it be like to touch that sunburned flesh?

'I don't know. Nothing. It will all go on just the same.'

'Come with me.'

She pulled her hands out from under the fur and rubbed her eyes. They ached from the candlelight, but more than that she needed the moment of oblivion the darkness brought. Her fears and desires rioted inside her; she had no idea what she was going to do.

The next moment she reached out and grasped Holofernes' hands.

He sat still for a several seconds then, deliberately, he

uncurled her fingers and slid his hands up her arms and over her elbows.

'Does this mean you'll come?'

Judith was trembling. His hands were strong and pulsing with life. She could feel the sinews and the warmth of his blood under the skin; it shocked her and spread a strange heat. It made her want to burst into tears.

'Come where?'

'To Rome.'

'And what would I be? One of these companion women?'

'If you like. Or you could be my wife.'

Judith looked into his shining eyes; they were asking something of her and offering something in exchange. She could not begin to understand it.

'Yes, I'll come.'

'Companion or wife?' He was laughing softly.

'Wife.'

For another long instant, Holofernes remained still. Then his grip loosened and, very gently, he began stroking the soft skin inside her arms. Judith felt each touch as a tiny sting; she arched her back and the sensation intensified. Then Holofernes was on his knees before her; he took her face in his hands.

CHAPTER ELEVEN

A bell was ringing in the main courtyard. All the bells in the palazzo had a low, buzzing tone which was surprisingly penetrating. The sound travelled round the little garden, thrumming in the bushes and the clambering vines. Cathy focused in the greenness that surrounded her and allowed it to swallow up the other vision.

She had been asleep – and she had been dreaming. A hot tide of blood rose to her face. The rawness of the dream was still with her. She felt as if someone had stripped off a layer of her skin and made free with her senses. She also felt watched. Cathy twisted round in her chair and peered up at the windows above her but they were all blank. Of course. The only occupied rooms to look into this small garden were hers and Matthew's; no one could have seen her.

The bell sounded again. It was ringing close at hand, she realised, too close for it to belong to the southern wing or the offices. Was it Matthew, back on one of his visits without his key? Cathy struggled out of the chair – standing up made everything go black for a second – and hurried up the back stairs to the apartment. 'Coming,' she called as she entered the hall. There was no reply and she slowed down, pausing opposite the mirror. Her reflection stared back at her.

She didn't think it was Matthew. He'd told her not to expect him until tonight; having started work on the Giuditta yesterday afternoon, he was eager to press on. In fact, this morning he'd seemed in a hurry to leave the apartment. Whereas Cathy was only too pleased to linger there and put off the moment of going to the studio.

So who was this, calling her out of her dream? Cathy knew, of course. When she'd sat down in the garden, she'd been thinking about him, wondering exactly what he'd meant by those mysterious parting words on Monday. Perhaps he was coming to tell her. She went forward slowly and her hand shook as she turned the catch.

Danilo stood there, his suit jacket slung over one shoulder, his shirt very white against the olive of his skin.

'Hello.' Cathy tried to sound affably surprised. It was difficult when her breathing was uneven.

Danilo smiled. It was a friendly smile, almost affectionate. 'I hope I didn't disturb you,' he said.

'No, not at all. I was lazing in the garden. I didn't realise it was our bell at first.'

As soon as Cathy said 'our bell', hers and Matthew's, she felt embarrassed. Suddenly she couldn't meet Danilo's eyes.

Danilo stepped forward and kissed her. It was as light a touch as ever, but his nearness made her blood sing.

'I've just come from the auction house,' he said. 'A meeting's just been cancelled, and I'm free for a few hours. My father mentioned that Matthew's hard at work on the painting, so I wondered if you'd like to come for a walk around the Ghetto. I could show you some of the places I mentioned last Friday.'

Cathy thought of polite ways in which she might refuse and

realised with a mixture of fear and relief that none of them would do.

'Yes, thank you,' she said. 'I'd like to do that.'

'Good. We can have lunch together too.'

'That would be nice, if you're sure you've got time.'

'Oh yes, we have time for that sort of thing in Rome.' Danilo was laughing at her, almost as Matthew might do.

Cathy smiled back, heard herself laugh, and opened the door wider. 'Come in. Can you give me a few minutes to get ready?'

'Sure. Would you like me to leave and come back in a while?'

'No, I won't be long. Would you like a drink?'

'Yes please, some water.'

Danilo followed Cathy into the kitchen. He moved easily, there was none of the tension she'd sensed last time. He was behaving as if she'd invited him, she thought, as she took the bottled water from the fridge; but then perhaps in a way she had. She had listened to him closely on Monday, and on some level she had been waiting all week for him to come and explain himself.

'Pasta, wine, olive oil,' Danilo said, looking at the shelves. 'You've got the basics already. How do you like living here?'

'Oh, the apartment's wonderful.'

'And the palazzo?'

'That's beautiful, of course. But I don't have very much to do with it, on the whole.'

'I rang the tower door first. I thought you might be in your studio.'

Cathy passed him a glass of water, withdrawing her fingers quickly so they wouldn't touch his.

'No, I haven't started work there yet. I'm still getting bits and pieces for it.'

Danilo watched her as he took a long drink. 'It'll be good to have someone in the studio again,' he remarked. 'I used to like going up there and watching my mother paint, when I was a little boy.' He straightened up. 'I'll go and wait in the sitting room, shall I?'

Cathy slipped into the bedroom and closed the door behind her. Quickly she made the bed and tidied away Matthew's clothes; she had an obscure feeling that it was important to cover their tracks. She felt guilty enough about having Danilo in the flat as it was. She checked herself in the mirror. Yes, she was heavy-lidded and there was a telltale flush on her cheeks. For God's sake, cool it, she said to herself. Nothing's happening. Nothing's going to happen.

She changed quickly and joined Danilo in the sitting room. He was standing by the open window, looking down into the courtyard.

'There's a bird nesting in the vine below here,' he said. A blackbird, I think. She's sitting now. You can see the top of her head through the leaves. I wonder how many eggs she's got in there.'

Cathy looked down. When she followed his pointing finger, she could just make out the brown feathers and one unwinking eye.

'When will they hatch?' she asked.

'Any time now. Then they'll be here for several weeks until they learn to fly. I'll have to tell Giovanni not to get the vines trimmed here.' Danilo glanced at her. 'Unless of course the nest bothers you.'

Cathy blinked. It appeared to be a serious question. Did

Danilo really think she was the kind of person who'd object to a nesting bird? She felt dismayed.

'No, why should it?'

'You never know,' said Danilo. 'With Italians, at any rate. My countrymen aren't sentimental about birds. In some regions, fledglings are eaten as a delicacy.'

Cathy grimaced, then remembered how, when they were children, she and Matthew used to steal eggs from nests and blow them. They knew they shouldn't disturb warm nests because then the mother would abandon the other eggs, but they used to do it all the same. Afterwards they would carry the hollow shells to school as trophies. Remembering her childish cruelty disturbed her.

'Oh well, I dare say I've committed my share of crimes against nature,' she said lightly. 'Shall we go?'

The Ghetto had come alive for the lunch hour. They strolled through the maze of passageways and streets, Danilo manoeuvring instinctively to keep Cathy in the shade. She was grateful for it, the heat was blistering. They followed a meandering route around the quarter, stopping here and there for Danilo to point out an architectural feature or to explain the history behind a particular building.

He was a good guide, relaxed and enjoying himself, chatting rather than talking. He spoke of events hundreds of years ago as if they had happened to people he knew and family names cropped up repeatedly: Piperno, Massini, and of course Bonaventura. It was a very personal slant on history, yet all the time Cathy felt that he was skirting round the edge of something still more personal. Behind the easy talk, she sensed that he was concentrating hard. It was almost as if he was reaching out with his mind and trying to touch her.

'You're very lucky, you know, to have roots in a place like this,' Cathy said, as they dabbled their fingers in the fountain in Piazza Mattei. 'To know there's somewhere you belong. I suppose wherever you are in the world, you always have this in the back of your mind.'

'Yes, I do.' Danilo shook his fingers sideways to make a shower of droplets. It was a practised move and Cathy wondered if he'd played here as a boy. 'Though I don't know about belonging. Some people would say the Bonaventuras are still interlopers. It's only since my father married my mother that there's Jewish blood in the family.'

'But your father seems very at home here. He's accepted, isn't he?'

'He's accepted for what he is, Armando Bonaventura's grandson who lives in the palazzo and heads up the auction house. He's a well-respected man and there's great sympathy for him too. Our neighbours in the Ghetto were very good to him after my mother died.' Danilo paused. 'It's ironic. You'd think that his marriage to a Jewish woman would have brought him into the fold, but it was her death that did it. I don't remember what the atmosphere was like immediately after she died. I was only seven, and bewildered by everything; but I do recall coming back to the Ghetto eighteen months later when my father finally called a halt to our travels. I remember people's faces when they came up to us in the street. They would nod as if we'd done something to satisfy them.'

Danilo removed his fingers from the water and, taking a handkerchief out of his pocket, dried them methodically. Then he rolled the handkerchief into a ball and rubbed at one of the decorative bronze turtles on the fountain bowl, trying to remove a stain. He did it unselfconsciously, like a man taking a mark off his car.

'Damn it, it won't come off,' he said. 'Shall we have some lunch? Then if you feel like it I'll take you to see the synagogue.'

The restaurant was dark and unassuming from the outside. It was only when they were settled at their table that Cathy noticed the thick napkins and the air of discreet wealth about the other diners. She had heard that there was an expensive restaurant in the Ghetto. This must be it. For a moment she felt disappointment at being brought here – smart restaurants were not exactly intimate.

But then, watching Danilo go quickly through the business of reading the menu, consulting her and the waiter, and ordering wine, she realised that this place was probably his local. He was, after all, a very rich man. And there was a deliberation in the way he talked and glanced around, and then touched the base of his wine glass, that made her think he was working up to something, and drawing strength from familiar surroundings.

Apprehensiveness brushed her. She was drawn to Danilo, but she loved Matthew. If Danilo had anything important to say to her, it could only threaten that.

'I'm sorry,' Danilo said, 'did you ask me something?' and Cathy realised she was staring at him.

'I was wondering about your work,' she lied. 'I don't really have any idea what you do.'

Danilo gave a tiny southern European shrug. 'Anything that needs doing, I suppose. I'm managing director of our American operation, which basically involves extending our influence and making deals with associates. When I'm over here, I'm more closely involved in the art side of things.'

'Do you like it?'

'Well enough, yes. It isn't my heart's desire but I have scope and flexibility. And prestige. And money.' He spoke with a tinge of irony.

'What is your heart's desire?' Cathy asked. 'Do you have one – in work, I mean.'

There was a pause. 'I wanted to be an architect,' Danilo said quietly. 'I would have liked to work on very big projects – building a new town, for instance. Or complexes where industry and culture and recreation come together. I would have liked to create something completely new and planned.' His sombre face lit up as he spoke, making him look younger.

'But you went into the business instead?'

'Not at first. It wasn't quite as straightforward as that. As a matter of fact, until my mid-twenties I was all set for a career in architecture. I'd studied architecture at university with my father's sanction, if not his approval. He wanted me to go into the auction house but he didn't stand in my way when I refused. When I left, I was taken on as an assistant in a firm. That's how it's done, you know. I was going to complete my training while I worked there.

'Well, after I'd been there six months, my father announced that he was recruiting new people for Bonaventura's and he asked me to sit in on some of the interviews. I did, and it was immediately clear that he was looking for a protégé, someone he would work with closely and groom to take over eventually. Coincidentally, they were all young men about my own age,' Danilo smiled wryly, 'and all arrogant, as successful young men in their mid-twenties are. They were full of ideas about how to develop Bonaventura's and how to use our private collection for the benefit of the business. I disliked all of them, of course, and one especially. My father watched my reactions and talked over all the candidates with me, and became most interested in the one I most disliked. I couldn't bear to think of our family's business in his hands, so I left architecture and joined the auction house. And I've been there ever since.' He turned the long stem of his glass between his fingers. 'It wasn't very subtle of my father, but it worked.'

Cathy stared. 'You mean he planned it? To make you feel jealous and go into the firm?'

'Clever, wasn't it?'

'But what about your architecture?'

'He didn't think it was a worthwhile ambition.'

'But you wanted to do it. It would have made you happy. Didn't he consider that?'

Danilo's eyes were guarded. 'He didn't believe it would make me happy in the long term. My father thought that if I joined the auction house and took my place in the family business, I would discover that it was my real vocation, that ultimately I would be more fulfilled.' Danilo stopped revolving his wine glass and drank from it. Then he shrugged again. 'My father's a very strong-willed man, Cathy. He's also something of a patriarch. He likes things to go according to his plans.'

'Obviously. And do they, usually?'

Danilo smiled. 'Oh yes.'

Cathy took a sip of wine and tried to match this Enzo with the hospitable man she knew. It was, she found to her discomfort, not so very difficult. She had always recognised him as driven and he had never pretended to be guileless. He had been very generous to her, but then being generous didn't mean he wasn't also pursuing his own ends.

And what might they be? He was getting the Giuditta restored, and by giving them the apartment he was ensuring

Matthew's company, which he obviously enjoyed. But was that enough of a gain to justify widening the breach between him and his son? Cathy had always sensed the breach was there; now she was beginning to understand its history.

Danilo leaned forward. 'Cathy, there's something I want to tell you about my father.' He broke off as the waiter arrived with their first courses. They were both silent while the plates were put down and their glasses topped up. Danilo's last words seemed to hang over them both, making small talk impossible. Danilo thanked the waiter with a nod and a gesture, and watched him walk away. His face was strained when he turned back to Cathy.

'My father,' he said quietly, 'loved my mother very much. He's never really come to terms with losing her. Nor with the way she was before she died. You could probably tell that from the way he talked about her last week, after he showed you the Giuditta.'

Cathy nodded, remembering Enzo sitting in the drawing room, a glass of brandy in his hand, his eyes remote.

'As he told you, my mother believed the painting was talking to her. She said that Judith was alive and pleading with her for help. That Judith was telling her to go to certain places and do certain things.'

'Yes, I remember. Hearing voices, it's common in schizophrenia, isn't it?'

'Yes, and that's what my father told my mother at the time. "You're ill. These voices are a physiological symptom. Take your medicine and they'll go." But she took the medication and they didn't go. I saw what they were doing to her. I used to go and sit in her studio while she painted. She did copies of the Giuditta and strange, exotic versions of it. They showed events which she said took place in Judith's life. They were almost like comic strip stories. She used to tell me that Judith was talking to her through them.' Danilo looked at Cathy with troubled eyes.

'I found it . . . exciting. Upsetting too because I could see how it upset my mother, but it was thrilling. I was a little boy. Here was my mother creating a new world in front of me, where people laid siege to one another and bargained and plotted, and kissed in vast colonnades – the scenes she painted were so vivid. I can see them now.

'But my father hated the paintings. He thought they were leading her further into madness and he tried to stop her doing them. He confiscated her paints and shut up the studio. So my mother took to visiting a house of artists she knew, and spending most of the day there. My father gave in and opened up the studio again, but my mother didn't seem to want it any more. She kept on going to the artists' house, and even when she was at home she wasn't well enough to take care of me. My father employed a nurse to look after me. Her name was Nadia, and ironically she and my mother became quite close. Sometimes my mother would come into the nursery and talk to Nadia while I was playing. They would talk very quietly, and often my mother would cry, without tears. It was terrible, a kind of gasping. And when Nadia asked her what the matter was, she would just whisper, "Help him."

'Then one day she didn't come home. Instead she ran away with one of the artists. I don't know what happened between them or how long it had been going on. I asked my father once but he wouldn't talk about it. But they didn't get far. My father contacted the police and they were sighted in Calabria. A car tried to stop them, there was a crash and the artist died.

'When they brought my mother back, she couldn't speak. My father brought in God knows how many doctors but it did no good. Three days later my mother locked herself in her studio, poured acid on her own paintings, defaced the Giuditta and hanged herself.'

There was a short silence. Cathy stared at Danilo but was unable to make any sense of his expression. Her mind was filled with images, splintered and incomplete. Judith on the hillside. Judith moving through the camp. Judith in Holofernes' arms. Herself, perched high above the Forum, her hand moving intently across the sketchpad.

'You're probably wondering why I'm telling you all this. It's very private and very painful, and I shouldn't be burdening you with it. But you see it's not over. After my mother died, my father grieved obsessively. He became convinced that he had let her down by not believing in her voices. He developed a kind of love-hatred for the Giuditta and would lock himself up with it and examine it for hours. He consulted psychics to see if they could hear what my mother had heard. He used to take them up to the studio; that's why nothing in it was ever changed, he wanted everything to be just as she left it.

'I didn't know this at the time. Nadia told me about it when I was eighteen. My father had involved her in some seances, or psychic sessions, Christ knows what. After the first couple of times she refused to go any more and she tried to talk him out of it, but she didn't think she'd succeeded.

'I tackled my father about it and we had a terrible row. He accused me of not caring about my mother or him, or about our heritage which he'd now convinced himself the Giuditta was. That was when I moved out of the palazzo. We didn't speak all summer, and though we resumed civilities after that, we were estranged for years. It's only recently that we've become close again and I'm still not in a position to ask him about his feelings. I'd hoped that the obsession had passed and that he'd finally forgiven himself. Giovanni told me that the studio hadn't been opened for several years, so I was hopeful. But then last Friday, you took out those drawings.' Danilo looked up; there was a painful intensity in his eyes. 'And I saw his face. I knew then that it was all still there.' He took a slow breath.

'I'm afraid for him, Cathy. And I'm worried about you and Matthew. I don't know what my father's motives are for letting Matthew work on the Giuditta, or why he's brought you into the palazzo and given you my mother's studio, but I don't think they're fully rational.'

Cathy's knife had grown slippery. She unwound her fingers from it and reached slowly for her glass. But her hand was shaking too much to lift it. 'You're saying Enzo's using me. That he thinks I'll be able to put him in touch with Alessandra.' Her voice was shaking too.

'I honestly don't know. Perhaps I've got it completely wrong, but you saw him last Friday night. What did you think of his reaction to the drawings?'

Cathy pressed her fingers against her chin to steady them. 'I thought he was shocked when I mentioned them. And then when he saw them, he seemed to change.'

'Yes, he did. As if a light went on inside him.'

Cathy looked up, startled. That had been the image in her mind, too.

Danilo shook his head bitterly. 'I wish this could end, Cathy, and I wish you'd never become involved. Too much unhappiness has been suffered in the palazzo. It's self-perpetuating. The place has an atmosphere. Sometimes I think, well . . .'

'What?'

'Do you believe in ghosts? Not people in chains and sheets but the echoes of old events. Sometimes I think I've felt it in places where violent things have happened, like the Forum. As if an imprint lingers.'

'You think the palazzo's haunted?' Cathy was surprised to hear her voice sounding quite calm. Her mind was splintering again.

'You saw Judith at a window,' Danilo said softly, 'before you ever set foot in the place.' His eyes were very dark. They seemed to be offering her something. Understanding? A bargain? Cathy knew their expression, but it seemed to belong to another person, in another time.

'When I was younger,' he went on, 'I used to have dreams . . .'

Whiteness dazzled Cathy's eyes. The heat she had been feeling for the last few minutes became unbearable and she swayed. Her hands clutched the table, slipping on the cloth, and then she felt Danilo's hands, cool and firm, steadying them.

'Cathy. Cathy. Put your head down. That's right. Have some water. It's the heat. You're not used to it.'

She concentrated on doing as the voice said. It had a note of quiet authority which was welcome; she wanted to relax into it and allow Danilo to take charge and banish her dizziness, her heat, the trouble churning in her mind.

'There, you look better now. Have another sip of water.'

Obediently Cathy sipped and bit by bit, the room stilled and her vision cleared. Danilo was watching her anxiously.

'Do you feel better now? Do you want to lie down? If I asked, we could go upstairs.'

'No thanks, I'll be fine. What did you say just then? The last thing?' His words were lost to her, swallowed up by the physical sensations, but she could remember that they had been important.

'Forget it. I'm sorry I upset you. I had to warn you that my father is . . . unreliable, but I shouldn't have dragged you into our private troubles.'

'No, I'm glad you did. Please go on, I want you to.'

'No you don't.' Danilo smiled. 'You have too much sense. Anyway, I 'm glad you stopped me. There's nothing to be gained by wallowing in bad memories. That way madness lies.' He paused and grimaced. 'Literally, in our case.'

'Danilo—'

'Could we change the subject?' He was still smiling but with a hint of desperation now. 'I'd really appreciate it. Tell me about your painting. When did you decide it was what you wanted to do?'

The sun was no longer overhead when they left the restaurant, but the streets were stifling. Danilo and Cathy walked slowly, not saying much. Cathy was trying, unsuccessfully, to think. The things Danilo had told her had changed the bond between them. It was complicated now and she felt more open to him, as if they were connected to each other by many different channels. There was so much in his story that touched on her. And at every point of contact was the same figure, slipping effortlessly from Alessandra's time to her own: Judith.

Could Enzo possibly be right? Was there some power locked up in that painting which had spoken to Alessandra and was now calling to her? The shiver travelled lightly along her skin, like invisible wings. Stop it. Don't be so bloody ridiculous. But was it ridiculous? There was no explanation for some of the things that were happening; even Danilo had admitted that.

Danilo. Cathy looked at him walking quietly beside her and wondered what he was thinking. He had that air of stillness again, just as when she had first seen him in the photograph, but now it seemed to be born not so much of confidence as of self-protection. She recalled his hands covering hers in the restaurant. There had been great comfort in that touch and she felt an irrational longing to feel it again.

'Here we are,' said Danilo. 'Just round this corner. I always like to come on it suddenly from this angle.'

Cathy followed the direction of his outstretched arm, turned the sharp corner and blinked. The streets had suddenly opened up. River light bounced off the cobbles and ahead of them pale walls rose impressively and a silver-grey dome glinted against the blue. They were at the synagogue.

'It's unexpected, isn't it?' said Danilo. 'It makes you realise how foreign the style of building is. We'll have to go in at the main door which is round that side. There shouldn't be – ah.' As they walked towards the synagogue's front, they could see lines of cars parked in the street. 'Damn, there must be a service going on. There isn't usually on a Friday afternoon.' Danilo stared at the synagogue. He seemed thrown; he hesitated, his body tensed, and Cathy was suddenly reminded of her first sight of him in the flesh, standing angrily in the drawing room at the palazzo.

'Perhaps it'll finish soon. We could wait awhile and see.'

Danilo nodded. 'True. We can't have you standing around for long though, in this heat. I tell you what, there's a driver waiting by that Mercedes. Why don't you stay here in the shade and I'll go and ask him when this is due to end.'

Cathy stood in the shadow cast by a tree and watched Danilo walk past the railings and the well-tended grounds to the synagogue entrance. He stopped and talked to the man. He was wearing a dark suit and was polishing the wing mirrors of the Mercedes.

Danilo glanced over at her as he talked and smiled. Cathy smiled back and looked hurriedly away. Watching Danilo in conversation made her feel uncomfortably as though she were spying. She gave her attention to the synagogue instead.

She had never taken the time to look at it properly before. Now that she did, she saw that it was quite different from the other buildings in the Ghetto. They were mostly simple Roman houses, some of them dating back to medieval times; this was elaborate and distinctly Eastern in flavour. Each façade had its own arrangement of pillars and pediments; acanthus leaves and geometric shapes were carved into the stone; and the dome was four-sided, its edges cutting sharply into the sky.

The longer Cathy looked at it, the more incongruous the synagogue seemed. One of the most disconcerting things was that the whole building seemed new. She stared at its hard silhouette – the corners zig-zagged and tricked the eye – and visualised it in some more southerly country, standing alone in a desert, with the wind blowing dust against it, wearing away the stone.

'It's an unlikely thing, isn't it?' Danilo had rejoined her. 'This is a Jewish temple of worship in the Christian capital of the world, and they built it in the style of Assyria and Babylon, two of Judea's most ancient enemies.'

'Assyria?' Cathy tried to echo Danilo's pronunciation: soft, with a resonance at the top of the throat. 'Is that the same as Syria?'

'In a way. Today's Syria is a much smaller descendant of Assyria. There was once an Assyrian empire, back in Old Testament times. It peaked in the eighth century BC, but it remained a power for long afterwards, really up until the Roman empire.'

'And what happened then?'

'Natural decline. While the Roman republic was consolidating itself, the Middle East was parcelled out between three main powers – Assyria, Macedonia and Rome. But Assyria and Macedonia were faltering. The territories they administered rebelled, and subject kings and rulers made alliances with each other and with Rome . . . I'm sorry, I'm sounding like a guidebook. Stop me if you're bored.'

'No, it's interesting. Please go on.'

'Well, Macedonia shrank to present-day Greece, and Assyria to Syria. There was a series of disputes between them and Rome, and each time Rome emerged the winner. As Rome grew more powerful, she drew the ambitious young men of the region to her. You must understand that this was a time when people were sick and tired of local invasions. They'd been living with them for generations – invasions and massacres and bitter factional wars. Rome offered the opportunity to rise above that. The Romans wanted to build a united civilisation, and if a man enlisted to fight for Rome in one of the overseas campaigns, and got himself noticed, he could make his fortune. So the young men went to Rome, and that hastened the end of the other powers.'

Cathy looked at the palm trees which stood tall and exotic in front of the synagogue. Danilo's words were resonating in her mind, filling it with half-formed pictures. Were they memories she couldn't quite recover or fantasies waiting to be created? One was clearer than the others: she could almost see Holofernes walking through the shadows of the palms, setting out for the new world.

'You know a lot about it,' she said.

'Yes, well, I'm half-Roman, half-Middle Eastern, so I have a personal interest.'

Cathy jerked round to look at him. Did Danilo really think of himself as Middle Eastern? It had never crossed her mind before, but now she called up the image of Holofernes and saw at once that there was a resemblance. They were both olive-skinned and strong, but Danilo disguised his physical strength by the way he carried himself.

Holofernes. Up until now, whenever she had carried thoughts of Holofernes into her waking life, she had linked him with Matthew. The timing had been right: she had dreamt of Judith moving towards Holofernes just as she, Cathy, had been making the decision to become Matthew's lover. It had seemed to fit so neatly.

But nothing fitted any more.

Danilo was watching her with interest, almost avidly. She darted her eyes away, but she could feel his gaze steady on her.

'Oh look,' she said vaguely, gesturing to the synagogue entrance. 'People are coming out. Perhaps we can go in soon.'

Danilo looked where she was pointing. Then he stiffened. After an infinitesimal pause, he turned to face her again, presenting his back firmly to the synagogue.

'Will you do me a favour?' he said. 'Can we postpone our visit there till another day? There's someone who's just come out who'll trap me in conversation if we go over, and I'm just not in the mood for her.' He smiled humorously, but there was tension in the way he stood.

'Of course.' Cathy stared over the railings, wondering who it was.

'Good, let's go.' His hand was suddenly on her elbow, turning her round, and simultaneously she saw a woman detach herself from the crowd.

'She's seen you,' she said.

Danilo continued to tug at her. 'Never mind, we'll slip discreetly away. It would seem ill-mannered to the dead man's family if I began talking to the mourners now. They'd wonder why I hadn't been at the service.'

'She's coming out.' Cathy resisted him. 'She's definitely recognised you. Danilo, it's too late to run now.'

Danilo stopped pulling her arm. He stared at her in frustration, then like a screen rolling down, his self-possession returned.

'You're right,' he said. 'We'll be civil.'

His hand was still beneath her arm, keeping her close for another second. 'It's Nadia,' he said quietly. 'Remember?'

As Danilo released her and turned to greet the approaching woman, Cathy stood bemused. Nadia? Remember what? And yet the woman did seem vaguely familiar.

She was in her late middle age, probably a few years younger than Enzo. She was dressed neatly in black and her face was fine-featured and carved into planes by two long stress folds that ran cheek to chin.

'Danilo, hello. How are you? I thought it was you, but I couldn't be sure.' She spoke very quickly and her Italian had a less musical intonation than the Roman one.

'Hello, Nadia,' said Danilo with impeccable civility. 'How are you?'

'Very well, thank God. It's a long time since you've been home. What brings you back now?' She spoke with the slightly censorious familiarity of an aunt or a teacher.

Of course. Nadia, the nurse. The woman who had looked after Danilo as a boy and known his mother.

'The usual things, Nadia. Family, business.'

Nadia nodded and her eyes travelled past Danilo to Cathy. Danilo turned and shot Cathy a swift, conspiratorial smile. 'Nadia, I'd like to present Cathy Seymour. Cathy, this is Nadia Razzi, a good friend of our family.' He was still speaking Italian, giving Cathy's name a lilting hard 't': Cat-ti. 'Nadia was my nurse when I was small, and she looked after my mother in the months before she died. My mother was very fond of her. And my father too.'

He didn't include himself, Cathy noticed. 'I'm pleased to meet you,' she said, also in Italian.

Nadia extended her hand. 'And I'm happy to meet you. Welcome to Rome.' She turned to Danilo. 'I've heard from your father, Nilo, of his plans for an exhibition. I hope it's a good idea.'

'So do I,' said Danilo expressionlessly.

'You're employed on the exhibition too?' Nadia asked Cathy.

'No, I'm here on holiday. At least, I came on holiday; now I'll be staying on awhile.' Cathy tailed off. She didn't want to have to explain herself, or her place in the palazzo, to a stranger.

'Cathy's a painter,' said Danilo. 'Giovanni is preparing a studio for her, so she can work.'

Nadia raised her eyebrows; they made two dark arches above her thoughtful eyes. 'Ah, your father will like that. Will she have Alessandra's old studio?'

Danilo looked at her blandly. Then to Cathy's surprise he said: 'I don't know. I don't live in the palazzo any more, Nadia. The daily running of the house goes on without me.'

'Yes, your father told me you prefer to stay in your apartment. Well, I think that's a good thing. Young people should be independent and not live too much in the past.'

Danilo nodded curtly. He made no attempt to encourage conversation and moved slightly closer to Cathy, so that the two of them faced Nadia like a barrier. Cathy was glad of it. There was something unsettling in the older woman, and it was reassuring to feel Danilo there, giving her unspoken protection. The sleeve of his jacket brushed very lightly against her arm.

Nadia seemed to recollect herself. 'I hope you'll enjoy your stay in Rome,' she said, extending her hand once more. 'Perhaps we will meet again. I sometimes visit Signore Bonaventura at the palazzo.'

'I hope so.' Cathy took the outstretched hand. Nadia had a light, strong nurse's grip.

'I'm happy to see you looking well, Danilo. Francesca Leli asked me about you last week, she said you didn't go to her daughter's birthday party. She asked me if you were ill.'

'I'm busy, Nadia, as always.'

'Of course. I should thank you for stopping to speak to me on such a busy afternoon,' she said with a stab of irony. 'But don't forget the Lelis and your other friends. There are many people here who like to see you.'

Danilo bowed his head respectfully to her embrace and

murmured goodbye. He watched her walk back to the other mourners, his face utterly blank.

'She takes a great interest in you still.' Cathy allowed the hint of a question in her voice.

Danilo shifted his jacket from one hand to the other. 'My old nurse and my mother's,' he said quietly. 'And my father's now. She thinks all Bonaventura family business is hers. I wish she hadn't seen us together. I'd be prepared to bet my father receives a visit from her soon.'

Cathy let herself into the tower staircase with one of the keys Enzo had given her. It was cool and quiet inside and as she climbed the stone steps, light fell onto her through the small square windows in the outer walls. They were set very high; she caught only glimpses of roof and sky as she passed them. At the top of the stairs she unlocked the door to the landing. It was empty, as it had been each time Enzo brought her here. 'You will rarely be disturbed up here,' he had smiled.

Cathy hesitated by the windows, looking down into the courtyard. Then she slid the third key into the lock of the studio door. She stood on the threshold, looking at the clean-swept room. It was peaceful and friendly. The shutters had been opened and on the table lay drawing paper, pens and charcoals. The desire to draw was like a thirst in her; smiling with relief, she stepped inside.

Chapter Twelve

The camp was on the move around them. In the pink-grey light of dawn, people were preoccupied with their tasks. They wrestled with heavy cooking pots and recalcitrant livestock, struggled to secure bundles to carts. They spared Judith and Endeyeh only mildly curious glances as the two women sat together on a rock.

Judith took no notice of the people passing by. She went on feeding Endeyeh sips of wine and chafing her hands to warm them. She had been doing this for over an hour, ever since she had returned to the tent at first light to find Endeyeh crouched in a corner, dry-eyed and tearing incessantly at the hem of her skirt. At first, Endeyeh had ignored all her questions. It was a woman from Gilead, whom Jonathan had assigned to watch over Endeyeh, who came forward and told Judith the story.

It seemed certain that Rechab was dead. He had never been here as a soldier, but when the army was still gathering, some Judean conscripts on their march here had met up with traders, travelling north. Rechab was among them. He had sold oil and flax to his countrymen, and he had promised to visit them in the main camp later. But he had never come. Some time afterwards, new recruits had arrived, and told of being ambushed by armed Judean merchants. The soldiers had killed several of their attackers including the leader, a young man wearing a bright cloak.

Judith had sent the woman away and set about trying to comfort Endeyeh. But nothing seemed to do any good. Endeyeh took the wine without protest and let Judith hold her, but she didn't cry. At one point she reached up and softly wiped away Judith's tears. When the men had come to take down the tent, she had followed Judith out into the desert morning and stood still while Judith wrapped furs round her shoulders. Now, huddled on the rock, Judith tried to help her friend grieve.

Nothing reached Endeyeh, not even Judith's news. She had given it a few moments ago, judging that she could not delay any longer. Endeyeh might not have heard, for all the response she gave. With growing urgency, Judith pressed on.

'Endeyeh, did you hear what I said? I'm going to move on with the camp. I'm going to be Holofernes' bride. And you'll come too. I'll take care of you, I'll look after you. We'll be travelling up through Rechab's route, and I'll get Holofernes to ask everyone what they know. If he's alive, we'll find him. If he's not, at least we'll discover what happened.'

Endeyeh finally looked up. Her eyes were bleak but completely comprehending. 'No, I can't come with you, Judith.'

'Yes, you can. I've told you, I'll look after you.'

Endeyeh shook her head. 'I'm going back to Bethulia.'

There was finality in her voice. Judith recognised it at once but she shied away from it.

'No, Endeyeh! There's nothing left for you there. I won't be there any more, you'd have to go back to Chabris and Sarra or find a new house. Please, we should be together now. Please come to Rome.'

Endeyeh shook her head. In the fresh light of new day, her

face was smooth. 'What would I do in Rome? If I can't have Rechab, I should be in Bethulia, where my family are. Someone will take me in. And just in case it isn't true, if Rechab is still alive, then I must be where he can find me.'

'But what will you tell people? They'll blame you for going back without me.'

Endeyeh looked at the wall of people moving steadily past them, carrying their possessions. Her faint smile was like a mocking echo of the vibrant one she had given last night. 'I'll tell them your story, that you offered yourself as a hostage to make Holofernes move on, and he accepted. That's what you'll be putting about, isn't it?'

Judith closed her eyes. 'Yes, that's it. I've got to. I can't stay.' She felt the touch of Endeyeh's hand and looked up. The sun was moving rapidly over the horizon and its rays made Endeyeh's face glow with a false radiance. 'Oh Endeyeh, please don't hate me. I don't want to go without you.'

'I don't hate you. And I know you've got to go. You'd have to even if you didn't want to. Bethulia won't have you back now.'

The marriage ceremony was over quickly. As she and Endeyeh walked from their own tent, behind the soldier with the sword, to Holofernes' canopy, Judith remembered her first marriage procession. Then it had been spring; all the neighbours cheered and sang, and the girls threaded flowers through her veil. This time she wore no veil, and the people who watched her were strangers.

Holofernes stood under the canopy with his lieutenants; Jonathan and another, grey-haired, Judean waited to one side. The tent had already been dismantled. Behind the men there was only an expanse of stained ground and a chariot, filled with heavy chests. Judith reached the edge of the canopy and Holofernes put out his hand to draw her in.

'You shall be my wife,' he said. They were the same words Manasses had spoken, but Manasses had also said, after the Bethulian custom, 'for all of my life.'

Manasses' life had been so short; Judith suddenly wondered how long Holofernes would live. He was a soldier, his trade was war, and his life was full of violent dangers. How long would she have with this man and where would he take her? She couldn't imagine anything about the life they would lead together. She felt a dizzying sense of helplessness, as if the desert had tilted and she was spinning through the wide air.

Holofernes looked across at Jonathan and his companion. The elderly man stepped forward and Judith realised that he was going to act as the priest or elder would. Had Holofernes remembered this much from his childhood, or had he asked Jonathan what should be done? That he had arranged this touched her, and bewildered her.

The old man placed a hand on each of their shoulders in turn and spoke the traditional blessing. 'From this day, you shall be her brother and she shall be a sister to you.'

Holofernes' hand tightened on Judith's. It was an unexpected spasm and it brought an answering one, deep inside her, as she remembered their love-making of the night before. It had been fleshy and passionate, the kind of loving she had once craved from Manasses. But her boy husband had refused to give it to her and now she thought that he must have been right, for the memory of Holofernes' acts disturbed her and filled her with fear. She felt stripped of her dignity and ashamed of the desires, the appetites she had discovered in the darkness.

The old man passed the marriage cup to her

'He did what?'

'Took me around the Ghetto and the synagogue. It was very interesting.'

'And bought you lunch.'

'Mmm.'

'Where?'

'I didn't notice the name,' Cathy said. It wasn't true, she had read it on the menu. 'It was up the hill, near the baker's.'

'Lorenzetti's,' Matthew said flatly. 'That's one of the most expensive restaurants in Rome. Well, well, and did you have a nice time?'

'Yes, thank you.' Cathy cradled her drink and looked gingerly at Matthew. He was trying for a sardonic note but he was pale and his hands moved restlessly among the knives and forks, searching for a corkscrew. 'The food was good,' she said brightly.

'Yes, it would be.' Matthew found the corkscrew and bent his head over the bottle of wine, hands gripping and twisting, apparently concentrating hard.

He was determined not to ask any questions, Cathy could see. Which made life easier for her in the most obvious way, but also left her feeling very alone. She was going to have to do all the talking here.

'Danilo knows a lot about local history. He must have steeped himself in it when he was younger. It's not just book knowledge either. He can tell stories about almost all the families, who married who and why the Cencis fell out with the Fesares eighty years ago, that sort of thing.'

'And why did the Cencis fall out with the Fesares?'

'They argued about who was supposed to run the Cencis' leather shop in the Via Frattini. The Fesares said Mr Cenci had promised it to Biaggio Fesare when he married Cenci's daughter.'

Matthew poured himself a large glass of wine. 'Fascinating,' he said, smiling.

'Matthew.'

His smile faded. 'Yes?'

'Danilo took me out because he wanted to talk to me about something.'

Matthew took a careful drink. Above the rim of his glass, his eyes were wary. 'Well? Go on.'

'He's worried about his father. He thinks he isn't quite rational about the Giuditta.'

'Why?' Matthew made a face. 'I suppose entrusting me with it is a sign that old Enzo's irrational.'

'No, Matthew, it's nothing to do with you, it's all to do with Alessandra. You see, after Alessandra died, Enzo fell apart. You know that already, but what Danilo told me is that Enzo blamed himself for everything and began to wonder if Alessandra's delusions weren't really delusions at all. He was so eaten up with guilt he began to think that maybe she really had heard voices from it. He even had psychics and spiritualists in her studio, holding seances over it.'

'*What?*' Matthew stared in disbelief.

'I know, it's ghastly, isn't it? It went on for several years before Danilo found out about it, because he was away at school most of the time. When he did find out, he tackled Enzo and there was the most God almighty row. Enzo accused him of betraying his mother's memory and not caring about what had happened to her. That was when Danilo moved out and that's the root of the trouble between them. They've never talked about it since. The Giuditta's stayed up in the studio and as far as Danilo knows, it's been undisturbed for several years. But now Enzo's brought it out again.' Cathy tailed off. Matthew had put his glass down on the kitchen table and was gazing at her incredulously.

'Don't you see?' she said. 'When we showed Enzo my drawings, we didn't know what we were dealing with. Though I felt – well, you know what I felt about it.'

'Yes, I know, and it seems that bloody Danilo knows too.' Matthew shook his head. He seemed speechless for a second, then he punched the wall viciously. 'Christ, he's clever. He doesn't miss a trick, does he? He doesn't miss a fucking trick.' He walked out of the kitchen.

'Matthew! What the hell are you talking about?' Cathy followed him into the hall but Matthew strode away into the sitting room. 'Matt, don't you walk away from me. What's the matter? I'm talking to you about Enzo.'

Matthew turned from the circuit he was making round the sofa and chairs. 'No, you're not. Danilo is. Every word you've just said comes from him, doesn't it? This is poor, hard-done-by Danilo's version of events and you've swallowed it all without so much as a grain of salt. God Cat, use your brain, can't you see what he's doing?'

'He's trying to protect his father.'

'Balls. He's trying to drive a wedge between his father and me. This is just an attempt to sabotage my relationship with Enzo, my work on the Giuditta – in fact, my whole position here at the palazzo. Danilo's as jealous as hell of me and he can't stand the way Enzo and I get on. He especially can't stand the way Enzo's working with me on the collection. He was always against the idea of the exhibition, I knew there'd be trouble from him sooner or later. Though I must say I didn't think he'd come up with anything so devious, so bloody insulting to his father.' Matthew's face was ashen with fury. Cathy had seen him like this once or twice as a child, but never since he'd become an adult. His vehemence shocked her.

'You don't know what you're saying,' she said quietly.

Matthew resumed his pacing round the room, his eyes fixed on her. 'Oh yes I do,' he said, his voice as soft as hers. 'I've known Danilo longer than you have. I've seen him in action in business dealings. Where his interests are threatened, he's ruthless.'

'This isn't business, Matt, it's his father. Danilo loves him.'

'Does he, though? I'm not so sure. He looks at him very coldly sometimes, and that night we saw the Giuditta for the first time, he could hardly bring himself to speak to him.'

'I didn't notice.'

'No, but I did.'

Cathy was silent. Matthew had himself under control now but she could still feel rage emanating from him.

'So let me get this straight. You don't believe what Danilo's saying about Enzo. You don't even believe Danilo believes it. You think he's making it all up as a deliberate plot to cause trouble between you and Enzo.'

'It's not as far-fetched as you make it sound, Cat.'

Cathy just raised her eyebrows. For a few long seconds they looked at each other, Matthew's face shuttered, her own sceptical.

'Danilo's a clever man,' Matthew said curtly. 'He's managed to make trouble between you and me as well.'

'Oh, for God's sake!' Cathy turned impatiently and marched out of the room, back to the kitchen. She refilled her glass so vigorously that she spilled wine everywhere. 'Shit, shit, shit,' she muttered, kicking a drying-up cloth onto the floor.

She felt agitated and cooped up. She was tempted to punch the wall, but Matthew had already done it.

Why was he being so unreasonable? What was it about Danilo that made him so touchy? As soon as she'd mentioned Danilo's name this afternoon Matthew's face had changed, as though a dark cloud had passed behind his eyes.

Cathy swallowed half the glass of wine in a gulp. Her thoughts were a loud babble, but not loud enough to blank out the little voice somewhere in the deeps of her mind, which told her that she was being dishonest. Matthew had plenty to fear from Danilo.

She remembered the heat under her skin where his hand had touched her arm. It had been like a memory.

'I don't want us to quarrel.' Matthew stood in the doorway. Still feeling the remembered heat, Cathy watched him. He leaned against the door jamb and reached for the bottle of wine. 'Have you been showering in this or something?' he asked, looking at the damp floor.

She returned his hardworking smile. 'More or less.'

'Look, I'm sorry I got so angry. I don't trust Danilo and I can't pretend I do, but you like him, so why don't we agree to differ?'

'Sure.'

'I mean, we can hardly act on what he said to you anyway.'

Cathy watched him pick up his glass from the table and add more wine. 'Can't we?'

Matthew shot her a quizzical look. 'What did you have in

mind? Asking Enzo about it? "Excuse me, Enzo, are you by any chance trying to raise ghosts through this painting? Oh, you're not. Fine, just wondered." Rather you than me, Cat.'

Cathy shook her head. 'No, obviously we can't ask him, but don't you think we should bear it in mind? For instance, I don't think I'll show him any more of my drawings, for a while at least.'

'It's up to you. If you're happy keeping them from him, go ahead. It seems rough on him, though, after all he's done for us.' Matthew paused. 'I thought you hadn't done any more drawings since we moved in.'

'No,' Cathy raised her glass to her lips and thought fast. Now was not the time to tell him of the drawing she'd done an hour ago. She wanted to tell him; she wanted to confide how, after Danilo had left her in the archway, she had gone slowly up the tower staircase to her studio. How she had opened the windows and sat for a while, listening to the sounds of the Ghetto. How she had felt the tingling in her fingers, laid out a piece of heavy paper, chosen a medium-point pen and obeyed the instinct to draw.

But she didn't dare tell him, because she didn't understand it herself. The scene she had drawn, of the makeshift wedding, was like nothing she had read. Nor was it anything she had imagined. But as it had taken shape under her pen she'd thought, yes, that's it, that's how it was. And she had thought it with such utter conviction that for a moment it was as if someone else was speaking in her mind.

Had she dreamt it and forgotten, until the act of drawing brought it back? Or had she conjured it up there and then, under the influence of Danilo and the somnolent afternoon?

Her dream life and her waking life no longer had firm edges separating them.

'No, I haven't done any more drawings,' she lied. She couldn't tell him, still less show him. This afternoon she thought she'd seen a resemblance between Holofernes and Danilo; what if it were there in the picture, too? 'But I feel as if I quite want to,' she hedged her bets. 'Perhaps I will once I've got used to the studio.'

She had the feeling he was only pretending to believe her. She drank the rest of her wine, avoiding his eyes.

'I'm hot and sticky and I smell of wine,' she said. 'And I'm fed up of thinking about the bloody Bonaventuras. I'm going to have a shower. Why don't you come too?' She asked it almost tentatively, not sure of her reception. When she looked up and saw Matthew's softened face, her heart squeezed.

'Yes, please,' he said. He put his glass down with a clatter and put his arms gently round her, his hands cupping her head. 'Let's not argue any more, Cat. I hate it. Why are we always on the edge of fighting suddenly?'

'I don't know. But I love you. I love you. Hold me.'

Chapter Thirteen

'What do you think of Nicanor?'

Judith looked at Holofernes in surprise. He was sitting on his copper-bound chest, his arms resting on his knees. He had been in the tent with her for a while, and she had known he was leading up to something. He had paced, stopped, cracked his knuckles, twisted a comb into her hair for her. Then he had sat down on the chest and pretended to muse.

As she went on oiling the arm bracelets so that they would slip on without grazing her, Judith had wondered what he was going to say. She'd assumed it would be something about her. Some detail of her behaviour perhaps. Holofernes was always telling her that she should hold herself more aloof from this woman, try harder to make friends with that one. Nothing she had discovered, was straightforward in this travelling town.

But now he asked her this.

'He doesn't speak to me, unless you're present. So I don't speak to him.'

'Yes, I'd noticed. Full of himself, isn't he?'

'He comes from a good family. People have respect for him.'

'Yes, that's what I was thinking about. If there was a split between him and me, how many people would support me?'

Holofernes was talking quietly. Judith felt apprehension grip her

'Is there a danger of that? I thought he was committed to your plan.'

'He is. But I was wondering, which one of us is seen as the best bet for the future? You're a newcomer here, how does it strike you?'

'The Achaeans would go with him. And perhaps Sirio's men. It would depend on what he was offering them.'

'Sirio's lot are disaffected? I didn't know that.'

'They've been on the march a long time without anything to send home.' Judith spoke matter-of-factly. She had been on the march a long time too, nearly two weeks, and day and evening and night she listened to the talk of the people around her. The men bargained and planned among themselves, and word of it got out immediately and circulated among the women, and she listened to it all.

As they moved north along the trade route, it sometimes seemed to her that they were like a desert within a desert, with their own shifting sands. From a distance they must look like one coherent body but within the camp rumour whirled incessantly, making one person mistrust another, altering allegiances, so that relationships were never quite the same from one day to the next.

Holofernes always talked to her as if she understood what was going on, and she answered him the same way. At first she had thought of it as a pretence – he was giving her a lead and she was making believe to follow it. But already she had begun to forget that.

In the great camp outside Bethulia, she had been truly at a loss. There, everyone but her had seemed to belong. Now, though, they were all in transit and everyone was uncertain. Of the three thousand who had struck camp outside Bethulia, two thousand had set off north with Holofernes, yet within a week nearly seven hundred of them had left the march – to go home, or to pursue rumours of ships off the coast, or to seek out new opportunities in the troubled borderlands of Syria. Judith had been dismayed to see them go, but Holofernes had simply shrugged.

'It was bound to happen. I'd like to arrive at Apamea with twelve hundred if I can, but the numbers aren't as important as who makes them up. I'd rather keep the Egyptians than the Galatians, for instance. So many Romans already have influence in Galatia. But if I can deliver a body of Egyptian soldiers to Lucius Tullius, then we're starting to be in business.'

Judith listened hard, both to Holofernes' laconic explanations and to the discussions and debates which took place endlessly in the camp at large. She had learnt a lot, very quickly. As Holofernes had pointed out to her the other day, she was in a position to know this makeshift community as well as anyone.

She heard what was being said among the women. She could watch, better than most in the camp, what was happening between the men. She shared the same discomforts, felt the same heat. She, too, calculated the miles to Apamea and speculated as to exactly what the city might offer, and who among them was best placed to take advantage of it.

This life was hand-to-mouth, lived minute by minute. At times they were frantically busy, setting up camp, buying provisions, cooking, eating, arguing, inviting traders and travelling tribes they met to tell them the news. Since they had entered Syria, Holofernes and Nicanor had been sending messages to their contacts, trying to find out what Demetrius knew of their actions. Between these bursts of activity there were the long hours of travelling when they walked on, heads swathed against the sun, stepping in rhythm until the ache spread all through their bodies and everything hurt, sometimes talking, sometimes silent, sometimes unable to tell whether they had spoken a minute or an hour ago.

There were times when Holofernes would travel beside Judith. At others, Naaman, one of the Syrian scribes, would walk alongside her and teach her simple Latin phrases. In the evening, after dinner, Naaman would teach her written Latin for a while, and then Holofernes would claim her. He liked her to join the men and listen when they talked about tactics and plans, 'like Cornelia Gracchus', he said. Later on, alone in their tent, he would make love to her. Each night was as passionate as the first and as troubling. Judith twisted fiercely in Holofernes' arms, longing to escape but unable to let go.

It sometimes seemed to her that the last two weeks had gone on for ever and that before that, nothing had been real.

This afternoon they had arrived at the grateful shade of an oasis, and they were to stay here overnight. An envoy from Demetrius was expected, and that was why Judith was preparing herself with special care. She would not be sitting with Holofernes during the talks and the feast, but she might be asked to join the men afterwards. And she would undoubtedly be pointed out to the envoy as Holofernes' woman. His wife. She tried to convince herself that the word had a dignified ring.

She wiped the excess oil from the bracelets and began to ease the coiled silver onto her upper arm. It was good to do something while she talked; it stopped her showing her anxiety. In these weeks as Holofernes' wife, she had struggled to throw off her Bethulian responses. For Holofernes, this expedition was an adventure, bristling with opportunity. If she were going to survive in her new life, she would have to learn to become like him. The old Judith was dead, the new Judith was hard-headed and unafraid and perfectly capable of discussing defections from the camp.

'What makes you think Nicanor's planning to leave?' she asked.

'He's not planning to leave, but he might have to.'

'What do you mean?'

'Nicanor's got his eye on Lucius Tullius too. I reckoned he'd be content to use him, and me, as a passage to Rome, but now I'm not so sure. He's been talking to people behind my back, criticising the way I've led them. I knew his Achaeans would follow him anywhere, but if he's turned Sirio's men too . . .' Holofernes rocked back and forth, frowning at his feet.

Judith watched him surreptitiously while she twisted the bracelets into their least painful position. Of all the people in the camp, Nicanor discomforted her the most. He was courteous to her in Holofernes' presence, but otherwise he didn't bother to disguise his disdain. He didn't go out of his way to insult her, that would require too much energy. He just took it for granted that she lived on a lower level and that they both recognised the fact. It had occurred to Judith before now, watching him, that he felt much the same way towards Holofernes. But this was the first time Holofernes had shown himself aware of it.

'Do you think he'll try to take over from you?'

'Not yet,' said Holofernes. 'Not while we're in the middle of my country, with Timochus on his way here. I've got too many friends hereabouts. But once we're within range of Apamea, he might well try.'

'But he wouldn't succeed,' said Judith, rapidly adding up Nicanor's supporters and Holofernes'. 'Would he?'

'Better not to take the risk.' Holofernes stood up. 'Here, let me help you.' He bent over her and stared at the bracelet, now clamped uncomfortably tight on her arm. He unwound the lowest loop and then, taking the band of metal carefully between his fingers, he worked his way up its length, stretching it at each painful curve. The relief was immediate.

'There.'

Judith looked down at her arm. She didn't know whether to laugh or cry. The bracelet had lost its symmetry and the lower end stuck out at an angle.

'I bet that's more comfortable.'

'Yes, it is.'

Manasses had given her this bracelet shortly after their marriage. For both of them it had symbolised the bright future they planned to share.

'No point wearing things that hurt you.'

'No. Thank you.'

'Your poor arm, it's bruised.' Holofernes stooped and kissed it. His hand crept round her waist. 'Oh well, I'd better go and work out how to settle Nicanor.'

Judith held him for a second, although she was relieved that he was going.

'What are you going to do?'

He smiled. 'Wait and see.'

'What's going on?'

'It's a row.'

'Nicanor's refused to lend Holofernes his servant.'

'So he should.'

'No, that's not it. Holofernes' man Bagoas took Nicanor's wine into their tent and Holofernes is claiming it.'

'No, no, Holofernes took Demetrius's envoy into his tent without Nicanor and then they sent out for more wine . . .'

Judith moved unobtrusively through the clusters of people. All afternoon, in the heavy shade of the oasis, Holofernes had been talking to the envoy. It was true that Nicanor hadn't been told of his arrival. She knew that because she had seen him playing dice half an hour after Holofernes had gone out to meet the envoy. But he had found out soon afterwards. She'd watched his angry progress to the tent.

Since then, they had all been in there together. They had sent out for more wine. Various men from the different companies had gone in to join them; some stayed, some came out with unsettled expressions and reports that the generals were starting to quarrel.

It was now evening. The heat had dropped and a warning tinge of violet had entered the air. Within an hour, darkness would be closing down on them. Judith had wondered if Holofernes would wait till tomorrow; he surely wouldn't want to provoke a crisis in the dark. But the sounds coming from the tent were unmistakable and as she watched, people moved away from the entrance and Nicanor burst out. His lieutenant came on his heels, and half a dozen of the Achaean men.

'Get my armoury!' Nicanor said to his lieutenant. His face was taut with anger and a dark flush had spread across his throat. 'Pack up the mules. Go and find me Sirio. He can come with us or not, but we're not staying here with that son of a slut.'

He was walking swiftly away from the tent, and the crowd popped and shifted alongside him, some people running to keep up. 'Tell the women to pack. Where's Nessus? He's got to take a message to my brother.' Nicanor's eyes swept the people on either side of him, seeking out those he needed. They came to Judith and for an instant they registered contempt. 'Come on, let's get out of here. There's too much vermin in this place.'

He surged off, taking some of the crowd with him. Those who stayed seethed in front of the tent, hurrying back and forth and trying to get information. Long minutes passed before Holofernes came out. He seemed relaxed and in no hurry. He had Jonathan with him, and Achior, his other lieutenant.

'Give the order for free passage,' he was saying to Achior. 'No one's to attack them or stand in their way unless they try to take what's not theirs. Put some men on guard.' He turned to Jonathan. 'Send someone to the settlement to let them know what's happening, and that it's no threat to them. All right, all right!' He raised his voice above the querulous din. 'Nicanor and his Achaeans are leaving. He's got ambitions that aren't healthy for the rest of us, so we don't want him here any more. That's all there is to it. There's nothing to get excited about. There'll be duty for some of you to ensure an orderly departure; the rest of us can get on with dinner.'

He looked around, hands on belt, apparently amused. He caught Judith's eye and gestured her towards him. She went as swiftly as she could, weaving through gaps in the crowd. The men were already splitting into groups around the lieutenants and organising themselves. They were small groups compared to those that had massed outside Bethulia. Judith realised that with Nicanor gone, they would be losing four hundred people at a stroke. Their army was shrinking steadily.

'That's done,' Holofernes said easily as she reached him.

'Come into the tent. I want you to greet Jason Timochus, the man Demetrius sent.'

In the tent a young man was sitting on the ground, spearing figs on a knife. He put the knife down when Judith approached, bowed and murmured a greeting to her, crossing his arm over his chest in the Syrian fashion.

'He's off,' Holofernes said to him succinctly. 'He'll be clear of us by nightfall. Let's drink to it – my wife will fill your cup.' Judith took the cup, replenished it and presented it to the young man. He accepted it with another bow. Holofernes grinned at him and signalled for Judith to sit behind them. One of the women servants came forward to give her a cup of wine.

'That went well,' Timochus said. He raised his cup to Holofernes and drank; his eyes were laughing.

'Yes, he's got too much pride for his own good, that one. He'll be straight off to Antioch now, to get in first.'

'Demetrius will give him a warm welcome.'

'Serve him right. Demetrius has several scores to settle with him over the Parthian business last year. Will it keep them both busy for long enough?'

'If you set off first thing tomorrow and go straight to Apamea, yes. From what the scout told me, Lucius Tullius will be there in two days.'

It was a long time before they were alone in their tent and Judith could ask Holofernes to explain.

'Timochus knows all about my plans to join forces with Lucius Tullius,' he said. 'He supports them. So when Nicanor began making trouble with the men, I got word to Timochus and we agreed we had to get rid of him. Today was a set-up. Timochus arrived on so-called urgent business and after we'd kept Nicanor waiting long enough to get him angry, we let him overhear us discussing a plan to go behind his back. We pretended to have set up a meeting between King Demetrius and Lucius Tullius and me, in Antioch.

'Nicanor burst in, we denied it all and you heard the rest. He believes I'm trying to cut him out, so he's rushed off to Antioch with all his men, to try and get to Demetrius and Lucius first. But Lucius isn't there,' he went on cheerfully. 'He's still heading for Apamea to meet me. By the time Nicanor has finished explaining himself to Demetrius, Lucius and I will be allies and no one will dare touch us.' Holofernes smiled wickedly and lay back on the cushions.

'Timochus isn't really Demetrius's man then? He's in it with you?' Judith drew the thongs off his legs carefully. She wanted to keep them both clothed as long as possible, so she could think.

'Timochus *is* Demetrius's man.' Holofernes bent his knees and shook his sandals off. He rolled on his side and caught Judith's arm between his hand and his mouth. 'In fact, he's Demetrius's cousin. But he's a realist and he knows that Demetrius can't hold on for more than a few years. For all its wealth and its past successes, Syria is under pressure. The Parthians are attacking us from the east and getting stronger all the time. We're having to rely on Rome more and more to help us out, It's only a matter of time before the Romans send a standing army in and Syria is ruled like a province, with Rome's ambitious young men coming out a year at a time to run things – with local help, of course.

'Now, I want to be in a position to provide that local help. That's what this is all about. Timochus wants that too. Whoever stands in well with the Roman governors will have huge power and influence, especially if they can deliver the backing of fighting men. Timochus would rather it was me than one of the generals from the older families because I'll reward him better, and he'd certainly rather it was me than Nicanor, who isn't even a Syrian. If Nicanor gets his hands on power in Antioch, Syria will be drained of everything. You can bet it's Syrians who'll be sent to Rome as slaves, it'll be Syrian money that goes to pay for Rome's expansion, and only Nicanor's Achaeans will benefit.'

All the time he was talking, Holofernes had been moving his mouth softly across her bare arm. Judith shivered involuntarily and his eyes flickered up to her face. He slipped his hand under her girdle.

Judith placed her hand on Holofernes', trapping it as his fingers worked to untie her girdle knot.

'But what has Lucius got to do with all this?'

'Lucius Tullius Bestia,' Holofernes gave a mocking bow, 'son of a senator, young man of morals and learning, is extremely ambitious. He has clearly decided to make his name in the east. My spies tell me that he's been very active on this campaign in Mesopotamia, making deals, getting what the Romans call *clientelae* – people who pledge their loyalty in return for protection.'

'Like allies, you mean?'

'Yes, except allies pledge loyalty to the head of a tribe or a state. Clients give it to an individual man. Noble Romans have had clients ever since Rome began. They used to be fellow Romans who voted for their patron and were protected by him but nowadays new clients are often recruited from the overseas provinces and their patrons are the Roman generals who led the campaigns there. These clients give their Roman patron money, arms, men, horses. They'll even go to Rome with him to give him support and a show of strength. It all helps a man who's keen to build a political career.'

Holofernes finished untying Judith's girdle. He placed both hands flat on her belly; deep inside her, something shifted in response to his touch.

'And that, my wife, is what Lucius Tullius is up to. Which is why now is the perfect time to strike a deal with him.'

'Why?'

'Because he needs me. I told you before, he's not naturally a military man. If he's to deliver protection to his clients, he's going to need someone who's fought in the region, who knows the terrain and understands the strengths and weaknesses of the various enemies. And that – is – me.'

In between words, Holofernes drew her robe apart and pressed his mouth to her skin.

'We'll be in Apamea in two nights' time,' he said, smiling against her stomach. The wiry hair of his beard scratched her flesh. In contrast, his tongue was very soft. The pleasure, always shot through with shame, made Judith put her arm across her eyes. 'And that's when you'll have a part to play. I've got to convince Lucius Tullius that I have not only military expertise, but authority in the area. So if he asks, you were sent into my camp as a token of esteem by your elders, and our marriage took place with their knowledge and their blessing.'

'Yes,' said Judith faintly. It felt strange, almost wicked, to think back to Bethulia and her old, sheltered life, the unending round of prayers and household duties, her censorious neighbours' eyes always on her.

What was it like there, now that the siege had ended? What was Endeyeh doing? Had they allowed her to go on living in her former mistress's house or was she back with Chabris and Sarra? For a second Judith fought to keep her mind there, but it was no good, Holofernes' caresses and his softened voice were dragging her away and all she could see were the walls of the tent and his bare limbs and, propped up against the chest, his sword.

The great ridge rose in the west, dark and knife-sharp. All day it had kept pace with them as they travelled. Now, however, as the train spread out across the hillside, Judith's eyes were all for the city.

It gleamed in the late afternoon light, square stone building on square stone building, with flights of steps, roof terraces, cisterns and conduits, all arranged in what seemed a purposeful pattern around the soaring, dizzying colonnade. The pillars were taller than any house, taller then the temple in Jerusalem, and they marched away down the centre of the city, further and further until Judith could no longer see the spaces between them.

'Apamea's not as rich as Antioch,' Holofernes had told her, 'but it's grand. The Greeks began building it and then some Greek-loving Romans carried it on. They keep adding to it – you know what they're like once they fall in love with the Greek way of doing things.' Judith didn't, but she had nodded all the same. 'It's a big trading centre now, and a garrison town. The Romans keep a legion there most of the time.'

Apart from the colonnade, two things struck Judith as she picked her way across the ground towards the city gate: the confidence of these people, living here with no walls to protect them; and the sheer number of soldiers swarming all around.

Holofernes had gone ahead with his various officers and

was talking to the soldiers at the gate. A man in a Roman toga and cloak was there too. 'Travellers' rooms,' the word was going round. 'The city's got lots of them. Who'll get them?' Judith thought of the one guest room in Bethulia, built into the wall by the gate; she had always been fascinated by the people who climbed up out of the desert and were admitted there. Surely as Holofernes' wife she would be one of the people taken into this city. She heard her name mentioned as people around her began speculating, and as she waited she noticed that movement was taking place in the train. People were gravitating to one side or another, and when she craned her neck she could see that at the gate, Holofernes' lieutenants were signalling. Bagoas was working his way back through the crush towards her, calling Holofernes' servants around him as he came. For the first time, Judith realised, she was about to taste Roman hospitality.

It wasn't a city guest room but a house, the house Lucius Tullius was staying in, no less. Holofernes was quietly jubilant.

'It shows he takes me seriously,' he said. 'And it shows the world as well. It's looking good.'

The house was large but, unlike a rich Judean home it didn't seem to be built round a courtyard. From the street it looked like a solid block, with a passageway burrowing into it. A few yards down the passageway, a door was opened to them and they stood in a small room, decorated with masks and busts. A second and more elaborate door was opened and they were ushered through. Suddenly they were in the light; here, after all, was a secret courtyard. Roof shelters offered shade along each side but the centre was open to the sky.

Holofernes, his lieutenant Achior, Bagoas, Judith and her servant were led across the courtyard, up onto a wooden platform at the end and through a curtain. The corridor was dim after the atrium but Judith could clearly see daylight filtering through from the far end. Men's voices came from a room to her left. Holofernes walked in, followed by Achior and Bagoas. Judith started to follow but one of the house slaves bowed in front of her. 'I'll take the honoured guest to her quarters. The women of the house will attend her there.'

Judith was tired and her head ached with a sharp silver pain. The women of the house all spoke to her in Latin and she could understand very little of it. She could ask simple questions but then she couldn't follow the answers. She was unsure whether the women were servants, slaves, prostitutes, 'companions' or people of note in Apamea. The one thing she had established was that they were not of Lucius's own family.

They came and went from her small room with polite explanations which she couldn't understand. At the moment all but two of them were gone, though she could hear their voices distantly, sounding sweet and clean as if they were out of doors.

Judith wished she was out of doors, but the male servant standing before her was carefully explaining that she must get ready. The household was preparing a feast to welcome Holofernes. The general himself was now being bathed and dressed in the ceremonial honoured guest's toga; the servants would be bringing ointments and perfumes for his wife to bathe too. Then she was to join her husband and their host Lucius Tullius in the triclinium, the dining room. Judith thanked him and pressed her hand against her eyes.

'Is the honoured guest sick?'

Judith hesitated, trying to summon up the Latin words she needed.

'Are you ill, madam?' To her surprise, the servant switched into her own language.

'I have a headache,' she said tentatively. 'We walked a long time in the sun.'

'Perhaps you'd like to walk in the peristylium? It's cool at this time of evening and you could wait there while the staff prepare your bath.'

The peri—?'

'It's a garden, within the walls of the house. Some of the other women are there now.'

The other women. Judith thought she would rather stay inside after all, away from the noise.

'My bath's nearly ready. I'll just bathe and dress.' She put out her hand as the man turned away. 'Are you Judean?' she asked curiously.

'I'm from Macedonia, madam.'

'You speak my language well.'

'I speak four languages. Many of us do.' And he was gone.

Many of us? Who were 'us'? The servants? The Macedonians? The people who inhabited this exotic, Greek-Roman-Syrian city, glittering on its hilltop?

As she watched the water and oils being brought for her bath, she could almost feel the city pressing in through the walls of the house making its raucous, polyglot demands. Trade routes converged here. Armies marched through. Judith of Bethulia, holding out her arms for scented oils to be poured over them, was lost.

It was still light when Judith followed the servant to the garden. Complicated shadows were interlaced in the doorways and corridors and she could hear the sound of running water ahead.

Lucius Tullius was with Holofernes in the peristylium, the servant had told her; he would receive her there. His tone had implied that this was an honour and Judith tried to remember what Holofernes and the scribe had told her about Roman manners. The house of nobles was a private place, and the atrium, the square room half open to the sky, was where visitors gathered. More important guests were received in the inner room, where Holofernes had gone. From then on, the deeper you penetrated into the house, the more of an honour it was. Unfortunately she had lost her bearings and couldn't tell which way she was going.

The servant turned a sharp corner and ducked sideways and Judith stepped between two pillars into a beautiful enclosed courtyard. A colonnade ran all round it; fish swam in a pool, two fountains played, marble statues lined the paths and bushes were dotted all around, many of them covered with dark pink blooms.

Standing by the pool were Holofernes and a pale man with short dark hair and a face like a hill cat. His eyes were set far apart, his nose was fine and as he turned to look at her, his face flickered with quick intelligence.

Judith stared at him. She heard the servant speak her name and realised that he was leading her towards her host. She glanced from Lucius Tullius to Holofernes and saw that her husband was looking vigorous and pleased; he seemed twice the width of the Roman.

Holofernes stepped out to meet her and took her hand.

'I present to you my wife, Judith of Bethulia,' he said in Latin. It was easy to recognise the phrase; he had taught it to her. 'She's honoured to be in your house, Lucius Tullius.'

'I'm honoured to receive you.' Lucius's voice was light; it

made the Latin sound more fluid.

'And I to be here,' she said.

Holofernes smiled and she realised that she had made a mistake with the simple response. 'My wife's just learning to speak Latin,' he said.

Lucius said something incomprehensible to Judith but it sent ripples of recognition over her. Greek, the language she had heard spoken in Jerusalem all those years ago when she had first met Holofernes. The language they had been forbidden to study in Bethulia.

'She doesn't speak Greek either,' Holofernes said, still in Latin. 'In her city the priests don't allow it.'

'It's as well you rescued her then.' Lucius switched into their language. He spoke it swiftly enough but with the emphasis in odd places. Holofernes looked surprised then pleased, and glanced at Judith as if to say, 'See, Aramaic now! He's everything I told you and more.'

'We'll speak your Aramaic for a while, madam,' Lucius said. 'We'll take it in turns to speak our languages, here in the city of travellers. But after that, you must learn the language of Rome quickly.'

'I will,' said Judith, returning his gaze. His eyes were grey-blue, unlike any she had ever seen. They were cool and yet in the blackness of the pupil an intensity burned.

He had turned now and was leading the way to one of the colonnades, his sandalled feet weaving through the bushes. Judith couldn't take her eyes off him; she had never seen anyone so alive.

The triclinium opened onto the colonnade, so that cool night air reached them as they sat on the couches. For the beginning of the feast, Holofernes' lieutenant and two of

Lucius's sub-commanders had joined them, but they left when the servants began to bring out the main dishes.

Holofernes and Lucius Tullius had been speaking Latin again. Lucius had slipped into it unconsciously when they began to discuss affairs of the senate and the consuls in Rome. Judith wasn't able to follow, though she listened as if she could understand every word.

Now the conversation had reached a pause and the two men turned back to her. Aware of their master's attention switching, the servants who had withdrawn to the shadows hurried forward and began lifting dishes of soft-cooked meat to her. Judith took small amounts; all the meat was cooked to a mush and though the taste was good, the softness revolted her. Lucius Tullius looked at her consideringly. 'How do you like our Roman food?'

'It's delicious. Your cook is very skilful.' Holofernes had told her to praise the cook if she could. She thought she saw amusement in their host's eyes. 'Most people in the east find the texture too soft,' he said. 'But this food is tough compared to what we eat in Rome. There, we eat shellfish fattened from the river, so soft and warm it dissolves in the mouth.'

Judith tried not to shudder. 'I'll look forward to it.'

'It will be one of many things you'll find different. Your husband tells me he's been teaching you how our state is run. So you understand about our consuls and senators and magistrates?'

'Some of it,' Judith said.

'And do you believe it's a good way to govern?'

Judith glanced at Holofernes. What did he want her to say now? She knew he had reservations about the Roman system – 'Too many high-born men jostling for position; too many ambitious sons of powerful fathers,' he had told her. But she could hardly say so to Lucius Tullius who was just such an ambitious son. Holofernes looked up from the date he was splitting and gave her a faint wink.

'Oh yes,' Judith said serenely. 'It's made Rome great, and your eastern provinces seem to live at peace under it.'

'Because we don't force them to live under it. We send them *propraetors* and governors, take tribute from them in the form of wealth and soldiers, but we don't impose our system on them. In many ways, the people of our provinces have more freedom than the nobles of Rome.' Lucius shot Holofernes a speaking look. 'As we were just saying.' He turned back to Judith. 'When you come to Rome, you'll find the young men less prominent than in the east. We have something called the *cursum honororum*, a path of deeds and public positions men have to follow before they can have influence. Our elders are the most important people in our society, as they are in yours, I think.'

Judith blinked. For a confusing moment, she wasn't sure what he meant by her society.

'The Judeans I've met are always talking about their elders,' Lucius added. 'And Holofernes tells me that you come from an elder's family yourself.'

'Yes,' said Judith, Chabris' face suddenly and unwelcomely clear in her mind's eye.

'Respect for one's elders is a strong social force,' Lucius remarked. 'And a moral force too. But in Rome, young men's abilities are being wasted. Young men themselves are being wasted. All they are allowed to do is fight endless campaigns. We have to serve in ten campaigns before we can put ourselves up for election to even the most junior magistracy. I have five more campaigns to go. Or I should have.' He turned his eyes from the flickering tapers to her face. 'Do I shock you?'

'No.'

'You surprise me. I'd have thought that coming from one of the old priestly families you'd have a reverence for tradition.'

'I do, for the good traditions.'

'Aren't all traditions good, in Jewish teaching? Your city is famous for its strict adherence to the old laws, Judith, and I understood your elders sent you into General Holofernes' camp as an example of all that was good and upright in the old Judea.'

There was a softness to his voice which wasn't entirely friendly. Judith thought again of the hill cat.

'In Bethulia I tried to lead my life according to the elders' teaching,' she said warily.

'And succeeded, it seems. So how did your husband convert you to our ways?'

'Oh, I've never tried to convert my wife.' Holofernes cracked open a walnut cheerfully in his palm. 'I have too much respect for her, and besides, I don't need to. She's given me her loyalty and that's enough for me.'

'Yes.' The taper flame was reflected, white and burning, in the depths of Lucius Tullius's eyes. He gazed at her for another instant before, with a tiny gathering of his muscles, he looked away. 'Yes, of course. In Rome, too, a wife's loyalty to her husband is political as well as personal. That's one thing you will find the same.' He looked from Judith to Holofernes, his expression volatile in the leaping light. 'A toast to that,' he said, making a gesture with his hands.

The servants glided forward. One lifted the ladle from the bowl of water and wine; another passed the men's cups to him and back again, brimming, into their outstretched hands. Lucius Tullius raised his deftly. 'To the loyalty and honour of wives in Rome, and the achievements of their husbands!' He and Holofernes tipped their heads back and drank.

'Clever, isn't he?' said Holofernes with satisfaction. They were in the guest room; from just outside came the noise of servants clearing up, from out in the City came more various sounds – voices, harp music, the cries of a moneylender.

'Very.'

'Don't be like that. Take it from me, you can't be too clever in Rome. We'll need every bit of his political skill, just as he'll need my military expertise.' He pulled at her girdle, and it fell to the floor. 'It's a good plan, Judith,' he said, 'We're thinking in the same terms – long ones. Lucius Tullius wants to be elected *propraetor* of one of the provinces across the Euphrates, in Mesopotamia. That's why he's started recruiting *clientelae* out there. Officially he's too young for a *propraetorship*, but if he can prove himself in a big eastern campaign and send lots of booty back to Rome, they might turn a blind eye to his age. For all they go on about honour and austerity,' Holofernes lowered his voice, 'money gets you anything in Rome.'

'We haven't got any money,' said Judith. She folded her arms across her breasts; she felt uneasy and jumpy.

'No, but we've got a thousand armed men. And we offer the promise of money. If we can get Lucius the command of a campaign against the Mesopotamians, I can bring off enough victories and treaties for Lucius Tullius Bestia to sail back to Rome on a tide of gold. After which you can bet he'll get a whole series of *propraetorships*. He'll be able to hop from one to another, all over the east, with me as his military commander, until we end up in Syria. Or perhaps even in Judea.'

Judith walked around the room. The earlier heat had dissipated and she was shivering. 'And what about me? I thought we were going to settle in Rome.'

'You will. You'll stay there while I'm away on campaigns and be a political wife.'

'They won't accept me.'

'Why not? Lucius Tullius did. You heard what he said about marriages in Rome being political. Oh, you won't be moving in the most exalted circles. But as long as Lucius needs me, there'll be other men's wives who'll want to be good to you, don't you worry. Anyway, if you don't like it, you can come and join me. You've had experience in the field now.' Holofernes grinned at her.

Judith stood still and looked at him. It was odd seeing him in a stone-built room after the weeks in a tent. The straight lines of the wall and the doorway framed his muscular body harshly, as if, now put together as a hospitable bedroom, they could also act as a prison. She was suddenly and unexpectedly anxious.

She walked up to him and laid her hand fleetingly against his cheek. 'Be careful.'

CHAPTER FOURTEEN

She saw Enzo from across the courtyard. He raised his hand in greeting and began walking steadily, unhurriedly towards her. Cathy might have thought he was simply strolling along taking the morning air if she hadn't caught his eye. Enzo's expression was pleasant but compelling. He intended to speak to her.

So, she thought, it had indeed been Nadia who came visiting yesterday. Rising late from their bed, drugged with sleep and love, she and Matthew had seen a neatly dressed woman cross the courtyard and ring Enzo's private bell.

'I wonder who that is, visiting on a Sunday.' Matthew had said. 'I've never seen her before.'

Cathy had said nothing. She couldn't be sure, after all. She and Matthew had been away from the palazzo for the rest of the day, exploring the Pincio Gardens and the Villa Borghese on the other side of Rome. On their return, however, Cathy had looked up at the south wing and seen Enzo gazing down at her. He had turned away and seemed to hesitate, irresolute. By the time he turned back, Cathy had tucked her arm possessively through Matthew's and was staring up into his face, with eyes for no one else.

Now it was Monday morning and Matthew was working in

the lab. And suddenly Enzo had materialised from the ground floor of the north wing.

'Good morning, Cathy. Are you on your way to the studio?'

'Good morning. What a beautiful day. Yes, I am.'

'I'm so glad. You've already had a fruitful time there by the look of it.' His smile travelled from her face to the portfolio she carried under her arm.

'Just sketches,' Cathy said vaguely.

'Ah. Studies for abstracts, may I ask? Or something rather more familiar to me?'

Cathy's heart started to pound. She had already decided to lie but with his eyes on her, it was harder than she'd expected.

'Abstracts.' She nodded and smiled pointlessly.

Enzo continued to look at her. She thought his face became less friendly.

'You don't mind my asking, do you?' he said, with just a touch of accusation in his voice. 'I'm naturally very interested in your ability to . . . reinterpret the Giuditta.'

'Of course. Naturally. But I'm afraid I haven't done any more of that since the drawings we showed you.'

'That's a shame. I wonder why. Perhaps all the attention frightened your muse into hiding.' He smiled very faintly. 'Well, I mustn't keep you.'

The studio was stuffy after the weekend. Hesitating in the doorway, Cathy was struck by the stillness of the atmosphere. She felt the air might ripple like water when she stepped in. She shook herself. *Don't start imagining things.* She walked briskly across to the far wall and set about opening the shutters. Light poured in but for the first few seconds it seemed only to intensify the stillness.

Determinedly, she opened the windows too. That was better:

cheerful weekday noises floated in, on a tide of warm air.

Now that the world felt within reach, Cathy shut the door to the corridor. She cleared a space on the worktable and opened her portfolio. The new drawings nestled in there, between other sheets she had put in for protective covering. She had done two over the weekend, in brief, snatched moments of solitude, the first when Matthew was in the kitchen making lunch, the second in the Pincio Gardens when Matthew had gone to buy ice creams. And there was a third, incomplete drawing, begun early this morning while Matthew still slept and then abandoned when he awoke. Cathy had been shaken to realise how compulsive the drawing was becoming. She had crept out of bed to begin this last sketch, thinking of nothing but the need to create it.

As yet, she had only the most fleeting impression of the scenes she had drawn. They had flashed onto her mind like frames of a film, running too fast for her to understand. It was only now, in the half inviting, half oppressive quiet of the studio, that they would be able to come into their own.

Cathy's hands shook as she laid them side by side. The camp at the oasis, with Holofernes squaring up to another man. Great pillars rising up on either side of a pavement. And the half-finished one: two men in a courtyard, drawn in silhouette only.

Cathy was already reaching for her pen. She couldn't stop herself; the need to draw was overpowering, like a thirst or a longing to sleep.

Matthew, she thought, as if to try and stave it off. Matthew. But then, when she looked at the figure of Holofernes, she thought she saw Matthew's eyes looking back at her. How could this be? On Friday, after she had seen Danilo, she had thought he resembled Holofernes.

As she looked, Holofernes seemed to shift, reminding her now of Matthew, now of Danilo. And as she began to draw in the features of the slender man in the courtyard, they too seemed familiar, teasing her with an impossible double likeness.

Matthew sat up straight to ease his aching back. His muscles were cramped from hunching over the painting, but it was a good ache, the physical cost of his work. He would willingly pay it again.

On the easel in front of him, the Giuditta was beginning to emerge. Her outline was clear now and he gazed at it. There was something throat-wrenching about the figure's beauty, the despairing strength in the arms, the tender way her fingers curved round the awful object. The swathe of hair, dark on dark.

He would be ready to lift the topmost layer of overpainting from the face next. Matthew stood up and reached out very gently to the canvas. He touched his fingertips to the disfigured face, tracing the line of the cheek, then moving across to rest where her mouth must be.

Under the clinical light of the overhead panel, Judith's eyes glowed.

Matthew found it hard to pull his hand away. As the contact broke he felt a distinct pang of loss. He walked restlessly over to the sink and started boiling the kettle for coffee. Once he was no longer immersed in the Giuditta, he would think about Cathy, and that troubled him.

It had been a beautiful weekend. They had locked themselves away in their apartment and made love for hours; got up and dressed and gone roaming through different quarters of the city; lazed in gardens, idled round galleries, held hands in cafes and restaurants, watched the lights of the riverside dim the stars as the night grew late. Cathy had been loving and passionate and funny. And it had all been slightly feverish.

Matthew sighed and spooned coffee into the jug. Don't think about it, he told himself. Don't go looking for trouble. There was enough out there already, with Danilo fighting his little war of attrition against his father. Could there be any truth in what Danilo had said? Matthew's instinct was to mistrust him, especially when it came to Cathy or the Bonaventura collection. But there was something uncomfortably persuasive in that story he'd given Cat. Certainly there was a darkness in Enzo's relationship with his son. The longer Matthew knew Enzo, the more he became aware of it.

He switched off the kettle, counted ten to let the water stop bubbling, and poured it into the jug. It smelt wonderful. He carried the jug and his cup back to the workbench and sat down at some distance from the easel. He wondered what Cat was doing now and instantly banished the thought, turning instead to look at the Giuditta. God, she was beautiful. Gratefully, almost guiltily, Matthew gave himself up to contemplating her.

Cathy raised her head from the drawings. She was exhausted. She blinked in the sunlight, trying to grow used to the sight of the studio furniture again. She had been far away, in a desert world.

She had been working for over two hours and the drawings had changed. They were no longer simple sketches but elaborate scenes. She had been moving from one to another, adding characters, details, expressions and gestures, even drawing plants and rock formations into the landscape. Her hand had moved obsessively, and as she drew, the events surrounding the drawings came back to her. The sights and sounds flowered in her mind, not in any orderly sequence but expanding all over the place, as memories do.

Now she felt drained, but her body wouldn't obey her desire to rest. Blood buzzed through her veins and her senses were sharp.

At least doing the drawings had brought one kind of relief. While she'd been in that world, her confusion about Matthew and Danilo had dropped away. There had been only Judith's feelings, and for Judith, Holofernes and Lucius could not have been more distinct. Holofernes was energetic and battle-tough; his touch was warm and he insisted that she should learn fast, shed her Bethulian ways and be his match. Lucius was a mystery. Outwardly calm, he seemed to Judith to burn with a secret fire. She thought he watched her but he said nothing.

In Judith's world, these men were opposites; it was only Cathy who confused the two. And, she saw bitterly, she continued to confuse them. She looked into those two male faces in the last drawing. Physically very different, and yet . . .

Her head snapped up. She could hear footsteps coming along the corridor, from the far end. Giovanni? Someone from the offices? Cathy slid the drawings into a neat pile and put her portfolio on top of them.

There was a knock on the door. 'Hello,' an Italian voice called. 'Is anyone in there? Something's been delivered to the office for you.'

'Coming.' Cathy glanced around the studio. No, there was nothing private on show. In fact, with the drawings covered up, the place looked unnaturally still again as if no one had worked in here for years.

Sylvana, one of the administration staff, stood outside.

'Sorry to disturb you, but this has just arrived.' She held an irregularly-shaped package, wrapped in brown paper. 'I brought it up at once because I thought it might be a piece of equipment you needed.'

'Thank you, that's very kind,' said Cathy. It didn't look like anything she'd ordered from the art shop; besides, their deliveries always came in boxes stamped with their name. Sylvana was holding out the package gingerly.

'There's something sharp,' she warned. 'Sticking through the paper there.'

Cathy thanked her and closed the door. She weighed the parcel in her hands and listened to Sylvana's retreating footsteps. When the heavy door at the end of the corridor had swung back into place, she carried the wrapped object to the table.

It rustled and something sharp pricked her finger. The pain was tiny and familiar. Suddenly Cathy was surrounded by a soft whirl of memories, like a dust storm.

Slowly, she peeled off the sticky tape and unwrapped the paper. Inside was a small bush, planted in a pot. Its leaves were toothed and grew in a rosette; from their midst rose a spike of pale yellow flowers, each one protected by a thorny, green and purple bract.

Cathy had never seen acanthus before, but she knew it. She put her shaking hand to her mouth and sucked the spot of blood. Then she picked up the card lying among the leaves. 'Acanthus Syriacus' it read. 'Found on the hillsides of Syria, near the ancient city of Apamea. From Danilo.'

* * *

Cathy swallowed the last drop of Martini and leaned against the bar. She wanted another, she could have drunk a whole bottle, but the second glass had already caused Bruno's eyebrow to lift.

Besides, she should get back to the studio. In her sudden panic she had left it unlocked; she hadn't even closed the door. The air in the room had seemed so close, as if it were trying to hold her in, and then in the stillness she had heard something, a sound like a human whisper. She had slapped her hands over her ears and run to the door, jumping out over the threshold and racing down the stone staircase, not thinking of anything except getting away.

Now, with two Martinis inside her and the familiar fittings of Bruno's bar all around, she had been able to think a little. She didn't understand what was happening to her and she was especially bewildered about Danilo's role in it, but she had made one decision: she would tell Matthew what was going on before it went any further.

It would take careful phrasing. She wouldn't let him see the extent of her attraction to Danilo, of course; that would be to hurt him pointlessly. Oh God, it was such a stupid accident of timing. If she and Danilo had met a couple of years ago things could have taken their course naturally. By now, any affair they might have would be long over, a fading memory.

But then she and Danilo would never have met if it hadn't been for Matthew. If she hadn't followed Matthew to Rome.

Cathy counted out money for the drinks, with much fumbling. She would go and seek out Matthew as soon as she'd closed up the studio; she would take the plant with her and hand it over to him in a kind of symbolic gesture. And the drawings? She felt an instinctive tightening in her belly and paused, her hands still crumpling lire notes. Yes, she told herself, the drawings too. She would put them together in the portfolio and take them to the lab

Cathy said goodbye to Bruno and walked quickly back across the road. The tower staircase was cool and musty and she was reluctant to enter it again. She shut the door behind her and set off up the stairs at a trot, which quickened to a running lope. She was breathless by the time she reached the top and the blood roared in her ears. She leapt in through the open landing door and stopped, dismayed. Enzo was standing just inside her studio, with his back to her.

Cathy's reaction surprised her. After the first consternation, she felt a protective fury. She wanted to rush past Enzo, push him back into the corridor and slam the door in his face. As he turned, she raked the room with her eyes. Her portfolio was still covering the drawings, thank God, and the plant was where she had left it on the table. She had got here just in time.

Enzo met her gaze coolly. All this morning's cheerfulness was gone from him, yet Cathy had the impression that he wasn't so much angry as shocked. His eyes had a sunken look.

'Hello, Enzo.' She was unable to control the aggressive edge in her voice. 'Have you come to see me? What can I do for you?'

Enzo raised one eyebrow. He did it slowly and it was very effective; all the same, Cathy sensed that she had the advantage.

'You can explain to me why you've been out, leaving all the doors and windows open.'

'Yes, I'm sorry. I wasn't thinking. But I did shut the door to the courtyard, and I was only across the road. I would have seen if anyone tried to get in.'

'That's hardly the point, Cathy. I asked you to be very careful about locking up.'

'I know, and I will be in future. I usually am. I apologise, Enzo, it won't happen again.'

Enzo nodded. His eyes were still on her face. 'It's not just the insurance, you know. We have press attention from time to time. Once they hear about Alessandra's collection, they'll start pestering us again. They've tried to get in here before now.' Enzo gestured to the courtyard. There was something tense in the way he moved.

What was it they said about people who looked you straight in the eye? That they were trying to fix your attention where they wanted it, to stop you noticing something else. Cathy looked to either side of Enzo and stiffened. The portfolio was still on the table but now she saw that it had been moved. One corner of it was wedged up against a stack of books and an edge of drawing paper showed beneath it.

Enzo hadn't believed her about the drawings; he'd been going through her things.

'I understand. I'll be careful.' Cathy heard her voice distantly. 'Was there anything else?'

'Yes.' Enzo's eyes were like black pebbles. He was going to ask her about the drawings now. What the hell could she say? She didn't know herself why she'd lied to him. 'I notice you have all the windows open. Is it too hot in here for you? I can ask Giovanni to bring up an electric fan.'

Cathy's heart beat wildly; what was Enzo playing at? 'It's fine, thank you. I just like to hear the sounds of the street.'

'The noise doesn't distract you?'

'No. I like hearing life going on around me.'

'Yes, it must be very quiet for you up here. And of course,

working alone as you do, I imagine you can feel quite isolated.'

'Sometimes. But then it's good to have the space to myself. And the solitude to concentrate.'

'Yes,' said Enzo very quietly. 'That's what Alessandra found.' He suddenly looked exhausted. He moved aside to allow Cathy into the studio. They stood without speaking, measuring up to each other like combatants.

Deep lines had settled round Enzo's mouth, marks of weariness, and for a moment Cathy passionately wanted to confide in him. He was only an old man after all, struggling to come to terms with his grief, and he had never shown her anything but generosity. She didn't want to fight him, or even resist him.

But just as she decided to speak, Enzo said, 'I shall leave you.' His voice was as dry as old leaves and as brittle. He nodded to her, with a faint wraith of a smile, and walked to the door.

He was holding himself very erect, and she had the impression it cost him a great effort. He held the door with his right hand and turned awkwardly; as he disappeared into the corridor, Cathy saw his left hand move to his jacket pocket and slip something small and white into it. He had taken Danilo's card.

Matthew recognised the authoritative double rap at once. He pushed his stool backwards and put some distance between himself and the painting just as the door opened.

'Good afternoon, Matthew.'

'Hello, Enzo,' Matthew took a last look at the canvas as he stood up. Was it afternoon already? He had been too rapt to notice. He hadn't done any more actual work on the painting –

he had to wait for this last lot to dry – but he'd been looking at it, sunk in concentration about it, though it was difficult now to say exactly what he'd thought. He tore his gaze from it and turned to Enzo.

'I've lifted a lot of damage from the neck,' he said. 'You'll see it at once. The colours aren't quite what I expected; there are deep olive tints, unusual for the period.' He watched Enzo's face as he approached the easel. What he really wanted to see was an answering light to the one he knew shone in his own eyes. What he really wanted Enzo to say was, 'Beautiful. Beautiful.'

But Enzo looked troubled. He stopped five feet away from the painting and stared at the emerging flesh without speaking. He nodded. 'You're making good progress.'

'Well, so far I've been doing the easier parts. The hair's going to be a problem. It shades into the background anyway, and the overpainting's so thick there that it's going to be difficult to lift it and keep the integrity of the painting.' Matthew gestured to the dark halo round the Giuditta's head and shoulders. He enjoyed tracing that subtle line through the air. Enzo nodded again, but his attention wasn't on the painting.

Matthew, looking down at him from what he felt to be a great height, thought Enzo seemed diminished. The energy that usually emanated from him was out.

'Matthew,' said Enzo, 'do you know that Cathy's still drawing the Giuditta?'

For a second, everything seemed to stop. Matthew had the impression of vast tracts of time and space stretching out around him and isolating him. It seemed curiously familiar.

'Yes,' he replied, 'I think I do.'

'What do you mean, you think?'

Matthew had stood up from the stool; now he sat down again. 'Cathy said something on Friday that made me think she'd done more drawings. I asked her if she had and she said no. But,' he looked at Enzo, trying to work out just why he was telling him this, 'I don't think I believed her.'

Enzo was standing on the other side of the workbench, regarding him with an expression of utter bleakness. 'You think she lied to you?'

Matthew looked at his hands. 'Not lied exactly. Well, yes, I suppose it was a lie technically, but I probably shouldn't have asked her. Perhaps she just wasn't ready to talk about the drawings.'

'Does she usually talk to you about work in progress?'

'Yes, she does.'

'Do you have any idea why these drawings should be different?'

'Not really.' Matthew shrugged. 'They seem to have touched some personal response in her.' The figure of Danilo loomed in his mind and he had to peer through it to see Enzo. 'Has Cat shown you some more drawings, then?'

'On the contrary, only this morning she denied having done any more. But half an hour ago I saw them in her studio.'

Matthew watched Enzo in silence. 'You saw them?' he asked eventually.

'I found them hidden under her portfolio. Rather hurriedly and ineffectively hidden. I got the impression that she had been interrupted in her work by a delivery.'

Matthew laughed incredulously.

'Hidden? You mean you searched the studio?'

Enzo's face was grey, and he ignored the question.

'Matthew, I must ask you something. Has Cathy been seeing Danilo?'

Matthew's mind went blank. His only thought was that he was cold, and that in the heart of the coldness burned a small, fierce heat. When he spoke, his voice sounded far away. 'She saw him on Friday. He took her round the Ghetto and told her about the history of the quarter. She said it was very interesting.'

'And you don't mind?'

'Why should I mind?'

'Matthew. You and your stepsister are obviously very close. The exact nature of your relationship is a matter for the two of you alone and I have no wish to pry, but I know my son. He's interested in Cathy. He's also been hurt very badly by what happened to him as a child.'

'Scarred,' murmured Matthew bitterly. Weren't romantic heroes always scarred by some long-lost injury?

'No, not scarred. That implies healing. Danilo's wound is still open. He still bleeds. Matthew, I know how melodramatic this must sound to you but try to put aside your Englishness and your very correct schooling just long enough to believe me. Danilo is seeking recompense and such people are always dangerous, to themselves and others.'

'Oh, I believe that,' said Matthew. 'But why is he interested in Cathy? Is it just out of rivalry with me?'

'No. Danilo has . . . ' Enzo looked through Matthew. 'He has certain ideas about the Giuditta. That's why the painting has been locked away for so long. He and I reached an agreement, years ago, that it should remain under lock and key and be seen by no one but ourselves. Cathy's drawings have changed that.' Enzo's eyes refocused on Matthew. They were weary. 'The palazzo is a strange place, full of memories, stained by tragedy.

Danilo saw his mother suffer and he suffered with her; he's haunted by the knowledge of what she went through, as am I. But whereas I have been haunted only through the second half of my life, the pain has grown up with him. His longing for his mother and the fantasies which comforted him in adolescence are still potent for him. They've been reawakened by Cathy's drawings. But Danilo is a man now, and a powerful one and I'm worried about where this will end.'

Matthew swallowed; his rational mind told him Enzo was talking morbid nonsense, but his throat was dry as sand and that sense of isolation was on him again.

'Enzo, I understand that you're worried about your son,' he said carefully. He took comfort from the patronising croon in his voice. 'It's natural. But all he's done is take Cathy out to lunch and give her a guided tour. Cat's an adult and if anything else develops, I'm sure she can handle it.'

The old man regarded him for several seconds. Matthew felt his foolish bright expression stiffen in place.

'Other things are already developing. Cathy's drawings are no longer of Judea, they're of the Syrian desert and the ancient city of Apamea. Alessandra, too, painted Judith in those settings, and she talked about them to Danilo. They became part of his emotional landscape – I suppose you might call it his private world. This morning, the office staff tell me, they took up a package to Cathy. It was a gift from Danilo. I've seen it. It's a strange-looking plant with spiky leaves, like a cross between a thistle and an orchid.'

Enzo took a small white card from his pocket and put it on the bench. Danilo's handwriting stared up at Matthew.

'Acanthus Syriacus, he tells her,' said Enzo. 'Now that's a coincidence, isn't it?'

* * *

Night had fallen and Matthew was hungry, so much so that he had a pain in his gut. Or was that anger? It was like a white line, clamping everything together.

Cat was lying to him. The loving weekend had been a sham. And now she was waiting for him to go back across the courtyard to their apartment so that she could lie some more.

She had already come over here to find him, just before eight o'clock when the light had begun to fail. She had knocked on the door and tried to open it, then, discovering it locked, she'd called out to him. He hadn't answered and eventually she'd gone away.

He looked at the Giuditta. He'd been working at it on and off for hours, in spates of furious activity. When he was close up to it, squinting to see and using his hands as gently as he knew how on the roughened surface, the woman seemed to escape from her outlines and hover all around him, dwarfing the canvas and engulfing him in a subtle glow.

But he couldn't do any more on her; he was too tired, he risked harming her further. Besides, he would have to face Cat some time. He didn't want to talk; he didn't want to think. He had thought that if he played it carefully, he could manage to have everything, but it was all going wrong.

'Matt, please talk to me!' Cat's face was white. Her skin seemed to have stretched tight over her cheekbones and jaw.

'Why?'

'I need to know what Enzo's said to you. He's said something awful, hasn't he?'

'You tell me. What is there exactly that he could say to me?'

'He has. Why didn't you let me into the lab? I knew something was wrong.'

Matthew had never seen Cat like this. She was jumpy and her voice cracked across two notes. Despairingly, he walked round her and down the hall. She followed, plucking at his arm.

'I've got to talk to you, Matt. I'm frightened, I don't know what's happening.'

'And I do,' said Matthew quietly. Cathy stood back and let him go into the kitchen ahead of her.

'Look,' she said, 'I can guess what Enzo said. He's angry because I've been doing more Judith drawings and I didn't tell him. Then Danilo sent me a plant today, with a message on it connected to my drawings, and Enzo saw it. He stole the message, Matt. First he came into the studio when I wasn't there and went through my things, then he stole the florist's card.'

Matthew spun round to look at her. She stood framed in the doorway, her eyes wide, panting slightly.

'You've been seeing Danilo.'

'No, how could I have been? We've been together all weekend. I only saw him on Friday and I told you about that.'

'Then much more must have happened on Friday than you said.'

Cat shook her head. 'No, I've been thinking about it too, and there wasn't anything.'

Matthew put his hands to his temples. 'Why are you lying to me, Cat?'

'I'm not.'

'Yes, you are. You've been doing these drawings and lying about it. And you've been dreaming and denying it. It makes sense now. I knew there was something not right about the weekend. I'm not an idiot, Cat.'

She crossed her arms and clutched at her shoulders, a curious gesture that seemed to belong to a different kind of woman. She was shivering slightly. Matthew's heart felt as heavy as a rock.

'Don't lie any more, I can't bear it. I know I've rushed you into this. I was always afraid you might not go through with it. Tell me two things honestly. Are you still having those dreams?'

'Yes,' said Cathy through trembling lips.

'Is Danilo in them?'

Cathy just looked at him. He wasn't sure if it was pity or shame in her eyes.

'I see,' he said. He picked up a bottle of wine and a corkscrew, pushed blindly past her and shut himself into the spare bedroom.

Chapter Fifteen

To the south, the sea was dark blue, a calm unfathomable expanse, unmarked by their ships' passage. The island of Lesbos, round which they had sailed, looked as mysterious from this height as it had done from the water. Its wooded slopes kept its secrets close, and according to Lucius its secrets were great ones, for among those trees had lived some of Greece's greatest poets: Arion, Alcaeus, Sappho.

Judith lifted her face to receive the welcome buffeting of the wind and watched Lucius. He stood a few feet away from her, his back to the sea, and his eyes feasted on the great terraced marketplace, the agora, crowded with people, on the gymnasium beyond it, and on the pillared temple built on the very summit of the hill.

'Assos,' he said wonderingly. 'What do you say now, Judith? Wasn't it worth coming out of our way to stop here? Didn't I tell you this was one of the beautiful places of the world? I sailed here once before and recognised it at once for what it is – a place of truth. It was built by great men for great men. Aristotle, the philosopher, lived here. He stayed three years, as a guest of the city's ruler. He married the ruler's daughter.'

'It is very beautiful.'

It was, but not in the splendid way of Apamea, with its

pavements and colonnades and buildings raised to a pattern. This was a simpler beauty. The hilltop city had been carved out of the cliff and laid with carefully dressed stone. The agora was long and broad, walled with two tiers of stone blocks. Shallow steps led out of it at each end. Beyond it the gymnasium was protected by semi-circular walls. Wide stone walkways, flagged and levelled, linked the public spaces, while on either side of them the houses clustered.

'Do you see how it works?' Lucius said. 'You can pass from the agora to the gymnasium directly. From either you can go straight up to the temple. Every part of the city is open to every other part, and all the people, high and low, pass through the agora constantly. The plan of the city encourages debate, and contest.' He looked at her. 'These are Greek arts worth learning. This is what I mean when I say I want to take the Greek gifts home with me.'

Judith nodded. She was used to hearing Lucius extol the Greek arts, but today for the first time she felt she understood why. She had been apprehensive about leaving the ship and making the steep climb to the outlandish city, perched high above the sea. All the elders' warnings against decadent Greek ways had returned to her and she had walked up the path between Lucius and Holofernes reluctantly, fearing that she would be shocked or frightened by what she saw, or that her ignorance would be exposed.

But the men standing talking in the lower segment of the agora – debating, Lucius said – had a pleasing dignity, and the steady stream of men and boys making their way to the gymnasium drew her eyes after them enviously. Holofernes had already followed them, pausing to make Lucius promise that he would come too. Meanwhile, Lucius seemed content to stand here on the lower edge of the agora with her.

But no, Judith thought as she looked at the Roman; content was too weak a word to be applied to him. Rather he looked exultant, transfigured by what he saw. And as she often did, Judith found his intensity disturbing.

The weeks in Apamea, followed by another couple of weeks at sea, had thrown Judith a good deal into the company of Lucius Tullius Bestia. She was no longer afraid of him – she had no reason to be. As Holofernes had explained to her, Lucius had entered into a partnership with him and therefore Judith, as his wife, had an immediate claim on Lucius's respect and his protection. Lucius had lived up to this. In Apamea he had treated her with unfailing courtesy and arranged for her to have servants, clothes and jewellery. Since they had been at sea, the courtesy had changed into a more open friendship. The cramped conditions had made anything else difficult. When Lucius wanted to talk frankly to Holofernes, it often had to be in front of Judith. And so as they sailed westwards, Judith had discovered that Lucius admired Greek learning passionately; that he regarded several senators in Rome as his opponents; that he had defied his father by refusing to go on a third campaign to Numantia and coming east instead; and that he suffered, when moods were on him, from a dark sense of obligation to his ancestors. At such times he would argue angrily in support of the very traditions that were holding him back.

Holofernes sometimes mocked Lucius then, or tried impatiently to chaff him out of it. And Lucius would turn his clear grey eyes on Holofernes and Judith would wait, partly nervous, partly in anticipation, to see whether he would withdraw into his peculiar cold silence or break into the sudden, equally peculiar laughter.

Judith might not be afraid of Lucius any longer, but she was not sure of him. He was fierce in everything he did and sometimes Judith felt the pull of his personality so strongly that she had to concentrate in order to resist.

He was looking at her now, his face alive with smiles, and he was speaking.

Judith smiled back. 'I don't understand the Greek language, Lucius Tullius.'

'No, but you should. You've learnt Latin quickly enough. I'll tell one of the Macedonian slaves to teach you Greek too.'

'You're very ambitious for me.'

'You'll need Greek if you're to run a governor's house in Syria. But you should learn for the sake of the tongue, and the ideas that are expressed in it. The Greek arts, together with the Roman virtues, are the future of the world. And people like us – you and I and Holofernes – should be people who belong everywhere.'

Judith raised her hands to her hair which was blowing loose from her combs. The combs were her own, from her marriage chest in Bethulia; but on her wrists jangled bracelets studded with Syrian carbuncles and round her neck hung a Greek neckchain of pearls and rough emeralds. These were the outward signs that she no longer belonged to just one place.

'I thought you said that a Roman always belonged in Rome.'

'Ah yes, Rome first and last. But Rome can be carried to other countries, just as other countries can be carried to Rome. So we link lands and peoples and grow strong.' Lucius was looking at her intently. His cheeks were touched with colour as if he had been running and his eyes were bright.

Judith laughed suddenly, feeling very free. It seemed a daring act; she was so used to thinking before she spoke and listening hard, fitting her words to those she heard other people say. Holofernes expected it of her, she knew; she saw the gleam of approval in his eyes when she rose to a new occasion. It pleased her but it wearied her too. She was glad that Holofernes wasn't with her now, to witness this. He would have laughter buried in his eyes at the sight of Lucius Tullius Bestia, young scion of Rome, talking to Judith of Bethulia as if she were a queen. Lucius's gaze was clear and free of mockery and she allowed herself an instant to forget Holofernes and her past, and the memory of her shame in Bethulia.

'Help me learn Greek,' she said.

The sky was overcast and as the carriage lurched along the road between strips of cultivated land, long shafts of light appeared round the clouds, then vanished again. The noise had risen among the ranks of marching men behind them; here in the leading carriage a tense quiet reigned.

Holofernes leaned against the side of the carriage, his fingers drumming on the painted wood and his back very straight. Judith could tell that he longed to be out of the carriage and marching at the head of the ranks. For the third time in as many minutes, he signalled to Marcellus Paullus, the young officer leading the march, and pointed out to him something amiss on the cart piled high with eastern merchandise.

By contrast Lucius seemed scarcely aware of the procession. He sat rigid, his eyes fixed on the hills of Rome that were now drawing nearer with every bumping clatter of the carriage. Judith watched him gazing at the slopes and wondered what he found to hold his attention there. She had been staring just as long as he had, trying to make out what he was seeing. The hill to the right was heavily wooded at the top and covered with dwellings below. Was that the Palatine hill Lucius had told her about, where the nobles chose to live? There were certainly no palaces that she could see, but then Lucius had also said that it was considered dignified for powerful men and their families to live modestly. Or was the hill to the left of that the Palatine? There were some large houses towards the summit, but they appeared to be jumbled among smaller buildings, and there was nothing stately about the streets.

Holofernes had finished talking to Marcellus Paullus now, and Judith moved towards him to claim his attention.

'Which of these hills is the Capitol?' she asked quietly. 'That's the holy hill, isn't it, that looks over the Forum? I thought we were going to enter the city that way.'

'You'll see it in a moment.' Holofernes gave her an amused glance. 'The land plays tricks coming into Rome. You see that low hill there, which looks as if it's the other side of the river? It's this side, and it's blocking the view. Once we're clear of these terraces, you'll know what you're looking at all right. Meanwhile,' he dropped his voice, 'don't look so disappointed.'

Judith moved away from him with dignity. She wished that Holofernes' eye were less acute; he was almost always able to read her reactions and it made her feel at a disadvantage. She knew that he expected her to live up to him, yet it was difficult to do so when he made comments like that. She turned away from him and went back to surreptitiously watching Lucius.

He met her eyes briefly but made no sign of recognition. Ever since they had been within sight of Rome, he had been growing more withdrawn. Judith had the impression that he was bracing himself to bear a heavy load, and that it was descending on his shoulders now, even as she watched. It was not the exultant homecoming she had expected.

The carriage swung round a bend in the road, a noise like a sighing shout went up from the men around them, and suddenly, across a plain and a dark brown river, the city had doubled in size. There was what must be the Capitol, a smaller hill than the others, with two peaks, each crowned with a temple; and spreading out at its foot a collection of great buildings, some pillared, some blank-walled, some raised on high steps.

Judith caught her breath. The sight of the Forum struck her like a physical blow, and then the next moment she was thrown onto the floor of the carriage and Holofernes was shouting and clambering over the side. She saw Lucius's white face hanging at a strange angle, as if it was the sun turned human and come down from the sky. It took her some time to lever herself out of the carriage onto the ground where the splintered wheel had come to rest.

It was a whole hour later when Judith stood on the far side of the river, listening to men's strange cries.

'Oh, what a terrible misfortune!'

'Jupiter, what a terrible misfortune!'

'Jove! What a misfortune has befallen me!'

The soldiers' exclamations rose into the air, one after another, as they each tore their cloaks and stepped onto the bridge. Two hastily woven wreaths of fig and olive floated on the water beneath, and three men stood by the devotional fire, tending the flames to make sure they stayed alight as the crossing continued. Judith, Holofernes and Lucius, having gone across first without mishap, waited together. Not until all the men were safely across and all propitiatory gestures completed would the three resume their journey at the head of the procession. Meanwhile they stood clustered around the small temple to Concord which overlooked the bridge. Lucius turned his amulet continually between his fingers. At regular intervals he intoned the same prayer: 'Jupiter, if we have offended you, we offer amends. Bless our entry into Rome and turn the bad auguries to good.'

Judith shivered as she watched the long line of men march towards her, then turn onto the northward road. Face after face flashed onto her eye and all looked stricken. It was a bad omen to stumble at the beginning of any undertaking, but for their leaders to crash to the ground just as they were approaching Rome was enough to strike fear into the bravest.

She, too, raised her hand to her neckchain and touched the amulet which Lucius had given her. It felt cold and unfamiliar, and she asked it for protection silently, not knowing what she, a foreigner, could expect from these Roman gods.

Once they were further along the road, crowds began to gather. People surged around, calling out greetings and pointing at the cart piled high with merchandise. Boys ran alongside the Syrian men and called questions to them. 'Where have you come from? Are you from the east? Are those Syrian spears?' Older men and women cheered the soldiers they recognised.

To Judith, it seemed that the city was growing in every direction and that it now surrounded them, threatening to swallow them up. To the right, the public buildings of the Forum towered; away to the left spread the lower city, a jumble of rickety buildings leaning against one another, many of them falling down. Higher up past the Forum, crowded streets ran amok over the hillsides. It was hard to get her bearings with the people pressing on all sides and pointing at her and Holofernes.

She was not sure exactly when the procession broke up and they left the wide road to climb the narrower streets, but suddenly she realised that she was entering a different kind of space. She and Holofernes and Lucius, with Marcellus Paullus behind them, were crossing a wide pavement. People swirled about them in a businesslike manner, drawing aside to let them pass. Around the edges of the space, in the shade of the great buildings, citizens talked energetically, pursued transactions, bought and sold. Richly dressed women were carried through the throng in litters; behind the pillars of one of the larger buildings, moneychangers were at work. At the foot of a flight of steps leading down from a plain-walled building, men in striped togas were in austere conference.

They were in the Forum. Holding herself very erect, Judith walked behind Lucius and Holofernes until they came to a halt at a small temple, standing alone. Here, unassumingly and briskly, Lucius gave thanks for their safe homecoming.

'Lucius Tullius, it's good to see you back. We were expecting you more than a week ago. Did you have trouble?'

The man who had just entered the atrium was tall and broad, and a good fifteen years older than Lucius. He had a soldier's air about him, and held on vigorously to Lucius's elbow as he spoke.

'No trouble,' said Lucius, smiling. 'We sailed off course to stop in Assos.'

'Oh, naturally.'

'Yes, naturally.'

The man shook his head. 'You recruited more than a thousand Syrians and brought them all back via Assos? Did they appreciate it?'

'This one did.' Holofernes stepped forward and held out his hand to the older man. 'Do you remember me, Marcus Strachus?

It's an honour to meet you again.'

Marcus Strachus's face split into a grin. 'General Holofernes. I heard you were on your way back, but I didn't know whether to believe it or not. So it really is you.' He clapped his hands round Holofernes' arms. 'Well, well. You've had success in Crete and Judea, I hear.'

'The east is changing, Marcus Strachus. I told you that last time we met.'

'And you mean to make it change some more. Well, I'll join you in that.' Marcus glanced at Lucius. 'And Lucius Tullius, of course,' he said hurriedly.

Lucius nodded. He looked from Marcus Strachus to Holofernes with interest and, Judith thought, a degree of caution. 'It will be a privilege for me to work with two such proven generals,' he remarked. 'Tell me, Marcus Strachus, how much of our plans has become public? I was very careful in what I said to you in my message, as you know.'

'Yes, and I've kept your counsel. But army gossip is a terrific thing. Even before you set sail from Syria, we'd heard you'd recruited from Mesopotamian and Syrian *clientelae*. And by the time I received your letter, Holofernes' name was already being bandied about. So people have drawn their own conclusions and it's widely believed that you're planning some joint campaigning east of Antioch.'

'In which case, we'd better get our heads together and regain the initiative.'

'My thoughts too. By Mars' shield, I'll be glad to get to some practical work. When shall we start?'

Lucius spread his hands apologetically. 'As you see, I've been back only an hour. There are four clients over there who need attending to,' he gestured to three men and a boy who were being served drinks on the couch just inside the vestibule, 'and before I can settle anything, I must go and see my father. He was in the Comitia when we came through the Forum so I haven't been able to pay my respects yet.'

'Ah yes, good idea,' said Marcus Strachus. He looked awkward. 'An honourable man, your father. But I should warn you, rumours of your plans have reached him too. He's not best pleased, by all accounts. He still believes you should do another campaign in Numantia.'

'I'm well aware of that.' Lucius turned abruptly and signalled to the servants to bring wine and water. 'Marcus Strachus, if you'll stay here in my absence, General Holofernes will tell you how our ideas are advancing.' Lucius paused, and for the first time in the conversation, looked at Judith. She had been standing quietly all this while, knowing that she must be presented sooner or later, concentrating meanwhile in order to understand the visitor's gruff Latin. Now she tried to control her discomfort as the older man stared at her with frank curiosity.

Perhaps Lucius saw it, for a smile flickered across his face. 'General Holofernes has brought a new wife with him,' he said lightly. 'She is Judith of Bethulia, an elder's daughter from the Judean town our friend besieged.'

'I'd heard of a wife,' said Marcus Strachus. He bowed with heavy grace. 'I'm honoured to meet her, General Holofernes. We'll make her welcome in Rome.'

'Judith is renowned in Judea for her beauty and her virtue,' Lucius said musingly. 'She comes to us as a symbol of success in the east.' Then, still looking at Judith with a hint of speculation, he bowed and walked away.

Marcus Strachus shifted from foot to foot and looked uncertainly at Holofernes.

Holofernes frowned and shrugged. 'My wife,' he said. He reached out briskly for Judith; as his hand closed on her wrist, she felt his sudden irritation. 'Our marriage was one of the more unexpected things to come out of my commission for Demetrius.'

'Well, marriage is like that,' said Marcus Strachus. 'I wouldn't be married to Valeria Iulia if her brother hadn't been consul during the Pergamum trouble. But she's been a good, loyal wife, much better than I'd have thought. Honoured to meet you, madam,' he said, enunciating clearly into Judith's face. 'Welcome to Rome.'

'My wife Judith is educated,' said Holofernes drily. 'She speaks Latin quite well.'

'Oh, good, good. I didn't realise. Look, let me send one of my slaves back to our house to tell Valeria to come and call on her.'

'Yes, do that.' Two slaves approached with wine and water and Holofernes dropped Judith's arm. He took one of the offered cups and swallowed quickly. Then he seemed to recollect himself. He held up his cup to the older man. 'Your health, Marcus Strachus. May we prosper together.'

'Your health, General. And our shared prosperity.'

'Now,' Holofernes dropped his voice. 'Let's take this into the study, the tablinum, shall we? We don't want to be talking strategy in here with all these clients around. And Judith can go into the peristylium till Valeria Iulia comes.'

Now that the heat had gone from the afternoon, the city was teeming. Judith walked alongside Valeria Iulia, trying to keep one corner of her stola draped over her head as the other woman did, and wondered if she would ever find her own way around Rome.

It wasn't only that the place was vast and busy, the city itself seemed designed to baffle. Streets had no pattern. Lucius's house was on the Palatine hill with the dwellings of other nobles, but big houses and humble shops stood next to each other; flights of steps, which must once have led somewhere, broke off short; buildings stood aslant and crosswise, making a nonsense of the streets. Valeria was Roman born and bred but she had already lost her way once and they had walked through streets of leather tanners, book makers, sandal makers, silversmiths, copper makers, dye blenders and gemstone traders before one of Valeria's slave women had led them back in the right direction.

Now the Forum came into view beneath them and Valeria paused to instruct Judith in its institutions. Judith turned her head obediently and listened to Valeria's light, slightly sardonic voice. Valeria was younger than she had expected, only a few years older than herself, but she was disconcertingly sophisticated. And she was obviously a political wife. She seemed to take it as a matter of course that Judith would be active on Holofernes' behalf, just as she was for Marcus Strachus, and she was wasting no time in educating Judith in the workings of Roman public life.

Judith listened hard, anxious to keep up. She strained her eyes trying to distinguish one great building from another and tried to memorise their functions. There was the Curia where the senate met and the Comitium where men converged to make political alliances and trade favours; in the long, pillared Basilica Porcia, businessmen carried out deals. The Macellum was that huge low building, under whose roof the ancient provisions market was now unified. And dotted between these buildings were trees, fountains and temples, all of which,

Valeria informed her, tended to become the focus for certain groups of people at different times.

The Forum was even more crowded now than it had been this morning when Judith had seen it for the first time. But now its character was noticeably less austere. Within the imposing precincts, people strolled and jostled, hailed one another, laughed, whistled and, most of all, loitered.

'This is the rumour hour,' Valeria said as they resumed their downward path. 'The formal political business happens in the morning. That's when men bring their clients here to press for measures in their interest; when debates are held and judgements are read out, and sometimes assemblies are called. Wives aren't supposed to be present at the political business unless it's a matter that affects their family – or unless it's something of great importance to the city. But if there's something interesting going on, we simply come down to the market. That way we can both keep an eye on what's happening to our men and hear what all the merchants and slaves are saying. You'd be surprised what they can tell you sometimes; they don't miss much.

'But now,' Valeria smiled with satisfaction, 'it's rumour hour when everyone comes here, to listen and talk and pick up the latest news. Oh look – no, don't look, just keep on walking. We're being watched by Cornelia Gracchus, no less. She's the mother of the two most up and coming men in Rome. They'll be successful if she has to kill for it. Now if *she's* staring at us, this alliance between Lucius and your husband must be as promising as my Marcus says it is. How exciting. Perhaps we'll be invited to her atrium one of these days.'

'Holofernes told me about her,' said Judith, looking surreptitiously at the stern-faced woman peering from between the curtains of her litter. 'She's influential with all the powerful men, isn't she, and has them to her house to discuss business of state?'

'Yes, she's started quite a fashion for it,' said Valeria. 'Not that I've been in her atrium, and Marcus isn't received there very often. He's a new man, you see. Lucius's father is a regular, of course, being a senator, and I dare say Cornelia will be wanting to have Lucius himself there more often now. She likes to keep a close watch on young men who might rival her sons.'

'What do you mean, a new man?' Judith asked, puzzled. 'I thought Marcus Strachus came from a long line of generals.'

'Oh, that's true, he does. And his great-grandfather was a consul and a senator. But to be truly noble in Rome your last *three* generations must have held a high magistracy. And although both Marcus's grandfather and father were generals, neither of them lived long enough to hold high office. They both died in battle before they could be elected. So the family had to start again and that makes Marcus a new man.' Valeria drew breath and smiled mischievously at Judith.

'You'll come to understand it. Oh, look. There's Lucius. He's talking to a friend of his father's. There's no sign of Aulus Tullius himself, though. I wonder how the interview went. Aulus Tullius, Lucius's father, is a great stickler for tradition. He won't take kindly to his son going into partnership with a Syrian, I'm afraid. Lucius will have a lot of persuading to do.'

Judith followed the direction of Valeria's gaze and, with a small jolt, immediately recognised Lucius. He was talking to a grey-haired man and he had a concentration about him that was unmistakable. It set him out from all the other men around him. Lucius radiated vigour, but it was not like Holofernes' irrepressible physical energy. This was controlled, much more of an inward fire.

Watching him hold the attention of the grey-haired man, Judith felt the force of his will as if she had been standing next to him.

'I think Lucius Tullius is probably well suited to persuasion,' she said.

'Yes.' Valeria sounded amused. 'He is a self-possessed young man, isn't he? He has quite a reputation for celibacy, you know – or at least for discretion, which amounts to the same thing in Rome. And yet I hear that when he's roused he can be quite passionate.' She dropped her voice. 'He had an affair with one of our most celebrated courtesans, but he was very secretive about it. He used to deny that he had ever visited her house.'

'Perhaps he thought his father would disapprove.'

Valeria shrugged. 'It's hardly a crime to sleep with a courtesan. No, I think he sees physical passion as weakness so he doesn't want to admit to it.'

Judith nodded. 'It could be,' she said lightly. She thought uneasily of Lucius's parting remark that afternoon, about her virtue and beauty. What had he meant by it? It had been an odd thing to say, sounding almost like a taunt. Perhaps it was the effect of the long journey, and the exhausting homecoming. Judith felt so alien here in this vast city; could it be that now Lucius saw her here among his peers he was beginning to question whether she was really all she claimed to be?

Pain twisted inside her. She had thought Lucius Tullius was her friend and she wanted him to think well of her.

At that moment, Lucius looked up and, coolly scanning the

crowd, his eyes alighted on Judith. Suddenly he seemed to quiver into a fierce alertness.

Judith stared back at him, unable to move.

'He's seen us,' came Valeria's wry voice. 'Or at least,' she added more slowly, 'he has seen *you*.'

Judith felt rather than saw Valeria turn to observe her. She used all her willpower to keep the blood from rising to her cheeks, while she held Lucius's gaze.

Chapter Sixteen

'Danilo Bonaventura's office, can I help you?' It was the familiar female voice, light and expressionless.

'This is Cathy Seymour. We spoke two days ago. I was wondering if Danilo Bonaventura was back yet.'

'Hello, Miss Seymour. We're expecting him back today, but he isn't in the office yet. Shall I leave him a message to telephone you?'

'No, thank you. I'll try again later. Will he be in this afternoon, do you think?'

'As I said, we're expecting him.'

'Thank you.'

Cathy banged the receiver back onto its cradle and put her hands to her face. It was hot and she was trembling. Each time she spoke to Danilo's office she felt more furtive. She couldn't resist glancing over her shoulder now, to check that Matthew hadn't come in unheard.

This made the fourth – or was it the fifth – time she'd telephoned the office. She always spoke to the same person and she never left her number, because she couldn't risk Danilo calling the apartment.

It wasn't just that Matthew might answer; she was worried that Enzo would find out. Cathy was sure Enzo was behind

Danilo's sudden absence on business in Milan. She remembered Enzo turning away from her in the studio, pocketing the card. And then he had gone straight to Matthew and told him.

Enzo had worked fast to wrongfoot her. She was isolated now – Danilo was away, Matthew wasn't speaking to her. Enzo himself hadn't come near her since Monday. But he kept an eye on her; Cathy had seen his silhouette in the windows of the south wing, watching her as she crossed the courtyard to the tower staircase and as she went forth on her restless, lonely walks around the city.

The instinct not to trust Enzo was strong in her, and it grew stronger with each of Nadia's visits to the palazzo. She came nearly every day now. Cathy would see her arriving or leaving, sometimes both, as she kept her own vigil at the windows of her studio. The atmosphere in her studio frightened her now, but she had made herself go in there each day this week, not to draw or paint but to watch the street. Ever since Monday night, when Matthew hadn't come back out of the spare room, she'd had an irrational terror that he would leave the palazzo without telling her, never to return.

If he had gone on being angry with her, Cathy would have found it easier to bear, but he had simply retreated into himself. He spent long hours working and periodically went out into the city on his own. He ate out every evening. And each night, when he finally returned, he slept in the spare bedroom again.

'Look, I don't want to talk about it,' he'd said when she pleaded with him. 'You need space, you can have space. I'm giving it to you.'

'But I don't need space, I need your help!'

'I can't help you, Cat,' he'd said in a choked voice. 'It's up to you. I can't decide things for you.'

And he had turned his back, leaving her as she had been ever since – alone. Except that she wasn't really alone, because within her solitude this week she had been conscious of another presence. Judith was there somewhere, leaking her story into her blood, urging her to take up her drawing pens and give it shape. And Cathy obeyed. It was no longer in her power to resist.

But now Danilo was coming back. This afternoon she would be able to speak to him; within a few hours she might be able to see him. She was beyond knowing what she felt. She walked up and down the sitting room, her hands crossed on her chest, while quarter after quarter the church bells meted out the time.

'It's excellent, Matthew, truly excellent. But why don't you leave it for today and go out?'

'No need. I enjoy it.'

'I know you do.' There was a troubled note in Enzo's voice. His hand settled on Matthew's shoulder and gave it a shake. Matthew suppressed a sigh and looked away from the canvas, up at his employer.

'There's no need to worry about me, Enzo.'

'Of course there is. You and Cathy have quarrelled. She slips around the place like a thief, looking hunted. You shut yourself away in here all day – it's midday now, did you know that? I saw you come in at eight. You're sweating, your eyes are dilated and an impartial observer would think you were on drugs.' Enzo leant down so his face was within a few inches of Matthew's. 'Matthew, take my advice. Get out of here for a while.'

Matthew blinked. Enzo was right, he was sweating, his

vision had gone cloudy. 'Why?' he asked.

'Because you're in bad shape. Apart from anything else,' Enzo straightened up and stepped away, wrinkling his nose humorously, 'you could do with a shower.'

'Thanks.'

'I'm serious Matthew. As your employer, I'm telling you to take the day off. You can clear up now, and I'll be back in half an hour to lock up. Then you're to go out of the palazzo for the day, preferably with Cathy.

'Having a shower is optional.'

'No,' Matthew said, more loudly and rudely. It registered this time; Enzo's heavy smile went askew.

Good. What Matthew wanted more than anything at this moment was for Enzo to go away and leave him alone. He turned pointedly back to the painting and focused on Judith again. Now that he was looking at the familiar figure once more, his vision cleared.

'Matthew, I know that coming to live in the palazzo has been a bad thing for you. Our family tragedy has come between you and Cathy. The last thing I want is to interfere further—'

'Don't then.'

'But there are things I must make you understand. Once Danilo saw Cathy's drawings, I knew he would pursue her. He can't help it, the Giuditta has enormous emotional significance for him and once Cathy showed herself influenced by it, that was that. He couldn't keep away. I asked you both to come here so that I might keep you all under my eye, and try to prevent a disaster.

'Danilo has been away all week because I sent him away. He's been kept extremely busy in Milan and as far as I know he and Cathy have had no contact. Matthew, don't shut yourself away and lose the advantage. Cathy's had a week to cool down and think. I've seen the way she is, and I'm sure she's ready to turn back to you. Danilo will be back later today and he'll seek her out. You must understand that your best chance of saving the situation is to go to her now, before he does.'

Matthew shut his eyes. There was a pit of misery in his stomach, sucking all his emotions into darkness. This was what his new life with Cat had turned into: a squabble between the Bonaventura father and son. Enzo manoeuvred and talked of tactics and gave advice as if this were some kind of business deal and meanwhile he and Cat stood on opposite sides of a gulf, with no trust or confidence between them any more.

'I'm sorry Enzo,' he said bitterly. 'I know it would be very convenient for you if Cathy and I kissed and rode off into the sunset, but I'm afraid we can't oblige.'

'Talk to her, Matthew, that's all I'm asking.'

'I can't.'

'You can if you—'

'I *can't*,' said Matthew, staring straight ahead at the Giuditta. He concentrated on the flesh tones beneath the overpainting, on the underlying structure of bones and muscle hinted at by the brushwork. At moments like this, when the pain was very bad, he found release by losing himself in the detail. 'And you know, Enzo,' he added quietly, 'you may be my employer but in the circumstances I don't think you have any right to ask.'

There was a long silence, followed by the sound of Enzo moving slowly towards the door.

'I never intended you and Cathy to be hurt.' His voice seemed very small in the big room. Matthew didn't look round.

* * *

She would go out and walk. She would visit churches and mingle with nuns and tourists and try to work out what she was going to say. Cathy's head was a mass of unresolvable questions and her body seemed to thrum with energy. She wished she were on a deserted beach somewhere northerly and grey, where the sky was endless and gulls cried over mudflats and she could run herself into oblivion, outdistancing all the watchers and chatterers, all the people who reached out and tried to pull her back. She would be free, hurtling towards the wide horizon and . . . who? Someone waited for her there but she couldn't see who it was.

In the courtyard beneath the office windows, several of the Bonaventura staff loitered. It was twelve thirty and the Roman lunch hour had begun. Cathy was glad of the cover they offered her; she walked casually towards them, lifting her head in their direction and preparing to exchange greetings. She was so intent on them that she didn't hear the footsteps coming up behind her.

'Caterina. Caterina, how are you?' It was Nadia, wearing the dark blue dress and white cape of the nurse's uniform.

Cathy looked from her to the door of the southern wing, from which she must have emerged. A peculiar fear gripped her.

'What's happened? Is someone ill?'

'No. I'm working at the hospital this afternoon, that's all.' Nadia looked closely at Cathy. 'You were worried?'

Cathy met the scrutiny as coolly as she could; she had to suppress an urge to step backwards. 'I was surprised. I haven't seen you in your uniform before.'

Nadia nodded, as if considering Cathy's statement and

passing it. 'You've noticed me here this week, though, haven't you? I've come several times.'

'Yes, I recognised you.'

'I've been coming to see Enzo. To talk to him, to have consultations. You know why, don't you?'

'No. How could I possibly know?'

'But you do.' Nadia stood too close to her, her cape making hard white curves in the air like wings.

Cathy said nothing. Nadia's eyes were sympathetic.

'I don't begin work until two o'clock. Why don't we go somewhere and talk? My apartment isn't far away.'

'I don't understand what you want to talk to me about.'

'You do. You don't look well. Enzo shouldn't have left you to struggle alone for so long, it was cruel. I have things to tell you which will help you understand.' Nadia turned towards the archway. 'I'm going home anyway, for some lunch. There's a subsidised canteen in the hospital but I don't like to use it, it's so crowded.'

The noonday light bounced off the stones into Cathy's eyes.

'You're not really on your way anywhere, are you, Caterina?' Nadia's voice was sympathetic and in the dimness under the archway her face was full of repose. Cathy was suddenly seized with an impulse to go with her. She would like to talk to another woman, and to an older one, who looked as if she had fought her own battles in her time.

And perhaps Nadia really could help her. She was an old friend of the Bonaventuras who obviously cared about them; she had been Alessandra's confidante before she died. Danilo hadn't actually said anything against her. But Cathy remembered his reluctance to speak to his old nurse and knew that he would not want her to go.

They were at the mouth of the archway now. Cathy hesitated before stepping into the sun, still trying to make up her mind.

'This way,' Nadia said. 'We'll be there in five minutes.'

The piazza was busy with shoppers and lunchers, a car had parked across a shop entrance and was causing an argument and two cats were having a stand-off outside the bakery. Walking quickly down the hill towards them was Danilo.

The sight of him acted like an electric charge. Every inch of Cathy was suddenly alive; colours seemed brighter and noises sharper and when she looked at Nadia, she saw that far from being relaxed, the nurse was concentrating on her fiercely. Above her smiling mouth, Nadia's eyes were commanding.

'Don't go to him,' she said, but Cathy stepped back and pushed away Nadia's reaching hand. Then she turned, stumbling, and ran towards Danilo.

'Cathy, I was just coming to see you.' Danilo steadied her and kissed her on both cheeks, all in one fluid movement. He glanced at Nadia and his hands tightened on her arms. 'It's all right,' he said quickly. 'Something's happened, hasn't it? What's she been saying to you?'

'She wants to talk to me.'

'We need to talk to each other first.' Danilo looked down at her for a few seconds. 'You've realised, haven't you? Will you come to my apartment?'

Cathy nodded. She was beginning to tremble and that made it hard to speak. What did Danilo think she had realised? He was tucking her arm under his and, with great economy, turning her round to lead her up the hill. He looked over his shoulder at Nadia and gave her an open-handed salute. It was the friendly parting gesture of young Romans, but his face was defiant.

'I didn't want to go away,' he said as they climbed the hill.

'My father engineered a crisis in our Milan office with one of our American clients. I had to be there.'

'Yes, I guessed.'

'I told you my father knows how to get what he wants.' He looked down at her. 'I didn't refuse to go because I didn't want a fullscale row. It would have meant talking about you.' He paused. 'I wish I hadn't gone now. What's happened?'

'Enzo came into my studio while I was out and found some more drawings I'd done. I hadn't told him about them. He found your plant too. He didn't say anything about it, but he was furious. He took your card away with him and showed it to Matthew.' Cathy began to shake in earnest. The facts sounded quite trivial and yet they had turned her life upside down. 'Matthew isn't speaking to me and neither is Enzo. Nadia's been coming every day and vanishing into huddles with your father, everyone's angry and tense and I don't know what the hell's going on.'

'Is that why you telephoned the office?'

'Yes. At least,' Cathy stared at the cobbles passing under her feet, 'it was part of the reason.'

Danilo took her hand 'I wanted to call you back,' he said, 'but I didn't dare in case I got Matthew. I'm sorry you've had to go through all this alone.'

'Through all what? Can't you tell me what's going on?' It was a relief to be touched by him at last, and yet it was also disturbing, it set off such a chain of emotions.

'Not here,' Danilo said gently. He nodded at a narrow building just ahead of them. 'We're nearly home. Let's get to the apartment then I'll tell you everything. Or at least, everything I know.'

Danilo's apartment was high and airy. Most of it was taken

up by one big living room whose windows looked west over the roofs of the Ghetto to the city. Cathy stood in the middle of the polished wooden floor and wished Danilo would come and touch her again. But he stayed just inside the doorway, turning his keys over.

'Cathy,' he said at last. He pronounced it Cat-ti, as when he'd introduced her to Nadia; it had a caressing sound. 'I don't know how to begin. I don't even know how much I need to tell you. By now you must have recognised so much of it for yourself.'

Cathy tried to read his face. It was both wary and eager, very unlike the self-possessed businessman of his photographs. 'I don't know what I know,' she said. 'I seem to know things all the time without understanding them. It's as if – as if I'm having someone else's memories.'

Danilo smiled slightly. 'Someone else?'

He wanted her to say the name and she was reluctant to. She felt as if, once spoken, it would take her over a boundary into uncharted land.

'Yes. I think I'm feeling some of what your mother felt. I'm drawing pictures in the way you said she painted them. Of the people and the places in her story – Judith's.' There, she had said it now. But there was none of the expected response from Danilo. He seemed to be waiting for something.

'Danilo, does Judith haunt the palazzo?'

Danilo didn't move his eyes from her. 'My father thinks so,' he said. 'But I believe people are more important than places. Look, Catti, I don't know the answers any more than you do, but I do know that you and I are important to one another. You've been important to me for years – I was just waiting to meet you.'

'Danilo, I do feel something for you. But don't you think that it's the circumstances? The fact that you and Matthew don't get on, and that I've been doing those same drawings, like your mother did, and that we've allowed the mystery to take over?'

Danilo unclenched his hands and stared at the keys, then at Cathy. 'Is that what you honestly think?'

Cathy struggled to think and failed. She shrugged wretchedly.

Danilo moved to a small table and put down his keys. He half turned, made an oddly familiar gesture with his right arm across his chest and bowed. His smile was full of laughter. 'Welcome to my tent,' he said softly.

Cathy gasped and failed to draw in any breath. There was a vacuum in her lungs. It was as if the universe had wrinkled and in Danilo's place stood a man she knew from another world – Holofernes, looking at her as he looked at Judith: mockingly, wickedly, intimately.

Numbly, she watched Danilo leave the room and heard the sound of running water. She couldn't think; she couldn't feel. Then he was back.

'I'm sorry,' said Danilo, 'I shouldn't have done that. But it made me angry to hear you rationalising it away. I've lived with it so long, you see, and I've had to listen to my father and Nadia saying just that sort of thing and I've had to pretend to believe it. Look, stay here, I won't be long.'

In the large room Cathy sat alone on the sofa and sipped her water. Danilo was down the corridor somewhere; she could hear noises of drawers being opened. She was light-headed and everything around her looked preternaturally clear.

She put her fingers to her mouth to stop her teeth chattering on the glass.

Danilo came back in. He seemed to move in a more muscular fashion than before. He stopped halfway across the room.

'Are you all right? Are you ready to talk?'

'Quite ready.'

'That sounds as if you think I'm playing games with you. I'm not, Catti, far from it. I don't know how to say this. How can I explain? He was moving towards the sofa now. 'I've always felt like a foreigner. My father's family are outsiders in the Ghetto, for all the generations they've been here. My mother's family is Jewish, but they come from Torino, which is so different from Rome as to be practically another land.

'After my mother died, I was sent to school in England and from seven until eighteen I split my life between the two countries. In Italian, the word for village and for country is the same – *paese*. I have no *paese*, except for the one my mother passed on to me. It's a *paese* of the mind, a land made of visions and inner knowledge, of secret disclosures. In the last few months of her life, my mother inhabited this land almost entirely. It overlapped with her everyday life and conflicted with her relationships with me and my father, and that conflict destroyed her.'

Danilo sat down on the sofa, keeping an arm's length between himself and Cathy. His face had lost its set lines and looked very young.

'I think I knew, in those last months, that she would die of it. And I felt guilty because what she told me about this secret land, what she showed me in her paintings, was so beautiful to me that I didn't want to surrender it. I knew, the way children do, that it was killing her but I couldn't stop myself loving it and wanting more of it.

'She died and my father took me away for a year, travelling.

We went to all kinds of busy, cultured places in western Europe and then in America. Even then it struck me that we didn't go east or south; it was as if my father wanted to turn his back on it, in the most definite way possible. We came back here for a few months and then I went to prep school in England. And that was when the dreams started.'

Danilo looked at his wrists, which rested exactly aligned on his knees.

'At first I dreamed the same thing, always. A girl, standing lost at the roadside in an old city. I asked her if she needed help and I gave her some of my drink – in the dream it was called wine, but it was much fruitier than any of the wines my father had let me sip, almost like juice. The girl and I would talk and tell each other who we were, and bicker.

'The dream didn't come very often. About once a term, perhaps not even that. And it kept pace with me. As I grew older, my dream self grew older. Sometimes I was wearing slightly different clothes; once I remember being very pleased because I was carrying a longer knife, with a newly sharpened blade. I cut my thumb on it, testing it.

'At the time, I knew it was part of the world my mother had shown me. I didn't question it. I was just pleased it was still there, and it made me feel closer to her. All the same, I didn't realise just how close the connection was. I was eleven when names came into the dream and I was very shocked to recognise that in the dream I was the young Holofernes and the girl was Judith.

'That was when I mentioned it to my father. He reacted quite badly. He tried to take it in his stride but I could see how shaken he was. He told me they were morbid dreams, a part of the process of grieving for my mother but one I should try and get through as soon as possible. He tried to get me to see a psychiatrist but I had no intention of talking about it to anyone else, my father's response had been negative enough. I kept myself very active, as he suggested, and to his great satisfaction the dreams stopped.

'They stopped for two years. Then, when I was thirteen and moved to my new school, they began again. This time, they were different. I was older, so was Judith, and we met not on a roadside but in an army camp. And I was laying siege to her city.'

Danilo sat very still, gazing into the quiet room. Cathy watched his profile. How could she ever have thought he was enigmatic? It seemed to her now that she could see every emotion as it struggled with all the others and submitted to his will.

'They were incredible dreams. Violent. Funny. Terrifying. Some of the events were the same as my mother had described to me, but it was so different, because in her inner land, Holofernes was a man from her own life – the artist she ran away with eventually. In my land, I was Holofernes, and the way he did things was as I do, his desire for Judith was my desire, and she – she was my woman.'

Danilo went on looking straight ahead. His face, which had looked so young at the beginning of his story, was now crevassed with emotion.

'My dreams took us out of Judea together, through Syria into Apamea, and across the sea to Rome. After that, they turned into nightmares. I would wake up sweating and dizzy. I'd cry. I'd wake on the floor, clinging to the iron bedstead. The dreams were no longer coherent dreams, but fragments all jumbled out of order. There was violence in them, and cruelty, and darkness. They reminded me of my mother's last paintings, which I saw only in glimpses. In the end there was only one dream, which came again and again. I was in a large white room with Judith. What had happened beforehand I didn't know, but I was in danger. I was at the very end. Judith was the only one who could save me. I wanted to live, but it was up to her to give the word. I waited for her to give the sign; I thought she would. And then there came this second when I understood she wasn't going to.'

Danilo lifted his head and looked at her. In his dark eyes, a tiny light seemed to recede. The moment of comprehension was back on him; Cathy felt part of its horror.

Danilo put out his hand and, without asking, took her water glass. He drank thirstily.

'That was that. The story went no further. I tried to understand what was happening. I read around the subject of the Judith story; in the holidays I went to see Nadia and tried to pump her about my mother's last weeks, but she wouldn't talk. What was worse, she told my father and he started asking me all kinds of questions. I was relieved to get back to school in the new term.

'I was fourteen then. My friends were becoming interested in girls; I began to meet their sisters at half-term, and for special dances. Some of them were nice and I enjoyed being with them, but I always felt I was just playing at being interested. Then I dreamed of the modern girl.

'There was no story in this dream, she was just there with me. It was a dream that came several times, and each time we were getting to know another part of each other. We didn't usually talk very much; sometimes we walked, sometimes we were in a house, once we were doing prep together. There was a deep happiness, which I had no words to describe. She was Judith, of course.' Danilo looked at the remains of the water and drained the glass. 'I'm sorry, I've drunk all your water. Shall I get you some more?'

Cathy shook her head. Her lips felt parched but she wanted Danilo to go on. She felt that she was falling down a long, long drop and there was nothing for it now but to reach the bottom.

'Go on.'

Danilo glanced at her. 'Go on? Do I need to? Really?'

'Yes.'

'There's not much more to tell. I didn't understand then and I don't understand now exactly why this has happened to us. Where it's come from, why it's happened this way. I don't feel possessed. I am Danilo Bonaventura, not Holofernes the Syrian, and I was sure of that at fifteen. That's how I knew that the modern girl must exist too. She was herself as I was myself, but we were linked. We needed to find each other. So I looked.

'I was very logical about it.' He smiled mockingly. 'A business mind at work, even then. She looked British to me and in the dreams we spoke English. I reasoned that if I was drawn to the Judith legend, she would be too, so at half-terms and when I stayed with friends in the holidays I began a Judith trawl. I visited exhibitions which included Judith paintings, I saw plays and operas about the story, I went to museums of Middle Eastern life. I became an expert.' He laughed sheepishly. 'I became bloody bored.

'I kept it up for three years, and there were times when I wondered if I'd simply become obsessive, like a train spotter. Then in the Easter holidays of my last year at school, I found her. It was in the National Gallery. I had walked through the whole thing as usual, and ended up in the back rooms where, at the time, they had some rather lurid Dutch paintings on show. Do you remember them? There were some martyrdoms, and the slaughter of the innocents, and a peculiar Judith who had obviously been modelled on a man.

'You were standing in front of the Judith painting, with a boy. Seeing you like that was the most extraordinary sensation. I was surprised at how young you were, I'd thought you'd be eighteen, my own age, I wasn't expecting a fifteen-year-old. I didn't know how to react. I stood and watched you from the far side of the room. You and the boy were joking about the picture and holding hands, but you stayed in front of it quite a while and when he moved on, you looked at it over your shoulder.

'I followed you both out of the room. You were obviously finished there. You went all the way back through the gallery to the main hall. I had to get my camera out of the left luggage but I watched you all the time – the boy was reading a poster and you were buying cards at the desk. I turned to take my camera from the attendant and when I looked back, you were gone. I rushed out after you but there were so many people on the steps I couldn't see you. I fought my way down one flight of steps – it was the wrong one. When I reached the pavement I saw you and the boy a hundred yards away, climbing on a bus. I ran but I didn't get there in time. All I could do was take this, as proof and as a pledge that I would find you again.'

Danilo picked up the envelope he'd laid on the cushion beside him and placed it in Cathy's hands. She had to make several attempts at opening it. The flap was creased with much handling. There were two photographs inside. The top one was a small print showing the corner of Trafalgar Square and two people boarding a bus. The figures were only a centimetre high and unidentifiable. The second photograph was twice the size; Trafalgar Square was gone, and the bus had been enlarged to fill the picture. The texture was grainy and the colours had suffered but the two people jumping onto the deck were unmistakable now: herself at fifteen, with jeans and tangled hair, hand in hand with her stepbrother.

Chapter Seventeen

Judith walked through the atrium, her sandals making no sound on the tiled floor. There were five people in here today, three of them Lucius's clients, two of them other nobles whom she knew Lucius had been discreetly pursuing. Holofernes was talking to the nobles, and laughter came from the couches where they sat. Lucius glanced across from his place among his clients and caught Judith's eye. He bowed to her, and she to him. Then she walked swiftly on to the vestibule where Daria, the youngest of her slaves, was waiting with a pair of shoes.

She had no desire to join the group in the atrium. Besides, it wasn't a place for respectable Roman women. True, some of the more ambitious political wives had begun holding salons after the manner of Cornelia Gracchus, but Judith was not in a position to emulate them. Instead, she had modelled her life on Valeria's and now occupied a position on the edges of her circle. In the morning, Judith would call on Valeria at her house, or on Fulvia or Clodia or Flora, the wives of other nobles. They would sit in the peristylium or one of the rooms in the back of the house, embroidering and discussing the news of the day. Valeria was skilled at turning the conversation round to discover titbits of information which might be useful to Marcus, and Judith was learning how to do it too. She was also acquiring the art of evading the questions which might expose her, or which might lead her to reveal too much about Holofernes and Lucius's activities.

If word came of interesting business at the Forum, the women would call their slaves and hurry down to the Macellum, to watch and listen under the pretext of buying household provisions. They would descend there again in the afternoon, for 'rumour hour'.

Every evening, almost as a matter of course, the nobles would dine together, and to Judith's surprise wives were expected to take their places alongside the men. So night after night she sat on the third couch, with the other wives. She ate things she had never dreamt of: fish disguised to look like chicken; large birds stuffed with smaller birds stuffed with mice; soft, repulsive oysters which trickled a rank aftertaste onto the tongue. She drank small cups of watered wine. She heard Greek slaves recite poetry and professional musicians play their lyres. In the more daring houses, clowns performed tricks, acrobats tumbled and women from eastern countries, who bore a faint resemblance to Judith herself, danced sinuous dances. And sooner or later during these banquets – usually later, once people had lost count of the number of toasts – Lucius would draw her into conversation.

Judith looked forward to these talks, and feared them. They talked sometimes of the east, sometimes of Rome, at other times of Greek learning. Lucius had kept his word and every day his favourite Greek slave, Polymene, would spend an hour instructing Judith in the teachings of Hellenism. She was surprised to find that she recognised several Greek ideas from life in Bethulia – the elders had not been as successful as they supposed in cutting out the Greek influences. This new understanding helped her in her talks with Lucius. By drawing on all her perceptions from the time she lived in Chabris' house and by using her wits, she could speak quite fluently on his chosen subjects. And while they conversed, Lucius's grey eyes would study her face, and hidden within his cool voice would be a caress. Each communion with him left Judith feeling excited and guilty, and increasingly, irresistibly reckless.

But there was no room for recklessness. She knew that as well as anyone, and once she was away from Lucius, she would observe Holofernes anxiously to see if he had noticed anything amiss. Holofernes was her husband and had a right to her support. In Rome, as Lucius had said, wives gave their husbands political loyalty. Valeria, for instance, worked for Marcus Strachus's success even though he spent his nights in the house of Flavia, a freedwoman, by whom he had two children. Judith had sworn to herself that she would make Holofernes a worthy wife. He had taken her out of Bethulia and brought her to Rome; so far he had treated her well. Judith knew that Holofernes was proud of her beauty and her courage and if he was exacting, it was no more than she might have expected.

And still, every night, Holofernes came to her room and made other, more intimate demands on her body. During those hours, Judith felt herself cut off from the world around her. Her hands left her control; her eyes were full of shadows and flame-lapped flesh, and her breath ebbed and flowed to a foreign rhythm. Sometimes she wept without knowing why.

Judith was bewildered by the way she behaved during these night hours, and Holofernes did not speak of them afterwards. He did not seem repelled by her, as Manasses had been, but he obviously thought it best not to acknowledge what they did.

Judith felt torn. Sometimes during the day she found herself looking ahead to the night and anticipating with an excited shiver the sound of Holofernes' footstep, the touch of his hand on her breast. Then shame would course through her and she would think instead of Lucius. His clear face and flashing energy seemed pure in comparison with Holofernes' dark passions. And in those moments, despite her wish to be loyal, Judith felt that whereas Holofernes' desires dragged her down, Lucius's might release her.

In the vestibule, Judith sat on the ledge seat and allowed Daria to remove her sandals and fit her shoes. She was going to call on Fulvia, one of the more fashionable of the respectable young matrons, so she had chosen shoes with red straps and a small buckle. These were the most ornamented of all the pairs of shoes Judith had bought under Valeria's guidance and Holofernes had frowned with disappointment and asked why she hadn't bought any decorated with gemstones. Lucius had explained to him that such elaborate shoes were worn by the wives of rich merchants and by courtesans, not by the more traditional, high-born Roman wives.

'We're not traditional,' Holofernes had said, grinning. 'Or Roman. We're from the decadent east; why not enjoy it?' But he had given in and agreed that they should follow Lucius's lead and be discreet.

Now, from the atrium, came a burst of wicked laughter. Holofernes' voice was the loudest – discretion did not come easily to him. Judith listened for Lucius to follow suit, but she couldn't hear him. She wasn't surprised; all too easily she could imagine him standing among his clients, looking sharply across at Holofernes and the two nobles. He would be annoyed by Holofernes' entertaining them so loudly, and anxious to know what he was saying. For although the two men were making good progress in winning the support of nobles and military figures, there was tension between them over their methods. Holofernes was impatient with Lucius for being so cautious; Lucius was angered by Holofernes' tendency to go off alone and make separate deals with officers from former campaigns.

There had been several arguments. Lucius emerged from them expressionless and narrow-eyed; Holofernes either came out shouting or treated the discord as a joke. 'Don't worry,' he'd said to Judith after the last row, 'we just have different ways of doing things. His is the politician's, mine is the soldier's. You'll get used to it.'

'I don't want to get used to it,' Judith had said nervously. He had laughed at that.

'You don't have a choice. I'm not educated in the arts of subtlety like Lucius is. If you wanted that, you married the wrong man.'

Daria finished fastening Judith's shoes and, hearing movement within the atrium, Judith stood up hurriedly. Footsteps were coming towards the vestibule and she did not want to be found here. Lucius's clients always stared at her with an open curiosity she found disconcerting; and if it was the nobles who approached, then Holofernes might well be with them. She thought it would be wiser not to be drawn into discussion with them in front of Lucius.

Judith devoted much of her energies these days to maintaining an equilibrium between the two men – outwardly at least. Inwardly, she sympathised with both of them; she was pulled from one to the other like the tides of the sea that flowed first this way and that, turning ceaselessly in answer to the phases of the moon.

* * *

The visit to Fulvia's house was profitable. Valeria arrived soon after Judith, then Clodia came; and finally two older women appeared, whom Judith had never met before. From Fulvia's expression, Judith could tell that the visit was a mark of favour, and an unexpected one at that. The two matrons, Lucceia and Geggonia – who turned out to be the wives of a senator and aedile respectively – settled themselves in a dignified manner, took out their embroidery and proceeded to question the younger women about their husbands' activities. Eventually Lucceia turned to Judith.

'Your husband, I believe, was active in Pergamum two years ago. My husband, Marcellus Galba, had dealings with him. He speaks highly of General Holofernes' ability.'

'And my husband admires Marcellus Galba,' said Judith, hoping Lucceia would not ask for details.

'Marcellus Galba has many friends in the east,' Lucceia went on. 'And he knows the terrain well. He has particular influence in the region of Cappadocia.'

'I know that my husband would like to consult Senator Marcellus Galba,' ventured Judith. 'When the senator is not too burdened with affairs of the state.'

'Marcellus Galba is at a meeting in the Curia this morning,' said Lucceia austerely. 'I do not know when it will be finished.'

Ten minutes later, Lucceia and Geggonia left. When Fulvia returned from bidding them farewell, she and Judith talked excitedly. The visit was a clear sign that the two women's husbands wanted to be approached by Lucius and Holofernes. Pausing just long enough to be sure that the visitors had left the street, Judith and Valeria called their slaves and set off to look for their husbands.

* * *

'Hush!' Judith raised her hand to stop Daria's question and strained to hear what was happening outside. Raised voices had been reverberating along the central corridor which linked the atrium with the back of the house; now, though, angry footsteps had taken over. Lucius's voice sounded again, quieter this time but clipped with controlled violence.

A silence followed, in which Judith could distantly hear sounds of movement, and then the door to her room opened and admitted Holofernes.

He grimaced and shut the door by leaning against it. 'You know what they say, Bel help the Syrian who deals with Rome. These people aren't normal.'

'What's happened?'

'You'd think Lucius would be pleased that we've got a senator and an aedile queuing up to be in on our plans. I spoke to Marcellus Galba and Sertorius and they each have pressing reasons for wanting to join a new eastern campaign. They see it as a chance to bring back huge amounts of booty and secure wealth from clients, which of course it is. So they're willing to help convince the senate and the consuls; in fact Sertorius himself suggested that he make a start today. He went off to talk to some of the senators, and the next thing I know, Aulus Tullius gets wind of it, summons Lucius to see him and tells him he's a disgrace to his family for trying to buy upstanding Romans with the whorish wealth of the east. As if the old hypocrite hadn't bought enough men himself in the past. Just because he bought them with magistracies and contracts to do public works, he thinks he belongs to some higher moral order. It's jealousy, that's what it is. He's an embittered old bastard who can't bear to see his son on the rise.'

'And Lucius is upset?'

'Upset? You should see him. His face is milk-white and as tight as a drum. He says it's my fault, of course; I shouldn't have talked to anyone without consulting him first. I should just sit around smiling enigmatically while he goes back and forth to Aulus Tullius mouthing Roman pieties.'

Holofernes batted at his hair with an impatient hand.

'I listened for a while then I lost my temper. I've told him that we're going to this dinner with Marcellus Galba tonight whether he likes it or not. And I've also told him that he'd better come if he wants to keep up with the way things are developing. I'm the one with the military record in the east, not him, and he'd do well not to forget it.'

Judith flinched. 'What did he say to that?'

'He said, "Leave me alone," through his teeth.' Holofernes shrugged. 'Bel's balls, it's a pleasure.'

Judith held out her hand for the mother-of-pearl combs Daria was holding, and began to twist them into her hair. 'Will Lucius come to the dinner with us?' she asked anxiously.

'Who knows? I hope so. It won't look good to have to go without him. But I'm not asking him to come, not after the way he spoke to me.'

Judith looked at her reflection in the beaten silver mirror as the combs nestled one by one into her dark hair. Holofernes was reflected behind her, an angry figure playing restlessly with the long fold of his toga.

Judith eyed the forward thrust of his body and imagined Lucius, equally angry but upright, out in the peristylium. The picture made her throat tighten apprehensively. She linked her hands in her lap.

'Shall I ask him?'

Holofernes looked up and met her gaze in the mirror. 'What, you think you can persuade him without losing face for me?'

'I don't know, but I can try.'

He went on looking at her. 'Yes, you can, can't you? You've had enough practice talking to him at all these dinners, after all. And it won't be the first time you've talked round a stiff-necked man.' He flashed her a smile that was tinged with anger.

Watching him leave the room, his toga bundled inelegantly under his arm, Judith was unable to tell whether the anger was directed at Lucius or herself.

Lucius put down his cup and pushed it across the polished stone table top. He made a tiny sign with his hand, barely perceptible to Judith, and a slave came forward to ladle more wine from bowl to cup.

'Have you come out here of your own accord, or at Holofernes' request?' Lucius said.

'Both.'

He smiled. 'You, at least, are honest.'

'I think we're all honest, aren't we, Lucius? It's just that we don't always agree.'

'Which raises a debatable point. If we disagree about what is honesty, which of us can be said to be honest? All of us? None of us? Or perhaps just one.' He took another drink. His hand was steady and his voice measured but Judith realised Holofernes was right: Lucius was rigid with tension. 'You're in a difficult position, aren't you, Judith?' he said. 'You're married to Holofernes and will therefore work to support him. But you see very well that he's jeopardising our chances here. He's too rash. This crudeness is all very well for the Syrian army where the generals can dictate terms to the king, but we are in Rome. We govern ourselves with more complexity, as I think you understand.'

Judith spoke cautiously. 'I'm beginning to understand how things are done here.'

'Yes.' His clear eyes regarded her. 'But your own experience has already taught you the principles.' There was a gleam in his face which disconcerted Judith.

'My own experience?'

'With the elders of your home town. They didn't choose you as the bearer of their good will, did they? You had to put yourself forward. You had to plan it and select your moment and then argue your case in order to convince them.' Lucius observed her with a needle-sharp calm. Judith drew breath; it came thinly and she clamped one hand over the other in order to keep herself steady.

'Who's been spreading these rumours?' she said, attempting to sound amused.

'Oh, no one's spreading anything.' Lucius's amusement was more convincing. 'It was told to me in confidence, for my ears alone.'

'By whom?'

Lucius lowered the cup which had been about to touch his lips. 'By your husband, the general.'

Judith clung to her own fingers, feeling the texture of the knuckles and the smooth nails. 'Why would Holofernes say such a thing?'

'He grew exasperated one day when I told him that he should follow your example and be more discreet. He said that you could afford to be discreet now that it was others' turn to act, but that you had seized your moment when you had to.'

Lucius was no longer smiling. He looked thoughtfully at Judith. 'You see, both of you were dishonest with me in the beginning. Then, by revealing the truth to me, Holofernes became dishonest with you. And now I've told you what Holofernes confided, I've put myself in the position of being dishonest to him. So Judith, tell me, whom do you trust now? And why should I trust either of you?'

Judith's mouth was dry and she couldn't answer. She stared at Lucius. His face was changing, but she couldn't interpret the ripples of muscle and the altering expression in the eyes. Was he preparing to condemn her? Was he summoning his voice to shout for Holofernes and order them both out?

But when he spoke, it was softly. 'You must have wanted to leave Bethulia very badly. What was it that made you take such a risk, Judith?'

Lucius was watching her quietly, eagerly; colour had crept into his cheeks. Judith thought of Chabris and the disapproval of the citizens, and the hours of lonely prayer, and felt that they were reaching out to pull her back.

'I wanted to live,' she said desperately.

Slowly Lucius nodded. His eyes, darker suddenly, moved across her face.

'And now you are here in Rome,' he said, 'where your life can begin again.' He paused. 'I'm looking for a new life, too, Judith. For achievement, for honour, for the strength to break old bonds. We are very alike, you and I.'

Judith was muddled with wine and the conviviality of Marcellus Galba's feast. In the rich interior of the senator's triclinium, the conversation had soared and dipped and triumphant notes had been struck. She had not spoken to Lucius, nor indeed to

Holofernes. She had remained firmly in the company of Lucceia and Geggonia, answering their questions – at first austere, becoming more and more inquisitive – about life in the east. But throughout the evening she had secretly watched Lucius and Holofernes, and in turn she had felt their eyes on her, marking her, caressing her in their different ways.

And now, as Holofernes entered her bedroom, took the oil lamp from his slave and dismissed him, Judith felt herself torn between desire and resentment.

'A successful evening,' Holofernes said, waving Daria out of the room. 'They're with us. More than that, they need us. Even Lucius seemed pleased. I'm glad you were able to persuade him to come.' He put his hands on her shoulders to unfasten her tunic. 'What did you say to him?'

Judith looked across at their reflection in the mirror. Holofernes was bent over her, smiling as his hands worked at the tunic fastenings. She could feel his breath on her skin.

'I told him he could trust us.' She paused. 'And then he told me that he knew we had already lied to him.'

'When?' Holofernes' head jerked up. 'We've never lied to him.'

'He said,' Judith removed herself from Holofernes' grasp, 'that according to you, I had argued and persuaded to be allowed to leave Bethulia.'

'Ah. That.' Holofernes straightened. 'I suppose he was angry when he told you that. There was no need for him to pass that back to you, I'm surprised at him.'

'Why did you tell him?' Judith walked across the room. 'You know it's a lie.' The assertion, which she had meant to sound dignified, came out too fast. Judith glanced at Holofernes and found him looking levelly at her.

'People talk, Judith, and I have a lot of contacts. I don't think any the less of you – more, in fact. That's why I told Lucius. He needed to realise that in the real world, no matter how many noble ancestors you have and how many statues of them clutter up your house, you've got to act if you want to get anywhere.'

Judith began to tremble. 'You betrayed me.'

'No. I said nothing to let him know you needed to leave Bethulia. He thinks only that you wanted to.'

It wasn't so much his words that humiliated Judith as the compassion in his face. Holofernes saw her wince and moved quickly towards her.

'Judith of Bethulia, I don't care what you did to your husband. He was a fool and Bethulia is a vicious-minded prison. I told you years ago that you were too good for that place and you've proved me right.'

He loomed in front of her, blotting out the light. Judith took a step backwards and came up against the wall. Holofernes reached out and she tensed herself but he neither grabbed her nor pulled her to the bed. Instead he gently slid the combs from her hair and held up his hands so that her heavy locks fell over them.

'You're a brave woman, Judith – my kind of woman.'

He dropped his hands down to her neck and her breasts; he stroked her, his fingers sliding over her sides and into the small of her back, pulling her haunches against him.

Judith fought to keep from responding, but the familiar, treacherous hunger took over. She hung in Holofernes' arms, wanting him and hating him at the same time. This Syrian husband of hers knew too much about her; as long as she was bound to him, she was tethered to her past, and her shame. She struggled for one last second above the dark tide that was engulfing her and thought of Lucius who also knew what it was to want to be free.

'All is not well in the confederacy. Is it?'

Valeria's face was bland as they strolled through the rumour-hour crowd, but her voice was knowing. Judith sighed.

'No. Lucius and Holofernes seem to disagree about everything suddenly.'

'So Marcus tells me. Of course, he thinks it's a clash of temperaments – Lucius's caution against your husband's vigour.'

'It is.'

'Are you sure there's nothing else behind it?'

'Nothing I know of.'

Valeria flashed a long look sideways. 'Hmm. You know, when we were all together two nights ago, I thought Holofernes wasn't too pleased about Lucius talking to you.' She paused, and when Judith didn't respond, added, 'Perhaps it will be as well when you're no longer under Lucius's roof. Have you been to see Aufidius Metallus's house yet?'

Judith shook her head in bewilderment. 'No, should I have done? Who's Aufidius Metallus?'

'He was chief centurion two years ago. He died of fever and his widow is going out to the country. Don't tell me you don't know. For the last few days, Holofernes has been negotiating to take over his house.'

Judith stopped dead and Valeria had to stop with her. The vivacious face stared up at her, wary for once.

'You didn't know, did you? Oh dear, if you and your husband are no longer talking, it's serious.'

'Don't be ridiculous, Valeria, of course we're talking!' Judith snapped. 'Holofernes knows I've been wanting a house of our own. We've discussed it several times. He did say something to me about a possible house, but he didn't go into any details. And why should he? I trust him to make arrangements for us.'

'That's good,' said Valeria drily, 'because as far as I'm aware, your husband is with Aufidius Metallus's widow at this moment, doing just that.'

As soon as the door opened to admit her to the vestibule, Judith heard their voices. They were both loud and in full flow, shouting over one another in some distant part of the house. She clutched the wall as Daria removed her shoes and slipped on her sandals.

Balbas, one of the Greek house slaves, stood mutely in the corridor. Judith beckoned him.

'Is there anyone in the atrium?' she whispered.

'No, Madam Judith. When Lucius Tullius came in, he told them all to go. Then he sent Trincio out for your husband the general.'

'How long have they been arguing?'

Balbas pulled his mouth aslant. 'Quite a while.'

Judith moved past him into the atrium. There was a sudden silence from the heart of the house, and then both voices resumed, pitched lower than before but if anything even more furious.

Judith put her hand over her mouth and sat on the edge of the nearest couch. She was still out of breath from hurrying up the hill to get here and there was a pain in her side like a spear-head. Her heart thudded ominously.

For six days now, ever since the feast at Marcellus Galba's, the tension had been running high. Lucius and Holofernes struck sparks off one another constantly, while Judith hardly dared meet the eyes of either if the other were in the room.

She had lied to Valeria. It was true that Holofernes had spoken of getting their own house, but Judith had not encouraged him. The thought of going away from Lucius dismayed her and she had responded vaguely to Holofernes' suggestions, murmuring that she still had much to learn about running a Roman house.

Yet he had taken the step nonetheless. Why?

There was a crash as something was hurled to the floor, and footsteps pounded along the central corridor towards her. Judith jumped up as Holofernes burst into the atrium. He was ablaze with anger.

'There you are,' he said, walking straight past her to the bowl of scented water and splashing his face. 'Tell your slaves to pack your belongings. We're leaving. We have a house beyond the silk merchants' street, a fine, modest, suitably austere house which was the home of a respected chief centurion.' He spat out the words, evidently in continuation of the row with Lucius. 'A house for a distinguished man of arms, no less, and his loyal wife. We shall be very well suited there. I've already taken leave of Lucius. When he comes to his senses and realises that I too am entitled to my own roof and walls and atrium and shouldn't be condemned to live under his jurisdiction for ever like a slave, then we'll invite him to a feast to bless the house. And perhaps from somewhere in his arrogant, dried-up Roman soul he'll find the grace to come!'

He splashed more water on his face. 'Trincio! My shoes, *hurry*!'

Judith lurched towards him to grab his sleeve but he was too quick; he snatched her wrist, kissed it angrily and was gone.

Judith went cautiously down the central corridor, making no noise. She felt as if she were stalking Lucius. In the wake of Holofernes' loud departure she had heard movement among these rooms and now, pausing in the doorway of Lucius's study, she saw the shards of lacquered pot scattered on the floor. Otherwise, the room was empty. Lucius must have gone in the opposite direction from Holofernes, into the small peristylium.

As soon as Judith stepped into the colonnade, she saw him. He was sitting on the stone seat by the bed of violets and he had his back half turned to her. It was the hour of evening when the rows of herbs gave off their scents. Judith was suddenly reminded of the first time she had seen Lucius – in the grander, more ornamented peristylium in Apamea. Then, standing by the pool and surrounded by splashing fountains in the Syrian dusk, he had emanated a wild vitality. Now he sat very upright and still.

Judith stood in the shadows, waiting for him to move, but he might have been carved in stone. She took a step forward and her foot struck a pebble.

'Judith.' Lucius stood up and peered into the shadows of the colonnade. 'Is that you?'

She pulled her stola round her protectively. 'Yes, Lucius.'

'You've just spoken to Holofernes.'

'Yes.'

'Did you know about this house?' There was no anger in his voice; there was no emotion at all.

Judith couldn't control a gasp as she answered, 'No, Lucius, I didn't.'

He must have heard, for he made a movement towards her, quickly reined in. 'I lost my temper,' he said at length. 'I thought you and Holofernes were abusing my hospitality and going behind my back. But it seems it was your husband acting alone, once again.'

'I'm sorry,' said Judith. She wanted to say more; the thought of leaving Lucius's house was painful. It put a hollow inside her, surrounded by a tightness.

Lucius, staring into the dimness of the pillars, nodded. His eyes found her face and dwelt on it with a sudden, frustrated hunger.

'Come out where I can see you, Judith.' His voice was urgent. 'Stop hiding in the shadows.'

Judith walked into the fading light. Small stones rolled from under her feet and the hem of her stola, dragging across a herb bed, sent a lizard scuttling. As she drew closer to Lucius, she saw that although he stood still, he was breathing hard.

'Come closer,' he said when she stopped a few feet away. 'We must speak without being heard.'

Her next steps brought her within the compass of his arms. Yet he didn't touch her; he only looked at her.

'We've both been waiting, haven't we?' he said. 'For the moment to speak to each other. For Holofernes to give a sign. I've afforded him enough openings, but he ignores all of them. Yet he knows Roman ways well enough to realise what's expected. He's resisting me deliberately.'

Judith stared up at him. She knew that she should deny what Lucius was saying, but it was too late. Her face, and her nearness, had given her away.

'Lucius,' she said. It was half in joy that he had spoken, half a plea for him to stop. He smiled and she looked away, feeling tears threaten. 'You forget, I don't understand all Roman ways yet. What is it you're expecting?'

Lucius shook his head. 'Judith, please look at me. You realise, surely, that one of the traditions among Roman nobles is that we give one another gifts of regard. Swords, horses, houses; and where the regard is very great, wives. Valeria, for instance, was married to Lectinius Publius before he gave her to Marcus Strachus. She had borne Lectinius two living sons, you see, and Marcus was his cousin and a distinguished brother officer, and he needed an heir. You knew that, Judith. Well, that's what I intend with Holofernes.'

Judith saw his face very clearly: every muscle, every angle of bone.

'You want to marry me.'

'Ah, Judith, marry you, no. I must marry a wife from the Roman nobility. But I want to take you as my woman. I want to live with you here, and build you a villa in the country, on our family land. I want you to entertain for me like Drusilla does for Appius Paullus, and Octavia for Terence. I want you to return with me to the east and live with me in our governors' palaces. Becausc I mean to be governor of many provinces, one after another, to build up influence and fortunc, and I want you to share all of them.'

Judith gazed into his eyes, mesmerised. They were darkened and dazzling and in them she saw brilliant images of the life he offered her.

She felt his hand touch her cheek before she noticed him move; it was cool and light, and beneath it her flesh thrilled as if sluiced in icy water. She shuddered – she hardly knew whether from longing or fear. Lucius wanted her, but he was not offering, could not offer her marriage. If she went with him, she would be stepping outside respectability and honour for ever.

Yet she had already done that once, when she became Holofernes' wife. In the eyes of Bethulia, she knew, she was Holofernes' whore. Did it matter what she did now?

Holofernes had been good to her. He had made her no promises but he had looked after her well. He had lied for her, and claimed the respect of other men for her. He had brought her with him – so far. But he had also concealed his knowledge of her past from her, and then betrayed it to Lucius. Holofernes lived dangerously and as long as she was with him, the danger would threaten her too. It was a danger from inside as well as out; Holofernes called up the most violent responses in her, the most unwomanly feelings.

By contrast, Lucius's touch concentrated her senses into one pure brilliance. She felt like the evening star, shining so brightly that she repelled the darkness.

'Judith, we must be together. Do you agree?'

'How do I know you'll keep me with you? You might get tired of me and cast me off, and then I'd be just another eastern prostitute.'

'How do you know Holofernes will keep you as his wife? He could divorce you tomorrow, or more likely next year when he's doing deals in the east and needs to make a diplomatic marriage with the daughter of some Mesopotamian prince. And then where will you be? Abandoned in Rome.'

'No,' Judith said quickly. 'Holofernes wouldn't do that to me.'

'You trust him then?'

'For that, yes.'

'And me?'

'I don't understand you,' Judith said helplessly. 'I don't know how to judge you.'

Lucius remained very still, his palm resting against her cheek. His face seemed almost translucent in the blue light.

'Test us,' he said at last. 'Let me ask Holofernes for you in your presence, then you'll be able to see just how far each of us values you. What price he puts on you, what sacrifice I'm willing to make to have you. Put us to the test.'

Judith felt his hand begin to tremble against her cheek. At first she thought he was shaking, then she realised it was herself. She was shaking with terror and with exhilaration, because she recognised that she had come too far along this road to turn back.

'When?' she whispered.

'At the feast for your new home. The one your husband has already invited me to, so graciously.' Lucius's mouth twisted into an ironic smile. 'Go to him now and tell him that I heard, and I accept.'

CHAPTER EIGHTEEN

Cathy opened her eyes and was halfway off the sofa within a second, not understanding what she saw. Lucius was bowing before her, strange objects in his hands.

Then she saw that it was Danilo, setting down two plates of prosciutto and artichoke hearts. A box of breadsticks, an open bottle of wine and two glasses already stood on the low table.

'Lunch,' he said simply. 'It's three o'clock, you know.' He straightened up and looked at her. 'Take your time. You've been a long way under.'

Cathy sank back into the cushions. 'How long have I been asleep?'

'Less than an hour. Don't you remember, you wanted to be on your own for a while, to think, so I went out to do some shopping. As soon as I left the building I realised I'd forgotten my wallet and came back up for it. You were already asleep. It's the shock, I expect.'

'Yes.' Cathy looked away. Danilo's face was eager; he had seen at once that she'd been dreaming. She didn't want to hear his questions; not yet.

She looked fixedly at the desk over by the window. It was a beautiful piece of furniture, curved and made from wood with an undulating grain. She would have expected Danilo to opt for something more austere. In fact, almost everything in the room was lighter and less functional than she had imagined. She realised that up till now all her ideas about Danilo had been based on what Matthew had told her. Matthew, his antagonist.

Danilo was speaking, asking her whether she wanted water as well as wine.

'Just wine, thanks.' Cathy watched him pour it. His hands were golden, the wrists dusted with fine black hair. What was Matthew doing now? She remembered his longer, more loosely jointed hands reaching for his own bottle of wine on Monday night, and the blind way he had turned towards the door.

'Thanks.' She took the glass Danilo gave her, and felt her stomach twist as their fingers accidentally touched. She drew her knees up onto the sofa and retreated behind them. She felt as if her insides were separating, tearing her between Danilo and Matthew; just as Judith was feeling the impossible love grow between herself and her two men.

It was no accident that Cathy had dreamt that last scene here, and now. But it was beyond her to know which was the mirror and which the authentic image. Was Judith's story a reflection of hers or was hers unfolding in response to Judith's?

'It's all right, I'm not going to ask you any questions.' Danilo placed her plate on the edge of the table and put a knife and fork beside it. 'I know you're not ready.'

Cathy looked at his profile as he busied himself with breadsticks. 'You might as well ask now as later,' she said, wondering if she meant it. 'I don't suppose I'll get much readier.'

'Really?' Danilo's quick glance showed her the blaze of hope in his eyes. It kindled an exhilarated fear in her.

'Really.'

'In that case . . .' He looked at her and then shrugged, his smile ironic. 'After all that, I don't know what to say. I can only guess what a shock it must be to you. I've had years to live with this and get used to the insanity of it, but for you it's only a couple of weeks old.'

'Not quite. It started before then.' Cathy thought back, staring into her wine. 'I saw a picture of you before I came here – Matthew showed it to me when he'd just got the job. I felt odd about it at the time. I thought I knew you. And there were other things too. I had a nightmare on the plane which made me feel I was somewhere I knew, except it was all foreign. And that was like a nightmare I once had years and years ago, when I was a teenager . . .'

She broke off and looked at the rim of her glass. It bore the smeared imprint of her lips. Why had she forgotten it, that terrifying dream which now came back to her, absolutely clear but miniaturised and remote? Herself at fifteen, sitting up in the darkness gasping, trying to push away the branches that were twining round her arms and shoulders, growing across her face. They grew strong and yet they were dry and sapless; her nose was full of their dusty smell. Sweat sprang from her skin. She had tried to scream for what felt like years; then at last she had felt a rush of cool air and a hand lifting the branches from her face and Matthew was there, his hair tousled from sleep, saying, 'Wake up, sis. It's all right. Ssh, you'll wake the parents.'

Matthew. He was with her now; he had been with her then.

She looked up at Danilo. 'It's not just us, is it? Matthew's in it too.'

Danilo was sitting on the far edge of the sofa, watching her.

He nodded reluctantly. 'He seems to be.'

'No, it's more than that.' Cathy scrutinised his face. 'And you know it's more than that. Matt's as deeply involved in all this as you and I. He brought me here. I'd never have come if it hadn't been for him. He introduced me to the Giuditta – he recognised her as something special even from the photo, and then he saw the likeness in my drawings. And anyway,' Cathy paused, 'I felt it. When I had my first dreams, I knew they were connected with him. I told him so – that's why he didn't like them; he said I was being guided by them and if Judith turned against Holofernes, I'd turn against him.'

'Holofernes.' There was an edge of sharpness in Danilo's voice. 'You thought he was Holofernes?'

'Yes. It – it seemed to fit the circumstances.' Cathy looked away, thinking of the bus ride out to the country village, Matthew's hands closing over hers in the bedroom, the hours of love-making as the radiance died from the light.

Several seconds passed before Danilo spoke.

'I could see you and Matthew were lovers. I'm not blind. But somehow I never thought you'd get us confused.'

'Everything's confused for me,' Cathy muttered. She didn't want to talk about Matthew to Danilo; it felt like a betrayal of both.

'Is it? Do you still think Matthew's Holofernes?'

Cathy looked up and flinched from the pain in his face. 'No,' she said softly.

'But you wish he was?'

'I don't know. Oh, God help me, I don't know anything.' She pressed her glass against her forehead; its coldness gave her an instant headache. 'I only know I've been in love with Matthew half my life, and just as we become lovers I meet you.

And I can't ignore what I feel for you, and I can't disbelieve what you tell me and show me.' She gestured towards the prints, now lying on the desk. 'You're haunted by the story of Judith and so am I. You have dreams, I have dreams. Does Matt have dreams too? He's certainly in some kind of communion with the Giuditta, locked away in the lab with it day after day. I think he's talking to her now, Danilo, rather than to me. He's angry with me.'

She put her glass down and turned to look at Danilo. She spoke slowly, articulating the thought that had been slipping round the edges of her consciousness all afternoon.

'There are three of us here, just are there are three of them in Judith's world. Judith, Holofernes and Lucius; you, me and Matthew. I'm dreaming Judith's story and you're dreaming Holofernes'. So that makes Matthew Lucius.'

'Yes,' said Danilo at length. 'I believe so.'

'Do you know what happens to them all?'

Danilo shook his head. For the first time since she'd known him, Cathy thought she saw fear in his eyes. 'I've told you all I know.' He rubbed his forehead as if his head ached. 'My dreams were always jumbled after they reached Rome. I still have them now and then, more like impressionistic flashbacks than anything else – except for that last dream, of course. That's always clear.'

'The dream when Judith won't save you.'

'Yes.'

'And you don't know what she needs to save you from?'

Danilo hesitated. 'No, not exactly. But I know who my enemy is.' He didn't speak the name; he didn't need to.

'That's the old story,' Cathy said quickly. 'In your version. It might be different in mine.'

'Yes, it might.'

'And as you said earlier, we're not possessed by these people. We're just linked. It could be that we influence them as much as they influence us.'

'Yes,' said Danilo more doubtfully.

'I need to talk to Matthew. I've got to find out how much he knows.'

'And what he's said to my father.' Danilo met her gaze levelly. 'We know what my father's said to him, don't we? That you've been lying about your drawings, that we've been having secret meetings. But what is it that Matthew's been telling my father?'

'You think Matthew might be having dreams and has told Enzo instead of me?'

'You said yourself that Matthew's angry with you. And that he's been trying to get to the Giuditta from the start. He's an ambitious man, Matthew, and he goes after what he wants pitilessly.'

'Matthew's not pitiless!'

'Isn't he? He worked very hard to persuade you to stay out here with him, even though it meant you giving up your business and all your friends. He had to persuade you to show my father those drawings, didn't he? Yes, I thought so, I could see you were uneasy about it. And now he's got access to the Giuditta, who knows what he's saying to win more and more of my father's trust?'

'That's not fair.' There was an ugly knot in Cathy's chest which made breathing painful. 'He's genuinely fond of Enzo. He hated the fact that the drawings upset him.'

'I'm not disputing that. I believe he is fond of my father, but he won't let it stand in the way of what he wants. Just as I know he loves you, passionately – anyone can see that. But he's doing his best to hurt you now. He didn't like you dreaming because it was out of his control, and now he's punishing you for keeping secrets from him. Catti, your stepbrother wants to own you.'

'No! That's not true.' Cathy got to her feet and went quickly to the window. She leaned against it, looking from Danilo to the rooftop view outside. 'Please don't do this to me,' she said. 'Please don't try and turn me against him. Everything's frightening enough without that.'

Danilo sat very still on the sofa. His broad shoulders looked peculiarly helpless.

'I'm sorry,' he said eventually. 'Don't leave, I need your help.'

Cathy didn't move. 'Of course I won't leave,' she said. 'I need you too.'

'You dreamt again just now, didn't you?'

Cathy nodded.

'What was it? Can you tell me?'

'It was Lucius and Judith,' she said. Over the top of the buildings she could see the green-brown waters of the Tiber and the Janiculum hill beyond. 'He was courting her, asking her if she'd leave Holofernes for him.'

'What did she say?'

Cathy looked at him. Inside her, a dark flower was unfurling its petals: guilt, grief, loss. 'She said yes.'

Danilo looked down at his hands. Cathy twisted away from the window and went over to him. Her arms ached; her mouth was speaking his name long before she was close enough to touch. He half rose and as she came round the side of the sofa, he pulled her into an awkward embrace.

Their tongues met; their hands held on to one another desperately. Cathy tried to pull herself closer against him, but the sofa was in the way. With each touch, it was as if she lost another part of him; she was almost crying when he finally scooped her legs from beneath her and pulled her across the cushions onto his body.

It was the strangest love-making she'd ever known. Her flesh ignited in a string of tiny flames. As their clothes came off, their nakedness was overpowering. Cathy felt she wouldn't be able to touch Danilo's bare skin; that her own was too exposed to stand it. But they were already touching. They stood by the sofa, stroking, exploring, burrowing fingers and mouths into one another.

Each part of Cathy's body seemed to have its own appetite. And each time it was able to satisfy itself in a small explosion of pleasure. They triggered one another like memories or laughter. Energy coursed through her. At some stage – was it before or after he came inside her? – she felt Danilo laughing too.

CHAPTER NINETEEN

Judith paced around the atrium of her new home, gazing distractedly at the hangings and statues. The house was more ornate than she was used to in Rome, and many of the decorations were from the east – the fruits of Aufidius Metallus's successful campaigns. Oil lamps with long plaited stems, mother-of-pearl bowls, a rug woven of silk threads – they were at once familiar and alien.

She crossed her arms over her breast; there was a chill in the air. Yet beneath her fingers the flesh of her upper arms was hot. Soon the guests would arrive. Marcellus Galba was coming, and the aedile Sertorius, with their wives Lucceia and Geggonia; Marcus Strachus with Valeria; and, of course, Lucius.

She had not seen Lucius since that fevered discussion of the day before. She knew he would keep his word and come tonight; Holofernes had returned from the Comitium this morning and confirmed it. 'You were right,' he said. 'He is going to come. And the Romans say we're volatile. I wonder . . .' He had looked at her in a way that disturbed her.

'Yes? You wonder?' Judith had turned from him, pretending to inspect the newly plucked birds which the cook had brought out on a tray.

'Oh, it's a waste of time. How can anyone who's not

Roman fathom the way their minds work?' And he had gone off, back to the Forum to attend the slave market and bring them back 'some young and good-looking and experienced slaves. It'll have to be one of each, it's all I can afford now.'

All day long Judith had worked in the house, organising the slaves, consulting uneasily with the cook and receiving calls from Roman matrons. Valeria had been among them.

'What's this we hear about a fight?' she'd asked, with a touch of agitation. 'Marcus was told Lucius threw Holofernes out of his house and has sworn never to come into this one.'

'Nonsense,' Judith had said dismissively. 'Lucius thought Holofernes should have taken a smaller house, or been content to stay under his roof. You know what Lucius is like. They argued about it last night but it's over now. Lucius is coming to the feast this evening.'

'Good. Because any breach puts us in a difficult position. After all, we've lent you three of our slaves for this feast.'

She had departed as the next callers arrived, leaving Judith perturbed. But she'd had no time to dwell on Valeria's anxiety. There was too much to do to ensure that the house was correctly arranged, the special tributes to the house gods ready to be lit, the food rich enough and the slaves graceful enough to do honour to their guests. And beneath all her domestic activity, beating like the heart of some great beast, was the knowledge of what Lucius meant to do.

It was now the hour before dusk, and time Judith bathed and dressed. From the inner house she could hear Holofernes talking to Trincio and Balbas, the two slaves he had bought from Lucius. She could tell from his voice that he was pacing as he talked – he seemed invigorated by this new house. At any rate, he was very determinedly taking possession of it.

He came out of the triclinium as she passed.

'Judith, I'm giving Marcellus Galba the place of honour. I'll seat Lucius as the joint host. That should satisfy both of them. But will Marcus take offence?'

'I doubt it. I think Marcus is worried about offending Lucius himself. Valeria was here earlier, saying what a difficult position we'd put them in.'

Holofernes rolled his eyes. 'What a time for them to lose their nerve. It's in the Roman character, you know. They hate making any kind of new beginning. They believe that every time they start something new, they disturb their gods and risk making them angry.' He grinned and then looked more closely at Judith. 'Are you all right?'

'Yes. Just a little anxious about tonight.'

'That's natural. It doesn't mean anything. Look at it this way, we're entertaining a senator and an aedile. Lucius will be here, just like all the other times, and old Marcus is as solid as ever. And you, my Judean wife, are beautiful and brave as always.' He moved close, screening her from the slaves, and kissed her softly on the lips. 'This is for later,' he said. 'For much later, when these stiff-necked Romans have gone.' His hand brushed her cheek, smoothing the skin which Lucius had touched yesterday.

Judith stood still for a few seconds. The unexpected gentleness took away her self-possession. Suddenly she was full of doubts. She wanted to press herself into Holofernes' arms, confide in him what Lucius was planning, but he was moving away from her.

'You must get ready, Judith,' he said. 'There's not much time.'

Her skin was lightly perfumed; her hair was rolled onto her

head and fastened with combs. She wore earrings, neck chains and rings. On one of the chains round her neck she carried the amulet Lucius had given her when they were still on the voyage west. And at the last moment she wound round her arm Manasses' coiled bracelet which Holofernes had pulled out of shape in his attempt to stop it pinching her.

Why was she thinking about that now? A warning to herself, perhaps: remember, even in his tenderness, Holofernes imposes his will. Not that there had been many tendernesses, Judith thought, as she stood beside Holofernes in the atrium, ministering to the guests. Holofernes had never cherished her. He treated her like an army comrade or a younger brother, encouraging her through difficulties, laughing her out of her fears. It was often helpful – such as the time he'd brought shellfish to her privately in Lucius's house, to teach her how to eat them – but no more.

The only time he treated her as a woman was when he came to her room at night. She wouldn't think of such things; not now, not with the guests here. Marcellus Galba was complimenting Holofernes on the house and showing a keen interest in the silver dishes which had once belonged to a prince of the east. Geggonia and Lucceia were exchanging eloquent looks. Marcus Strachus was talking to Sertorius with a furrowed brow and Valeria sat beside the older women, valiantly attempting to make conversation. And Lucius, whose step Judith had recognised as soon as he entered the vestibule, had just walked quietly into the atrium.

It was late. The food had been delicious. The flesh of the birds, soaked in wines and berries, had been soft, and the fish delicate and white-bodied. Once the meal was finished, the men had drunk toast after toast in deep cups of wine, and the woman had joined in, allowing the slaves to half fill their smaller cups.

The wall hangings in the triclinium shifted in the draughts, and the tapers played tricks with the coloured threads.

The slaves were not graceful, but it didn't matter because the men were too busy talking to notice. Valeria made everyone laugh with her dry observations and even Geggonia and Lucceia had unbent. The Greek slaves had recited their poems; the musicians were about to play their lyres for the third time, to usher the important guests out.

Judith sat on her couch between Geggonia and Lucceia, presiding over it all with a fierce grace of her own. She had never felt so free. Nor so beautiful. She knew the others saw it too. Both Holofernes and Lucius kept turning to her, and now the other men also seemed to feel her thrall. Marcellus Galba's heavy-lidded eyes kept flickering towards her in puzzlement.

There was a dizzying sense of power in knowing what Lucius was going to do. The others probably thought it was the wine that made him combative, alternately silky and spiky as he raised his eyebrows at their comments and invited them to justify their opinions. Judith alone could discern his purpose. He was taking issue again and again, sometimes humorously, sometimes seriously, with Holofernes, drawing him steadily down the road towards the challenge.

Once again the lyre music rippled through the room. It gave Judith a peculiar feeling, like secret laughter. She looked at Holofernes. He was watching her, as he so often did, with a gleam of complicity. It intensified the odd sensation inside her and she looked swiftly at Lucius beside him. Not by a muscle did he betray himself, but in his composed face his eyes blazed.

Marcellus was going, and Sertorius with him. The whole party accompanied them to the atrium where Judith and Marcus and Valeria bid them farewell. As Holofernes and Lucius escorted the guests to the vestibule, Judith felt Valeria's hand laid gently on her arm. She looked at her, startled; her friend's face was worried.

'Judith, I think it's best if we go now, and take Lucius with us.'

'Why? It's not so late.'

'The men have drunk a lot, and I don't like the way Lucius is behaving with Holofernes. I'm afraid there's going to be a quarrel.'

'You must go if you want, of course, but I don't think Lucius will want to leave with you.' Judith heard the confidence in her own low voice and saw anxiety turn to suspicion in Valeria's eyes.

'In that case we'll stay,' Valeria said. 'Oh Judith,' she added in an urgent whisper, 'this is so dangerous for all of us.'

'What is?'

'You know very well. You're jeopardising everything, do you understand? Everything.'

Judith glanced over her head at Marcus. He was too far away to have heard his wife's words but he was watching her with the same tense air.

'I understand you don't mean to stay with us much longer, Marcus Strachus,' she said. 'We'll be sorry to lose you from our party.'

'In that case we'll wait,' Marcus said bluntly. And then, glancing at Valeria, 'I wouldn't want our departure to spoil anything.'

His face was grim and for the first time since Lucius's

arrival, Judith felt her unease return. Why were they so afraid? But it was too late to ask, for Holofernes and Lucius were coming in side by side.

Back in the triclinium they resumed their former seats except for Holofernes, who remained standing. He seemed preoccupied.

'Congratulations on a successful evening.' Lucius reclined Greek-fashion on his couch, leaning on his elbow. Holofernes nodded, but said nothing.

'You're pleased, surely,' Lucius persisted. 'Marcellus Galba is well and truly committed to us now. And Marcellus naturally brings Sertorius with him, which means we're likely to get the support of all the contractors Sertorius favours. Not to mention some of their money.'

Holofernes reached for a cup of water. 'Yes,' he said. 'It's not bad going for someone who's about to be charged as a criminal.'

Lucius laughed. 'You'll survive to have them cheering your chariot home. They'll be begging you to commit more crimes against the state than even you have the stomach for.'

Holofernes gave him a brooding look. 'I never set out to commit crimes against the state. And that's not what I'm doing.'

'What crime?' Judith felt a knot rise uncomfortably into her breast. 'What are you talking about?'

Holofernes shrugged. 'There's a rumour out that I'm going to be arrested.' He drank the water down thirstily and passed his cup to the slave for more.

'What rumour? I haven't heard it.' But from the stillness which had descended on Marcus and Valeria, Judith realised that they, too, knew of it.

'You've been busy in the house all day,' said Holofernes.

'It's what everyone's talking about in the Forum and it's been gathering detail in a way I don't like. There's a name to it now.' He turned back to Lucius. 'Balbas brought me a message in the vestibule. My accuser's supposedly going to be Gaius Nepos, the ex-chief centurion.'

Judith felt her skin tighten, as if in a blast of cold air. 'Why didn't you tell me?' she asked.

'Because it might be nothing. And the feast had to go ahead anyway.'

'It *is* nothing,' Lucius said and held his own cup out, but towards the wine bowl. 'It's just the rumour mill at rumour hour. At the worst, someone's deliberately started the story to try and frighten you and see what support they raise.'

'Yesterday you seemed to think that would be a lot, what with my recruiting unofficially and offending everyone by taking my own house.'

Lucius's smile illuminated his face. 'And you swore that even Romans wouldn't be so – what was it? Puling and pusillanimous. Yes, and unmanly.'

Holofernes squared his shoulders. 'All right, let's not bear grudges against each other.'

'I agree. We're partners, and now's the time for us to prove it. Come on, Holofernes, stay still for a moment and let me toast our venture.' He indicated the couch and Holofernes sat down, rubbing his hand across his eyes. Judith saw a flash of teeth; he was grinning.

'I expect you're right,' he said. 'Puling and pusillanimous, did I really say that?'

'You did.' Lucius spoke easily and Holofernes chuckled, his hand still over his eyes. But Judith saw no amusement on Lucius's face; he was watching Holofernes without expression.

She felt another tremor of unease and moved restlessly, but Lucius was speaking again.

'We must all drink to this toast – fill everyone's cups. To Holofernes, his courage and his forthrightness. May he guide our venture to glory!'

Judith drank, keeping her eyes on the men. She could hear Marcus echoing the toast warily.

'To Lucius.' Holofernes raised his cup abruptly into the air. 'He's a brilliant and honourable man. Syria salutes Rome.' And Marcus's voice again, more definite this time.

'All the same,' said Lucius as the cups came down, 'we must make a gesture without delay. Something to consolidate our success and bind you close into the fabric of Rome.'

'I could be elected as a magistrate,' said Holofernes facetiously.

'You need to forge a bond with a Roman family,' Lucius went on. 'Unfortunately, mine is out of contention because of my father. But there is a suitable family, poor but well-respected, now led by Titus Labenius. His father fought honourably in the last war at Carthage and Titus was a superb advocate in his day, who helped hundreds of clients. The family lost their property when the harvests failed and the land was seized in payment for debts. I advised Titus Labenius at the time and he took his case to the people; he won recompense by popular acclaim and he has been indebted to me ever since. He has a rather beautiful daughter.'

Judith held herself very still. Holofernes was looking puzzled but amused. 'Yes?' he prompted Lucius.

'Titus Labenius promised her to me then.'

'Congratulations.'

'She was very young then, only ten. Now she's sixteen,

which is the age at which I always intended to marry her.'

'It's a good age.' From his voice, and his carefully grave face, Judith could tell that Holofernes was suppressing laughter. He must think Lucius was drunk.

'Indeed. In fact, wasn't it the age at which your wife was married for the first time?'

Holofernes glanced at Judith. 'It was.'

'Livia will make an excellent wife,' Lucius mused. 'She's well-educated and accomplished but her father has kept her sheltered from the world. She would be an ornament to any Roman man who married her.'

'I'm sure she would,' Holofernes grinned and reached for his cup. 'Another toast, it seems. To Lucius and his bride!'

'You don't understand.' Lucius raised his hand. 'I'm not proposing to marry Livia myself. I'm offering her to you.'

Holofernes's cup stopped in mid-air. He stared at Lucius. 'What?' he said in bafflement.

'I'm proposing that you should marry Livia,' said Lucius calmly. 'She's promised to me; I am giving her to you. It would be a good alliance for you. It would join you to one of our most respected families and it would win over many people who now regard you as a foreigner. And the fact that I'm willing to let you marry her will show everyone how highly I think of you. It will leave them in no doubt of the bond between us.'

The silence which followed was broken by Holofernes' embarrassed laugh. 'Well friend, I'm honoured that you think me worthy of your promised bride, and I see that there might be advantages, but aren't you forgetting something? I have a wife.' He turned and looked at Judith. His face was quizzical but no more. Beyond him, Valeria and Marcus sat as still as statues.

'You could divorce Judith without dishonour,' Lucius said coolly. 'She's been your wife for half a year now and there's no sign of a child. That's reason enough to divorce her, and there need be no stain on her or you.'

Holofernes' cup clattered down, spilling wine. 'My wife isn't a hen to be killed when she fails to lay fast enough,' he said sharply. 'It might be the Roman way to cast wives off and let them take their chance, but it's not mine.'

'I'm not suggesting you cast Judith off. She would come to me.'

There was a silence. Holofernes had his back to Judith and it communicated nothing.

'*What?*' he said at last, very quietly.

Lucius's smile flashed out like fire. 'I'm proposing an exchange. It's an honourable deal – more than honourable, in fact. My promised bride goes to you; your wife comes to me. In that way, we truly prove our partnership.' Lucius looked radiant. He seemed to have gathered all his energies into himself and now he sat very erect opposite Holofernes, as brilliant and fierce as a naked blade.

Holofernes looked slowly round at Judith. There was something in the movement that disturbed her, a heaviness, almost a raggedness. She recognised it but had no words for it; she had waited for this moment, but now it was coming too fast and she had no time to work out what she was seeing, or feeling.

Holofernes' face was shocked. 'I see,' he said. He looked at her searchingly. Judith felt herself begin to crimson. It was as if a tide were washing through her, making her unable to speak or move. 'I see,' Holofernes said again.

His eyes were full of pain. Judith was stunned; she hadn't

expected this. She leaned instinctively towards him but he flinched. It was a tiny movement, imperceptible to anybody else. He continued to look at her steadily and his chest rose and fell; then he reached out and took her hand. Her fingers jerked as his grip closed firmly on her.

'Right, Lucius.' He turned, a businesslike note suddenly in his voice. 'This honourable deal. You want to marry my wife.'

Lucius's face shimmered in the taper light. 'I'll look after her. You can trust me for that.'

'That isn't what I said. Is it part of your honourable deal to marry Judith?'

'I shall marry her in the Syrian sense, certainly. You know we can't have a Roman marriage. Here we can have only one wife at a time, and my wife must be Roman and bring me a political alliance. But Judith will have everything you could ask for her – respect, position, honour.'

'But not a Roman marriage. In other words, you want me to give you my wife for you to use her as a courtesan.'

'Be careful what you're saying, Holofernes.'

'You insult me and you insult my wife. You suggest that I should be grateful for marrying your cast-off bride while you turn my wife into a prostitute – and *you* tell *me* to be careful!' Holofernes laughed incredulously.

Two hectic spots began to burn on Lucius's cheeks. Marcus leaned forward and said, 'Come on now, brothers—' but Lucius silenced him with a gesture. 'How dare you,' he said to Holofernes, deadly quiet. 'I'm offering you my bride, a pure girl of noble Roman family. You, a foreigner, are in no position to refuse her. And how dare you suggest that I, as a Roman, will not keep my word by your wife?'

He looked at Judith as he spoke, a quick, anxious look.

'As a Roman,' Holofernes said thoughtfully. 'What about as a man? As a man, what do you say to a woman whom you're proposing to remove from her husband and put into your bed? Go on, Judith's here, she's listening. Tell her, as a *man*, what you're going to do with her.'

Emotions warred in Lucius's face, fury, resentment, triumph. Finally he smiled. Deliberately ignoring Holofernes, he fixed his eyes on Judith.

'I already have,' he said softly.

Holofernes' hand clenched so hard on hers that Judith's knuckles ground together. The next second he had released her. He stood up. 'Get out.'

'It's a little late for—'

'Get out. You're not fit to be under my roof.'

Lucius rose, like a spring uncoiling. 'I'll go, with pleasure,' he said. Every muscle in his face had tightened, though his voice was steady. 'But when I go, I'll take Judith with me.'

Marcus was on his feet too. 'Brothers, this has gone far enough. It's been a long night and we've all drunk a lot of wine. Let's go to our own houses now.' He took Lucius's arm but Lucius shrugged him off.

'Leave me alone, Marcus. I'll leave when I'm ready. No uneducated Syrian bandit is going to order me out of a Roman house.'

Holofernes walked quickly across to him and struck him on the face with his open hand. Lucius staggered and fell over the edge of the couch,

'It's all right,' Holofernes said contemptuously as Marcus threw an arm in front of him, 'I won't slap him again. I wouldn't hit him with my fist, let alone draw a sword on him. He's just a stupid boy.' He walked back to Judith. Behind him

Lucius, now back on his feet, lurched after him and was held back by Marcus.

Holofernes took Judith's hand. His expression was unfathomable as he looked at her, full of dark and violent emotions. 'You see Judith and you want her,' he said, turning back to Lucius. 'Well, want away. Judith is married to me under Syrian and Judean law, and she remains my wife, for all that you've been sneaking round her.' He paused and looked Lucius up and down. 'Your father was right,' he said dismissively. 'You're a disgrace to your ancestors.'

Beneath Judith's fingers, Holofernes' hand was shaking. This was not as she had imagined it; everything was different. She had thought Holofernes would argue, then negotiate, then hand her to Lucius with a wry salute. She had been wrong.

Confusion made a whirl of her thoughts, like a sudden storm out of season. But although she couldn't think, she was glad; there was a fire of gladness in her. She clung to Holofernes, and her mind was suddenly full of visions of the past – herself and Holofernes by the Acra in Jerusalem, Holofernes sitting on his wooden chest in the encampment, the view of the sea from Assos, and Holofernes coming laughing from the gymnasium, shaking water drops from his hair.

In front of them, Lucius still struggled to recover breath. He was white and sheened with sweat. His nostrils dilated and his shoulders heaved with the effort to take in air; he was seeking her eyes, but Judith looked away, panic and guilt seizing her.

'You'll regret this,' he said to Holofernes at last, very quietly. A question hovered in his tone; he was waiting for her to give him a sign.

'I doubt it,' said Holofernes contemptuously.

'You will.'

In the background, a noise was growing. Judith had been aware of it for some time: it was a murmuring, scuffling sound with a steady beat in it, and it had slipped into her senses so that she hadn't stopped to question it. Now, though, it broke off and resumed again much louder and nearer.

'They're at the door!' It was Valeria who cried out.

'No! No!' Marcus muttered under his breath. 'In the name of Mars, not now.' He looked over Lucius's shoulder to Holofernes. 'I was afraid of this.'

Judith turned in bewilderment to Holofernes; different reactions were chasing one another across his face and she couldn't read them. But when he relinquished her hand and set his shoulders, her confusion turned to fear.

There was a cacophony of voices at the front of the house and the running footsteps of a slave down the corridor.

'I know,' Holofernes forestalled the boy as he appeared in the doorway. 'Gaius Nepos is here, with the guards. I'm coming to meet them.'

They hurried along the corridor, robes swishing and their breathing loud in the narrow space. Ahead of them, light spilled into the atrium from the torches carried by the guards. There were four guards, a knot of supporters and a stocky, grey-haired man who stood in the central, uncovered part of the atrium. When Holofernes entered, he walked up to the stocky man and bowed.

'Gaius Nepos, welcome to my house. It's late to come visiting, but welcome all the same.'

Gaius Nepos ignored Holofernes' outstretched hand. 'I haven't come visiting, General Holofernes,' he said gruffly. 'I've come to arrest you, in the name of the Roman people, on charges of subversion of the state, taking property, and sedition with the Roman army. You're a traitor to Rome, General, and a dangerous criminal.'

'I'm not and you know it.'

'You'll answer charges tomorrow morning. Take him.'

The guards handed their torches to the supporters and surrounded Holofernes.

'In the name of all the gods!' exclaimed Marcus. 'There's no need for this. If you want to bring a charge, man, bring it in the Forum tomorrow. General Holofernes will answer it there.'

Gaius Nepos scowled. 'The Syrian's a traitor,' he said, 'and a Syrian. We can't trust him. Take him.'

'No!' The cry burst hoarsely from Judith. 'You can't take him, he's not a traitor. He has friends who'll vouch for him – Marcus Strachus here, and Lucius Tullius. And Marcellus Galba the senator. Ask them.'

'We're here to arrest you too, madam.' The battered face looked uncomfortably into hers.

'My wife?' Holofernes looked at him in disbelief. Two guards had wrenched his arms behind his back, but he ignored them. 'You're arresting my wife?'

'I'm sorry, General.' Gaius Nepos frowned at the wall hanging. 'It wasn't my idea. It's the law.'

'The law? When you charge a Roman, you don't charge his wife.'

'But you're not a Roman, General.'

'No,' said Holofernes, staring at the older man. 'But I am a general. An army man.'

Judith watched the two men exchange glances and felt herself spinning into the dark. Why was Gaius Nepos arresting Holofernes when she could feel the sympathy between them? And why was Lucius silent?

'Let her stay with us.' Valeria had stepped forward. Her touch on Judith's arm was tense. 'We'll bring her to the Forum at dawn, to hear the charges. You can count on us.'

'Yes, I think I can.' Gaius Nepos turned quickly at the sound of unrest among his supporters, and they fell silent. 'All right, Marcus Strachus, it's your responsibility to guard Judith, the Syrian's wife, tonight, and to bring her to the Forum to hear charges against both of them tomorrow. General Holofernes, you'll come with me.'

He turned, military style, and marched to the door. Holofernes turned in time with him, making the guards stumble. From the midst of them, he shot a look at Judith, an angry, defiant, vulnerable look. She stood with her arms crossed over her chest, trying to pull strength from her own body, and gazed back at him.

Then he was gone and there was only his voice from the vestibule, saying tauntingly, 'Why don't you shackle me? Then I could walk at your pace.'

Judith was shocked to hear herself laugh aloud. She put her hand over her mouth and looked at her companions: Valeria, frightened; Marcus, grave; and Lucius, deadly calm.

Chapter Twenty

The telephone's ring pulled Danilo from the shallows of his dream. He'd been trapped there for some time, unable to break through the surface and reach Cathy. He sat up quickly and looked at her. She lay turned towards him, her face troubled and her breathing irregular. Her dream continued, uninterrupted by the noise.

Danilo found it disturbing to see how deeply she went into the dreams. It made him realise that she was alone in there. Alone and beyond his reach.

He heard the answering machine switch on. He slid out of bed and walked into the living room, taking Cathy's scent with him. He listened to his own recorded voice requesting a message and in the short silence had time to wonder which of them it would be.

'I know you must be there.' His father's voice, speaking in English. 'Danilo, Cathy, one of you pick up the phone. I don't intend—'

Danilo grabbed the receiver, praying the words wouldn't have pierced Cathy's sleep.

'Yes, Father,' he said quietly, in Italian. 'I have picked up the phone.'

Again, a short silence, then Enzo said, 'This has gone far

enough. I can't stand by any longer.'

'It's none of your business.' Danilo looked at the matt black panel of his answering machine; it made a strange contrast to his naked body.

'I was like you once.'

Danilo thought of his father standing by his own telephone. He would be in his study, surrounded by possessions and documents, wearing a suit.

'No, you weren't,' he said brutally. 'Your trouble was, you were nothing like me. You didn't even know what you had. It was all handed to you on a plate and you destroyed it, and my mother with it. *I've* waited years. I've searched for Cathy and worked for her, and now we've finally come together, you're trying to take her away. You know it was your fault that mother died and now because of that, you can't bear to let me have Cathy.'

'I am not going to talk to you about your mother.'

'No, you never did.'

'I'm talking about Cathy. She has to know.'

'She does know. I've told her.'

'Everything?'

'Yes, Father,' Danilo said softly. His chest was rising and falling fast, but he didn't think it could be heard in his voice. 'Everything.'

'Then you've got nothing to fear from bringing her to me.'

Danilo put the receiver down and turned off both telephone bell and answering machine. The hair on his chest and under his arms was damp. He knew from his father's voice that he was going to act; he, in turn, would have to decide what to do now.

'Ahhhhh.'

The sound came from the bedroom: a wild, low laugh. He stared at the door. 'Ahhhhhh.' The same again, but this time with a sobbing rhythm.

Danilo knew he should be running to help her but he had to force himself to cross the floor and step back into the room.

Cathy was crouching in the bed, holding the sheets round her. Her mouth was open in an empty smile.

'Cathy.'

She gazed at him. 'No,' she whispered. 'Oh no,' and covered her face with the sheets.

Danilo sat on the bed and held her tentatively. He was afraid she might flinch, but she stayed huddled and motionless in his arms.

'Catti. Can you tell me about it? It's all right, you're with me.'

She shook her head. 'You weren't here,' she said.

'I was only in the other room.'

'I thought I heard you talking.'

'I was on the telephone. My father called.' Through the sheets, he felt her stiffen. 'Listen, he knows you're here. Nadia must have gone straight back and told him. If we stay here, I'm sure he'll come looking for us.'

'No!' Cathy twisted free and began scrambling out of bed. 'He mustn't come here! What if he brings Matthew?'

Danilo caught her arm. 'What if he does? You and Matthew have to be honest with each other some time. You can't go on denying what's happened between us.'

'I'm not denying it. But Matthew mustn't come here and find us or something awful will happen. I know because of the dream. Please . . .' She looked down at his hand gripping her arm; Danilo saw that her skin had turned white under the pressure of his fingers. Hastily he released her.

'We'll go out,' he said, striving to sound reassuring. 'Here's your shirt. You're right, we need to get out.' He reached for his clothes and glanced over her head to the window. 'It's a beautiful evening out there.'

Beyond the glass, the sky was green and gold and the shadows were lengthening. This should have been his time of greatest happiness: with Cathy come to him at last, the two of them naked in his quiet room, their skin still warm from one another's love. And yet they were running.

Cathy held tightly onto Danilo's hand as they climbed the hill. She wished he'd slow down; he was walking fast, and asking so many questions.

He wanted to know about the dream and she had told him most of it: the successful dinner, the toasts, Lucius's proposal and the row that had followed. As she spoke, the choking violence of the scene returned to her.

She did not tell him about the arrest. She couldn't bear to. The picture of Holofernes being marched off was so strong in her mind, and so terrible, that she couldn't find the words for it. And she was frightened. Hatred had broken out in Judith's world; at any moment it must cross into her own. What was going on between Matthew and Enzo within the palazzo walls?

Fear beat steadily in Cathy's mind, scattering her thoughts. She must tell Danilo about the arrest: she owed it to him. He of all people had a right to know. But she couldn't bring herself to do it. Not yet. He would rush off to the palazzo and confront Matthew, and she had to speak to Matthew first. She had to find out how much he knew and give him a chance to come clean.

Cathy was too deeply bound to Matthew to stand aside now. Whatever he was doing or planning to do, whatever he understood, she had to hear it from him.

She no longer knew what to believe. When she looked back now over the way things had happened, Matthew seemed to flicker ahead of her on the path, drawing her onwards with his firefly light.

Danilo shifted his fingers within her grip and she realised she must be hurting him. He was frowning, looking down at her with puzzled attention.

'This row,' he persisted. 'Did it end with Holofernes' hitting Lucius?'

Cathy nodded.

'And Lucius didn't retaliate? He didn't go for his sword?'

'No. He tried to go for Holofernes, but Marcus held him back. Then he told Holofernes he'd be sorry.'

'And that was it? Lucius just walked out after that?'

'Yes.'

'You're sure?'

'For God's sake, yes, why do you ask?'

'I heard you waking up, Catti. You sounded devastated. That couldn't have been just because Lucius walked out.'

'I was frightened,' Cathy said evasively. 'I was frightened because Judith was frightened, and because the hatred between them was so terrible. You didn't see everything in your dreams, why do you think I should?'

They had reached the top of the hill. The Ghetto and the river lay behind them; evening sunlight gleamed off hundreds of windows and cars. Danilo put his arm round her shoulders and steered her into the narrow street ahead.

'I don't expect you to see everything.' His voice was steady;

Cathy realised he was trying to soothe her. 'But you do see different things, don't you? I suppose I hoped that between us we might be able to put the pieces together and come to some kind of shared understanding.'

They were nearing the end of the street and the cobbles were no longer level but tilting down. Through gaps in the houses, the verdigris sky pulsated.

'Where are we going?' Cathy asked suddenly. It was a reflex question, she knew where they were heading. She had walked these streets once before, in the other direction, on the day she'd done her first drawing of Judith.

Danilo stopped and made a slightly bewildered gesture with his hands. 'As you see, we're above the Forum. I'm sorry, Catti, I wasn't really thinking, but I seem to have brought us – home.'

The hill sloped deeply downwards and at its foot stretched the ruins of the ancient city.

'I don't want to go down there!' Cathy felt a sudden visceral panic.

'All right, we won't go into it. Look, we can take this road down and cut across the top end of the Forum, then we'll turn into the Piazza Venezia. Catti,' as she tried to pull away, Danilo held on to her hand, 'you're not asleep now. You're awake, with me; it's the rush hour. Nothing can happen to you.'

Cathy nodded and forced her hand to relax in Danilo's. She mustn't get hysterical; she should talk sensibly, reassure him, then slip away to the palazzo as soon as possible. But the great ruins grew taller and more threatening as they descended the hill, and Cathy hung back, using Danilo's body as a screen.

'It's fine,' Danilo was giving a running commentary, like

an airline pilot, 'we've got down as far as we're going and we're crossing the Forum now; we don't get any closer than this. You're with me, remember.'

The road across the Forum was raised on a bridge. Immediately to the left was a wall of rock; on their right, iron railings guarded the drop down to the ruins. There were tourists all around. Cathy squeezed Danilo's hand and began to take her bearings. Up to the left, on the hilltop, was where she had sat during her first week here, sketching. That was where Judith had first appeared under her pen.

She looked up at Danilo to tell him so. He was looking intently at her, the expression on his face a curious mixture of calculation and need. Beyond him the road was in shadow from an overhanging rock. It wasn't deep shadow, Cathy could see dust motes circling in it and sunlight played on its outer edges, but the sight of it made her quail.

Danilo's grip tightened and he pulled her forward.

'No.' Cathy braced her legs. Danilo's left arm went round her waist, driving her on. 'No!'

'It's time to be honest, Catti.' With a twist of the mouth, as if he too were afraid, Danilo pushed her into the shadow.

The two of them were alone on a wide pavement. A great distance separated them. Across it, Cathy saw Danilo watching her. She saw desire, fear and enmity in his face. And hope. A little, sharp white flame of hope burned in his eyes.

She put her arms up round her head to shield herself and staggered towards the sunlight. It burst over her like a tide of warmth. But already – or was it still? – Danilo's arms were round her.

'What did you see? You must tell me. You *must* tell me.'

Danilo's arms were strong and warm. They held her close,

as he had held her naked this afternoon, as Holofernes had held Judith . . . but he was not Holofernes.

Cathy stared into his dark eyes. In the depths of the pupils the hope was still burning, steadily, defiantly. Lucius's hope.

Oh God, what did it mean?

'I saw you,' she said quietly.

His face changed. It altered gradually, relaxing. The stillness left it; his heavy features seemed to become narrower and lighter and when he smiled it was swifter than before. 'And you know me now.'

Cathy could feel herself begin to tremble. She tensed her muscles to keep it from him, but the reaction was too violent. She was shaking and he felt it; he frowned, his eyes still smiling, and moved his hands over her back.

'You're shocked. But you knew already, at some level.'

Cathy nodded. She was sick and giddy and didn't know anything, but instinct warned her that she shouldn't argue. 'It's just, you said you were Holofernes. Today when you imitated him, you were so like him.'

'Ah well, I know him intimately. I've been dreaming of him for years.'

'But why did you pretend?'

Different expressions shifted across Danilo's face. Cynicism, resentment, pain. 'Because Lucius loses Judith,' he said bitterly. 'Lucius always loses. My father was Lucius and I watched him lose my mother. When the dreams passed to me and I discovered I was Lucius too, I swore I wouldn't let it happen again.'

Cathy stared at him. 'You're not Lucius,' she said, desperately trying to reassure herself. 'You're Danilo. And I'm not Judith, I'm Cathy.'

'Yes.' Danilo cupped her face. 'You're Catti, the girl I saw in my dreams, the girl I found in the National Gallery. I knew you could love me if you had the chance. If you hadn't known anything about Judith, I wouldn't have told you, but your own dreams had started and the drawings, and you knew about Holofernes. I could see you were already half in love with him, so I identified myself with him. I wanted us to have a chance and I was right, wasn't I? Once you could see me clearly, you came to me. You are in love with me, Catti. It's too late to ignore it or pretend it hasn't happened; and that's what I wanted.'

There was longing in Danilo's eyes. Cathy remembered the way he'd laughed as they made love, and her own fierce desire. Despite all that swirled around them, she had been happy then.

For a moment she thought that perhaps she could go back to being happy if she simply stood here with him, shutting out everything else. But there was one person she could not shut out.

'Matthew,' she whispered. 'This means – that he's Holofernes.'

A screen seemed to fall over Danilo's face. 'No, it's as you said – it's not possession, only a link.'

'Matthew's in danger.'

'It was all a long time ago.' Danilo stroked Cathy's cheek and for several seconds it was as if Matthew didn't really exist. Danilo's face was before her and she struggled to conjure up Matthew's features too. Then she became aware of her heart beating harder and suddenly she could see Holofernes being taken away between the guards, and Matthew walking blindly into the spare bedroom.

'Let me go! It's going to happen again!' Cathy tore herself free. Danilo grasped instinctively at her, then stopped. She could see him bringing himself under control, remembering he was in a public street.

'Catti.' His voice was quiet and compelling. 'Don't leave me now.'

'You said that before.'

'Because it's important. We can't afford to lose each other now.'

Cathy looked dumbly at him. She knew that he was right. If she went now, they might never find each other again.

'Oh my love, I've waited so long. There are so many things I have to tell you.'

Cathy took a faltering step towards him, stretched out her hand, turned and ran.

Save him. The whisper was close up in her mind, so close she might almost have said it herself. *Save him.*

The streets lurched by; her feet hit the ground again and again but the buildings went past so slowly. To her blurred eyes they seemed to dissolve and show glimpses of another landscape: the road gave way to red-brown earth, in place of tall buildings square villas stood higgledy-piggledy. A goat looked out of a first-floor window. A woman crossed her path wearing robes and sandals.

She was going mad.

Save him. Save him.

Cathy came into the Ghetto from the north-west and lost herself in streets that only this morning had been familiar. The sun had been sinking beneath the roofs as she ran; by the time she reached the palazzo it had gone. The courtyard was blue and silent and there were no lights in the apartment.

But in the east wing the laboratory blinds glowed. Cathy's

feet were loud on the cobbles as she ran to the east wing door. She pressed the bell once, and then again, more insistently. As she slammed her sweating hand onto it for the third time, the door opened and Enzo stood there. He looked hunted, and his eyes slid from Cathy to the courtyard behind her.

'Where's my son?' he said warily.

'He's not with me, I left him at the Forum. Please, Enzo, I must see Matthew!'

'Is Danilo all right?' Enzo's face twitched.

'I think so. I was with him until ten minutes ago. Enzo, I must see Matthew.'

Enzo shook his head and then stepped wearily aside. 'You can try if you like. He's in there,' he gestured to the lab.

Cathy went quickly to open the door. It was locked.

'Matthew?' she called. There was no answer.

'He won't let me in either,' said Enzo.

Cathy rattled the door, panic seizing her.

'It's all right,' Enzo added. 'He's not dead. He's been speaking to me.'

'Why won't he let you in?'

'He says he's not ready. He's working on the Giuditta and he's reached a very important stage. He doesn't want to be interrupted.'

Cathy breathed out. 'That sounds like Matthew.' She smiled shakily, but Enzo's face was bleak and in her mind the whisper was gathering again. 'What's the matter?' she asked quickly.

'You've been recognising things today, haven't you? That's what Matthew's doing too, alone in there with the Giuditta. When we recognise each other – that's when it becomes impossible to escape.'

The finality in Enzo's tone terrified her. Cathy took a deep breath. 'For God's sake, Enzo, what are you trying to say?'

'You're not the first, you know. It happened to Alessandra and me before you. Danilo knows that. And to Annalisa Genzanese – that's why she painted the Giuditta. And to who knows how many others these two thousand years, who left no record behind. Judith and Lucius and Holofernes live on through us, and die again through us, too. I tried to warn you from the beginning. First I tried to keep you and Danilo apart, then I brought you and Matthew here under my eye to keep you safe, but it hasn't worked, I haven't been able to stop it.'

Enzo's matter-of-factness was the most frightening thing. He might have been talking about a failed business strategy. Cathy swallowed.

'What's going to happen to us?' she asked.

'I don't know. You'll do what is in your natures to do; I can make no difference now.'

Matthew could hear Cat's voice outside the door; she and Enzo were talking in low, urgent tones. The sound agitated him, plucking his attention away from the painting – or should he say, the woman – in front of him.

Yes, he should say woman. She was Judith to him now. After hours of painstaking work, he was finally going to lift the punishing dark mask from her face.

He hadn't expected to get to this stage today, but he had worked as if inspired. He'd added tiny, vital repairs to the eyes and mouth. He had brought up the gold of a ring on the right hand. And as the hours went by, he had worked patiently on what remained of the overpainting, treating, blotting, brushing.

Now it was ready to come off. Matthew put his hand over his ears and hummed, to rid himself of the noise outside. Then, still humming, he picked up his tools and went forward to the canvas. His muscles cracked with the effort of holding steady as he performed the delicate motions.

He eased; he lifted; he inserted the edge of his scalpel and guided the molecules as they relinquished their hold on the canvas. First one corner of the mesh came loose, then the whole thing shivered and at last it fell away, leaving only a faint shadow on Judith's skin. Through the shadow, Judith's flesh glowed. Her eyes were incandescent. She seemed to grow larger and move towards him, out of the frame.

Cathy was calling him now and shaking the door handle. But Matthew was gazing, awed, at Judith. It was as if she were too vibrant to be contained in the picture. He felt her all around him, in the solid lab furniture, in the bright artificial light that seemed to beat against the windows.

Judith was alive. God, she was here, in this room; he could feel her breathing. Was this what Cathy had meant? How stupid he'd been not to realise before. Why had he been so stubborn when she'd tried to explain?

But then she hadn't tried very hard. Jealousy cramped inside him again. No, Cathy hadn't tried to help him understand. From the beginning, she'd been secretive about Judith. It was Danilo she'd chosen to confide in, Danilo who murmured intensely over lunches and sent her secret gifts. Desert flowers, Enzo had said. No doubt the two of them had played at being Judith and Holofernes during their trysts.

Danilo was coming back today. Perhaps he was out there now, standing silently behind Cathy as she battered on the door. That was the pattern, these days: Cathy and Danilo running around together, Matthew shut away on his own.

Except that he was no longer on his own. Judith had finally

come to him too. And she had come to him more gloriously than she had ever appeared to the others. Cat might have glimpses, but they had distressed her as often as they'd made her happy, and all Danilo's intimations of Judith seemed to be dark ones. Yet the lab was ablaze with Judith's presence. She was here exultantly, triumphantly, winging her way through Matthew's blood. As well she might, because it was Matthew who had set her free.

Cathy was shouting angrily to be let in. It was as if she sensed the new intimacy between himself and Judith and was determined to break it up.

Matthew threw down his tools and marched to the door. He had spent all his adult life fighting to make Cathy accept his love and she had rejected him. What did she want of him now?

'Cat, Enzo. I'm sorry you've been waiting so long.'

Cathy stared. Matthew leaned against the doorpost smiling defiantly. He met her eyes and his smile became mocking. 'Oh dear, you both look very serious.'

'We'd like to come in, please,' said Enzo.

'Of course. That's why I've opened the door.' But he didn't move; in fact, he folded his arms like a barrier.

'Matt.' Cathy searched his face. It was silhouetted against the brightness of the open doorway and his hair was wild.

'Cathy. What, no Danilo? You seem to be one Bonaventura short of a pack. Didn't the reunion go as planned?' Matthew looked feverish. Cathy was reminded of times in the past when she had seen him sick or in trouble and her heart twisted.

'I need to talk to you,' she said urgently. 'Why wouldn't you let me in?'

'I've been busy.'

'Doing what?'

Matthew's eyes narrowed. 'I tell you what,' he said. 'I'll tell you about my day if you'll tell me about yours. How did you spend the afternoon?'

Cathy felt that he was looking right into her. She could feel her expression crazing into misery.

'Jesus,' Matthew said. 'You bitch. You've just got out of his bed, haven't you?'

'Matt—'

The doorbell screamed briefly and cut off her words.

Matthew raised his eyebrows. 'Well, well, the son of the house. Aren't you going to let him in, Cat?'

The bell sounded again, a longer blast. Cathy stared beseechingly at Matthew. Enzo seemed unable to move.

'I know.' Matthew suddenly strode out of the doorway. 'Why don't *I* go?'

Danilo came in without a word. He was pale and breathing unevenly; his close-cropped hair was damp. He looked desperate. He walked straight up to Cathy and put his hand to her face.

She shrank against the wall. She didn't know if fear or pity was uppermost in her.

'Touching scene,' observed Matthew from behind him. 'Or do I mean, non-touching? Don't mind me, Cat, go right ahead.'

'Shut up,' said Danilo without looking round.

'I'm so sorry,' said Matthew. 'I forgot I was just a servant. I'll leave you two lovers together, shall I, and go back to my chores.'

'No, Matt!' Cathy lunged at him as he went by. 'I must talk to you. There are things I have to tell you – about me and Judith.'

Matthew paused in the lab doorway. His smile was triumphant. 'I know,' he said. 'But the thing is, you're too late. I've done it on my own.'

Danilo went very still. 'Done what?'

'Set her free,' said Matthew simply.

Cathy saw Enzo's colour change. He made a stumbling movement towards Matthew and took hold of his arm.

'Matthew, Cathy's right, we all need to talk. And I think it would be better if you and Danilo took some time to cool down, apart from one another. Why don't you and I go into the south wing—'

'What have you done?' Danilo was staring at Matthew. There was a curious expression in his eyes, dread and excitement mingled. He looked slowly from Matthew to Enzo and Cathy saw the excitement grow fiercer. 'In God's name, Father, what have you let him do?'

There was a long moment's stillness. Then Enzo released Matthew's arm and seemed to brace himself. 'Take us in there please, Matthew,' he said.

After the corridor, the lab was dazzlingly bright. All the overhead panels were switched on and the light fell mercilessly, without shadows. Cathy could see no painting at first, and for a wild moment she wondered if Matthew had destroyed it. Then she realised that he was leading them round the long workbench and that the easel stood at the far end, at right angles to them so that only the edges of the picture showed.

Matthew was moving confidently. A reckless vigour emanated from him. Like Holofernes, Cathy thought fearfully; oh God, just like Holofernes.

'Stay there,' Matthew ordered when they were several yards from the easel. 'You'll see it better for keeping,' he looked tauntingly at Danilo, 'your distance.'

With three easy paces he reached the easel and turned it round. He bowed mockingly, and when he straightened up, his smile was radiant.

Then all Cathy saw was the painting itself. Where Judith's eyes had once gazed out from the lattice of black paint, her own face now looked at her. It had been daubed rather than painted, but it was horribly recognisable. Her fair skin blotted out Judith's olive tones; her grey eyes sat uneasily between Judith's lids. Judith's right hand now wore Matthew's signet ring, and the head she cradled, hacked about and streaked with blood and dirt, was Danilo's.

'You maniac. Jesus Christ, you maniac.' Danilo spoke hoarsely.

Enzo had turned grey; he moved his mouth but no words came out.

'Matthew, what have you done?' Cathy's voice seemed to escape into the room without her. It had a high swoop in it, and a crack. 'What have you done?' it said again.

Matthew stared at her, his face falling, and his eyes ranged from her to Enzo, to Danilo. 'What's the matter?' He turned to gaze at the painting and touched the still damp mouth fleetingly with his fingertips. 'Can't you see how beautiful she is?'

Danilo stared at him. 'You're mad,' he said slowly. 'Or evil, or both. You're going to pay for this.'

Enzo turned abruptly to his son.

'He'll pay, Father,' said Danilo, as if the old man had spoken. 'Yes, he will.'

'No,' Enzo shook his head, his hand tugging at his collar. 'Mother of God, no.' He turned to Cathy and she saw first the sweat on his forehead, then the blue tinge to his lips. As she watched, he pulled frantically at his collar and his fingernails darkened.

'Help,' he choked. 'You must help—'

Cathy leapt forward just as his legs buckled. She smelled his sweat as she struggled to hold him up, then they were falling and the pain in her head sent everything white.

Chapter Twenty-One

The atrium was very bright. It seemed to Judith that more tapers were burning than usual and their flames hurt her eyes. She had stopped her panic-stricken laughing now and in the quiet she stared at her three companions, at the slaves who clustered nervously round the walls. Balbas stood by the vestibule as if there was still a chance he could bar the door.

Marcus turned to Lucius. 'This is very bad.'

'Yes,' said Lucius expressionlessly.

'I was worried – but you seemed so sure. An hour ago you were confident it wouldn't come to this.'

'I was wrong, evidently. Holofernes must have made more enemies than I imagined.'

'Yes. Gaius Nepos wouldn't bring the charge unless he had backing. We'll know who we're up against tomorrow, when his accusers gather.' Marcus tugged his beard. 'We'll need to prepare his defence carefully,' and then, with a quick glance at Lucius, 'You'll be his advocate, of course.'

Lucius raised his eyebrows. He turned away from Marcus and began rearranging his toga.

'Lucius Tullius,' the army officer suddenly sounded in Marcus's voice, 'you must represent him. Who else is there?'

'Plenty of people.' Lucius sounded very remote. 'Rome has

no shortage of clever young advocates; you'll be able to find someone.'

'But no one with your skill or your understanding of the case. We've only got a few hours, man. And besides, we need you. How will it look if Holofernes' partner won't defend him?' Marcus spoke bracingly, like a man chivvying a horse.

In answer, Lucius lifted his head. It was a small, sinuous movement and it put despair into Judith. 'How do you imagine,' he said softly, 'that I can go on being the general's partner? He has insulted me and all Roman men. You may be able to march alongside such a man and call him friend, but I will not.'

'Lucius Tullius.' It was Valeria who spoke. She stepped hastily in front of her husband and clasped her hands, looking earnestly into Lucius's eyes. 'General Holofernes behaved wrongly this evening, of course he did. But from his point of view, he might have felt he had provocation. You see, I believe he thought he had to defend his wife's honour – he didn't understand the full meaning of your offer to him.'

Lucius glanced down at her, then away. 'He understood very well.' Although she could see only one side of his face, Judith felt his rage and humiliation.

Valeria hesitated. 'Lucius,' she said, 'as a friend . . .'

Lucius didn't move. Marcus shifted and cleared his throat.

'We need to put that behind us now,' he said. 'There's too much at stake. We stand to lose all the support we've built up – the campaign will go and so will our own reputations.'

'Not necessarily.' Lucius looked from one to the other. Then a muscle began to flicker in his cheek, pulling his mouth askew. 'Everyone underestimates me,' he mused. 'Everyone assumes I can't mount this campaign without Holofernes. People have always thought I lack something. Brilliant, yes, but no stature. Not a natural leader.' He turned to Judith. 'Madam? You've been able to observe Holofernes and me side by side. What's your opinion? Do I have the qualities to run this campaign alone?'

Judith could not speak. A bar was across her tongue, pinning it down, while her thoughts roared far above. Valeria was moving her head, trying to communicate something, but Judith couldn't see her clearly. She was alone in the emptiness except for her fear. It swirled like a duststorm, gathering about Lucius's slight figure.

She hung on to the sight of his eyes. They were unwavering and hot, like coals. She remembered when she had thought he burned with a cold fire. She had been wrong. She had not understood. Lucius's fire only seemed cold at first because it did not reach out to others. But she had gone seeking it, drawing closer and closer, and now she felt its true heat. And she knew it could consume them all.

'I see.' Lucius's voice was hoarse. 'You don't have the courage to speak but your silence does it for you.' He snapped his fingers for his slave and walked towards the door, his eyes scorching a path ahead of him.

Valeria and Marcus were arguing. Marcus had despatched slaves into the city to try and pick up news about Holofernes' arrest, and as messengers reappeared and vanished again, the wrangling went on. Judith heard some of it: Valeria wanted them all to go to Lucius's house; Marcus said they should concentrate on finding another advocate for tomorrow. Judith's own name sounded repeatedly on both their lips, but Judith didn't follow what they said, she was thinking of Holofernes.

Where was he now? They had mentioned the underground

prison in the Forum. Would they really put him in there, in the dark and the filth? Yes, of course they would. He was charged with treason, a crime which carried the punishment of banishment for Romans, and death for foreigners. They meant to kill him.

Judith saw him again, marching out between the guards. And she saw him at another, earlier moment in the evening, the lull after the senator's departure, when he had stood in the triclinium, brooding over the rumours. She could see her husband's troubled face, the furrows in his skin, so clearly that she felt she could touch them. Had it been then that she'd begun to understand?

She could no longer remember the order in which things had happened. Nor did it matter. If only she could think what to do next. But bewilderment kept engulfing her, and a rage against herself and Lucius so intense that it doubled her up in pain. Between them, they had betrayed Holofernes utterly. Judith had discovered her love for her husband too late.

Too late; too late; her thoughts scurried like rats over the dungeon floor. It wasn't altogether too late. As long as Lucius still wanted her, there was a chance that she could influence events. She thought of him leaving the house, and the inferno that had shown in his eyes. He still wanted her – probably more to punish than to love. She must go to him and bargain.

'I need to see Lucius.'

Marcus broke off from his hurried instructions to a slave. 'What for?'

'I have to persuade him to defend Holofernes.'

'You had your chance to do that earlier. I didn't notice you saying much then.'

Valeria was on her feet. 'Do you mean it, Judith? You're

not just going to Lucius on your own account?'

Judith closed her eyes. 'You have every right to suspect me of that. But I swear I want to help my husband.'

Valeria scrutinised her. Then she glanced back at Marcus, but he was busy speaking to Balbas who had just reappeared. Valeria moved quickly to Judith.

'I don't understand you,' she said in a low voice. 'You knew Lucius was going to ask for you tonight, didn't you? What did you think would happen?'

'I – I didn't know. I suppose that's what I wanted to find out.'

'Well, now we've all found out.'

Judith stared down into Valeria's pinched face. 'I'm sorry,' she whispered.

Valeria turned back to her husband. 'Marcus, I think she means it. In any case, we have to take the risk. Lucius certainly won't listen to us; our only chance is if Judith can change his mind.'

Marcus nodded slowly. His shoulders were hunched and he chewed his lip as he looked from one woman to the other. 'It seems so. In fact, if Balbas's news is correct, Holofernes' only chance has always been Judith.'

'What is Balbas's news?'

'Nothing good. Gaius Nepos's chief backer in bringing the charge is Senator Aulus Tullius himself, Lucius's father. Lucius must have known an arrest would be attempted tonight.'

'He knew?' Judith tasted nausea. 'Lucius knew? But he told Holofernes it was just a rumour.'

'Yes, he did, but it wasn't very convincing, was it? And then immediately afterwards he sprung his "offer" on him. I expect,' said Marcus grimly, 'Lucius thought the prospect of arrest would concentrate your husband's mind. He's right, people do underestimate him. When this young man wants something, he leaves nothing to chance.'

Someone was talking in the distance. Strange voices, speaking in an exotic tongue. Here and there Cathy seemed to recognise words but she had to struggle to hold on to them. She opened her eyes. She was in a small space, with several other people. She knew that back, it belonged to Danilo; she could tell from the broad shoulders and the way his hair curled at the nape of the neck. Besides, that was his watch on the wrist which lay poised on the blanket. Not her blanket, someone else's.

It was Enzo's blanket. He was on another stretcher a few feet away from hers and he was one of the people talking; Cathy recognised the cadence of his voice. It was quieter than usual though, and he kept pausing between phrases to take long breaths. An unfamiliar voice interrupted him and by concentrating, Cathy could work out that it was saying: 'Don't talk. Please, Signore Bonaventura, lie quietly and don't talk.' Enzo fell silent for a moment, then he began murmuring again. He was speaking swift Italian and Cathy allowed the words to pass her by. Enzo was alive then and so was she, although her head hurt. But what peculiar dreams she'd had.

Except that they weren't dreams, of course; it was the other world. She had been with Judith again and bad things were happening there. Too bad to think about now. Gratefully, Cathy let them go.

Everything seemed curiously softened. It was nice lying here like this. She was in an ambulance, she realised that now. She must have cracked her head when Enzo fell on her; the last thing she remembered was his weight and the frighteningly suffused colour of his skin. Cathy shifted so that through half-closed eyes she could see Enzo's profile. A dark flush still stained it.

She saw Danilo grope along the blankets until he found Enzo's hand.

'Hush, Father,' he said in Italian. 'Try to rest. We can talk later.'

'No, Nilo. I might not be here later.'

'You will be, Signore Bonaventura.' It was the unfamiliar voice again. 'It was only a mild attack, and you're receiving the best attention now.'

'Yes, yes,' Enzo muttered angrily. 'Do you *have* to listen? Do you understand English?'

'I'm afraid not, signore.'

'Good,' said Enzo, switching promptly into English. Cathy laughed and a second unfamiliar voice spoke immediately behind her.

'The young woman's conscious.'

Enzo turned with an unwieldy motion of his head and shoulders, and Cathy saw that he had leads attached to his chest.

'Cathy, my dear. Are you all right?'

'Yes, thank you.'

'You sound drowsy. I fell on you; you might be concussed. Do you know where you are?'

'In an ambulance, I imagine.'

'Yes. And do you remember what happened?' Enzo was looking at her urgently, his body propped up on one arm. The scene in the lab, which had been just the other side of the muffled feeling, burst onto her memory. Cathy wished she had the energy to shut her eyes.

'Yes, Enzo, I remember it all.' Then, after a second's wondering what she should say next, she heard herself cry out, 'Matthew! Where is he?'

'Gently, gently,' said an Italian voice into her ear. Its owner, a young man in a tunic, peered into her pupils and put his fingers to her wrist. 'Don't excite yourself,' he said and Cathy lay obediently limp.

'Matthew's following us by car,' said Enzo. 'Isn't that so, Nilo?'

Danilo nodded. He hadn't spoken a word to Cathy yet, but he had turned, still holding his father's hand, so that he could watch her. He looked oddly peaceful; there was no trace of his earlier desperation.

'He's right behind us,' he said.

Cathy stared into his eyes. 'Is he on his own? He didn't seem – I'm not sure he knows what he's doing.'

'He doesn't,' Danilo said flatly. 'God knows what happened to him while he was working on the Giuditta, but he isn't making any sense about it.' He paused and looked reluctantly at his father. 'He's very worried about you, to give him his due. He doesn't understand why you reacted so badly to the Giuditta, but he realises he's responsible.'

'He isn't.' Enzo gripped Danilo's hand to pull himself more upright. 'Give me a pillow,' he wheezed at the ambulance crew. 'Now! No, not a word, I intend to talk to my son and Miss Seymour in comfort!' He leaned painfully forward while the pillow was supplied. 'Matthew isn't responsible,' he switched back into English, 'because Judith has pulled him in now. He's no longer free to see things clearly. That's what happened to us in the end, I believe that's what always happens each time the old force comes to life, and that's why I need to talk to you both now, while there's still time.

'No, Danilo, don't try and silence me now. You said your mother would be alive if it wasn't for me and it's true, but not because I didn't love her. It's because I loved her too possessively. I tried to control her. I was afraid of the Giuditta and the things it was showing her, and I locked up her studio to try and stop her going on with them. Then, when she found Benedetto and fell in love with him and told me he was Holofernes, I tried to stop her seeing him. Finally, when they ran away together, I tried to bring them back and killed Benedetto in the process.'

Danilo was white. The sight of him suddenly brought back the image of Lucius from her dream. Lucius. Cathy's heart began to hammer. But Danilo was speaking, too forcefully.

'It was a car crash, Father. You didn't kill him.'

'I did. I set the police onto him. I used all my influence to get them to chase that car. I didn't think about Alessandra's safety, only that Benedetto shouldn't take her away from me. He was trying to outdistance the police when he crashed the car. I killed him, just as Lucius killed Holofernes.'

'No, Father, stop it. The two things aren't the same.' Danilo tried to withdraw his hand from his father's, but Enzo tightened his grip.

'They are,' he said quietly, not lifting his eyes from his son's face. 'You see, I had known for some time that I was taking Lucius's part, just as you know it about yourself. And like you, I was blinded by the injustice of it. Alessandra was my beloved wife, I loved her above anything. God forgive me, Danilo, but at the time I loved her even before you. Why should I be drawn in on the side of Lucius the destroyer? I fought it. I fought her. I did everything in my power to come between her and Benedetto, and in so doing I turned myself into Lucius.'

'I don't believe it.' Danilo snatched his hand away and rubbed his sweating forehead. 'You're just saying this because you think somehow it will help me. But it doesn't, it makes a mockery of everything.' He turned to Cathy. 'He pretends to understand but he can't. When I first told him about the dreams, he tried to send me to a psychiatrist – that's how much he really believes in them.'

Enzo's eyes were anguished. 'I know I failed you, my son. I was wrong not to tell you at the time. But I was so shocked. It had never occurred to me that you would inherit the curse. And afterwards, when you didn't mention it again, I thought perhaps it had passed from you. I prayed it had. But when I saw you and Matthew together I began to be afraid, and when Cathy arrived, I knew.'

Cathy's pulse was like hailstones, setting up a terrible rhythm inside her. Lucius the destroyer; the full truth of the dream was on her now and she could feel Judith's fear bleeding into her own.

'It's true, isn't it?' Her voice sounded as if it belonged to someone else.

Enzo stared down at his hand, which was trembling, then turned to Cathy. 'It is. I'm sorry.'

Cathy felt a touch on her shoulders and looked round. One of the men in tunics was pushing at her gently, saying 'Please, you must lie down.' She shook him off angrily and, sat up further, hugging her knees.

She felt almost too afraid to speak. 'Please – it's starting again, I can feel it – what are you trying to tell us?'

The exertion of speaking was taking its toll; Enzo's breath

came in gasps. 'The past will consume the present if you let it. Don't let it – get yourselves away. Cathy, you should leave Rome. Danilo, you must let her go.' Enzo looked pleadingly at his son. 'Nilo, I know you love Cathy. Believe me, I've watched you and understand. But you must allow her the freedom to make her own choice. Don't do as Lucius did. Don't make his mistake and mine, and the mistake of God knows how many others who have had to play out his part. This time, release them.'

Danilo had shrunk back against Cathy's stretcher. 'Release who?' he asked in a shaking voice. 'Judith and Holofernes?'

'Cathy and Matthew. Let them go together, and then if in time Cathy chooses to come back to you, you'll be able to love her freely.'

There was a long silence. Danilo stood pressed against Cathy's stretcher, gripping the side bar. His body was twisted and he stared at his father like a trapped man. Eventually he looked away.

'And if I did that,' he said quietly, 'would you come back to me, Catti?'

His face was turned from her, but even so Cathy could see the mingling of dread and hope. The same emotions were intertwining inside her, almost choking her.

'I don't know,' she whispered.

Danilo covered his eyes. Then he dropped his hand with a defeated gesture and straightened up. 'Go,' he said, glancing swiftly at her. Cathy couldn't tell if he'd really seen her; there wasn't time to meet his eyes before he turned back to his father. His face was sheened with sweat – or was it tears? 'They can go.'

They spent the rest of the journey in silence. Danilo didn't look at Cathy but sat by his father, holding both his hands. Enzo clung to him, his face working, and didn't object when the paramedics came forward and began making anxious checks of his pulse and respiration.

To Cathy, pressed gently back into a lying position by one of the paramedics, those minutes felt like the pause in a film, just before the music swells to celebrate the climactic scene. She could see everything very clearly; each gesture, each facial expression of the father and son was magnified. She knew what was supposed to happen. But hope and dread were still tangled inside her and the dread was growing stronger. Her pulse continued to patter out its unyielding rhythm. Something was amiss in this scene of reconciliation. As the ambulance continued to lurch through the city and Enzo stared hungrily at his son, Danilo quietly rearranged his Father's blankets. His movements were sharp, like flame.

They drew up in the hospital forecourt and the older paramedic opened the ambulance doors. 'We'll take Signore Bonaventura first,' he said. Night had fallen and the darkness was hectic with illuminated signs and car headlamps. 'I'll ask a nurse to come and sit with the young lady while we send out some porters for her.'

'It's all right,' said Cathy quickly. 'I can walk.' She slipped off the trolley and stood unsteadily, bracing her hands against the doors.

Help him, Judith's voice whispered inside her head. *Help him.* She must get away from Danilo and find Matt.

As if he'd heard the thought, Danilo leapt in from the forecourt and grabbed her arm. His fingers locked hard.

'Sit down, Catti, you've probably got concussion.' Still holding her, he turned to the paramedic. 'I'll bring Miss

Seymour in. Where can I get a wheelchair?'

'By the sliding doors over there.' The man stepped hurriedly aside as Danilo pushed past him and went striding towards the doors. 'We'll need you to come in with your father,' he called after him. 'You have the details of his medication.'

'My son likes to act on his decisions,' Enzo said heavily. He met Cathy's eyes. The exhaustion in his face was more than physical. Cathy wondered if her fear showed as clearly in her face.

'Evidently,' muttered the second paramedic, taking the foot of Enzo's trolley. 'Excuse us, signorina.'

The two men unlatched Enzo's trolley and wheeled it, together with its wires and monitor, carefully down the ramp. Cathy stood up and groped her way hastily after them.

Lights dazzled her and the smell of petrol muddled her senses. She peered at the cars that drove by, looking for Matthew.

'Cathy.' Enzo's voice was on a level with her elbow. She stooped abruptly.

'Yes, Enzo?'

'I didn't want to say what I did. I know how much Danilo loves you. Whatever you do, you mustn't doubt that.'

'I don't.'

'Where's Matthew? I should speak to him, too.'

'I don't know. I can't see him.' Cathy's eyes darted here and there across the forecourt. 'I'll look . . .' She began to sidle away.

'Ask Danilo. He'll find him.'

Cathy turned, to see Danilo pushing a wheelchair fast towards them. His face was taut.

'What are you doing, keeping my father waiting out here?'

he demanded. 'In God's name, you said you'd take him in at once!'

'We are, we will,' protested the younger paramedic. 'Signore Bonaventura was just speaking to the young lady.'

Danilo swerved the chair round behind Cathy. His eyes swept warningly over hers. 'Sit in it, Catti,' he said. 'You're not well enough to be on your feet.'

'Stop!' Enzo wheezed as his trolley began to move. 'Where's Matthew?' He struggled to push himself up on his elbows. 'We can't see him. Isn't he here yet?'

'No. He was calling a taxi, he's bound to be a little delayed.'

'A taxi? I thought you said—'

'There he is!' Relief hit Cathy like a fist as she saw Matthew in the back of a dark blue car which slid to a rapid halt a few yards away. 'There's someone with him. Is it Giovanni?'

'That's not a taxi.' Enzo's voice crackled with alarm. 'That's a police car.'

'Take my father inside,' ordered Danilo. 'Now.'

'Come along, Signore Bonaventura. Now please lie still.'

'Danilo, what have you done? What in God's name have you done?' Enzo was overtaken by rasping breaths. 'Nilo, you promised . . .'

The paramedics looked at one another and whisked his trolley round. 'Cesare, quick, get him inside.'

Enzo's face was darkening and his open mouth gulped for air. The trolley clattered as the paramedics raced it towards the doors.

'Your father's pills!' one of them shouted. 'Bring them! We need to know exactly what he takes!'

'I'm coming,' called Danilo. Cathy had begun to stumble towards the car, but Danilo scooped her into his arms and sat her in the wheelchair. 'I'm coming,' he called out again, but he stayed leaning over her, his hands hard, his eyes irresolute.

'What are you doing?' Dread pulled Cathy's voice out of shape. 'Why aren't you going to your father?'

Danilo removed one hand from her arm and smoothed her hair back. 'My father, what was he saying to you just now?'

'He said he knew you loved me.'

'But?'

'There was no but. He just said that whatever happens, I mustn't doubt it.'

'Whatever happens. That's a useful phrase, so impersonal. It absolves us all of any responsibility. I wonder what he meant by it?'

Out of the corner of her eye, Cathy saw the driver of the blue car get out. Under the lights of the forecourt, she couldn't tell if he was wearing a dark suit or a uniform. He opened one of the back doors. Danilo took hold of her chin and forced her to look at him.

'And do you doubt that I love you, Catti?'

Cathy gazed at him.

Help him, urged the voice. *Speak; save him.*

Cathy shook her head. 'No,' she said, gasping. 'I don't doubt it.'

'Then what about your love for me?'

'I don't know.' No, not good enough; Judith had told her to speak. To lie. 'I love you, Danilo. You're right, I do love you. But what's going to become of us?'

The darkness in Danilo's eyes deepened and glowed. 'We'll be happy together, I swear.'

'But what if Enzo's right, and we put each other in danger?'

'My father's a sick man, and a bitter one. He's had so much

tragedy in his life he can't believe anyone else can escape. But we can. If we're strong, we can get away from him and from Matthew.'

Running footsteps, urgent and officious, came to a stop right next to them.

'Signore Bonaventura? Is there a problem?' The young nurse was agitated. 'I've been sent for the pills.'

Danilo straightened up, still looking at Cathy. 'Yes,' he said. 'Yes,' he repeated under his breath. He turned to the nurse. 'The pills,' he said, frowning. 'Of course. You'd better take them in ahead of me. I have them all here.' He began taking small bottles out of his pockets. He scanned each swiftly; in the lamplight his pupils were huge. 'These are his regular daily pills, so are these. He takes these only when he has chest pains. These are . . .' He hesitated and frowned at the label. 'Oh sorry. Stupid of me. These are mine. And these yellow ones he takes when he can't sleep.'

The nurse took and checked the bottles hurriedly. 'Thank you. That's all? I have to take them in at once.'

She ran back to the doors. Danilo made no move to follow; he stood staring after her, his hand turning the bottle he'd kept. In the silence, Cathy heard the dry clicking of the pills.

She could also hear sounds from the blue car. Danilo blocked her view of it, but she'd recognised the shuffle of people emerging, a murmur of male voices. And there was something else, a metallic noise, light and intermittent. It seemed to play in counterpoint to her heartbeat.

Danilo glanced down at her. 'Your stepbrother,' he said. He blinked at the bottle he still held and then dropped it into his breast pocket. 'At least my father will be spared all this.'

He stepped out of her line of vision. A knot of men was

coming towards them. Cathy saw two uniformed carabinieri, one man in a dark suit and standing shoulder to shoulder with one of the uniformed men, Matthew. He was ashen and appeared dazed.

'Cat!' he said as soon as he saw her. 'Oh my God, what have they done to you?'

'Nothing,' said Cathy. 'I'm all right.' The words died in her mouth as Matthew tried to reach her and was jerked back by the man in uniform. The handcuff round Matthew's wrist hit its mate with a loud clink and the policeman swore.

Danilo and the suited man were speaking in rapid Italian. Cathy tried desperately to follow but her mind was full of Judith's soft clamour. *Save him. Help him. Save him.*

She tried to stand up but Danilo's hand was on her shoulder at once, keeping her in the chair.

'Matthew,' she cried in panic, 'what's happening?'

'I don't know.' Matthew pulled towards her again and was once more yanked back. His mouth was unsteady. 'They say I've killed Enzo, but I haven't. I haven't, Cat, have I? You tell them.'

'Of course he hasn't . . .' But the suited man was gesturing towards the sliding doors and the carabinieri were already taking Matthew away. Then the man shook Danilo's hand and walked briskly after them.

Cathy put both hands to her shoulder and pulled and wrenched at Danilo's fingers, dug her nails into his wrist. He dropped his left hand over both of hers and cupped them easily.

'What are you doing? What are you doing to him?' Cathy's voice rose hysterically.

'I'm not doing anything. It's a police matter. They're

interviewing Matthew about why he deliberately damaged our most cherished work of art.' Danilo gave a crooked smile. 'Except that I gather it's not only a question of the damaged painting now, but also of assault on my father. Matthew's been very honest. He's told them that he was fully aware of how much the Giuditta meant to my father. Apparently, if they decide that Matthew acted maliciously, they could bring a charge of attempted murder.'

Cathy's mouth was dry. 'You know that's not true.'

'Do I?' He looked down into her face. He was still imprisoning her hands on her shoulder and was directly above her. He was so close that Cathy could see all his smile lines, and the groove by his mouth that she had kissed this afternoon. Yet he was as distant as the moon.

'Where have they taken him?' she asked fearfully.

Danilo straightened up and took hold of the wheelchair. 'Inside, to the emergency waiting area. They asked if I could go to the police station to make a statement but of course it's out of the question. So they're going to take over an office in the hospital for the time being.' He began to push her over the tarmac towards the doors which had swallowed up everyone else. 'They're going to ask a psychiatrist to make an assessment of him. They say he's been talking very wildly; they wonder if he might be mentally ill.'

'Please, don't do this.' Cathy spoke despairingly into the soft Roman night. Above the roof of the hospital, the sky was violet-orange where the Forum's floodlights spilled upwards.

The night was vivid with torchlight and knots of people clustered in the streets. They pressed in on Judith and her escort, and from all sides as she walked she heard their eager questions.

'What are they doing?' she asked Marcus Strachus.

'Waiting for you and Holofernes.'

'But why?'

'You're news. A charge like this is a big event – a Syrian general up for treason, powerful Romans ranged on either side.' He glanced at her. 'And a woman involved.'

The faces rose and fell; it wasn't only the motion of her footsteps, people were jumping to look at her. At Marcus's order, the slaves closed in round them.

Judith could hear excitement in the muttering, a fervid note. Who were these people who had come onto the streets to witness her downfall? She recognised none of them, yet they stared back at her with knowing eyes and she heard her name spoken proprietorially. 'Judith of Bethulia . . . she's the widow . . . there goes the Syrian's wife . . . she's under guard too.'

'Are you looking for Lucius Tullius?' she heard someone ask Marcus. 'Are you arresting him too?' And Marcus's reply, bitten out, 'Don't be ridiculous, man!'

'Lucius Tullius.' The name was taken up quickly. 'Lucius Tullius . . . hc had them in his house, you know . . . Lucius went this way . . . they betrayed him, I heard, plotted against Lucius . . .'

The story was dancing from mouth to mouth, changing as it went, and she had no redress against it. What would they be accusing them of by tomorrow?

Did Lucius know? Had Lucius even started the rumours? Judith felt at a loss, pushed and pulled by forces she didn't understand. Marcus was bleak-faced; he had retreated behind his soldier's manner, as if to say, 'This is a bad business; we'll just have to go through with it as best we can.' He was distancing himself, Judith sensed. He thought there was no help for her and Holofernes.

Judith could not allow that to be true. She would not believe it. But if Lucius had deliberately allowed Holofernes' arrest to go ahead, then it must mean that he saw Holofernes as a rival who threatened him. A rival for Judith, and for the glory of leading the campaign. The terrible irony of it was coming home to her, for it was Holofernes who had brought both these things within Lucius's reach and made him realise how much he desired them. Yet Holofernes also stood between Lucius and his possession of them.

Judith bitterly regretted her silence in the face of Lucius's last appeal to her. For it had been an appeal, he had been seeking her support. If she'd only had the wit to extemporise an answer, to give him some taste of what he wanted, then he might have stayed and talked and between them all they might have persuaded him to help Holofernes. Instead she had added her own rebuff. Now she would have to fight through Lucius's anger in order to reach him.

How was she to do that? Should she throw herself on his mercy and weep? Should she plead for Holofernes in the name of the friendship between the two men? She had a terrible feeling that Lucius would only be angered by both.

Suddenly she saw Holofernes in her mind's eye. He was standing in her bedroom, his head lapped by the light of the oil lamp, his eyes full of secret laughter as he called her brave.

Judith straightened. Her husband had faith in her and she wouldn't let him down. She and he were two of a kind. It had taken her a long while to realise it and her obduracy had put him in danger. Now she owed it to him to use all her courage and calculation, all her gambler's instinct, to save him.

By the time they were admitted to Lucius's house, Judith had attained an outward calm. Lucius received them in the middle of the atrium and did not invite them further in.

'I'm surprised to see you here,' was his greeting. 'I assumed you'd be busy preparing for your defence tomorrow.'

Judith ignored his words. Looking him full in the face, she walked quickly away from Marcus and the guards and went up to where he stood in the middle of the atrium. She glanced at the sky, showing through the open roof.

'We can't speak here,' she said with a hint of anger. 'This is where you talk to clients who want tiresome favours. We need to speak in private.'

Lucius looked at her coldly but he did not move away.

Judith lowered her voice. 'There are too many stories circulating already. They can damage us.'

'Stories always go round when a charge is brought. Get a good advocate and you can rebut them.'

'You'll need one too, then,' said Judith. 'There are grounds for suspicion to wreck all of us. By tomorrow it will be too late. In the name of Jove, Lucius,' she allowed an angry intimacy to flare in her tone, 'we need to talk. And not here, in front of everyone.'

Lucius hesitated, then turned away abruptly, but not before she'd seen hope spark in his face.

'I'll speak to Judith in the study,' he said to the room at large. Judith was already moving, giving Marcus and Valeria no time to react. She had managed to take the initiative and she would not let it slip; she must dazzle and challenge Lucius, she must beguile him with his own desires.

She followed him into the corridor, then into the study, and as he paused she stalked past him to the very end of the room and stood with her back to the table round which Lucius and Holofernes and Marcus had so often gathered to discuss tactics.

'This is an impossible situation.' She spoke low and fast. 'What are we going to do? Do you know what people are saying?'

'Many things, I imagine, most of them absurd.'

'They may be absurd but they're also very damaging. They're saying that you're behind the arrests because you're after Holofernes' possessions – his fortune, his command. His wife.'

The lights were too dim for her to see Lucius's expression but she heard him draw breath.

'Yes,' she said. 'You see the position this puts us in. If Holofernes is found guilty, then I can't come to you with honour. And whatever you do with the campaign, you'll always have the people's suspicion dogging you. Didn't that occur to you? What were you thinking of, announcing your intention to take command back there at Aufidius Metallus's house, in front of everyone!'

Lucius was breathing quickly. 'So it's Aufidius's house again now,' he said. 'You seem to have dispossessed your husband already, yet a few hours ago you were acting the lady of that house, protesting Holofernes' innocence to Gaius Nepos.'

'He knows as well as we do that Holofernes is innocent,' said Judith impatiently. 'But I also know that if public opinion's running against him, he'll be found guilty. The first thing he needs to do is give up the house, to show he respects people's feelings. I shan't stay there tonight; I'll go back to Marcus Strachus's house.'

'Is this your idea or Marcus's? He seems to be a very amenable jailer.'

'He's trying to get us all clear of this situation. He stands to lose heavily if the campaign's discredited.'

'Your concern for the campaign seems surprisingly strong. I'd have expected you to be more worried for your husband and yourself. Do you know the punishment for treachery against Rome?'

'Banishment and confiscation of possessions.'

'That's the punishment for Romans. I'm sure Marcus has told you what happens to foreigners.'

Judith looked into Lucius's face. He was dangerous in the way a wounded animal is dangerous – still, hiding his injury, eyes dark with rage.

'Would you let us die?' she asked incredulously.

He stared back at her for a long time. Judith allowed first doubt, then pain, to register fleetingly in her expression; then, praying that she was timing it well, she drew herself up and let anger rush through every limb.

'I am an honest woman,' she said, 'and if I must, I'll die alongside my husband. It will be an honourable death. I thought you were his friend. I believed you when you said you wanted to be my protector. And,' she lowered her voice, 'I believed that you loved me.'

Lucius made a jagged movement towards her, then pulled himself up. His features were twisted. 'I've given Holofernes everything he asked of me,' he said, 'and you saw how he repaid me tonight. He said things no man could forgive, and he struck me like a slave. And you'd be proud to die beside him.'

Judith shook her head. 'I'd be prouder to live beside you,' she whispered. 'If you would forgive what Holofernes said in anger and prove his innocence, if I could come to you without shame, we could live together in honour. I could give you children,' she added longingly.

There was a rush and Lucius's hands were on her shoulders, then cupping her face. His touch was light but Judith could feel the tension in his fingers. Her head tipped back in response. Above her, the grey eyes were inchoate.

'Do you swear you love me?'

'I love you.'

'And you'll come with me, whatever the result of the trial tomorrow?'

'If I can come with honour, yes.'

He tipped her head further and bent over her so that their mouths were almost touching.

'What do you feel for your husband?'

'A wife's loyalty. Respect. Admiration for his achievements.'

'But not love or desire?'

'No.'

'Do you think I'm a better man than he is?'

'Yes.'

'Say it.'

'You're a better man than Holofernes.'

Lucius made a strange noise, like a laughing moan, and kissed her. A deep shudder ran through Judith; she pressed herself against him, hoping to still the revulsion or turn it into a semblance of passion, but for long seconds her body fought him. She had to pull her lips away, or she might have been sick. Desperately she smiled and stroked Lucius's mouth, imitating tenderness.

'My Roman,' she whispered.

Lucius was watching her. He went on watching, without a word, his eyes scrutinising, his hands moving against her neck and back as if they were reading her flesh. His features seemed to have cracked apart to reveal the naked need beneath. Afraid to look any longer, Judith laid her face against his neck.

She felt him gently stroke her hair.

'You're right.' His throat vibrated against her cheek. 'I am a better man than Holofernes. A nobler one. Tomorrow at the trial, I'll prove it.'

Under the harsh hospital lights, Cathy watched Danilo. They were sitting side by side on a bench seat, and Danilo had his arms stretched out on either side of him, his head tipped back against the wall in the posture of a desperate man.

Cathy leaned against his shoulder and felt the sweat soaking through his shirt. She both feared him and longed to comfort him.

Did he know why she was seeking his touch? When she had first left the wheelchair and taken his hand, he'd looked at her attentively and she had wondered then if the figures were appearing to him too. Could he see Judith and Lucius, here in front of them, between the waiting area and the reception desk? Did the linoleum and the noticeboards waver in his eyes too, and gather darkness? If Danilo saw, he didn't say. And prompted by Judith, Cathy gave him no chance to hesitate.

She turned restlessly and rubbed her head against his outstretched arm. She took to stroking his wrist again, and a minute later she laid his hand on her forehead and tried to be still. She made no passionate declarations – she knew he wouldn't believe them. Instead she concentrated on pouring into her touch all the perverse tenderness, the impossible, might-have-been desire she had felt in the last twenty-four hours.

She did not have to pretend. The emotions still weltered inside her. Surely she must be able to make him feel them if she hung onto these feelings and shut out the others – shut out anything to do with Matthew. Matthew was behind one of those doors in the far wall, being interrogated by the police. No, don't think of that. If you let in the fear and hatred, they'll reach Danilo. And they must not reach him. The only thing she could afford to show Danilo now was that he had won her. She must convince him that she loved him. He must believe that she was troubled, bewildered, guilt-tormented – but his.

It was Matthew's only chance. Judith told her so, not in words but in the way that she spun her desperate pretence round Lucius; in the way that she pulled Cathy across the boundaries of their worlds so that even now, once again, the large wall clock was becoming indistinct and the shadows cast by the fire extinguishers were hardening into two familiar figures: Judith and Lucius.

Cathy was not dreaming, or imagining. Judith's urgency was reaching into her world, here in the hospital waiting area. Judith was playing out her own life-and-death game, and insisting that Cathy follow.

Cathy shot a look at Danilo. He was staring ahead, watching in horror the shadowy place where Judith and Lucius were forming. So he hadn't seen them before, but he was seeing them now, for the first time. And they seemed to be seeing him. As Cathy watched, Lucius turned to look directly into Danilo's face; the shadow man's mouth set in a line and he took a step towards the light, towards Danilo.

'What is it? What's the matter?' Danilo was on his feet and speaking in Italian.

'I'm afraid there have been some complications.' The young doctor stood before them uneasily. He plucked at his white coat.

'What kind of complications?'

'Your father has had an allergic reaction to one of the drugs we gave him. It's been quite severe. I'm afraid he now has liver failure as well as the original heart condition.'

Cathy watched Danilo's skin tighten, making his features more prominent.

'You're sure?'

The doctor frowned. 'Yes, of course we're sure. I'm very sorry; we took every precaution to prevent it. We have his records here and we used only drugs that had been successfully administered before. But allergies can develop without warning and it seems that has happened here.'

Danilo was listening intently, his eyes on the young doctor's face. 'Is my father going to live?'

'We don't know. I'm sorry. Liver failure is a very dangerous condition. There's nothing more we can do for him here. We're transferring him to intensive care where he'll have the best specialist attention.'

'Yes, I see.'

Danilo appeared stunned. He stood opening and closing his hands until the doctor said awkwardly, 'I'll leave you with the nurse. She'll take you to the intensive care ward and tell you anything else you need to know.'

The nurse was flustered and not pleased to be told that Matthew and the carabinieri would have to go up to intensive care with them. 'No one's mentioned them to me. My instructions are to take you and Miss Seymour up to the ward, that's all. We don't usually allow police on the wards.'

'They'll have to come this time,' said Danilo shortly. 'My father might want to speak to Matthew. Besides, Miss Seymour and I both need to make official statements.'

'The staff upstairs won't like it at all. Which room are they in?'

In the grey and white side room, the police had removed Matthew's handcuffs. He was sitting at the far side of a square table. Next to him stood one uniformed carabiniero. The other sat by some filing cabinets ranged along the wall, and the third, suited man sat facing him. A small tape recorder was on the table, and the carabiniero sitting by the filing cabinets was writing in a notebook.

Matthew looked ill. His face was pinched and patches of scarlet stood out on his cheekbones. When he saw Cathy, he scrambled up and tried to get round the table to her.

'Sit down, Signore Forse,' said the uniformed man, grabbing his arm.

'Cat!' Matthew braced himself against the wall. 'Thank God you're here. Tell them the truth. Tell them that Enzo knew about Judith from the start, that it wasn't me who changed the painting, it was Judith. Enzo understood that, he'd tell them so himself.'

'Calm down, Signore Forse and sit down. You're not helping yourself.' The man in the suit spoke easily, but he raised his eyebrows at Danilo.

'They won't let me see him,' Matthew said. 'Where have they taken him? What if he asks for me?'

'I've told you, Mr Forse, Mr Bonaventura is seriously ill. You can't see him, and he's certainly not asking for you.' The man stood up and walked swiftly to the door. His face was respectful and wary. 'Is there any news about your father, sir?'

'He's developed liver failure. It was an allergic reaction to some drug they gave him. He's being transferred up to intensive care and we're going with him.' Danilo recited the information as if it had nothing to do with him. His eyes were on Matthew.

'I'm sorry, sir. And I'm sorry to have to bother you about statements at this time, but—'

'That's all right, I want to get everything sorted out. Bring Mr Forse upstairs and they'll find you another office. Cathy and I will give our statements as soon as you're finished with him.'

The man followed Danilo's gaze to Matthew. Matthew's eyes, wide with fear, were darting from person to person. Whenever he looked at Cathy, a terrible eagerness flared in his face.

'To be honest,' the man said wryly, 'there's not much more we can do with Mr Forse. He's not making much sense. In fact, he's sounding distinctly irrational. We'll need to get a psychiatric assessment before we can proceed with any charge.'

'You're in the right place for that,' Danilo said.

'Yes.' The man smiled uncertainly, not sure if it was a joke. 'Er, yes. Though we do have psychiatrists on the register at the police station. It might be easier to send Mr Forse straight there and I could stay behind and take your statements.'

'No!' Cathy couldn't stop herself. She stepped in front of the policeman and hugged her arms to control the sudden shaking. 'If you're taking Matthew away I'm coming with him.'

She turned to Danilo. *Touch him*, she told herself desperately. *Make a gesture to him. Don't lose him now.* She couldn't read his face at all; he looked blank and exhausted, but he had been like that ever since they entered the hospital.

'Danilo, please.' Cathy's teeth were chattering. 'I want to stay with you, but I can't desert Matthew.'

Belatedly, she managed to unstick her hands and held one

out towards Danilo. He looked at it for a second.

'Always protecting your stepbrother,' he said quietly. Then he took her hand and pulled her towards him, and settled her in the crook of his arm. There was a ragged movement from Matthew.

Danilo gazed across the room at him. 'Bring him upstairs,' he said to the policeman. 'We'll get a psychiatrist to him here. Now, if you'll excuse me, my fiancée and I would like to be with my father.'

In the lift, everyone was silent except Matthew. And Cathy willed him to be silent. She couldn't reassure him without betraying herself to Danilo and it tore at her heart to see Matthew's stricken face as he repeated his questions.

'Why did he call you that, Cat? Please tell me. Do you love him?'

'Not now, Matthew. Not here.'

'Is it because I wouldn't believe you about Judith? I understand now, though. She's alive, isn't she? She was alive all the time, she just needed to be set free. I'm sorry I didn't believe you before.'

'It doesn't matter.'

'Are you leaving me because of that? Or is it what happened to the Giuditta?'

'No.' Cathy tried to make her voice soothing for Danilo's benefit; with her eyes she signalled a warning. *Don't talk any more. For God's sake, my love, don't incriminate yourself.*

'Why are you looking at me like that?' There was dignity in Matthew's candour. He stood almost motionless, apart from a restive movement of his hands which set his handcuffs chinking. 'I'm not trying to take anything from you, Cat. I'd never do that. Please be honest with me.'

Cathy covered her eyes.

'Stop talking to her,' she heard the suited policeman say. 'I'm warning you, keep quiet.'

And though she wanted to leap forward and batter him and his henchmen, howl at them to leave Matthew alone, Cathy knew that the best thing she could do was to turn her head against Danilo's chest.

The ward was quiet and dark, with pools of dull orange spilling from lamps. Enzo was in a private room with modern prints on the wall and thick curtains. Cathy rubbed her fingers over the ridges in the fabric as she watched Enzo look into the face of his son.

'Father? Can you hear me?'

Cathy saw Enzo's eyes twitch.

'I'm not sure he's taking it in,' said Danilo to the nurse. 'He just winced, as if he was in pain.'

The nurse leaned over the bed and picked up Enzo's wrist.

'Father. I'm here, your son Danilo. Is there anything you want to say to me?'

Enzo's eyes stared up at Danilo and then moved, painfully, to where Cathy stood. His mouth quivered.

'Everything's going to be all right, Father.' Danilo spoke clearly, so that the carabiniero by the door could note it down. 'Cathy and I are here and we're going to look after you.'

'Matthew,' said Enzo, barely audibly.

'Matthew? What about him?'

'Matthew. Don't . . .' He shut his eyes, exhausted.

'We won't let him anywhere near you, don't worry. And he can't hurt the Giuditta any more.'

'No. No!' Enzo opened his eyes with an effort and tried to speak, making saliva bubble at one side of his mouth.

'It's all right.' Danilo stroked his father's hand, firmly, soothingly. He looked over his shoulder at the nurse. 'Get everyone out,' he said through his teeth. 'Can't you see he's dying?'

The nurse pulled Cathy away from the curtains and pushed her towards the door where she collided with the carabiniero. Then they were both swept into the corridor and Cathy found herself propelled towards a forlorn line of hard chairs, while the carabiniero gathered his notebook, checked his watch against the clock on the wall, and vanished into the side room where his colleagues were holding Matthew.

It took Cathy some time to come to terms with what she had seen. Danilo had lied. He had done it skilfully, so that only a person who knew his father well, and who knew the background to this evening's events, would have realised. But he had silenced his father when he tried to speak. He had denied him the opportunity to see Matthew. And out loud, so that the old man could hear, he had said that his father was dying.

What did it mean? Cathy gripped the edge of the chair, trying to think. Everything was going too fast suddenly; events seemed to be rushing on, sweeping the ground from beneath her. She knew it was Danilo's doing, but why? Was he working to set things right or make them worse?

She stared at the closed door to Enzo's room. She had to believe Danilo was setting things right. She could not afford to lose faith now. In the shadows by the far corner, Judith and Lucius were trying to break through again. She knew she must keep them at bay; they infected her with fear and it was then that she made mistakes.

Cathy turned towards the nurses' desk, at the corner between the corridor and the open ward. She looked deliberately into the low wattage light and listened to the nurses' voices. A new nurse had just arrived and the others were telling her about Enzo. Cathy had to strain to understand what was being said. She thought she caught the words 'heart attack' and 'complications' and, several times, 'police'. The new nurse was asking questions; as Cathy listened, they grew sharper. An argument was developing.

'No, he wouldn't have been given that drug,' the new nurse said. 'He couldn't have been given it, he was allergic to it.'

'They didn't know that at the time,' said one of the others.

'The emergency room had his regular drugs, didn't they? They would have known from those.'

'They didn't know. There was no indication. Dr Manani said he must have developed the allergy very recently. It might have been asymptomatic; he wouldn't have known about it.'

'He did know. It developed three months ago when he was in America and he was prescribed pills for the reaction. One look at them should have told Emergency.'

There was a pause.

'Well, Emergency didn't see them.' The second nurse sounded defensive. 'I don't know why. But it's nothing to do with this ward; no mistakes were made here.'

There was a silence.

Cathy's heart was thumping; she stood up and as the new nurse looked in her direction, she moved into the light.

'Nadia?'

'Cathy. I didn't see you there. Excuse me,' she said to her colleagues, 'I know Miss Seymour.' She came quickly down the corridor. 'Giovanni telephoned the ward where I was working and told me. I came at once, but if only I'd come sooner, before Enzo reached Emergency. There's been a terrible mistake.'

'Yes.' Cathy stared at the older woman. She wondered if her own face showed the same fear. She had to drink the air in order to go on. 'But it wasn't a mistake.'

'What are you saying?'

On the edge of her vision, Cathy could see the door to Enzo's room opening.

'Danilo brought Enzo's drugs in the ambulance, but he didn't give them all to the nurse. He kept one lot of pills back.'

The door opened wider but Nadia didn't see; she was staring at Cathy and a look of horror coiled across her face, aging her incalculably.

'You knew, and you let it happen?'

'I didn't realise. How could I? Danilo said they were his own pills.'

A figure filled the doorway.

'Nadia. Thank God you're here. Please come.' Danilo's face was working. 'My father's . . .' His mouth twisted in an attempt not to cry.

Nadia gazed up at him. 'No, Nilo,' she said. 'Oh no, not that.' Her hands groped in the air, suddenly clumsy, and Cathy seized them. She held onto them for her own support as much as to rally the older woman.

'Nadia.' Danilo's voice was supplicating. Nadia pulled herself out of Cathy's grasp and hurried towards the door. As she pushed past him, Danilo moved aside. He wiped his damp cheeks and said, 'Catti.' He sounded broken. 'Will you come and see him?'

Cathy backed away. Danilo's brow creased and he began to follow her into the corridor.

'Cathy? Please. He's so fond of you and it would mean a great deal if he knew we were together.'

Cathy shrank against the wall. 'Mean a great deal to whom?' she heard herself say.

Danilo stopped. 'To my father,' he said. 'Who else?'

'This isn't what he wanted.' Cathy told herself to hold her peace. Now more than ever she needed to dissemble, but she couldn't drive away her revulsion at what Danilo had done. She couldn't bear him to touch her. He looked strangely beautiful as he stood before her, as if he'd been washed clean of doubt. And from the intelligence that passed across his features, she knew he'd understood her thoughts.

'My father's an old man, Catti,' he said. 'His time is over. Ours is ahead of us and I'm only doing what I have to.' He reached for her and she side-stepped, but not quickly enough. His hand closed on her arm. 'You love me, you said so.'

'Danilo, you'd better come in.' Nadia spoke from the doorway. 'No,' she added sharply as he pulled Cathy with him, 'just you alone. Your father's trying to speak and it's you he wants.'

Further up the corridor, another door opened.

'Miss Seymour,' said the carabiniero, 'we'd like to ask you some questions.'

Cathy looked desperately at Nadia. Should she insist on going in with Danilo to try and get at the truth, to beg Enzo for help at the last? Nadia's steady regard was trying to tell her something but she could not decipher it.

'Come along, Nilo.' Nadia put a hand gently on his arm and at the same time detached Cathy from him. 'We must go and make our goodbyes.'

In the small office with framed certificates on the wall, the police-men were sitting close together. Matthew sat beyond them on a chair tucked into a niche. It was as if he were no longer important to them.

When he turned to greet her, Cathy saw that his right hand was fastened to a shelf upright.

'Welcome to the party,' he said. 'I thought you weren't coming.'

'It wasn't for want of trying,' said Cathy, speaking as fast as she could in order to confuse the police. 'It wasn't what it looked like earlier in the lift but I can't explain. What have they been saying to you?'

'Miss Seymour,' put in the suited man in fluent English, 'this interview isn't being held for the benefit of you and Mr Forse. Please don't speak to him again. Note this down,' he said to the carabiniero with the notebook and translated what Cathy had just said.

Cathy turned to Matthew again. 'Danilo's dangerous. He wants to have you locked up so for God's sake be careful what you say.'

'Miss Seymour!'

'Enzo'll help me,' Matthew said.

'Enzo's dying. Danilo—'

'That's enough, Miss Seymour! Or I'll have you charged with obstructing a police investigation!' The suited man's roar made Cathy flinch. 'Now tell me, do you wish to help your stepbrother?'

'Yes.'

'Then you will listen carefully to my questions and answer them. This evening, were you present when Mr Forse unveiled the work he had done on the Giuditta?'

'Yes, I was.'

'Did you think the work he had done was that of a responsible picture restorer?'

'It wasn't what I expected.'

'Why not?'

'I thought Matthew had made the face look a bit too much like me.'

'A bit too much like you?' The echo was incredulous. Cathy glanced at Matthew and saw that he was listening avidly.

'Yes,' she said, 'rather too much like me.' She put a judicious expression on her face. A glimmer of hope mixed with bewilderment showed in Matthew's eyes. He recognised what she was doing – this was a tactic they had used at school to cover for one another when they were in trouble. Pretend to be seriously considering the other's point of view, no matter how outrageous their behaviour. Move sideways when challenged; never deny but shift ground and see if you can lure authority along with you.

Cathy had no real hope of succeeding but at least she might draw attention away from Matthew onto herself. Perhaps she could muddy the waters enough to implicate herself, tie her fate to Matthew's. Then, she reasoned frantically, if Danilo still wanted her he would have to exonerate both of them.

'Do you think your stepbrother deliberately altered the painting to produce that effect?'

'I don't think he realised that the effect was quite so noticeable.'

'I see.' The policeman paused. 'And why do you think he did it?'

'Every restorer puts his own signature on his work, like any artist.'

The shadow of a smile flitted over Matthew's face. Her

questioner saw it. His eyes rested on Matt for a while and he riffled back through the notes before him.

'You like that, do you, Mr Forse? I agree that it's a better explanation than the one you gave, which was . . .' He found his place and read out, '"I restored the painting the way she wanted to be restored. Judith was guiding me. I didn't have to do anything. I just turned my hands over to her and she showed me what to do." Is that still your account of what happened? Or would you like to change it now?'

Matthew looked uncertainly at Cathy.

'Please answer to me, Mr Forse, not to your stepsister.'

'I told you,' Matthew said defiantly. 'That was what happened. God, Cathy!' He turned back to her. 'Why are you all denying it now? It was the rest of you who were so adamant about Judith in the beginning, you especially. You know I'm telling the truth so why won't you make a stand and say so?'

The two uniformed men exchanged glances; one of them discreetly tapped his head and the other smothered a laugh.

'What do you think of that, Miss Seymour?' the suited man asked, with elaborate courtesy. 'Do you agree that your stepbrother was guided by a ghostly apparition?'

But Cathy couldn't answer. For against the bare patch of wall beneath the shuttered window, human forms were taking shape. She saw Judith first, her head turned into the room, her features still indistinct. There were other people around her and as colours began to shoot through the shadows, Cathy recognised Valeria, Marcus, Balbas, Senator Marcellus Galba and his wife. Another figure stood slightly apart but it was not, as Cathy first thought, Lucius. This man stood sturdily and carried his head high but there was an unmistakable loneliness about him. It was Holofernes the captive.

A long shuddering breath came from Matthew; he was gazing at the figures too.

Don't, Cathy wanted to call to him; don't let them pull you in, we're not strong enough, but she could make no sound. The figures grew larger and brighter and were moving around the room. She could still see Matthew in handcuffs but the shelf upright was gone and so were the police. Then Matthew himself vanished and there was no room and no hospital, only the Forum, dazzling in the daybreak.

Chapter Twenty-two

Judith had expected more people. There were a hundred or so here already and more were trickling into the Forum all the time, it was true, but after the heckling in the streets last night she had thought the place would be packed. She'd imagined great banks of people, their faces avid with curiosity. Yet the spectators who'd turned up appeared an insignificant number among the huge buildings and they drifted around in an uncertain manner.

It was more frightening than a crowd would have been. Holofernes' life was on trial here, and possibly her own, yet Rome was only partially distracted from her business. Over by thc Macellum, early traders were setting out their wares. And even the well-known political figures she recognised were paying only patchy attention to Holofernes.

He stood with his wrists tied behind his back, flanked by Gaius Nepos's guards. A group of onlookers straggled round him, but he made no response to their catcalls. Nor did he look at Judith – he didn't seem to have noticed her arrival from the south side of the Forum; instead, his attention was focused on the part of the pavement where the aspiring young advocates gathered. He was scanning them, as if he expected one of them to catch his eye and approach.

He looked alone and defiant and stubbornly hopeful. Judith's heart twisted. Holofernes would never give up; even now he would be thinking of ways to come out fighting. But he didn't know the nature of the trap that had caught him, nor that she had helped spring it.

She hadn't understood the consequences but it was she, refusing to heed others and thinking only of herself, who had put Holofernes in this danger. Please the gods – all of them, Judean, Syrian, Roman – she had now done enough to save him.

'Where's Lucius?' Judith plucked at Valeria's cloak. 'Can you see him?'

'No, I can't.' Valeria's voice was thin with anxiety.

'Why isn't he here? He should be with Holofernes.'

'He's talking to the jurors,' said Marcus, jerking his grey head towards the small group by the Comitium. 'He'll be trying to find out their attitudes and test his lines of argument on them.'

'I don't think Holofernes knows he's here,' said Judith in agitation. 'Hasn't anyone told him Lucius is going to defend him?'

'Probably not,' said Marcus. 'Who is there to tell him? No one knows except us and we've been too busy to get messages through.'

'But he must be told! He'll think we've all deserted him!'

'He's about to find out now.' Valeria indicated Gaius Nepos who was making his way to the jurors, his back stiff but his legs covering the ground fast. 'Gaius looks worried, which must be good for us.'

They all watched as the ex-chief centurion marched up to the jurors, but he didn't address Lucius. He merely saluted him and turned on his heel to another, older figure who had appeared among the jurors. It was Aulus Tullius, Lucius's father, and with him were two secretaries, carrying documents.

Marcus drew a sharp breath. 'It seems Aulus Tullius is prosecuting.'

'What are they doing?' Judith whispered. 'Marcus, why are Lucius and his father talking? Is Lucius double-crossing us?'

'Of course not, they're bound to greet each other. You wouldn't expect them to cut each other dead.' But Marcus was staring at the father and son.

Judith saw Holofernes, too, turn in their direction, his attention caught by movement among the onlookers. As he saw Lucius he started, then almost immediately his shoulders went back and his head lifted. He was too proud to sag beneath the blow.

Judith lurched forward, almost pulling over Valeria who held her arm. 'Let me go!' she cried. 'I should be with him!'

'Yes,' said Marcus. 'You're right, he shouldn't be alone, it looks bad. And he shouldn't be tied. Come on.' He led them on, suddenly galvanised. 'There are men here who should be lining up on our side, behind Holofernes. Let's get moving on them. Hey!' he shouted as they bore down on the guard. 'Cut his bonds at once. He's no criminal; how dare you treat a respected friend of Rome like this!'

Holofernes turned at the noise and met Judith's eyes. The look he gave her was so intimate that Judith felt as if the ground had dissolved beneath her feet and she was running in mid-air. For a second there was no bravado in her husband's face, only anger, fear and a passionate gladness to see her.

Then she was at his side and clutching his arm.

'Judith. I'd hoped not to see you here.' The gladness had

gone, and an unfamiliar expression was taking its place: shame. 'Are they really charging you too?'

'I'd be here whether they charged me or not. I'm your wife.'

Holofernes moved instinctively to touch her, but his arms were still tied. 'But are they charging you?'

'Yes.' Judith turned to Marcus, unable to bear the tenderness in Holofernes' face. If he knew what she had done – but he mustn't know. To save him she must convince them all of an alternative truth. 'Marcus, make them cut him free!'

The guards stood irresolute, and with a curse Marcus himself stepped forward and cut the ropes. 'Hold your tongues or you'll answer to the chief centurion!' he barked at them. Then he squeezed Holofernes' shoulder. 'Friend, I'm going to get some of those people out there to come and stand by you.'

'Thank you.' Holofernes flexed his arms. 'You're a loyal man, Marcus, but it's going to be an uphill battle.' His jerked his head towards the Comitium and his smile was twisted. 'Haven't you seen, I've got two generations of the house of Bestia ranged against me.'

Marcus shook his head. 'Lucius is with us,' he said curtly. 'He's defending you.'

'What?'

'Yes.' Marcus met Holofernes' disbelieving eyes for a split second. 'We spent the night working on his approach. Excuse me, there's not much time.' He strode off, through the thickening crowd.

'Lucius?' Holofernes' face had darkened. He stared at Judith. 'Why would Lucius defend me after last night?'

His eyes were searching her face. Judith took his hands and Holofernes flinched as she unwittingly touched the weals left by the ropes. She remembered his flinch of the night before when he had suspected her. But Holofernes had not believed her capable of treachery. She must convince him of the same with regard to Lucius, otherwise he would never accept his help.

'You're right,' she said, speaking fast and low. 'Lucius didn't want to defend you at first. He was angry and humiliated and when Marcus asked him to be your advocate, he walked out. But we all argued with him – me, Marcus, Valeria. We followed him home and convinced him that his honour depended on it. Lucius isn't stupid, he could see how people would talk if he turned his back on you. And also I think he's ashamed of what happened yesterday. He was drunk and he behaved badly. If he deserts you now, he'll always know, and so will Marcus, that your partnership ended because he acted like a stupid boy. But if he defends you and clears you, and saves the campaign, then he's beyond reproach.' She was pulling the reasoning out of the air, but it had its own persuasive logic. Holofernes was listening hard.

'Yes,' he said abruptly, 'I see that. But all the same, how can it be honourable for Lucius to defend a man who knocked him down?'

'But no one knows about that, do they, except for you and me and Marcus and Valeria. And why would any of us tell?'

Fury showed briefly in Holofernes' eyes. 'No, if he gets me off and installs himself at the head of the campaign, I suppose we won't be able to. It's blackmail.'

'Whatever it is, it's our best chance. There are powerful interests up against us, Holofernes. Aulus Tullius is prosecuting, and he'll have many of the more traditional nobles on his side.'

'Father and son – I suppose it gives Lucius a chance to break free once and for all.' Holofernes looked over to where the two men were now surrounded by clients and supporters. Aulus was deep in conversation but Lucius was standing quietly, looking straight at them. As their eyes met, a charge seemed to travel between the two men, like invisible lightning. Holofernes wrenched his head back.

'No,' he said through his teeth, 'I won't let him speak for me. I'll do my own pleading.'

'You can't, you don't have the right.'

'Of course I do.'

'No you don't. If you fail to convince them, it's not just you and I who'll be condemned. All the men you brought from Syria will come under suspicion, and so will Marcus, and everyone who's helped us here. You're a leader, Holofernes, you're responsible for these people. You can't throw away their best chance.'

Holofernes gazed down at her, his face a mass of conflicting emotions. He'd tugged his hands free during her last speech, and now he adjusted her cloak on her shoulders and ran a finger down her arm, lightly stroking the coiled bracelet she had forgotten to remove.

'I've spoiled the shape of this bracelet, haven't I?' he said, frowning as if they were alone in her bedroom.

'No, you've made it better. It fits me now.'

Holofernes straightened slowly and put his hand on his belt where he usually carried his knife. 'Wasted on Bethulia,' he said softly. 'I always knew it. I should have got you out long before. You were made to be a general's wife.'

'I was made to be your wife.' Judith felt as though her tongue would bleed as she said it. Whatever happened, she would not be his wife for much longer. If Holofernes were cleared, she would have to keep her bargain with Lucius and go away with him. And if the people convicted him . . . She wouldn't think of that.

'I love you, Holofernes,' she said urgently. 'I know Roman wives don't say it, nor Judean wives. But I want you to know.'

'I do know. I've never doubted it.' He hesitated. 'Not really. You've taken your chance with me all the way through. And with luck there'll be many more chances after this.' He grinned at her suddenly, reminding her of another day when they had stood in a strange city and talked of the future. 'What's the matter?'

'Lucius is coming.'

His face clouded and he turned slowly to watch Lucius's approach.

'Will you let him defend you?' Judith asked. She was half in dread now, a terrible uncertainty beginning to obscure what had earlier seemed clear. Was she right to put Holofernes in Lucius's hands like this? Did Lucius want her enough to keep his word?

'I'll let him,' said Holofernes. 'But I don't trust him, and I mean to speak for myself as well.'

Lucius's eyes were like chips of stone in his exhausted face. They rested on Judith for a second, searing her. Then they turned to Holofernes. For a long moment neither man spoke. Then Lucius turned and clicked his fingers at the secretary who walked behind him with his papers.

'I'm here to defend you, General Holofernes. Are you ready to begin?'

The sun had risen up the sky but clouds swathed it; there was a chill in the air and Judith huddled inside her cloak. The warmth given off by the press of bodies around her was almost welcome.

Marcus had persuaded seven of Holofernes' supporters to come and stand by him, and with them came their clients and a taggle of onlookers. There was a much more substantial crowd around Aulus Tullius.

The rest of the spectators – and there were far more than earlier, two or even three times the number – thronged the broad pavement, committing themselves to neither party.

Aulus Tullius was speaking. He had a beautiful, measured voice and as he laid out the charges against Holofernes he walked up and down, his slight form leaning into the rhythm of his words.

'General Holofernes came to us with a reputation for brilliance in the field, for courage, and for strategic skills. He has lived among us for three months now and we've heard much of these skills. Some of our good citizens have been greatly impressed by them. Some of our neighbours, our friends, our sons,' he paused, 'have become his supporters. They have been won over by his plans for a rolling eastern campaign in the lands to the north-east of his native Syria.' He paused again.

'But Syria is not truly his native land. It is the land he adopted when he was growing up. He used that land to gain his education and experience in the army. He obtained access to powerful men. He was sent here to Rome on missions for the Syrian king. Some of his actions during that time benefited Syria, but by no means all. All, however, enriched General Holofernes.

'This is the pattern of the man's life. His prime concern is not loyalty to his country or to his allies; it is his own gain. He is a ruthless and devious man who has been the ruin of many people in his time. Now he is intent on using Rome to bring him power and riches.

'Ever since he has been here, he has been recruiting honest Romans to this task. They are persuaded by his arguments and his personal charm and they believe him when he says he is doing this for the good of Rome. But he is not. General Holofernes – and that is not even his real name – is a liar and a profiteer. More, he is a traitor to the noble state of Rome which has welcomed him to her bosom.'

After the senator's final words, a hush lay over the crowd. Judith stared at Aulus Tullius in horror. His quiet manner was convincing, almost mesmerising. She had never seen a strong resemblance between him and Lucius before, but then she had only ever seen the senator from a distance and had never heard him speak. Now she could see that both father and son had the same ability to channel all their energy.

Holofernes looked furious. He opened his mouth but Lucius had already stepped in front of him.

'I am proud to call this man Holofernes a friend,' he said clearly. 'He is a brave man and a brilliant one. He does indeed have all the qualities my father himself has acknowledged. But there is more to being a great general than physical courage and a strategic mind. You have to inspire men, and to do that you have to show yourself to be trustworthy. Soldiers won't be fooled by charm. They look for greatness of heart, steadiness of purpose. They look for a man who can see the potential greatness in all those around him and bring it into being at the crucial time.

'General Holofernes is such a man. He has seen the possibility for Rome to gain strength in the east. He has travelled in many of our provinces and lived in some of our allied states. For years he has helped strengthen the friendship between Syria and Rome – he has seen for himself that alliance with Rome brings peace to warring lands. He wants that peace for his own country of Syria, and for us. Those are his motives. They are honourable ones for he is an honourable man!'

Lucius's face was radiant. Judith watched him uneasily. He had raised a steady murmur of agreement from the men around Holofernes and some shouts from the crowd, but she could also hear a buzz of surprise. Marcus had told her that Lucius spoke with coolness and an unmatched quickness of argument. Yet that speech had been almost transported by emotion. What was he trying to do? Looking at Holofernes, Judith saw that he too seemed wary. When Lucius turned and held out his hand to him, Holofernes scrutinised him for several long seconds before extending his own.

Aulus Tullius took a sheaf of notes from one of his secretaries. 'My son, like many good Romans, has taken this man on trust. But let us examine some of General Holofernes' actions in the past. In Crete, for instance, ten years ago, he was fighting in the army of Mavros when he was condemned to death for stealing.'

'No,' Holofernes interrupted sharply. 'That's not true!'

'You were not condemned?'

'Yes, I was, but not for stealing. I took what belonged to me and the other soldiers in my company – our wages. We hadn't been paid for two months and we had nothing to eat while the commanders sat in luxury, selling off the war booty for their own profit.'

'That's a very convincing story, as all your stories are. No doubt you'll have an equally good justification for why, while you were in prison, you suddenly discovered a loyalty to Demetrius, the Syrian king's nephew then exiled on Crete.'

'I don't need any justification. Demetrius was the rightful

king of Syria. His uncle was a usurper and he was ruining Syria.'

'So you broke out of captivity with fifty of Demetrius's supporters, raided the house where he was kept under guard and escaped from the island with him.'

'Yes. And it was no easy thing to do.'

'Easier than being stoned to death, which was the punishment for profiteering.'

Holofernes looked scornfully at Aulus Tullius. *Don't*, thought Judith fearfully. *Don't underestimate him.*

'I'd be a liar if I said I was willing to die, especially for a crime I hadn't committed. But I didn't need Demetrius to get me out of prison. I could have broken out on my own.'

'Nevertheless, having fifty helpers made it easier. And, given that you had fallen foul of the army of Mavros who was a close ally of the king of Syria, you no longer had much of a future in the king's forces. It was convenient for your own interests to champion the rival claimant to the throne – which you did, very successfully. It was largely thanks to you, as I'm sure my son intends to point out, that Demetrius was able to take back his throne at the head of a small but skilfully deployed force of men.'

'Yes, in Bel's name, it was! And I'm proud of it.'

'So proud of it, and so loyal to Demetrius, that this year you betrayed his trust, abandoned the siege he had asked you to lead on Judea, and took your men over to my son, at Apamea.'

Holofernes went very still. 'Three years had passed. I'd been loyal to Demetrius for all of them, carried out his missions faithfully. But he was losing control of the country. We were being attacked by the Parthians; the siege was a desperate gamble I never agreed with. If I'd gone on with it, by now Syria would be torn apart.'

'Syria would be torn apart. So your motive for betraying the Syrian king and boarding a ship for Rome was not to serve Rome, but to preserve Syria.'

'It was both.'

'How very convenient – once again.'

'This is unworthy of us!' Lucius stepped forward, his face flushed. 'Anyone's motives can seem suspect if they are picked over endlessly, long after the event. And to us Romans especially the ways of foreigners can be difficult to understand. We have such a strong system of government, handed down from generation to generation on noble principles. It's hard for us to comprehend the subtleties and the – the shifts that men find it necessary to make in more troubled nations.'

He hesitated. He was breathing turbulently, obviously struggling with his emotions.

'I acknowledge that some of General Holofernes' methods seem devious to us. I have been troubled by a few – his informal ways of recruiting our centurions, for instance. But we – myself and his other partners – have censured him where appropriate and will in future be dealing with all matters relating to the legions ourselves. The brilliance of General Holofernes' strategy can't be allowed to go to waste because of his methods. Or his past record. Besides, it is in the tradition of our ancestors to take what is best from people, for the greater good of Rome. "Look with a noble eye and you will see nobility." I have always tried to live by that and I believe there are good things in General Holofernes. Many good things.'

Judith watched in dismay. Lucius, the most composed of men, was fidgeting. His head moved from side to side; his eyes lighted on many different people in the crowd but rested on no one, least of all herself.

She felt coldness steal through her. It came softly but irrevocably, like evening mist. Lucius was not trying to save Holofernes; on the contrary, he was feeding doubt into the crowd, echoing what his father said while seeming to deny it.

Judith turned to Holofernes, hoping that he would reassure her. But he wore an expression of sick comprehension.

'This is not right.' Her voice was inaudible; she couldn't make any impression on the murmuring that swelled from all sides. Yet somehow Holofernes had heard.

He looked straight at her. 'It wasn't that way,' he said. 'You do know that?'

'Yes, I know.' Again, barely any sound came.

'My son, Lucius Tullius, sees things as a good Roman.' Aulus looked austerely at Lucius. 'That is commendable and I would demand no less from him. But this general is not Roman. He does not share our noble values, and neither does his wife.'

Judith felt herself start to shake. She had been expecting to hear charges against herself earlier; she'd almost forgotten that she was here for any reason other than to support Holofernes.

'Since Holofernes and Judith of Bethulia have been here, I have met several men who were in Judea at the time of the siege. And they have told me a very different story from that which Holofernes puts about. Judith is no chaste young woman, sent into the enemy camp to plead for her city. She is an immodest harlot, a woman hated in her own home. She hunted her young husband to death and was afterwards kept in confinement by her father-in-law, scorned by all decent people, until she escaped into General Holofernes' encampment.'

'That's a lie!' Holofernes leapt forward and seized Aulus

Tullius by the throat. Instantly he was pulled off and forced to the ground by both Aulus's supporters and his own. 'You liars!' he shouted, and there came a crunch and a spitting noise. Then, almost incoherently, Judith heard again, 'You filthy liars.'

Lucius stood as if stunned, peering at Holofernes on the pavement. Then he crossed swiftly to his father.

'Father, are you all right? Did he hurt you?'

'No, son, I'm not injured. I'm just breathless. I wasn't expecting that.'

Lucius kept his hands firmly on his father, but Aulus shook him off. He glanced down at Holofernes, coughing on the ground. 'Let him up,' he said sternly. He raised his hand to quell the noise from the crowd. 'The trial must go on. If the Syrian general has any honour in him, he'll give his assurance it won't happen again.'

Holofernes got slowly to his feet. Only one of his own supporters stayed to help him; the others either moved to Aulus's party or dissolved into the crowd. One of his eyes was swelling and he spoke with difficulty out of his bloodied mouth.

'I've got plenty of honour in me. Just as my wife is decent in every drop of her blood. Not that that's a thing Romans could understand.'

Shouts, and a low snarling sound, overtook his last words. Judith stared at Holofernes, wondering why he sounded so strange, and then realised that his front teeth were gone. He looked desperately back at her, his eyes suddenly showing fear.

'Kill him!' shouted someone, and other voices took up the demand.

'Syrian scum! He should die.'

'And his woman.'

'No. Stop this. Speak, my son.' Aulus Tullius gestured to Lucius who had turned his back on Holofernes.

'He has insulted you, Father,' said Lucius in a choked voice. 'We must avenge the insult.'

'That can come later. Meanwhile, we are advocates. You have taken on this man's defence because you believed there should be a partnership between him and Rome. If you still believe so, you must go on with your defence.'

Lucius turned slowly and looked at Holofernes. An extraordinary mixture of emotions tussled in his face: disillusion, rage, reproach. And finally, shining from deep in his eyes when he glanced over at Judith, triumph.

'You have insulted my father, and I will pay you for that,' he said softly to Holofernes. 'But he's right. The campaign we have worked on together deserves to survive.' He hesitated and looked out at the crowd. 'Although Holofernes has just made himself the enemy of our family, I'm reluctant to believe that he is a liar and a traitor. I knew him when he was first in Rome several years ago and he seemed honest then. I travelled back from Apamea with him and his wife. And in all the time that we were together, I saw nothing to make me doubt Judith of Bethulia's modesty. Indeed, while we were in Apamea I met men who had been in Bethulia and their reports of Judith were that she was as Holofernes said, a devout young widow, well respected by her neighbours.'

He glanced at Judith; there was no sign that he was deliberately lying. He seemed to struggle with puzzlement and an honest admiration for her.

Hope and despair stretched Judith between them. Lucius was showing that he could save her if he wanted to. But was he going to, and if so, at what price? Holofernes had made as if to interrupt earlier, but he'd stopped when he heard Judith's name. Now he, too, looked at her, and she could see the same wariness on his face.

'Do you have any evidence to support the charges of bad faith?' Lucius asked his father. 'Other than the reports of some men who may be speaking out of malice?'

'The evidence of the facts,' Aulus Tullius replied. He also turned to the crowd. 'The general's conduct since he has been in Rome speaks for itself. He has insulted many of our most distinguished soldiers by neglect, and tried to suborn their men into joining his campaign. He has bought supporters with money. He has bribed people with promises that they will hold positions of wealth and influence in the provinces his campaign will create. Roman provinces, whose government can be decided only by Roman people.' Aulus Tullius had to raise his voice again to be heard above the mounting anger of the crowd.

'Lies!' said Holofernes. 'It's lies!'

'I have the names of men who will confirm it.'

'They're lying,' Holofernes repeated stubbornly. 'All this is just verbal combat. No one can prove any of it. For every charge that I've bribed someone, I can throw back a charge that someone on your side has bribed them to say so. You know it's true. What about Gaius Vespa last month? And the Aureliani brothers?'

He was shouting now, maddened and desperate, and Judith's heart hammered. But not all the shouts from the crowd were hostile. She knew very well that Holofernes had bribed people; she also knew that bribery was rife in Rome, and the crowd was aware of it. 'That's true!' came a cry. And someone laughed, 'Try them as well while we're at it!' Arguments began to break out between the onlookers. As she watched, the faces grew angrier and the noise swelled. The crowd pressed forward towards Holofernes and herself and the two guards restraining Holofernes were forced to move him several steps in her direction, so that now they formed one small group. In the chaos, Judith reached out and touched Holofernes' grazed arm.

'Separate them,' Aulus Tullius said sharply to the guards.

Lucius mounted a stone block that had appeared from somewhere. He held up his arms, demanding quiet. Gradually, the onlookers stopped shouting. In response to the urging of the guards, they began to shuffle back. In the clearing they left, Holofernes was marched away from Judith and made to stand on a second stone block which raised him above the crowd.

A tense silence now hung over everyone.

'I have spoken to my father and to the jury,' Lucius said, his voice as clear as water drops, 'and we are all agreed on a course of action. I am going to put a proposition to General Holofernes. It is a military proposition. Listen carefully to the way he answers.'

He turned to Holofernes.

'General Holofernes, you wish us to believe that you are not a traitor to Rome. I wish to believe that too. This court will now give you the chance to prove it. Is it true that the reason you abandoned the siege of Bethulia was because you thought the venture mistaken?'

'Yes,' said Holofernes angrily.

'You thought it was part of a generally misguided policy being pursued by Demetrius?'

'Yes, I've already told you. Syria was at war on the east; it would have ended up at war on the west too. I didn't want to be a part of it.'

'But you could have taken Bethulia for your country then?'

'Yes.'

'Then take it for your country now.'

Holofernes was absolutely still. The only thing about him that moved was his chest, rising and falling. 'I don't understand what you mean.'

'I'll explain it. You say that your loyalties are now to Rome. Rome needs a garrison town in Judea. Bethulia would be ideal, but the Judeans are refusing to make it over to us. As the first campaign in our partnership, Rome appoints you to win the town for us.'

Holofernes didn't speak. Judith stared at him; her eyes stung and the blood roared in her head, making it impossible to think. She didn't understand either. This was nonsense; military campaigns couldn't be decided like this. The consuls had to approve each one, Holofernes had told her so.

'I don't see the consuls here,' said Holofernes softly, echoing her thoughts.

'When it's time, you'll see the consuls. Meanwhile, we'd like your answer. Will you attack Bethulia and capture it for Rome?'

Holofernes looked steadily at Lucius. His skin had lost its colour; against the streaks of blood and dirt, it was grey.

'I'm not the right person for the job. My wife is from the town and her family live there. Generals aren't usually given command in such circumstances.'

'In the war against the Latins, Titus Manlius cut off his son's head for disobeying orders. We expect our soldiers to put country and proper conduct above family. It's the Roman way.'

At last, Holofernes' eyes moved to Judith. They rested on

her face and he seemed to hesitate; and she remembered the time in his tent outside Bethulia when she had seen his scars and had understood for the first time the blood and violence and hatred of war, the things that soldiers did to one another, and to the people who went down before them.

The same knowledge was in Holofernes' face. He looked like a trapped animal. He held out one hand towards Judith in silent pleading.

'General Holofernes, we're waiting for your answer. Will you attack Bethulia and capture it for Rome, and let no personal interest stand in the way? Give us your word now, and the charge of treachery will be proved false.'

Judith was still looking at Holofernes, but something in Lucius's voice alerted her. Her eyes flew to him. He was glowing with an inward light, watching Holofernes raptly.

This was what he wanted. Not Holofernes' death, but this moment: to see Holofernes ransom himself with the lives of her mother and father, her brother.

It was a trick; suddenly she was sure of it. There was no garrison, no attack planned for Bethulia. The only war being waged was Lucius's private one; the siege was his, against her love for her husband which she had not managed to hide.

Judith gasped with relief. She opened her mouth and cried 'Holofernes! Don't—' But she didn't need to tell him. Holofernes had understood too. He put his finger to his lips and though his face was still pale, he smiled.

'The charge of treachery *is* false,' he said, looking straight into her eyes. 'And what Rome has just asked me to do is beneath contempt. I will never do it.'

There was utter silence. The only sound was of birds twittering in a bush.

'Then you will die, General.'

Who did the voice belong to? Lucius? Judith looked at her husband. She watched a drop of blood snake its way across his forehead and mingle with sweat. Everything else seemed suddenly unfamiliar and remote.

Holofernes shrugged at her as if they were sharing a private joke. 'Be brave,' he said as they pulled him from the block.

The cliff rose high above the north end of the Forum. At the summit, slabbed rocks jutted out, casting their shadow over the ground. The darkness did not reach Judith. She stood several yards from its edge, flanked by guards.

Lucius was beyond them, with Aulus Tullius. And past him the mass of people curved, jostling and eager. She couldn't tell how long it was since Holofernes had disappeared behind the hill. Minutes? Half an hour? Longer?

She had stopped trying to plead. She hadn't spoken at all since Valeria had left her side. Valeria had said, 'We'll save you, Judith. At least we can save you.'

Figures appeared on top of the cliff. She saw Holofernes instantly. In the tangle of bodies she recognised his head and the curve of his arms, braced now, fighting.

The men seemed to spend a long time on the summit. They might have been wrestling or dancing. Then Holofernes broke free. Judith saw him outlined against the sky, his arms raised. He ran towards her, outstripping the others, and jumped.

The silence entered her bones. It remained there throughout the dull noise of his landing, the screams of the crowd, and the hoarse moaning that came afterwards. She looked at the ground. Broken but alive, Holofernes tried to move. His mouth was open, pressed into the stone. Judith could see his tongue.

She went slowly forward and stood in his blood. She knelt down and looked into his ravaged face. What was he trying to say?

Lucius was beside her, pulling at her arm. He was sobbing. 'For the love of the gods, Judith, get out of the way. Let me finish him.'

Judith turned and used his body to pull herself up. 'Give me your sword,' she said. Lucius looked at her but she didn't see him. She reached for his sword and felt him place it in her hand, then steady her. Judith looked into her husband's face, spoke secret words to him, and brought the sword down on his neck.

CHAPTER TWENTY-THREE

The silence was intense. Cathy looked at the three policemen, sitting like statues, and at Matthew next to her, and wondered how long they had been like this.

The policemen looked dazed. Matthew's free hand was clasped round hers but he stared at the floor and she couldn't see his face.

'What was she saying?' said one of the uniformed men. 'What was that?'

'Latin,' replied the other. 'At least, I think . . .'

The first man shook his head. 'What's happening here?'

The suited man reached for the telephone. 'I don't know what's happening. I wouldn't put it past her to have tried hypnosis, but it's not going any further. I want the psychiatrist here, now.'

Cathy saw the corner of Matthew's mouth lift.

'I wonder how much of it they saw,' he said quietly. 'Or did they just hear it?'

'Matthew?' she murmured. 'Oh God, are you all right?'

'I think so. My head's still on my body.' His laugh turned into a shudder. 'You've seen things like this before, haven't you?'

The suited man was busy talking into the phone and the

uniformed men were watching them blankly, unable to follow English.

'Yes,' Cathy said. 'But never so strongly before.'

'Does Danilo see them too?'

'I don't know. He sees his own versions perhaps.'

'Oh Christ. If only I'd understood sooner. It's been some kind of replay, hasn't it? You, me, him.'

'Yes.'

'And now we've come to the end. Why did it take me so long to realise?'

The end. Was that what he really thought? But then Matt had been seeing through Holofernes' eyes and now Holofernes was dead. Cathy realised that the wildness had gone from Matthew's face; he seemed restored to himself. But it was not the end of the danger. Keeping an eye on the suited man who was arguing into the telephone, she whispered urgently, 'Matt, do you remember what you did to the Giuditta?'

Matthew hesitated. 'I hope not. I've got two pictures in my mind. I can see the Giuditta the way she appeared to me when I was finishing her, so beautiful and alive. And then there's another picture. It's like some kind of awful joke.' He glanced at her, then away. 'I've been trying not to believe it. Is that really what I did?'

'Yes. Danilo called the police.'

'And Enzo?' His voice was barely audible. 'Is he really dying?'

'He seems to be.' Cathy squeezed his hand. 'But it's not your fault. Matt, listen.' She began to speak fast; the suited man had finished his phone call and was striding round the desk. 'Don't admit anything. Say you can't remember what happened. Danilo's dangerous—'

She gasped as she was seized roughly by the arm and pulled away from Matthew.

'Sit over there, Miss Seymour. And don't say anything, *anything*, until Mr Forse has been moved out of here. Then I'll interview you alone.'

The sharp double knock stopped them halfway across the room. The door opened before anyone could speak and Nadia stood there.

'What do you want?' the suited man snapped. 'We're carrying on a police investigation.'

'I need Miss Seymour and Mr Forse,' said Nadia emphatically. 'Mr Bonaventura is asking for them. He's dying; they must come at once.'

'Now? This minute?'

'This second, Inspector.'

The inspector dropped Cathy's arm.

'Attach yourself to the suspect, Versani,' he said to the taller of the carabinieri. 'I'll escort Miss Seymour.'

'We can only allow in Miss Seymour and Mr Forse,' said Nadia. 'Mr Bonaventura is dying. He needs peace at his bedside.'

'These young people are suspected of serious crimes against Mr Bonaventura. They can't be allowed to go in unattended.'

'They won't be unattended. Danilo Bonaventura is with his father and I shall be there.'

'I must insist on coming.'

'And I must refuse. My responsibility is to the wellbeing of my patient. I am not only a hospital nurse, Inspector, I'm an old friend of the Bonaventura family. I'm here at Mr Bonaventura's request and I intend to see that he dies with dignity.'

The inspector narrowed his eyes. 'Very well,' he said with ill grace. 'Versani, release Mr Forse. But we'll be waiting in the corridor,' he told Nadia. 'And if there's any trouble, we won't hesitate to come in.'

Nadia gave a peremptory nod, her eyes hostile, and stood to one side of the door, gesturing Cathy and Matthew to join her. Her movements were clipped and impersonal and though Cathy stared hopefully at her, her expression didn't soften.

What had passed between Nadia and Danilo? Cathy wondered. Danilo knew that she had found him out; did he suspect that she had told Nadia? If so, he would have been busy twisting the facts round, convincing Nadia of some version of his own.

There was no time to warn Matthew. Besides, she couldn't say anything without Nadia hearing. They were walking out into the corridor now, she and Matthew side by side and Nadia barely a pace behind them, like a bodyguard. And a few yards behind Nadia came the police. They were being ushered straight into Danilo's trap, she thought despairingly. Their only hope of a way out rested with Enzo.

Nadia spoke quietly over her shoulder to the policemen. 'You may sit in these chairs here and wait. Please don't talk more than absolutely necessary, or you'll disturb the patients. If you wish to hold discussions, I'll have to ask you to return to the office.'

The men stopped, and Cathy felt Nadia's hand placed briefly on her back. 'Further along, please.'

Cathy half turned, bewildered. Surely Enzo's room was the first one after the chairs? But Nadia's pressure increased and she walked on, into the dimness of the corridor. Perhaps she was mistaken; all the doors were identical, after all, and there was another group of chairs further along. Nadia stopped opposite them. 'In here, please.'

The room was identical to Enzo's; the same light was switched on and a screen had been pulled forward between bed and door. But the bed was empty.

Matthew stared at it, horror edging into his face. 'He's not here. Is he already—'

'No. Enzo is dying and Danilo's with him; it won't be long now. So we have very little time.' Nadia crossed the room to an inner door and opened it. She pressed a switch and a light came on, showing a small bathroom. 'Come in, quickly.' As they followed her, she was already at the other side of the little room, shooting bolts back from a pair of double doors. 'People in this ward are too ill to use bathrooms, but private patients like to have them anyway. This one used to be a store cupboard. This is the old door and it opens – if it opens,' she gritted her teeth and shoved the last bolt across, 'into the old porter's lift.' The double doors opened to reveal an iron grille and a deep lift. 'It still works but it's hardly ever used. Go down to the basement. From there, climb the stairs to the ground floor and on the right you'll find a side exit. Go out that way. If you're careful, it's unlikely anyone will see you.'

'What the hell are you talking about?' said Matthew. 'We can't do that. Where's Enzo? What about the police?'

Nadia gripped his wrist. She had to tilt her head back to look up at him. 'Listen to me, Matthew. You're in grave danger here. Once, years ago, I watched this happen and it's happening again. Enzo tried to intervene but he was too late, and now he's beyond helping you. You and Cathy have to save yourselves now. If you stay here, you will either go to prison or be committed to hospital as mentally ill. Danilo will see to that; he's gone too far to stop. You've felt the power of Judith's story, and how it lives on. It has you in its grip and through Danilo it's going to destroy you.'

'No.' Matthew was dead white, but steady. 'It's finished. We saw Holofernes die. Cat and I went through it together, in the office. It's over.'

'It's not over. Holofernes is dead and you feel released, but for Cathy and Danilo it continues. Danilo's still desperate for Cathy, and you're still in his way. Believe me, Matthew, I've watched this happen before and I know just how relentless this haunting is. Last time it was Enzo and Alessandra and Benedetto, her lover. He was a young, impulsive man like you, and he died.'

'It was an accident.'

'It was a car crash which would never have happened if Enzo hadn't been hounding him. But Enzo couldn't help himself; he was possessed. And do you know *how* Benedetto died? He was decapitated.'

Watching Matthew's face change, Cathy put her hand over her mouth to stop herself moaning. For a few seconds she had hoped that his steadiness might be well-founded and that she too would come to be sure that it was over. But now she saw the nightmare claim him back.

'You think Danilo's going to cut my head off?' Matthew tried to joke but failed.

'Listen, please listen. I owe this to you and to Enzo, and most of all to Danilo. I can't let him do this. You must get out of here at once. Get away. Take a train or a bus and go somewhere in the country. I have money for you,' Nadia dug in her pocket and pulled out a thick wad of notes, 'and I can get you some more once you've found a place to stay.'

'But this is insane. The police will find me – I'll have no papers. I can't stay hidden away.'

'You won't need to. If I have a little time, I think I can make Danilo give up hounding you.'

'How?'

Nadia glanced at Cathy; anguish showed for an instant in her eyes. 'I'm an old friend of the family,' she said quietly. 'I carry some influence with Danilo. And I understand certain things about him which he perhaps doesn't realise.'

The pills. Nadia was going to use her knowledge of what Danilo had done. Cathy stared at Nadia's tired, determined face; what must it mean to Danilo's old nurse to find herself acting as his nemesis?

'Oh Nadia. Be careful,' she said, though that wasn't all that she meant; she couldn't find words for the rest.

Sounds reached them from out in the corridor.

'Quickly!' said Nadia. 'You must go.'

'Cat?' Matthew stood irresolute. 'What should I do?'

'You must go. Cathy knows that you must both go. Don't you, Cathy?'

'Yes.' Cathy snatched the money from Nadia and kissed her hard.

'No!' Matthew stepped between them. 'Cat, you don't have to come. You mustn't. You'll be putting yourself outside the law and there's no need.'

'I'm coming,' Cathy said and pulled the grille aside.

Matthew grabbed her shoulders. 'No you're not.'

They grappled for a moment, fighting as they used to in childhood, and Cathy felt the threshold of the lift pass beneath her feet.

'Press the button for the basement.' Nadia's voice came

breathlessly as she slammed the grille shut on them. 'In a few days' time put an advertisement in the *Corriere della Sera* newspaper, for art lessons. Give a box number. I'll do everything I can.'

She swung the wooden doors shut. Matthew was still clasping Cathy, though he'd stopped pushing her away. She reached out and stabbed her finger on the lowest button and the lift started to move.

It wasn't over. The city was changing as they hurried through the streets. Shop windows became blank caverns, walls shifted, domes vanished and reappeared again and the people they passed seemed to tremble on the cusp of two worlds. Was that man wearing a jacket or a cloak? Did that young woman peer from a car window or the curtains of a litter?

Cathy clung to Matthew's hand and told him to guide her. 'I can't seem to find my way,' she said. She tried to stop her voice from trembling and prayed that Matthew could still see whole.

They didn't talk; there wasn't time for words, and besides, they had no breath. When they had put a maze of streets between themselves and the hospital, they hailed a taxi. They sat huddled in the back, frantically swapping the names of possible destinations. The rhythm of the taxi's engine turned into the lurching of a carriage; Cathy could feel the wooden wheels turning beneath her, shaking her.

They darted through the main hall of Statione Termini, camouflaging themselves among other travellers. The departure screens showed five trains due to leave in the next fifteen minutes: Venezia, Bologna, Perugia, Bari, Napoli. They had already decided to go south. They knew they should keep the first leg of the journey as short as possible and change tracks in a big, busy town. Cathy bought two French newspapers from a stall, concentrating desperately as the stallholder's muttered 'Thank you' took on the cadence of Latin and the handful of small change became heavier and winked ancient insignia at her.

Matthew was turning from the ticket office, his face ghastly. But he was holding two tickets and, arm in arm, they crossed the concourse to the platform where the Naples train stood.

Cathy looked at Matthew, leaning away from her, his forehead pressed against the window. He wasn't asleep; she could see his eyes flickering as the darkened landscape sped by.

They had talked as much as was useful. Explanations, recriminations, apologies had taken them through the first hour of the journey. Some of the things they discussed were almost ludicrously mundane now that they were hurtling into nowhere with enemies at their backs. And yet those details helped it become real.

They were fleeing. They were outcasts. There was no normality for them any more.

Matthew's hand lay on Cathy's leg and she put her own hand over it, clinging to his physical presence. At least when they'd been talking the other world had been kept at bay. But now it was breaking through again.

Cathy fought it, but she could not keep it away. Her eyes were full of confused visions, of long paved roads and lines of marching people, of ships and sea, of soldier's shields and women she seemed to recognise.

But shimmering behind all of these, its lines becoming clearer and harder the more she tried not to look, was Lucius's face, poisoned with self-loathing yet still illuminated by a terrible, implacable hope.

Cathy curled up and put her hands over her eyes.

'What is it?' Matthew's arm was instantly round her.

'I don't know. I'm just worried and confused, I suppose.'

'You're seeing something, aren't you? Don't keep it from me. Please, Cathy, tell me, let me help. Are they doing something to Judith?'

Against the pressure of her hands on her eyelids, Cathy could still see the images shifting, processing.

'No, I don't think so.' She was finding it hard to get enough air. 'I don't understand what's happening. I keep seeing places and people I don't recognise. It's as though Judith can't be bothered to explain it to me any more. But she's here, and she's trying to tell me something.'

'Slowly, Cat. Slowly.'

The heat in the compartment intensified and pressed onto Cathy's mouth and skin, blocked up her nose. She clawed at Matthew's arm. 'I can't breathe!'

'Yes you can. It's a panic attack. Listen, Cat! Look at my mouth and breathe when I do.'

Cathy watched and breathed, watched and breathed, and gradually, as her lungs expanded and oxygen flowed into her, Judith released her hold.

'There. Are you better now?' Cathy saw Matt dart a look over her shoulder as some people moved past their compartment. He smiled for their benefit. 'You're all right now.'

Cathy nodded and settled back against him, her head on his shoulder. She was sweating.

'What was that?' he said after a while. He sounded panicky himself.

'I don't know.'

'Have you seen anything? Do you know what might be happening to her?'

'No. I think she's going somewhere, travelling. I saw ships.'

'That would figure. Banishment was what they usually did to Romans guilty of treachery. And Valeria did say they'd save her. I wonder where they sent her?'

'She seemed to be with some kind of army. In a group of women.'

'Perhaps they turned her into a prostitute.'

Cathy waited for a tremor or a sigh, some kind of response from Judith, but there was nothing. 'I just don't know. She's not telling me.'

Matthew rubbed his head against hers and kissed her hair. 'You're safe,' he said. 'Holofernes died but I didn't. Whatever they do to Judith, you'll be all right. I'm here holding you.'

His arm tightened round her shoulders; he crossed his other arm in front of her so she was encircled. Cathy lay in his embrace, hoping he couldn't feel the sick pounding of her heart. It wasn't over. Judith was still struggling and behind them, in Rome, telephones would be ringing and angry men would be ordering the pursuit.

The carriage swayed back and forth, back and forth, as they sat on an silence. There was nothing left to say and after a while Cathy could not have spoken if she wanted to. Her tongue was weighted down and her eyes were dazzled with darkness.

Judith watched Chabris climb the mountain path before her. His dark head was grizzled now, but his back was as straight as ever. He sat erect on the donkey, shifting his weight easily to its stride. It was harder for Judith; she clung to her donkey's mane and her legs ached from gripping.

At the first turn of the path, Chabris looked round at her. 'The people will spot you from here. They'll come out to look at you. You are to say nothing at all, do you hear me? You'll look thankful to be home and properly grateful to God for bringing you back safe.'

Judith bowed her head. Beyond Chabris his third and fourth sons had halted and were waiting for them. They were out of earshot but they looked at her with their father's loathing. The men of her first husband's family were her jailers now. They had left her in no doubt that quietly, within the respected walls of their house, she would suffer.

Would it have been better to die? The punishment for adultery was stoning, and by Bethulia's laws what she had done by running away with Holofernes was adultery. She belonged to Manasses' family and they could demand her death under the law.

So Aulus had advised the praetor when he was considering her sentence. And the praetor had agreed with Aulus that Rome should send Judith back in disgrace, to be punished by her own people. They had made it sound like mercy but the praetor was uninterested, just doing the senator a favour, and Aulus Tullius's face had shown a chilly savagery when he had told her.

Judith had been in terror of dying by stoning. She had tried to tell herself that it was no worse than Holofernes' death, but she had once seen a woman stoned and the memory came back to haunt her now. It would be a slow death, at the hands of people who hated her, and her mother and father and Reuben would be looking on.

When Lucius had come to see her, the horror of it had been in his eyes too. He'd told her that he could save her; she was to be sent to Judea on a military vessel, in the care of a detachment beginning a tour of duty. He would arrange for her to be smuggled off the vessel before it left harbour. She would be taken to a house in the country. Later, when he went overseas with the campaign, she would be aboard his ship with him.

Judith had said nothing. Had she spoken, fear might have got the better of her; she might have wept and allowed Lucius to comfort her. She might have taken the escape route he offered. It would have obliterated her last shred of honour to find safety with her husband's killer. She had kept silent; she had never spoken another word to Lucius after Holofernes had died.

And yet even now, as she struggled up the mountainside towards the walled city that had once been home, Lucius was still with her. So clearly, she could see his face as he had looked at her on their last meeting, the day she left Rome.

'Let me save you,' he'd said. 'You can get word to me until the day you sail. Let me do it to make amends for Holofernes.'

Thc sound of Holofernes' name in his mouth was not the obscenity it should have been. Judith had seen the twisted thing that now lived in Lucius's eyes and understood it; after all, she had betrayed Holofernes too.

She had sent Lucius no message. She had boarded the ship that would take her home to death.

And there for a while she had seen another possibility of escape. Instead of being closely guarded, she was allowed to wander on deck. It would have been difficult to jump from the side, but with planning and timing, it could have been done. She had meant to do it too, until one of the soldiers had told her that she owed this freedom to Lucius. He had paid the ship's commander to treat her well and 'let you take your own way out, if you wanted'. After that, Judith had known she couldn't do it. She could no more owe her death to Lucius than her life.

So she had reached the Judean shore and waited obediently in the baking, filthy visitors' house while they sent for Chabris. And he had come.

They were not going to kill her. They had already put about another story, to save the family honour, and now she was going to make her entrance into Bethulia and lie for them.

She would not be stoned. Her parents and little Reuben would not have to watch her die and suffer the shame of what she'd done. But she would pay.

It would have been much better to have been dashed from the rock with Holofernes.

As they rounded the corner, Judith saw the people. They spilled out over the hillside, strangely quiet.

'Judith is home!' Chabris' sons were shouting, 'Our good widow is home! She's back safe from overseas and our enemy is dead! Give thanks to God!'

The people murmured.

'Our father comes behind,' they shouted. 'He brings Manasses' wife safe, and the threat from Syria is gone!'

A few cries of 'God be praised!' filtered down.

A small figure was moving down the hill, scrambling from rock to rock. He went straight past Chabris' sons and made for Judith. It was Reuben.

'Judith, have you come back?' he said, taking her donkey's rein. 'Have they really let you escape?'

'Yes, Reubi, I'm back.'

'I knew you would. I knew it wasn't true, what they were saying. I said—'

'Reuben,' Chabris interrupted warningly. 'This isn't the place for talk. Your sister is back, thanks to God's protection. It is a great day for our families and for the town. We must give thanks at once. Run back up and tell the people; they must get a goat ready for sacrifice, and prepare the altar. And find food for a feast.'

'Yes, Chabris.' Reuben looked at him with glowing eyes and ran back up the hill. 'Thanks to God!' he kept shouting excitedly. 'Thanks to glorious God! We're going to have a sacrifice! And a feast. Chabris says thanks to God for Judith coming home.'

The gate was packed with people, just as it had been when she left. Faces Judith had known all her life stared at her. Some called questions. Some said 'Thanks to God'. Some even cheered. But they were half-hearted and Judith could feel their suspicion. Her father came forward and embraced her, then her mother. They held her awkwardly and her mother wept as she welcomed her, and moved away again without meeting her eyes.

Judith could hear the story spreading assiduously. 'And she was a hostage, taken first to Apamea, then all the way to Rome . . . She couldn't escape, for fear of reprisals against us . . . And then when she was in Rome, she sought out all the important men and told them about Syria's treachery and Holofernes' wickedness, and in the end Holofernes was put on trial . . . She prayed three times a day, every day she was gone . . . the Romans had never seen such devotion . . .'

She had heard it before. All the way back from the coast, Chabris' sons had spread the story to anyone who would listen. They had grown very skilled at it; even as she followed Chabris through the slow-moving crowd, she could hear her neighbours' resistance giving way. Enthusiasm was beginning to enter into their voices. The details, carefully worked out by Chabris and his sons, were persuading them and giving the story a life of its own.

Over on the eastern side of the gate, the altar was being prepared for the sacrifice. People were beginning to run into their storerooms to pick out food and wine for the feast.

Chabris led Judith through the town to his house. From there, on the roof, he was going to address the citizens. Judith's mother and father followed behind her, and Reuben scampered in and out of the convoy. The enthusiasm of the crowd grew steadily; by the time they reached the courtyard of Chabris' house, Judith's family were being hailed and cheered along with Chabris. Reuben shouted louder and louder, but although her mother and father joined the ringing cries of 'Thanks to God!' there was still doubt in their eyes when they looked at her.

And it was there in the faces of all her old neighbours too. The town was accepting Chabris' story, but that was where the reconciliation ended. There was no warmth for Judith among the people she had left. In their hearts, they knew.

Suddenly, in the knot of people by Chabris' stores, she saw Endeyeh. She looked pinched and much older than when Judith had last seen her. She stared at Judith with sympathy and something like terror, and Judith instinctively held out her hand. Endeyeh glanced at Chabris, stayed very still and then, when Chabris turned to speak to someone on his other side, she slipped through the other servants.

'Oh Judith,' she whispered. 'Why did you come home?'

Judith clutched her hand. She couldn't speak. For the first time since Holofernes' death, she felt tears rising inside her.

'Holofernes was killed,' she said eventually. 'What have they done to you?'

'I have no freedom any more,' Endeyeh said. 'Chabris suspected me of helping you go and he gave me to Hannah, Simon's widow.'

'She's cruel to you?'

'I'm kept very close and worked very hard and—' Endeyeh gasped as Chabris turned and saw them. She backed into the crowd and was gone. Before Judith could call after her, Chabris gripped her arm.

'We will go onto the roof now.'

He led her to the steps, and she could smell the rage on his breath.

'Don't expect to see Endeyeh again,' he said calmly. 'She won't be allowed back in this house or anywhere near you. You're an evil influence on her and she needs guarding from you. She does penance for helping you in your debauchery. Her penance could be worse, you know; she could be found guilty of immorality herself and stoned. You can consider yourself responsible for her wellbeing. If you disobey us, Endeyeh will punished too.'

'I won't disobey you,' said Judith dully.

'Or displease us by being sullen. You will be an example to the whole town, Judith, in your constant rejoicing in God's goodness.'

Chabris stood back at the top of the steps to let her pass him. His face was very close and smiling.

Judith smiled in turn.

'Now raise your hands to God.'

She raised them.

'Now follow me to the prayer hut.'

Judith stood between Chabris and the hut of woven palm branches. The lattice was very dense and had been recently repaired; the smell of palm bark was overpowering and the wind that blew intermittently off the desert rustled the dried fronds heaped on the roof.

She looked out over the upturned faces below. Chabris had started speaking.

'We give great thanks for Judith's safe return. Her triumphant return! The wife of my firstborn, Manasses, risked her life, her virtue, her reputation in offering herself as a hostage to the vile Syrian Holofernes. We do not ask what she suffered at his unclean hands. But we know that God guided her safely and showed her the way to avenge herself and us.

'Judith prayed to God three times daily, each day of her exile. And he rewarded her by leading her to good men in Rome who listened to her story and believed what she told them of Holofernes' filthy blood lust, his ambition, his treachery against all and any master. The foul Syrian is dead, and Judith killed him. She herself struck his head from his body, smashed the loathsome flesh. Thanks to God!'

'Thanks to God! Thanks to God!' the crowd shouted.

Chabris turned to Judith. She lifted her hands again and cried. 'Thanks to God.'

'Later,' Chabris' voice soared above the noise, 'we will make offerings at the altar to celebrate God's goodness. Then we will rejoice in his glory at a feast. But before that, Judith will go into this prayer hut and make her private prayers to God. It will be the first of many hours of prayer. Judith is back with us, and she intends to devote her life to the praise of God.

'She will live with me and my family, here in this house. And she will spend much of every day in prayer, here in the prayer hut, where you can all see her enter and leave; where she can inspire you by the length of her devotions and the sound of her songs. She has much to be thankful for and she will give that thanks for the rest of her life.'

Murmurs of satisfaction rippled round the courtyard. Chabris pulled aside the curtain which closed off the hut and Judith stood on the threshold. The space was tiny, just wide enough for her to turn round in. Long needles of light criss-crossed it. She stepped inside and gasped as the heat closed on her face. Behind her, the curtain swished down.

The smell of palm dust and heat and drying sap was all over her. Outside, the people were calling their praises to God, and a chant was beginning: 'The vile Holofernes is dead. Praise God. Praise Him for killing the Syrian.'

Holofernes. Holofernes. Judith's eyes were wide open as she stared at the branches in front of her. She pressed her hands together and opened her mouth. She had to pray, but even if God would still listen to her, she had nothing left to ask. There was only one thing now; one prayer to make through the long life that stretched before her.

Soundless, stifling, she began to pray. I'm sorry. I'm sorry. I'm sorry.

'We're here.' Matthew spoke in a whisper, although they were still alone.

'Naples?'

'Yes, these are the outskirts.'

The night had been retreating for half an hour and a pale, dirty light filtered into the compartment. Beyond the window, industrial suburbs spread. The train was going more slowly now.

'This is it,' said Matthew. His voice was unsteady. 'If we can get out of the station safely, we've got a real chance. Let's just speak French from now until we're out, all right?'

'*D'accord*.' Cathy smiled stiffly and gathered up the French newspapers. Matthew was snapping into action, trying to convince them both that they could influence events. But Cathy's heart was beating to the rhythm of Judith's prayer, and she knew that Judith had been helpless at the end.

Cathy hadn't shared this last knowledge with Matt. The vision of the closing scene, Judith's punishment, had been vouchsafed to her alone. Cathy knew that whatever message it carried was for her. The message of guilt and things understood too late.

But it's not too late for us, she pleaded silently with Judith. *We still have a chance. Help us now. Tell me what to do.*

But there was only the faint rhythm of the endless, tortured prayer.

The train slowed and began to rock as it drew up to the platform. Cathy and Matthew joined the queue in the corridor and shuffled with the others down the steps onto the platform. The train was going on further, but several dozen people were disembarking here. Cathy and Matthew moved with the flow down the platform. It was nearly five o'clock, and the early risers of Naples were already beginning their day. Lights were on in the snack bars and waiting rooms, and on the surrounding platforms people in neat office clothes waited for trains.

The light was diffuse, and things lacked their true colour. Cathy flinched as she saw a man in a dark uniform, but it was only a station guard.

'Steady,' murmured Matthew in French. She could see the pulse beating in his throat. The passengers were funnelling into a narrow stream, heading for the exit. They took their place in the queue.

Were they moving slowly or was it her imagination? As they eased forward, Cathy peered round the heads in front and her stomach twisted. There was a uniformed carabiniero standing by the ticket collector.

'Policeman,' she whispered, the word coming out so high it was almost inaudible.

Matthew's face crazed into desperation. 'Where? Are you sure?' She nodded her head and he leaned out to look. Cathy saw him bite his lip.

'We'll go back up the platform and cross the tracks.'

Cathy looked over her shoulder. 'There's a station guard there. We wouldn't get past him.'

'We'll go down the other end then.'

Cathy looked ahead of them, past the exit and down the long platform. Between this platform and the next were wide swathes of track, every yard easily visible by the other passengers and railway staff. Beyond the next platform were more tracks and another platform, also dotted with people.

She said nothing. Every drop of blood had drained from Matthew's face. It seemed to Cathy that if the people around her glanced at him, they would immediately start shouting for police and ambulance, knowing something was terribly wrong.

She thought of Judith, looking at Holofernes as he stood on the block of stone in Lucius's trap. And, pitting herself against the maddened rhythm inside her, Cathy began her own desperate prayer. *Help us. It's not too late for us. I've done all I can, but it's not enough. Please don't let it happen again.*

The queue moved forward. They were only a few yards from the exit. Turning away, shielded by her hair, Cathy watched the carabiniero consult a sheet of paper headed by two reproduction photographs. Her own passport photo, and Matthew's.

'Go to the back of the queue,' Matthew said suddenly. 'I'll pretend I'm here alone. Perhaps you can get out. I'll make a fuss and keep them busy.'

Cathy slipped her hand into his.

Help us, she begged mutely. Her head felt as if it were drenched in tears, not of sorrow but of grief and rage. *Save him, you said, save him. I've tried. I've done all I can. I've lost everything, I've given it up gladly, I'd give it up again. The only thing we've held on to is each other. Don't make us lose that too.*

Nothing. Utter silence. Even the prayer had stopped.

Cathy squeezed Matthew's hand. For how much longer would she be able to feel his touch? Matthew turned to her; he tried to shake off her hand but she wouldn't let go.

Suddenly the people around them began to shift. They were staring this way and that; a few people broke out of the queue and began pointing at the tracks. Someone was shouting angrily. At the exit, the carabiniero craned his head to see.

Cathy turned. In the middle of the tracks, running away over the rails, were a man and a woman. They ran hand in hand, making for the end of the station and the open track, jumping and stumbling to avoid the rails. The woman wore Cathy's blue jacket, and her tangled brown hair flew around her shoulders. Tugging her onwards, steadying her when he could, was someone with Matthew's clothes and Matthew's hair, and two French newspapers in his free hand.

The carabiniero forced his way onto the platform; he rushed

to the edge, shouting. The guard from the far end came running towards him, warning him not to try and cross. Ignoring it, he jumped onto the gravel between two rails but the signal lights were changing and a train had appeared in the distance, coming fast. He hesitated and scrambled back.

The man and the woman continued running. They went in a diagonal line, trying to get beyond the end of the platforms. They saw the train coming and hesitated. Only then did they seem to realise what was going to happen. They made as if to go back, staggered, and at the last moment turned towards the platform.

For an instant, the two couples faced one another: Judith and Holofernes, Cathy and Matthew. Holofernes raised his hand in a flutter of newsprint; Judith put her arms round him and held him close. Then the train was on them, screams battled with the roar of the engine, and in the chaos Cathy and Matthew slipped unremarked and unfollowed into the waking city.

[illegible]

[illegible]

[illegible]

[illegible] had been [illegible] [illegible] they had [illegible] even in the [illegible]

[illegible] the edge of danger had never [illegible] by the police any [illegible] had been shaken [illegible]

AUTUMN

Cathy stacked her books and shivered. The sun was pale and failed to warm her through her thin sweater; the southern autumn had definitely arrived. Yet she had another half-hour to wait before Matt's bus arrived back from the neighbouring town.

He had been sure there would be a letter at the post office this week. He was beginning to feel restless; Cathy knew all the signs. Letter or no letter, they would soon be moving on again.

Nadia had written to say that Danilo had withdrawn the charges, so at least they'd been able to use their own names again. And after she'd sent them their passports, they were able to get work.

For several months now, Cathy had been teaching English as a foreign language; Matt, with his better Italian, had managed to get translating jobs. They worked hard. Living in even the most modest pensiones became expensive over time, and they were dutifully putting money aside each week to repay Nadia what she had lent them.

Life was very different now. The edge of danger had never left them. They might not be pursued by the police any more, but all the settled features of their life had been shaken up.

They felt like itinerants; they no longer fitted in. After a month or six weeks of living in one small southern town, doing short-term jobs, they would move on. Although Matthew sometimes talked about going back to England, he made no serious plans. Instead, he went every week to whichever main post office they were currently using as an address to see if Nadia had written again. He had the air of a man looking for something – answers perhaps.

Cathy no longer believed in answers. Those she had found only opened up more questions. She now knew, for instance, why Nadia had risked so much to help them: the clue had been there in the last dream, in Endeyeh's suddenly aged face. But to guess that Nadia had her own haunting explained nothing. It only made Cathy realise how many stories there were, and how subtle the intersections. Enzo had started out being haunted by Lucius. But that had been as a young man; as an older one, had he taken Aulus's part? Or even Chabris's?

It was too much. Everyone had a different story, and each story had its depths and passions; you could be touched by other people's, even endangered by them, but ultimately all you could do was hang on to your own.

Cathy's story was with Matthew. It was a choice she had made. And Danilo was an absence she would have to learn to accept.

He had been with her often as she and Matthew made their stop-start progress across southern Italy. It was not exactly Danilo's face she saw, nor quite his voice that she heard, but an atmosphere of him, composed of all the senses.

These past few days she had felt him more acutely than ever. Perhaps it was the coming of autumn that renewed the loss and made it sharp. It was a complicated loss: of the Danilo who might have been, the vital things that had become twisted against themselves.

Cathy wondered if Matt had sensed it. He'd seemed jumpy before he left this morning. She had found it hard to talk to him and had looked forward to an hour's solitude between the end of classes and his return. But she'd been sitting here nearly all that time now and she didn't feel rested.

She missed Matthew as if he'd been gone weeks. Since their escape they'd lived more closely entwined than ever and even so short a separation felt dangerous. Sometimes Cathy wondered how they could ever find their way back to a normal life after this.

The bus chugged its way into the square and stopped on the far side of the road. Dust billowed round its wheels, obscuring the passengers who got off. Cathy couldn't see Matthew among the old men and teenagers and she felt a sudden panic seize her.

'I'm here.' Matt had walked quietly up from the right. He stood by the table for a second, then put his newspaper down next to her books. A complex wave of emotion seemed to be emanating from him.

'Any letter?' Cathy asked.

'No. But there is something.' He glanced at her, then away, and pointed at the news story halfway down the page.

A photograph of Danilo looked out of the columns and Cathy knew before she read the print. On Tuesday night; an overdose of sleeping pills.

'They kept it very quiet,' Matt said, staring out across the square. 'He was on a ventilator until this morning apparently. But he was dead when they admitted him.'

Eventually he put his hands in his pockets and looked at

Cathy. His face was a battleground of emotions, and anger was one. 'I never wanted to win like this,' he said. 'I never should have— Oh hell.'

Cathy said nothing at all.

'I think we should move on soon,' Matthew said after a while. 'Just one more time, a move before winter. Then we might start thinking about going home.'

'Yes.'

'I don't want to leave Italy just yet though. I was looking at Bari, that might be an interesting place to stay. It's the port for places south.'

'It sounds good.'

'How are you fixed for work? Could we go at the end of the week?'

Cathy nodded.

'Well then. I'll go and tell them at the pensione.' Matthew hesitated. 'Will you be coming soon?'

'Yes. I just want to finish some marking first.'

He put his hand against her cheek; she caught it and kissed his knuckles before letting him go. Matthew walked quickly down the street, nodding greetings to the people they were soon to leave.

Cathy opened her notebook to a clean page and picked up her pen. She had done no drawing since they'd left Rome; once or twice she had tried but nothing had come, and she'd agreed with Matthew that perhaps, for the time being at least, it was for the best. Now, though, she thought that she might try it one last time, for Danilo.

She pressed the edge of her pen to the paper and began to draw. She could remember how it felt: the straight lines of the limbs, the curve of the head, the angles as they moved into independent life. But her pen wouldn't follow the memory.

She began to draw faster, shading, blocking out, pulling the drawing diagonally across the page.

After ten minutes, she had finished. She looked at the drawing in front of her. There was no trace of a human form in it, only abstract shapes, each one linked with another, mirroring one another, turning each other inside out, twisting and spiralling in a pattern which had neither beginning nor end.